PRAISE FOR MIMI MATTHEWS

Gentleman Jim

"A vigorous, sparkling, and entertaining love story with plenty of Austen-ite wit."

-Kirkus Reviews, starred review

"Matthews ups the ante with a wildly suspenseful romance..."
-Library Journal, starred review

"Readers who love lots of intrigue and historicals that sound properly historical will savor this one."

-NPR

Fair as a Star

"A kindhearted love story that will delight anyone who longs to be loved without limits. Highly recommended."
-Library Journal, starred review

"A moving friends-to-lovers Victorian romance... Historical romance fans won't want to miss this."

-Publishers Weekly, starred review

"Gentle, tender, poignant and deeply romantic, it's the best romance I've read this year."

The Winter Companion

"Fans of the 'Parish Orphans of Devon' series will adore this final installment, reuniting the orphans and their loves."

"Matthews once again delivers in her latest Victorian novel. Her love story is sweet and chaste, the characters well developed, and their relationship beautifully rendered."

The Work of Art

"Matthews weaves suspense and mystery within an absorbing love story. Readers will be hard put to set this one down before the end."

"The author seamlessly combines a suspenseful tale and a soaring romance, the plot by turns sweetly moving and dramatically stirring."

"If all Regency Romances were written as well as 'The Work of Art,' I would read them all...[Matthews] has a true gift for storytelling."

The Matrimonial Advertisement

"For this impressive Victorian romance, Matthews crafts a tale that sparkles with chemistry and impresses with strong character development...an excellent series launch..."

-Publishers Weekly

"Matthews has a knack for creating slow-building chemistry and an intriguing plot with a social history twist."

-Library Journal

"Matthews' series opener is a guilty pleasure, brimming with beautiful people, damsels in distress, and an abundance of testosterone...A well-written and engaging story that's more than just a romance."

-Kirkus Reviews

A Holiday By Gaslight

"Matthews pays homage to Elizabeth Gaskell's *North and South* with her admirable portrayal of the Victorian era's historic advancements...Readers will easily fall for Sophie and Ned in their gaslit surroundings."

-Library Journal, starred review

"Matthews' novella is full of comfort and joy—a sweet treat for romance readers that's just in time for Christmas."

-Kirkus Reviews

"A graceful love story...and an authentic presentation of the 1860s that reads with the simplicity and visual gusto of a period movie."
-*Readers' Favorite*, 2019 Gold Medal for Holiday Fiction

The Lost Letter

"Lost love letters, lies, and betrayals separate a soldier from the woman he loves in this gripping, emotional Victorian romance... Historical romance fans should snap this one up."

-*Publishers Weekly*, starred review

"A fast and emotionally satisfying read, with two characters finding the happily-ever-after they had understandably given up on. A promising debut."

-*Library Journal*

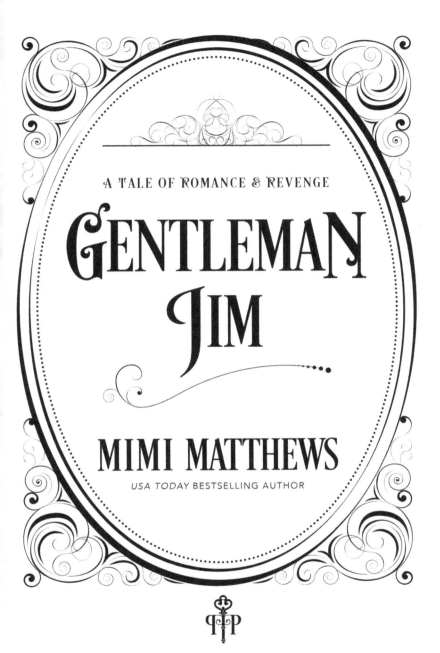

A TALE OF ROMANCE & REVENGE

GENTLEMAN JIM

MIMI MATTHEWS

USA TODAY BESTSELLING AUTHOR

GENTLEMAN JIM
A Tale of Romance and Revenge
Copyright © 2020 by Mimi Matthews

Edited by Deborah Nemeth
Cover Design by James T. Egan of Bookfly Design
Formatting by Ampersand Book Interiors

E-Book: 978-1-7330569-6-0
Paperback: 978-1-7330569-9-1

DEDICATION

For my mom, who instilled me with a sense of justice.

All human wisdom is summed up in these two words,
—'Wait and hope.'

ALEXANDRE DUMAS
The Count of Monte Cristo

PROLOGUE

Beasley Park
Somerset, England
Spring 1807

Beaten and bloody, Nicholas Seaton sat on the straw-covered floor of the loose box, his legs drawn up against his chest and his forehead resting on his knees. There was no possibility of escape. The doors of the loose box had been bolted shut and the wooden walls were made strong and thick, built to hold the most powerful of Squire Honeywell's blooded stallions. Even so, Nicholas had wasted the first fifteen minutes of his imprisonment trying to force his way out, slamming his shoulders against the doors and striking out at the walls with all of his remaining strength, earning nothing for his exertions but a fresh set of cuts and bruises.

He'd spent the next fifteen minutes pacing the confines of the loose box like a caged lion, clenching and unclenching his fists, grinding his teeth, and mentally cursing every member of the landed gentry and aristocracy.

"I'll see you hang for this, Seaton," Frederick Burton-Smythe had said after driving Nicholas into the loose box at the end of his whip.

And they would hang him. Nicholas was as certain of that fact as he'd ever been of anything in his whole life. Only two years ago a young man no older than himself had been hanged for the paltry crime of stealing chickens from Fred's father, Sir Roderick Burton-Smythe. To have stolen three priceless pieces of heirloom jewelry from Squire Honeywell's only daughter, Miss Margaret, was surely grounds for drawing and quartering.

It made no difference that Nicholas hadn't stolen anything. What good were his protestations of innocence? He was nothing but a lowly groom in Squire Honeywell's stables. A servant. Even worse than a servant, in fact, for he was the bastard son of Squire Honeywell's scullery maid, Jenny Seaton.

Jolly Jenny, as she was known, who—before arriving at the kitchen door of Beasley Park eighteen years ago, big with child and begging for scraps of food—had plied her trade at a hedge tavern in Market Barrow. A hedge tavern that had once been a favored haunt of the notorious highwayman Gentleman Jim.

"The mother a whore and the father a villain," the vicar's wife, Mrs. Applewhite, was fond of telling anyone who would listen. "Nicholas Seaton will come to no good, you mark my words."

No. No one would believe he was innocent. Especially when his accuser was Frederick Burton-Smythe himself.

Nicholas and Fred had been enemies for as long as he could remember, but in the past year their dislike of each other had escalated to raw hatred. As usual, Maggie Honeywell was at the heart of the matter.

The thought of her caused Nicholas's heart to wrench painfully. She was his best friend in the whole world. The one person he trusted. The only person he loved. A blood oath taken years ago had bound them together forever, when at Maggie's request Nicholas had gamely cut his hand and pressed it firmly against the matching cut in hers. But he needed no ritual to bind himself to Maggie Honeywell. She was everything to him.

Unfortunately, she was also everything to her widowed father, and as the years went by and she began to bloom into a strikingly beautiful woman, she became everything to Fred Burton-Smythe as well.

Sir Roderick and Squire Honeywell had long ago agreed that one day their offspring would wed, thereby joining the two greatest estates in the district—Beasley Park and Letchford Hall. Nothing had ever been formalized, as far as Nicholas was aware, but that didn't prevent Fred from behaving as if Maggie were already his own personal property. So when he'd come upon her and Nicholas in Burton Wood earlier that day, laughing gaily as they whirled about the clearing in each other's arms, Fred had seen red.

Maggie hadn't helped matters. At the best of times she was an impudent minx, and at the worst, a veritable hellion. Raised by Squire Honeywell as if she were his son and heir instead of his gently bred only daughter, she could outride, outhunt, and outshoot most of the young men in the county. Her temper was legendary and she'd learned at her volatile sire's knee that a profusion of oaths and various threats of violence were the means of solving most any problem.

"Nicholas is helping me practice my dancing," she'd said in that imperious, toplofty way of hers. "So you can bloody well piss off, Fred!"

And then Nicholas sealed his fate.

He burst out laughing.

On any other occasion, Fred would have charged him, intent on thrashing him within an inch of his life. Maggie would have leapt between them as she always did, verbally eviscerating Fred for attacking someone that he knew very well wasn't permitted to fight back.

Not that that had ever stopped Fred before.

In Maggie's absence, Fred had no qualms about cuffing Nicholas on the head and ears, brutally shoving him to the ground, or striking him on the back with his riding crop.

Nicholas was taller than Fred and broader of shoulder, but he was lanky and thin whereas Fred was as stocky and muscular as a bulldog. Nicholas liked to think that in a fair fight he could best his lifelong rival; however, the fights between him and Fred had never been fair, and as Fred was the heir to a baronetcy and Nicholas was a servant, he knew that they never would be.

"Master Fred's your better, Nick," Jenny said whenever he appeared with a bloody lip or a newly blackened eye. "You'd best stop provoking him."

But this time, Fred hadn't been provoked.

He simply pokered up, and in a fair imitation of his father, Sir Roderick, scolded Maggie for consorting with servants and conducting herself in a manner unbecoming to a young lady. "I shall inform your Aunt Daphne of your behavior," he told her sternly. "And when your father returns from London, I've a mind to speak to him as well."

And then he turned on his booted heel and strode away, pausing at the edge of the clearing only long enough to lock eyes with Nicholas.

There was murder in his gaze.

"How dared he threaten me?" Maggie seethed an hour later as the two of them lay stretched out on the grassy banks of the stream that ran through Beasley Park. "The jealous arse. Tell my father, indeed. As if Papa would ever hear a word against me."

"Your aunt would," Nicholas replied grimly.

Daphne Honeywell, the squire's widowed sister-in-law, had come to live at Beasley Park only two years before for the sole purpose of turning Maggie into a lady. Nicholas despised the woman. Because of her, Maggie's days were taken up with needlework and dancing lessons, and her head had been filled with thoughts of balls, routs, and assemblies. Because of her, Maggie no longer wore breeches and rode astride or stripped down to her underclothes to go swimming with him in the lake.

Now she dressed in pretty gowns, made of fabric so fragile and fine that Nicholas feared to touch it, and her thick mink-colored hair, which had once cascaded in a luxurious tumble down her back, was bound up in soft curls and silken ribbons. Even her complexion had changed. Carefully shielded from the sun with parasols and hats, it no longer glowed with a golden tan but had reverted to its natural hue: a flawless, creamy porcelain.

Two years was hardly any time at all, and yet the difference between a fourteen-year-old Margaret Honeywell and a sixteen-year-old Margaret Honeywell was as vast as the ocean.

More and more often, Nicholas found himself staring at his lifelong friend with a peculiar ache of longing in his chest. He'd never liked to be away from her, but now, whenever they were apart, he brooded over her to the point of melancholy.

And that wasn't the worst of it.

He'd been dreaming about her, too. Vivid dreams that surely no gentleman ever dared dream of a lady.

"Miss Margaret's not for the likes of you," Jenny had taken to warning him whenever she caught him sulking. "She's for Master Fred or some other fine gentleman. Ain't nothing going to change that."

Nicholas had never believed it. He and Maggie were soul mates. And yet, as he watched her slow transformation, there were times when he was stricken with an awful pang of sadness, a nagging worry that the day was fast approaching when Margaret Honeywell would take her rightful place in society and be lost to him forever.

"I shan't stop teaching you to dance merely because Fred and Aunt Daphne object," Maggie said as they lay by the stream. "I've always shared my lessons with you, haven't I? And dancing is really no different from reading or writing, I feel."

Nicholas levered up on his elbow and looked down at her. "When you taught me to read, you were seven years old. And we weren't required to touch each other."

"Why shouldn't we touch each other?"

He arched a brow at her.

She only laughed. "What hypocrisy. I'll wager no one would think it unladylike if I had been dancing with Fred. And he wouldn't have behaved half as gentlemanly as you do."

"Wouldn't he?" he asked, all of his senses instantly alert.

"You know he wouldn't. He always holds me far too close, and he's forever staring down at my bosom."

Nicholas suppressed the now familiar swell of jealousy and rage. The primitive urge to find Fred, and any other gentlemen who dared to look at Maggie, and beat them to a bloody pulp. "If anyone ever so much as lays a finger on you, I'll—"

"You never do," she interrupted, a hint of accusation in her eyes. "When we're dancing, I mean."

He was briefly diverted from his anger. "I never do what?"

"Stare at my bosom."

Heat rose in his cheeks. He looked at her a moment, dumbstruck, before giving her a crooked smile. "What bosom?"

Maggie responded to his teasing with a rare blush of her own. At sixteen, she had the beginnings of a figure that promised to one day be as glorious as that of her late mother, a lady who had often been referred to as the Somerset Aphrodite. "Naturally you wouldn't notice any of my endowments. You're too busy paying court to Cornelia Peabody."

"*What?*"

"Jenny told me so."

Nicholas scowled. "She wishes I would court one of the baker's daughters. I daresay old Peabody's offered to give her a discount on hot cross buns if I take one of them off his hands. Though how the devil either of them think I could keep a wife on less than five pounds a year is a mystery to me."

"It's not impossible," Maggie said.

"No, not impossible." He affected to give the matter a great deal of thought. "I suppose Miss Peabody could always find employment. Perhaps your father might even give her a job scrubbing out chamber pots up at the main house?" His smile reemerged. "Then there's the issue of lodging her, of course, but I'm sure she wouldn't mind living with me in that godforsaken little room of mine above the stable. Cornelia Peabody has always struck me as the sort of girl who longs to set up house in a small, rat-infested cupboard."

Maggie wasn't diverted by his teasing. "Then it's not true?"

"Gad, Maggie, what in blazes would I want with Cornelia Peabody?"

"She's very pretty."

Nicholas plucked a dark blue wildflower from the grass and twisted the stem idly between his fingers. It was a forget-me-not. The hearty little flower ran rampant at Beasley Park, decorating the grounds in a wash of blue every spring. The same arresting shade of blue as Maggie Honeywell's eyes. "So are lots of girls in the village. What does that signify?"

"And, by all accounts, a soft-spoken, well-behaved little lady, even if she is a baker's daughter."

He tickled her face with the forget-me-not, drawing its petals along the bridge of her nose, over the bow of her rosy-hued lips, and down to the delicate cleft in her stubborn little chin. "Do you mean she doesn't go about telling people to 'piss off' and calling them 'jealous arses' and 'confounded swine'?"

Maggie snatched the wildflower out of his hand. "I am sure she doesn't."

"Then more fool her," Nicholas said, lying back down on the grass. "Everyone knows high-spirited termagants are the only sorts of ladies I fancy."

"Such compliments. I believe I shall swoon."

A foolish grin spread over Nicholas's face, and as he gazed up at the clear blue sky, he reached out his hand halfway between their two bodies, turning it palm up in unspoken invitation. Almost immediately he felt Maggie's small, slender hand sliding into his.

"Can you get away tonight after supper?" she asked softly.

He shook his head. "I'm already behind in my chores. I'll have to catch up this evening if I'm to have any hope of meeting you tomorrow."

Maggie twined her fingers through his. "Tomorrow, then."

"Tomorrow, then," he'd echoed.

Tomorrow.

Nicholas squeezed his eyes shut against the oppressive darkness of the loose box. His chest burned with the effort it took to stave off an onslaught of angry tears.

There would be no tomorrows.

He was never going to see Maggie Honeywell again.

Within the next hour, Fred would return with the magistrate. And then Nicholas would be hauled off to jail. From there, he imagined Fred would see that things proceeded with the utmost haste. The Burton-Smythes had a great deal of influence in the West Country. There would be no delays in judgment, no last-minute reprieves.

How soon would they hang him? A week? Ten days?

Nicholas covered his face with his hands, feeling as if he'd been cast into a black pit of despair.

And then, the sound of creaking wood rent the darkness.

He sprang to his feet, instinctively backing as far away from the doors of the loose box as he could get.

Another creak.

Fred had returned with the magistrate.

Nicholas listened hard, ignoring the sound of his pulse pounding in his veins and the cold sweat that caused his torn linen shirt to cling to his back. Any moment now, the bolt would be thrown open and they'd try to take him.

Would he fight to his last breath?

Or would he go with them meekly and quietly, like a lamb to the slaughter?

He clenched his fists.

There was a soft rap at the wooden doors of the loose box. "Nicholas?" a voice whispered urgently.

Nicholas stood stock-still, not able to believe the evidence of his own ears. "*Maggie?*"

The bolts slid back and the doors to the loose box swung open.

Maggie Honeywell stood there, the dearest sight in the whole world.

She was wrapped in a red woolen cloak, and her dark hair, unpinned, tumbled about her shoulders in magnificent disarray. She held a lamp aloft in one hand, illuminating her pale, fiercely determined face.

He closed the short distance between them.

She set the lantern on the ground as he approached. And then her arms were around his neck, and Nicholas was embracing her so tightly that he feared he might crush her.

When he at last loosened his hold, she drew back just enough to bring her hands to his bloodied face. With excruciating care, she inspected him for injury, her hands moving lightly from his forehead, to his jaw, to his broad shoulders and chest.

"My God," she breathed. "What has he done to you?"

Nicholas caught her busy hands and held them firmly in his, preventing her from delving beneath his torn shirt. To his mortification, he felt tears stinging at the backs of his eyes.

No one, not even his mother, had ever shown him the tenderness and concern that Maggie Honeywell did. "How did you know where to find me?"

She gave his hands a reassuring squeeze. "Do you remember my telling you that Mrs. Applewhite was coming to supper? Well, Aunt Daphne invited her to stay the night, and after I retired to bed, the two of them must have dipped into the sherry. I could hear them laughing and carrying on all the way upstairs. And thank heaven I did, for when I went down to the drawing room to see what all the noise was about, I overheard my aunt talking about what had happened with you, and Fred, and my jewelry. I came as fast as I could."

"I swear I didn't steal anything from you. Fred must have taken your jewelry and hidden it in my room. How else would he have known where to look for it? He wanted to catch me with it. To get me out of your life once and for all. I saw it in his eyes when he found us dancing in Burton Wood. He wants me to be hanged or transported for life, anything to—"

"There's no time for that," Maggie said. "I've come to set you free. To help you get away before the magistrate comes."

Nicholas took a step toward her, his grasp on her small, slender hands tightening. "You have to believe me. I'd never steal anything of yours. Say you believe me!"

"Of course I do. And if I thought it would do any good, I'd proclaim your innocence to Aunt Daphne and the magistrate and anyone else who would listen. But they won't listen to me. You know they won't. They'll say our friendship has blinded me to your true nature, or some such nonsense. And then they'll accuse me of impugning Fred's honor by doubting his word as a gentleman."

Abruptly Nicholas let her go, not trusting himself to touch her any longer. "A gentleman. Your future husband, you mean."

Maggie's eyes blazed. "Why do you always bring that up? As if I want to marry Frederick Burton-Smythe."

"Look at what he did to me tonight." Nicholas drew aside the collar of his shirt, revealing the deep gash of blood running from the side of his neck down to the top of his chest. "I ask you, is this the work of a gentleman?"

Maggie's eyes widened. "Good grief! Did Fred do *that*?"

"Who else?"

"But why?"

"Do you think I'd just let him lock me up in here without a fight? He pulled me from my room after he found your jewelry. We were struggling with each other all the way down the stairs. I might have beaten him if he'd fought fair. Instead, when I drew back to hit him again, he lashed out at me with that blasted whip he's always carrying. I should have expected it. After all these years, I should have known…" He raked a hand through his already disheveled hair. "But I wasn't prepared, damn me. I fell backward into the loose box, and before I could regain my feet, he'd bolted the door."

"The blackguard!" Maggie's low voice trembled with fury. "The confounded coward! I shall show him what it feels like to be struck with a whip. When Papa returns from London, I'll—" She broke off with a muttered oath. "Devil take it, there's not even enough time for me to dress your wound. You must go, Nicholas. You must hide yourself from Fred and the magistrate until my father returns next week, and then, when you come back, we shall go to Papa together and explain—"

"Why should I come back?" Nicholas spat in a sudden burst of anger. "I hate this cursed place."

Maggie shook her head, denying the truth of his words. "Don't say that."

"I hate everything about it. I hate Sir Roderick and I hate Fred Burton-Smythe. I hate Mrs. Applewhite and your Aunt Daphne. I despise working in this stable and—"

"What about me?"

He felt a spasm of deep anguish. "You know how I feel about you, but how can one good thing outweigh all of this misery?"

"Well, you can't go away and never come back. As horrible as everything else is, Jenny's here, and I'm here, and you have someplace to sleep, and a chance to earn your living—"

"Earn my living? As what? A groom in your father's stable?" Nicholas laughed bitterly. "I'll never be a gentleman if I remain here. No matter how much you teach me about books and music and dancing. Bastards and commoners can never be made into gentlefolk, by no miracle. I'll never be anything more than a servant to you. And one day…" He looked at her, his chest constricting with torment. "One day you'll marry Fred Burton-Smythe, and you'll forget I ever meant anything to you."

"I would never!"

"I can't be here when that day comes, Maggie. I'd rather be dead. And if I remain here, I might as well be. There's no future for me as a servant at Beasley Park. Can't you understand that?"

"But where else can you go?"

"To Bristol. To the sea. I'll go to find my father."

"Your father?" Maggie repeated. "Do you mean… *Gentleman Jim*?"

"Jenny says that the last time she ever heard anything of him, he was on his way to Bristol. Perhaps if I can find him, if I can convince him I'm his son, he'll allow me to stay with him. To ride with him on his travels."

"But you don't even know for certain that Gentleman Jim *is* your father! Jenny has never admitted—"

"She's never denied it. And everyone who remembers what Gentleman Jim looked like says I'm the very image of him."

"Yes, I know that, but no one has seen him in ages. What if you can't find him?"

Nicholas's jaw hardened. "I *will* find him."

Maggie glared at him, her eyes shimmering with unshed tears. "Confound you, Nicholas Seaton, you know there's no time to argue!" She stamped her foot. "Oh, very well." She reached into the folds of her cloak and drew out a small, heavily filled sack. "If you insist upon going, then you must take this with you."

Nicholas eyed the sack warily. "Is that what I think it is?"

"Yes. Most of my pin money and all of the little tokens Papa has given me in the last several years. A shilling here, a guinea there. I daresay it has added up to a tidy sum. I was going to give you a few coins to sustain you until Papa returns from London, but under the circumstances I think you must take it all."

"No." Nicholas took a step back from her. "It's a king's ransom."

"Good. Then I'll never have to worry about you freezing to death or going hungry." She thrust the sack of money at his chest. "Take it. And take Miss Belle, too. Ride her as far as the crossroads and then set her loose. She can find her way back to Beasley Park from anywhere in the county."

Nicholas swallowed hard as he accepted the money. "Maggie Honeywell, you're an angel."

At his words, the first tears spilled over onto Maggie's cheek. She dashed them away with her hand. "I know I will never see you again."

Nicholas stepped closer, and reaching out, caught her cleft chin in his hand. It was an old habit. Something he'd done since she was a little girl. But this time the gesture wasn't playful or teasing. He didn't, as a brother would, give her chin an affectionate pinch and then let her go. Instead he gently tipped up her face so that her large blue eyes were forced to meet his. His thumb brushed away a tear, and then, before Maggie could guess his intention, he lowered his mouth to hers and kissed her very softly on the lips.

It was a brief kiss, and considering her tears, not a particularly romantic one, but it was the first kiss they'd ever shared. And it was nothing at all like the kiss that a brother would give to his sister.

"Wait for me, Maggie," Nicholas said. "I'll find Gentleman Jim, and when I make my fortune, I'll come back for you." He held her gaze for what seemed like an eternity. "No matter how long it takes," he vowed. "I will come back."

London, England
Spring 1817

Margaret Honeywell sank back into the velvet cushions of her father's traveling coach and closed her eyes. Last night had been spent at a rather inhospitable inn, the landlord of which had relegated her and her maid, Bessie, to a cramped bedchamber overlooking the stable yard, complete with a smoking fireplace, a lumpy mattress, and a door with a very unreliable lock. Between the noise, the discomfort, and the fear that they would be murdered in their beds, Maggie had hardly managed to sleep a wink.

"That's right, Miss Margaret." Bessie draped a carriage rug over Maggie's lap, tucking it in all around her. "You close your eyes and rest." She untied the ribbons of Maggie's bonnet and lifted it from her head. "And don't you fear dropping off to sleep neither, for there's a good two hours before we arrive at Lord and Lady Trumble's, and I'll wake you in plenty of time to put you to rights."

"You must rest too, Bessie," Maggie murmured without opening her eyes. "You slept as little as I did last night."

"Don't you worry about me, miss." Bessie settled her enormous bulk back into the seat across from Maggie. "A ten-minute nap, and I shall be as fresh as a nosegay."

The rhythmic rattling of the coach lulled Maggie to sleep. When next she awoke, they were within the city limits of London.

Bessie was at the ready with the dressing case, and having once again moved to sit beside her, combed out Maggie's curls and secured them with a few artfully placed hairpins. "Pinch your cheeks, Miss Margaret," she commanded in the same brisk, no-nonsense tone she used when directing Maggie to drink a vitamin tonic or to eat an extra spoonful of restorative jelly. "I mayn't be your nurse any longer, but I'll not have it said that you lost your bloom under my care."

Maggie dutifully pinched her cheeks, but when Bessie began forcefully tugging at her carriage gown in an attempt to straighten out the wrinkles, Maggie slapped her hands away. "Enough, Bessie! You're making me as nervous as a cat with all of your fussing. Leave me be for now. It's only Jane who will see me, and she'll not mind my hair and gown."

Undeterred, Bessie picked up Maggie's bonnet and began to dust off the crown. "Miss Trumble may not mind it, but you can be sure that dresser of hers, Miss Jenkins, will have something to say about your appearance. And any fault she finds will be hung round my neck, make no mistake. It's jealousy, is what it is. For all you aren't the daughter of a baron, she'd give her right arm to do for you instead of Miss Trumble. Not that Miss Trumble isn't a sweet girl—far sweeter than you are, Miss Margaret, truth be known—but she isn't what anyone would call a beauty."

"In *tonnish* circles, Jane is considered quite pretty."

Bessie snorted. "I'll wager no gentleman ever compared her complexion to Devonshire cream, or said her eyes were like two Indian sapphires."

"It would be rather silly if they had. Jane's eyes are brown."

"And what about those gentlemen during your come out, Miss Margaret? The ones that called you the Pocket Venus? I can't imagine anyone saying the same about Miss Trumble, no matter how many frills and furbelows Miss Jenkins puts her into."

"Naturally, they wouldn't. Jane is tall."

"A regular Long Meg," Bessie agreed without malice.

"And I might have been called the Pocket Venus at the beginning of my come-out season, but before I returned home, they were calling me something quite different, and well you know it."

"Foolishness," Bessie grumbled. "And don't think that makes Miss Jenkins any less envious of me looking after you!"

Maggie stared out the window of the coach as Bessie fitted her bonnet back on her head and tied the ribbons in a jaunty bow at the side of her face.

It had been over four years since Maggie had last traveled to London to visit her friend. She'd fully expected to make the journey the previous spring, but no sooner had she cast off her blacks after a year spent in mourning for her father than Aunt Daphne—in her typically disobliging fashion—had slumped over one morning at breakfast, as dead as the proverbial doornail, and Maggie had been forced straight back into her mourning clothes again.

Aunt Daphne had been the last of Maggie's family. There were no other relatives living, and consequently, no one left who might eventually need to be mourned. "Burn these," Maggie had instructed Bessie when she'd stripped off her mourning weeds for the very last time. "I shall never be needing them again."

For the journey to London, Maggie had donned a dark blue carriage gown. It had once accentuated the generous curves of her bosom and the narrowness of her waist. Now, it hung loosely on her small frame. She'd always been petite. Indeed, after the age of sixteen she'd never grown any taller. But following her illness, and the subsequent years of grief and isolation, there was altogether less of her.

Her mirror didn't lie. Instead of the voluptuous curves that had once inspired gentlemen of the *ton* to dub her the Pocket Venus, there was now a fragile delicacy to her face and figure that had never been there before.

She looked—or so she feared—very much like an invalid.

"A bit of good food and good company, and before you know it, Miss Margaret, you'll be as bonny as you were while your Papa was alive," Bessie said. "Mind you, you're still the prettiest young lady *I've* ever seen."

Maggie gave her maid a wry smile. At six and twenty there weren't many who would still consider her a young lady. Rather the opposite, in fact. She was well on her way to becoming an old maid.

It wasn't for lack of choice.

During her come-out season alone, she'd received six formal offers of marriage, including one from an impoverished earl who had hopes that Squire Honeywell's vast fortune would replenish his ancestral estates.

She had refused them all, just as she'd refused every offer since.

And if she still had any choice in the matter, she would continue refusing.

They arrived at Lord and Lady Trumble's house in Green Street a short time later. Jane was waiting on the front steps, a colorful Indian shawl draping her tall, slender frame. As a footman handed Maggie out of the carriage, Jane ran down to meet her, both hands extended in greeting.

"My dear friend! It's been far too long. How was the journey? Are you dreadfully tired?" She kissed one of Maggie's cheeks and then the other before linking arms with her and walking her into the house. "Aunt Harriet is fast asleep in her room else she'd be here to greet you. She's meant to be our chaperone, you know. Papa wouldn't consent to my coming to London otherwise. But you mustn't think she'll interfere with our fun. She's an absolute relic. She falls straight to sleep a moment after sitting down in a chair, and can't hear a thing without her ear trumpet. It will be as if we have the entire house to ourselves."

A footman in the entry hall took Maggie's hat, gloves, and cloak.

Jane chattered gaily all the while. "My eldest brother George is here in town already. You remember George, don't you? He keeps a set of bachelor rooms in St. James's Street. He's agreed to squire us to all of the balls and parties we attend during your visit. But you must be sweet to him, Margaret, for

I suspect he's only being agreeable for your sake. He's always had a bit of a *tendre* for you."

Maggie smiled at her friend. With fair hair that refused to hold a curl, an unremarkable nose and chin, and brown eyes set a bit too close together, Jane Trumble was, as Bessie had said, no great beauty. She was, however, both kind and clever, and when she talked, as she was doing now, her face lit up with such cheerful animation, it was impossible for anyone to think her plain.

They'd met during Maggie's come-out season in the ladies retiring room at a ball. Maggie's hem had been torn—trod on by a clumsy partner—and, in the absence of a maid, Jane had offered to mend it. The repairs were executed in a trice, but Maggie and Jane had remained in the retiring room for over an hour, talking and laughing. When at last they'd emerged, they were bosom friends, and had been ever since.

"As soon as you've rested from your journey, we must go shopping." Jane led Maggie up the stairs. "I'd wager that gown you're wearing is more than three years out of fashion. And your hat! How many times have you made it over? You look an absolute dowd!"

"I haven't bought any new clothes since Papa died. There's been little need. I've worn nothing but mourning." Maggie's mouth tugged into a frown. "Besides, it's Fred who controls the purse strings now."

Jane ushered Maggie down the upstairs hall and into the bedroom that was to be hers for the duration of her stay. Bessie had gone ahead of them and was already bustling about in the attached dressing room, seeing to the unpacking of Maggie's things.

Jane sat down on the edge of the bed and drew Maggie down beside her. Her expression became serious. "Does he really have so much control over your money? I know he was an executor of your father's will, but surely...?"

Maggie plucked at a stray thread on the skirt of her carriage gown. The mere mention of her father's will, the provisions of which amounted in her mind to nothing less than the worst betrayal a father ever perpetrated against a daughter, was still enough to send her into the deepest melancholy.

"Fred holds all of my money and property in trust until the date of my marriage. As long as that marriage is with his approval. And he'll never approve of my marrying anyone but him."

"How dreadfully unfair it is," Jane said. "Your father must be turning over in his grave."

Maggie gave a short, humorless laugh. "On the contrary. It's just the outcome Papa was hoping for. He couldn't force me to marry Fred while he was alive. In truth, he didn't have the heart to force me to do anything. But now he's dead, he leaves me no choice. If I don't marry within the time allotted, Beasley Park will go to Fred for good, and I'll be left nothing but a small income on which to live out my spinsterhood."

"Oh, Margaret. Your father doted on you so. I can't comprehend how he could give away your inheritance to a stranger. A man related to you by neither blood nor marriage. It makes no sense at all."

"Papa knew precisely what he was doing."

"Well, I can't understand it!"

"Can you not, Jane? Papa raised *me* to run Beasley Park. To love the land just as he loved it himself. He knew there was nothing on earth I wouldn't do to keep it. And knowing that…from the grave, he has forced my hand."

Jane shook her head in disbelief. "Then you mean to marry Fred?"

"Yes…I…" Maggie faltered. "I haven't told Fred my answer yet. I have a little time left."

"How much time?" Jane asked.

"The will stated that if I wasn't already married upon Papa's death, I would have two years in which to become so. That allowed for one year of mourning, and one year to find a husband. Unfortunately, it didn't account for the time I must spend mourning Aunt Daphne."

"Your aunt *would* choose to die the week after you finished mourning your father."

"Yes. And as a result, I have but six months left before I must wed."

Jane exhaled a deep breath. "Oh dear. No wonder you're looking so wan and sickly. I didn't like to mention it, but…"

Maggie wasn't offended. She knew full well how she must appear to her friend. "The Burton-Smythes believe in the strictest possible interpretation of the rules of mourning. I wasn't permitted to leave the house after Papa died except for walks in the garden with Bessie. And I wasn't allowed visitors or to…" She faltered again, raising a hand to her forehead. A headache threatened. "Fred already runs Beasley as if it were his own. He's joined it to the Burton-Smythe estate. I haven't any say, not even over the tenants that I've known my whole life."

"You have no power at all?"

"Not to speak of. Papa's steward, Mr. Entwhistle, keeps me apprised of estate matters as he can, and I know he still takes my opinions under advisement. He's promised to write to me during my stay here. As for my own personal needs, I must apply to Fred directly. And if I purchase something, even as small and personal as garters for my stockings, he insists upon seeing the receipts. He's not tightfisted. Indeed, he is *exceedingly generous* with me, as he's fond of saying. But he loves nothing more than making certain I recognize the power he holds. I have come to *hate* asking him for anything."

"He was always a vile worm," Jane said feelingly. "And I'm sure having to defer to any man seems intolerable to you, for unlike the rest of us poor females, you've never had to bear it before."

"Sometimes I think I cannot bear it. I'm so tired, Jane. And I have been so blue deviled."

Jane took Maggie's hand and held it in both of hers. "Poor dear. But you must take heart. I've just this morning heard some news that might cheer you."

Maggie proffered a weak smile. "Have you?"

"Oh yes. You'll be pleased to know that Frederick Burton-Smythe will be getting his comeuppance very soon. Tomorrow in fact." Jane leaned toward Maggie, lowering her voice so the servants going in and out of the dressing room couldn't overhear. "At dawn tomorrow, he is engaged to fight a duel!"

"*I beg your pardon?*"

"It's the truth. We ladies aren't supposed to know of such things, but I heard it from Mrs. Beauchamp, who heard it from her husband. He was present at the gaming hell when it all happened."

"When what all happened?"

"It seems that, while Fred was in the middle of a card game, one of the players gave up his seat to the Viscount St.

Clare. Well, St. Clare and Fred were at odds right from the start, apparently, for you know what a hothead Fred can be. Someone made a passing reference to a problem with the count of the cards. One thing led to another, and then, the next thing everyone knew, Fred was on his feet, shouting that St. Clare would answer for what he'd said. And St. Clare replied, as cool as you please, that he wasn't in the habit of meeting country nobodies on the field of honor, but that he'd make an exception in Fred's case."

Maggie's head was spinning. "*Fred* issued the challenge?"

"That he did, the arrogant fool." Jane laughed. "But I'm leaving out the best part. Lord St. Clare is the grandson of the Earl of Allendale!"

Maggie stared at Jane. "What does that signify?"

"Why, the earl was once considered to be one of the foremost shots in England, and his son, if all the tales are true, was even more deadly. He killed a man in a duel decades ago and was forced to flee to the continent, where he promptly killed another. Dueling is in their blood, you see. And I've heard that Lord St. Clare is the most lethal of them all."

Maggie rose abruptly from her place on the bed. She paced the length of the bedroom and back again. "But this is terrible, Jane! If Fred is killed, what will happen to Beasley Park? What will happen to my money?"

"He won't be killed. Only frightened, and perhaps humbled a little—or so I hope! That's why the tale is so diverting." Jane's smile faded. "Isn't it?"

"No, Jane. It's not diverting at all. It's maddening. Infuriating. Only think what the consequences might be if anything should go wrong." Maggie wrung her hands as she paced. "Oh, how utterly thoughtless of him—and how completely typical!

He never considers anyone but himself. He's the most selfish, inconsiderate man alive!" She stopped suddenly, turning back to her friend in a whirl of overlarge blue skirts. "I shall have to put a stop to it somehow."

"Put a stop to it? But how can you?"

"I shall...I shall summon Fred and tell him... Oh, what *shall* I tell him, Jane?"

Jane's brow creased. "I cannot think. I've never heard of a woman stopping a duel before unless... I suppose you could find out where they're to meet, and throw yourself between them. But that doesn't seem advisable, does it?"

"No, indeed."

"Well then, at the very least, you must summon him here. You must reason with him as well as you can." Jane paused. "And while you're at it, you must demand as much money from him as you require for the season, and then some. *You* have the moral high ground now, Margaret, and Frederick Burton-Smythe will not be able to deny you anything."

2

Maggie's note requesting Fred come and see her was taken round to his lodgings by a footman at half past four. The footman promptly returned with Fred's reply: Mr. Burton-Smythe would do himself the honor of calling upon Miss Honeywell in half an hour.

By the time Fred arrived, Maggie had washed and changed into a fresh gown and put her hair into some semblance of order. She received him alone in the Trumbles' drawing room, sitting composedly in a chair near the fire with a tea tray arranged in front of her.

"Margaret." Fred executed a smart bow. It caused the lines of his coat to strain against the brawny muscles of his back. "I'd have thought you had the good sense to rest after your journey."

Maggie had resolved to make an effort at civility, but at Fred's words, she couldn't refrain from a sharp retort. "You presume to lecture *me* on good sense?"

"You'll never regain your strength if you don't rest."

"How can I rest, when the first thing I hear upon my arrival in London is that you're engaged to fight a duel?"

Fred's face turned a mottled red—a particularly unbecoming shade when contrasted with his copper-colored hair. "I needn't ask how you heard such a rumor. Your friend Miss Trumble, no doubt."

"Do you deny it?"

He pokered up, his broad, stocky frame as stiff and unyielding as Sir Roderick himself. "I shall not admit it *or* deny it. Indeed, I shall not say another word on the subject. It's the height of impropriety to be discussing such things with you."

"Oh, do stop acting like your father!" Maggie glared up at him. "And why must you loom over me in such a disagreeable fashion? Sit down for pity's sake. Here. I shall pour you out a cup of tea, and then we'll talk like a lady of six and twenty and a man of thirty instead of bickering like two half-civilized children."

Scowling, Fred grudgingly did as she bade him. His expression slowly softened as he watched Maggie preside over the tea tray. When she held out a cup to him, his tea prepared just as he liked it, he took it from her with a complacent smile. "What a good little wife you'll be."

A flicker of temper sparked in Maggie's chest. "To whom, I wonder?"

"Why, to me, of course."

The flicker quickly kindled into a low, smoldering flame.

Fred drank his tea, oblivious to Maggie's worsening mood. He was dressed in what she assumed must be considered the first stare of fashion here in London. Skintight pantaloons, gleaming Hessians, and shirt-points so high that they inhibited the movement of his thick neck. To Maggie, however, he looked no different from the surly, squarely built bully of her youth.

She disliked him intensely. And yet, in six months, she would have to consent to be his wife. Mrs. Margaret Burton-Smythe. Then, he would not only have rights over her fortune, he'd have rights over her body as well. The thought of it had caused her many a sleepless night these past months.

"I didn't summon you here to talk about *that*," she said tightly. "I summoned you here to discuss this duel of yours."

Fred lowered his cup. "I can see you're concerned. And I can't tell you how much it gratifies me to know you care about my well-being. However—"

"I *care* about Beasley Park."

"However," he continued, unperturbed, "even if I were to engage in a duel in the morning, it doesn't follow that I'll be the loser."

"How not? When, by all accounts, the man you're dueling with is the most fiendish shot in all of Christendom?"

Fred's condescending manner gave way to a flare of masculine indignation. "Oh, that's what they're saying, is it? And how might anyone know, pray? St. Clare has been on the continent for the better part of his life. I don't recall anyone ever having seen him shooting at Manton's."

"If he's been on the continent for most of his life, it's because his father killed someone in a duel and they were forced to flee England. Dueling is in their blood, I hear."

"No more than it is mine. My father fought two duels when he was a young man."

"And in each one, he and his opponent deloped. I've heard the stories too, Fred. It isn't the same at all."

Fred glowered. "What do you know of affairs of honor? You're a woman."

Maggie answered him in a voice of perilous calm. "And women don't have honor?"

"Don't put words in my mouth, Margaret. Naturally a woman has honor. But a woman's honor is as different from that of a gentleman's as the sun is to the moon. You can't begin to compare them."

"On that I agree. You and I have exceedingly different notions of honor."

In the past, her words would have prompted an out-and-out row with Fred. But this time he didn't take the bait. Instead, with a visible effort, he regained his composure. He resumed sipping his tea, a mulish set to his jaw. "As I said before, this isn't at all a suitable subject for us to be discussing."

"No doubt," Maggie replied. "But we must talk about it, and we *shall* talk about. For if you're killed in the morning, what will happen to Beasley Park? What will happen to *me*?"

Fred's large fingers tightened reflexively on the handle of his teacup. "Having not spent a great deal of time contemplating my own death, I can't say with any certainty. I'd have to review your father's will. And as it's at the solicitor's, and I won't be at liberty to go into his office until tomorrow afternoon at the earliest, it's rather a moot point, don't you think?"

Maggie stared at him blankly. "What do you imagine happens, then? My money and property won't simply go up into a puff of smoke, will they? Who is to be in control of my inheritance if you're unable? Did Papa name someone?"

"No. I don't believe he did."

"Then…?"

"I expect if for any reason I wasn't able to fulfill my duties, the office would go to your distant uncle. That elderly fellow in Yorkshire. I can't recall his name."

"Mr. Arkham?" she said in tones of disbelief.

"Yes. That's the chap."

"Good lord, he isn't even a blood relation! He was married to some distant aunt, or half-sister of somebody or other, so far removed that Papa didn't even recognize them in our family Bible!"

Fred returned his teacup to the tea tray. He leaned forward in his seat. "Your cheeks are flushed. Shall I ring for Bessie?"

"No!"

Ignoring her protest, he rose and went to the bell pull by the fireplace. After giving it a sharp tug, he came to stand beside her chair.

Maggie fairly trembled with suppressed rage. The bloody nerve of Fred. Using her ill health as a means to win an argument. "I don't need Bessie," she said stiffly. "I am *not* unwell. I'm merely angry that you—"

"Enough of this now. I shouldn't have indulged you so. There's reason such topics are kept from women. I've told you there's no need for you to worry. That should be more than sufficient. I wouldn't have given permission for you come to London if—" He broke off his lecture as the doors to the drawing room opened and Jane entered. His eyes narrowed. "Miss Trumble."

"Mr. Burton-Smythe." Jane crossed the room to Maggie, seeming to register her overwrought state in one comprehensive glance.

Fred moved to intercept her. "A word, if you please. I am informed that—"

"Yes, yes, I daresay." Jane brushed past him to the tea tray. She swiftly poured out a cup, stirring in a generous helping of sugar. "Here you are, dear." She handed it to Maggie. "A few sips of this."

"I'm fine, Jane. Truly."

"Drink," Jane commanded. At that, she turned on Fred, drawing herself up to her full, and not inconsiderable, height. "This is *my* house, and Miss Honeywell is *my* guest. I'll not allow you to browbeat her into a faint or a fever. You know she's not been well since—"

"I'm perfectly aware," Fred said through gritted teeth. "I can only wonder that you, being so solicitous of Miss Honeywell's health, should have thought it a wise idea to burden her with a lot of baseless town gossip."

"It is not baseless!" Jane snapped back. "Everyone knows you challenged Lord St. Clare. And as Miss Honeywell's closest friend, I consider it my duty to give her fair warning when the man who controls her fortune is embarking on a course of action that will end with him getting his head blown off his shoulders."

Fred gave Jane a look of withering scorn before turning his attention back to Maggie. "Put it out of your head, Margaret. And from now on, restrict yourself to more feminine concerns."

Jane wasn't so easily dismissed. "Feminine concerns? Like supper parties and the theater and shopping for new gowns, do you mean?"

"Precisely."

"And how shall Miss Honeywell pay for these new gowns."

Fred shot a hard glance at her over his shoulder. "Not that it's any of *your* business, but Miss Honeywell is very well provided for."

"She's wearing ill-fitting clothes that are years out of fashion."

"She's been in mourning!"

"As that may be, to the rest of the *ton* it will simply look as if you've been unreasonably keeping her fortune from her. And when one sees you wearing a coat that appears to have been cut by Weston, and boots that have no doubt been polished with champagne, they'll further surmise that you've been enriching yourself at her expense."

At her words, Fred's face went scarlet. "If you were a man, an accusation like that would—"

"Hold a moment." Maggie placed a staying hand on his sleeve. "Jane isn't accusing you of anything. She's only telling you what conclusions other people will draw when they see how poorly I'm turned out. And you must own she's right."

Jane gave Fred an innocent smile. "In order to scotch these unfortunate rumors, Miss Honeywell will need a whole new wardrobe."

Fred fixed his gaze on Maggie. A muscle worked convulsively in his cheek. "I've never denied you anything, so long as you asked me in a polite and civil manner. Go to the dressmaker and the milliner, by all means, and have the bills sent to me. But not today. Today you're to retire to bed. Tomorrow, if you have recovered your strength from the journey, you may go shopping. But you're to take Bessie. I shall have a word with her before I go. She knows her duty."

He took his leave of them, then. Jane summoned a footman to fetch his hat and cane and show him out. As the drawing room doors closed behind him, she muttered, "How generous you are. We are both so *very* much obliged to you."

Maggie leaned back in her seat. As a girl, she'd been energized by arguments. Fueled by raised voices and heated words. Now such things only served to exhaust her. "What a colossal waste of time."

"Not entirely." Jane sat down across from her in Fred's vacated chair. "He's given you leave to purchase as many new clothes as you like. And if he thinks I mean to take you to Grafton House for a bargain, he's much mistaken. We shall go to Madame Clothilde, that new French modiste in Bruton Street that everyone's raving about. *Très exclusif*, apparently. She only dresses the richest and most beautiful ladies in town. You've lost a bit of your bloom, I know, but she'll not turn you away."

"How can I think of shopping? There's still the duel to consider in the morning, and I haven't the faintest idea what I…" Maggie closed her eyes, rubbing her forehead again.

"A headache?"

"No, no. Well, that is…yes, my head does ache, but I think I have an idea."

"To throw yourself between them?"

"Indeed not. But it occurs to me that, if I can't reason with Fred, the only course of action left is to try and reason with the viscount."

Jane stilled. "Lord St. Clare? But how can you? You haven't even been introduced to him. And even if you had…he's a single gentleman. You can't simply pay him an afternoon call."

"Of course not. By tomorrow afternoon, it will be too late. I must go today. Or tonight, rather, for I can't be seen paying a call on him in broad daylight."

"My dear, you cannot go at all. There's your reputation to consider."

"I suppose I shall have to go under cover of darkness," Maggie said, thinking aloud. "When I'm least likely to be observed."

"If you won't consider your own reputation, you must at least consider mine. I'm your hostess and responsible for your—"

"I won't ask you to accompany me, if that's what you're afraid of. And I won't involve your servants, either. I can very well take a hackney to the viscount's residence." Maggie hoped that would be enough to protect Jane's good name. "Unless...Gad, he doesn't live in bachelor rooms in St. James's Street, does he?"

"No. At least, I don't think so. I've heard he's staying at the Earl of Allendale's residence. A big mausoleum of a place in Grosvenor Square."

"But that's not very far from here at all."

"Yes, I daresay you might walk there," Jane said dryly.

"I know you disapprove, but you must advise me. Is St. Clare as unreasonable as Fred, do you think?"

"I haven't the slightest notion. We've never been introduced. Though I *have* seen him twice at the theater. He was sitting in a box with his grandfather. I must say, he didn't *look* like a particularly amiable gentleman. On the other hand, I can't conceive of anyone being as disagreeable as Fred."

Maggie considered this. "Well, I suppose the worst thing that can happen is he'll laugh in my face. Or refuse to admit me altogether. It's very likely a fool's errand, but if there's a chance he might call off this stupid duel, I must make the effort to see him."

"The worst thing that can happen...?" Jane was incredulous. "Margaret, no one knows the viscount well enough to judge his character. He's been on the continent for ages. For all you know, he's a rake and a libertine. A vile seducer. To go to his house alone—and at night, too—you're practically offering yourself to him on a silver platter!"

"I shan't go alone," Maggie said. "I shall take Bessie with me."

3

Maggie stood outside the monstrous structure in Grosvenor Square that the hackney-carriage driver had assured her was the town residence of the Earl of Allendale. It was cold and the mist had come up, blanketing the street in a gray fog barely penetrable by the glow of the gas lamps that lined it. She wrapped the folds of her fur-trimmed cloak tighter around her as Bessie paid the hackney driver.

Bessie hadn't been as reluctant to accompany Maggie on her errand as Maggie had expected she'd be. Indeed, her former nurse had taken the view that any behavior resembling that engaged in by Maggie in her wild and headstrong youth ought to be encouraged.

"You were never a frail, wilting sort of female, Miss Margaret," Bessie had said. "Not until you took sick. Who knows but that an adventure or two like you used to have might not put the color back in your cheeks?"

Maggie was oddly touched by her maid's loyalty. Especially considering Fred's all-too-frequent lectures to Bessie on the duty she owed her mistress, and his constant threat that, were anything to happen to Maggie, Bessie would be sent off without a reference. As if such a thing were in his power! He wasn't Maggie's husband. Not yet, at least.

"The driver has promised he'll wait here to take us back to Green Street after we've seen the viscount," Bessie said, approaching Maggie through the fog. Her own cloak, made of a nondescript drab, billowed around her large frame. "Though if you ask me, his lordship's as like to be in bed asleep as anything."

Maggie followed Bessie's gaze to the darkened windows of the house. "It's only one o'clock. I daresay there's more of a chance he won't be home at all. Most gentlemen hereabouts keep town hours."

Bessie pursed her lips in disapproval as she accompanied Maggie to the front door. "Wrap yourself up tight, Miss Margaret. No need for you to be getting a chill on Master Fred's account."

Maggie nodded, and while Bessie rapped at the door, she tugged the fur of her cloak up around her chin. It had been a gift from her father, given to her over six years ago when she returned home from her first season in London. A fine, deep blue velvet trimmed in sable. "The same blue as the wildflowers at Beasley," Papa had told her.

"Town hours, indeed," Bessie muttered, rapping at the door again. "Where are the servants, then, I ask you?"

Maggie briefly closed her eyes. Her cheeks were warm despite the cold, and within her chest was the familiar feeling of heaviness she experienced whenever she'd overtaxed herself. The journey *had* worn her down. She hated for Fred to be right.

She was just beginning to consider whether or not she should tell Bessie that it was all a mistake—that they should get back into the hackney and return to Lord and Lady Trumble's—when the front door opened and they were confronted by a stooped, white-haired butler with a candle held in his upraised hand.

He looked at Bessie first before dismissing her and turning his rheumy gaze on Maggie. His eyes swept her from the top of the sable-trimmed hood of her cloak to the toes of her kid half-boots. Seeming to have satisfied himself that at least one of the party was a lady, he lowered his candle. "Madam?"

Maggie stepped forward. "I'm come to see Lord St. Clare," she said in the same firm tones she used when directing the servants at Beasley Park. "It's a matter of some urgency."

The butler's face was devoid of expression. "Your name, Madam?"

She swallowed. "Mrs. Ives."

It was Jane who had suggested that Maggie present herself as a married lady. "Servants are prone to gossip," she'd said before Maggie departed Green Street. "It would be far better if St. Clare's servants didn't know you were *Miss* Honeywell. Indeed, it would be best if they didn't know who you were at all."

Bessie had heartily agreed, even going so far as to volunteer her own last name for Maggie's use. It was a small deception and would surely harm no one, but Maggie was uncomfortable with it all the same.

"I will see if his lordship is at home." The butler began to withdraw, moving as if to close the door.

Maggie delayed him a moment longer. "If he *is* at home, inform him, if you please, that my visit pertains to his dawn appointment."

The butler betrayed no signs of knowledge about the duel, but Maggie suspected her own knowledge of it underlined to him the urgency of her visit. He disappeared into the house, and after a short time, during which Bessie grumbled incessantly about the rudeness of servants leaving young ladies to wait on the stoop with no care at all for whether they would develop an inflammation of the lungs, he reappeared and welcomed them inside.

The entry hall of the Earl of Allendale's residence was far grander than that of Lord and Lady Trumble's house in Green Street. An enormous crystal chandelier hung from the ceiling, and a sweeping staircase curved up to the floors above. The floor was tiled in marble, and the silk-papered walls were lined with statuary and artifacts.

Maggie pushed back the hood of her cloak and looked around, her eyes settling first on a sculpture of a horse and then on an eerily shaped bust that, upon closer inspection, appeared to be some sort of a death mask. A shiver ran down her spine.

"His lordship will see you in the library." The butler guided them down the hall to a set of closed doors.

Maggie raised a self-conscious hand to her hair, smoothing any stray locks back into the simple chignon in which Bessie had arranged it before they left Green Street.

The butler opened the door for her, and Maggie preceded him into the library, Bessie not far behind her. The room was lit by only a few candles and the crackling fire in the hearth. Its dancing flames cast the bookshelves and furnishings in an ever-shifting pattern of shadows.

A tall, broad-shouldered man stood in front of the fire, his back to the room. Lord St. Clare, Maggie presumed.

"Mrs. Ives, your lordship," the butler said.

"Thank you, Jessup." St. Clare's voice was a deep, rich baritone. "You may leave us."

As the butler withdrew, St. Clare turned and approached his visitors. He was a big man, standing well over six feet, and had the sort of lean, well-muscled build that set off the current fashion for skintight pantaloons and close-fitting coats to magnificent effect. Unlike Fred, whose bulky frame had made him look oddly uncomfortable in his snug garments, the viscount seemed perfectly at ease, moving with a languorous, masculine grace that put Maggie in mind of a great, predatory cat.

A rake, Jane had said. A libertine. A vile seducer of women.

He emerged from the shadows to stand in front of her, promptly executing a slight bow. "Mrs. Ives. I don't believe I've had the pleasure."

Maggie stared up at him, her wide eyes meeting his stormy gray ones.

Her breath caught. "*Oh*," she said weakly.

And then, she fainted.

Strong arms caught Maggie before she fell to the ground, effortlessly sweeping her up and carrying her to the leather library sofa. A pillow was arranged behind her head, and long masculine fingers untied the ribbons at the neck of her cloak, revealing the modest kerseymere gown she'd worn beneath it.

"Fair exhausted, she is," Maggie heard Bessie saying as she slowly came around. "Only arrived in London this afternoon and refused to rest, no matter how much the master and Miss Trumble prevailed upon her."

"She's ill," St. Clare said.

"A nip of brandy will set her to rights. If you could spare a glass, your lordship?"

Maggie felt St. Clare rise. She heard the clink of crystal as a decanter was unstopped and a glass was filled. Then, before she knew it, a powerful arm was sliding beneath her shoulders, carefully raising her up. She smelled the familiar fragrance of horses and leather combined with a seductive, purely masculine scent that might have been the viscount's shaving soap. "Steady now, Mrs. Ives," he said, placing the edge of the glass to her lips.

"You mustn't trouble yourself, my lord," Bessie said. "If you'll allow me. I was her nurse long before I was her maid."

"Her nurse?"

"Aye, indeed I was. There's many who say she wouldn't be alive today if it weren't for my nursing." The glass was taken from St. Clare, and now wielded in Bessie's capable hand, pressed again to Maggie's lips. "Just a swallow, Miss Margaret," she urged, compelling her to drink it. "A sip won't harm you."

St. Clare's arm tightened reflexively around Maggie's shoulders. "*Miss* Margaret?"

"Oh, well, as to that..."

Bessie was saved from explaining by Maggie herself who, after swallowing far more than a sip of the proffered brandy, had not only been revived by it, but had also promptly proceeded to choke. "It burns like the devil," she gasped, opening her eyes and coughing. Thankfully, the aftereffects of the fiery liquid were short-lived. After a brief moment, she composed herself and, blinking several times, looked up at the figure of Bessie hovering over her.

And then she looked past Bessie, to the face of the gentleman cradling her in his arm.

Her pulse raced.

Lord St. Clare was a dangerously handsome man who, at first glance, put Maggie in mind of Byron's Corsair. He had well-formed features characterized by a strong, chiseled jaw, lean cheeks, and firmly molded lips that were inclined to curl into a sneer. His thick golden hair looked as if it had been tousled by a cold north wind. And his skin appeared to have been bronzed by the sun of some exotic land.

There was a faintly weathered look about him. A hint of world-weariness. Had he been a sailor, perhaps? An officer in His Majesty's Navy? Or was his appearance merely the result of years spent traipsing about the continent?

He was undoubtedly aristocratic, Maggie could see that quite plainly. His bearing was that of a gentleman who'd had wealth and privilege since birth. Indeed, it was that precise quality of subtle, patrician arrogance that, when combined with the healthy glow of his skin and the lazy, masculine grace of his body, gave him the look of a man who spent all of his time out of doors—riding, driving, and very likely dueling lesser men to the death just for the fun of it.

Good lord, how could she ever have thought this man was Nicholas Seaton?

He couldn't be, could he? It was impossible. He was too big. Too strong. Too old. Too highborn. Too...everything.

And yet...St. Clare's eyes were the same unique shade of stormy gray as Nicholas Seaton's, and they held within their depths that peculiar mix of humor, bitterness, and anguish that Nicholas's had had all those years ago at Beasley Park.

And he smelled like Nicholas, too. Not the expensive shaving soap—Nicholas had never had anything half so fine—

but the fragrance of horses and leather and that other scent that had so uniquely belonged to him.

Maggie met St. Clare's eyes, unable to contain the swell of longing within her.

How many years had she wasted waiting for Nicholas Seaton to return to Somerset? Too many to count. He'd been her first love. Her only love. She'd long ago resigned herself to the fact that he was dead. He'd have joined the army. He'd have been killed in the Peninsula or at the Battle of Waterloo. He must be dead. For if he were still alive somewhere in the world, he would have found his way back to her.

"The brandy was not to your liking, I see," St. Clare said. "Shall I send for a glass of wine? A cup of tea? Pray tell me what you require, Mrs. Ives, and I shall endeavor to supply it."

Maggie struggled to a sitting position. "I thank you, my lord, but I don't require anything. I'm much better now. Indeed, if you'll be so kind as to release me…"

St. Clare waited until she was fully upright before removing his supportive arm. He then drew back, taking a seat in a nearby chair. His gaze never left Maggie's face. "It *is* Mrs. Ives, is it not?"

Maggie straightened her skirts around her. Her gown, like all her others, hung loosely on her frame. She feared that whatever illusion her fine cloak had provided had now been dispelled. For all she knew, St. Clare thought her some sort of poor, grasping opportunist in ill-fitting clothes who went about pretending to be a fine lady. "No. It isn't," she admitted. "Mrs. Ives is, in fact, the name of my maid."

Bessie, who had remained near Maggie on the sofa, gave a nod to St. Clare but said nothing.

"I'm Margaret Honeywell of Beasley Park." Maggie thought she saw a flicker in St. Clare's gaze, but it was gone before she could interpret it. "I'm at present a guest of Lord and Lady Trumble in Green Street."

"So, not a Mrs. at all."

"No, my lord. But as I told your butler, my business with you is most urgent. It concerns your duel. And, as I only arrived in London this afternoon, time was of the essence. I had to contrive a way to call upon you without endangering my reputation. That's why I've come at this hour, and why I didn't give your butler my true name."

"Quite."

Maggie hesitated. St. Clare's expression was completely inscrutable. She couldn't tell for the life of her if he was one of those odious gentlemen who pokered up as soon as a lady mentioned such topics as duels or gaming hells or the demi-monde. She lifted her chin a notch. "I suppose you won't even acknowledge that you're having a duel with Mr. Burton-Smythe."

He shrugged one broad shoulder. "Why shouldn't I?"

She blinked. "Oh. Well... That *is* unexpected. But I must say, it certainly simplifies matters."

"I see no need to complicate them."

"Nor do I. However, there are some gentlemen who insist on making everything far more difficult than it need be."

"A tiresome habit. Tell me, Miss Honeywell, am I right in concluding that you're somehow affiliated with Mr. Burton-Smythe?"

"Affiliated?" Maggie gave a short laugh. "In a manner of speaking, yes." She rubbed her forehead with her hand.

"Does your head ache again, Miss Margaret?" Bessie asked, moving toward her.

"What? No. Please don't make a fuss. I'm perfectly well." Maggie turned her attention back to St. Clare. She hadn't thought it possible, but he seemed to be watching her even more intently now. "Yes, my lord. Mr. Burton-Smythe and I are affiliated. He is, in a manner of speaking, my guardian."

For a fraction of a second, St. Clare's mask of slightly bored affability dropped, revealing a glitter of outrage. "Your *guardian*?"

"More precisely, he's the executor of my father's will and has control of my property and funds until the date of my marriage. The provisions of the will are such that, if anything were to happen to him, there's a fair chance I would end up living in penury."

"Ah. This begins to make sense."

Maggie took a breath. She'd already fainted into the gentleman's arms. There was no need to stand on ceremony. "I understand that you're particularly proficient with a pistol, my lord."

He shrugged his shoulder again. "I'm a Beresford."

"I beg your pardon. A Beresford, did you say?"

"I'm John Beresford, Viscount St. Clare. My grandfather is Aldrick Beresford, Earl of Allendale. And yes, Miss Honeywell. The Beresfords are *particularly* proficient with pistols."

"Yes, of course. Your family name. Forgive me, I didn't know." Maggie dropped her eyes to her hands for a moment before raising them back to St. Clare's face. "I'll not beat about the bush, my lord. I've come to beg you to call off your duel with Mr. Burton-Smythe."

St. Clare seemed to consider this. "I assume you've already asked the same of Mr. Burton-Smythe?"

"Yes." She frowned. "For all the good it did me. He's utterly unreasonable. But you… Well, I don't know you, my lord, but I have every hope that you'll take my concerns seriously. If not, the only course left to me is to discover where your duel is to be held and to somehow arrange to appear there at the pivotal moment so that I might throw myself between the two of you."

He gave her a strange look. "Does that method usually work?"

"I don't know. I've never attempted it when pistols were involved."

"Do you mean to say that you *have* attempted it on other occasions?"

"Oh, yes. Before… That is, many years ago. But it was merely fisticuffs. And Fred—Mr. Burton-Smythe, I mean— only ever withdrew from fighting because I had some measure of influence over him then." She smoothed out a crease in her skirt. "It's different now. I have no influence at all. Indeed, I'm powerless to stop him doing anything."

St. Clare watched her awhile longer, and then, in a gentler tone than he'd used thus far, said, "Rest easy, Miss Honeywell. Much as he may deserve it, I don't intend to kill Mr. Burton-Smythe at dawn. It's a capital offense, you know, and having spent the better part of my life on the continent, I have no immediate desire to return there."

Hope surged in Maggie's breast. "You'll call off the duel?"

"Ah. No. That, I'm afraid, I cannot do. But I give you my word of honor that Mr. Burton-Smythe will not die at my hand."

Maggie had a poor opinion of a gentleman's word of honor. Even so, she knew better than to call it into question. A gentleman could be quite touchy on the subject. She supposed that St. Clare's assurances would have to satisfy her. "Thank you, my lord. I'm very much obliged to you."

"Indeed you are," he murmured. "One might even say that you're in my debt."

Bessie gave a sharp intake of breath.

Maggie cast a fleeting glance in her maid's direction before turning her attention back to the viscount. "In your debt? For sparing Mr. Burton-Smythe, do you mean? But you said you had no intention of killing him in the first place."

"So I did. And at the moment, that's very true. At dawn, however…" He shrugged. "Who's to say? Your Mr. Burton-Smythe can be devilish provoking."

"Of that I'm well aware, but I don't see how—"

"There's a good chance he'll say something to annoy me."

Her brows drew together. "He very well might."

"And when he does, the impulse to put a bullet in his brain may be too great to resist."

Maggie heard another gasp from Bessie. And no wonder. A gentleman shouldn't speak of duels at all in the presence of a lady, let alone be so lost to decency as to mention firing a bullet into someone's brain.

Perhaps St. Clare was trying to put her out of countenance?

If so, he was in for a disappointment. As a girl, Maggie had frequently heard her father threatening to blow this or that person's brains out, or to tear them limb from limb. Indeed, she recalled making similar threats a time or two herself. The Honeywells were known for their bluster.

"If he offends you in some way, can you not simply ignore him?" she asked. "It's what I try to do."

St. Clare leaned back in his leather chair and crossed his legs. The firelight reflected in the mirror-polished finish of his Hessians and glittered in the golden threads of his hair. He was the picture of an aristocratic gentleman at his ease.

Maggie wasn't fooled one bit.

His light-colored pantaloons clung to long, powerfully made legs, and his dark blue coat appeared to have been molded to his broad shoulders. The elegant sprawl he affected was an illusion. St. Clare was no more relaxed than a lion waiting to spring upon its prey.

"In other circumstances," he replied, "perhaps I could. But during an affair of honor a man's blood is running high. Even the most placid sort of gentleman often finds himself unable to refrain from violence when a pistol is in his hand. And I am not a placid sort of gentleman. In truth, I have a bit of a temper."

"As do I, my lord. What does that signify? Unless… Are you saying that your conduct at dawn hinges on whether or not Mr. Burton-Smythe can refrain from irritating you?" She was incredulous. "If that is so, then he's as good as dead. I have come here for nothing."

"Not necessarily. I believe, with the right inducement, I may be able to restrain myself."

"Inducement?"

"It strikes me, Miss Honeywell, that if I'm to do this great favor for you, the least you might do in return is to grant me a forfeit of some kind."

Bessie gave a puff of indignation. "Miss Margaret," she warned under her breath.

"It's all right, Bessie," Maggie said, still looking at St. Clare. If he hadn't reminded her so much of Nicholas Seaton, she might have been insulted. As it was, she could only be intrigued. "What sort of forfeit?"

"You've asked me to spare a man's life. A man whom I dislike excessively. The comparable forfeit for such a service would be great indeed. Far greater than anything a gentleman would ever ask of a lady. I propose instead, three more moderately sized forfeits to be collected at the time of my choosing."

"Miss Margaret!" Bessie hissed.

"Hush, Bessie. I ask again, my lord, what sort of forfeits?"

St. Clare gave her a crooked smile. "I don't know yet, but it will be nothing untoward, I assure you."

The sight of St. Clare's smile was like a lightning bolt straight through Maggie's heart. For a moment she couldn't breathe. She'd seen that same crooked smile thousands of times before. It worked on her in a powerful way. St. Clare wasn't Nicholas Seaton, she knew it, but to once again be the recipient of that smile and that stormy gray gaze, Maggie thought she would agree to practically anything in the world. "All right, then. I accept your terms."

4

"Jenkins has done wonders with your gown." Jane eyed Maggie's muslin walking dress from across the breakfast table the following morning. "Didn't I tell you? A stitch or two here, a bit of ribbon there, *et voilà!*"

Maggie cast a brief glance downward. Jane's dresser, while no skilled seamstress, was a dab hand at making minor alterations. She'd taken in Maggie's three-year-old white muslin in only a few strategic places, and now, instead of billowing about her like a shapeless sack, it skimmed softly over her curves. "It certainly fits better. Though I'm afraid no amount of ribbon can disguise how thoroughly out of fashion it is."

"Indeed. It is very plain. And not a single flounce. But the fabric is exquisite, and in that shade of white your complexion fairly glows. Who made it for you originally? Mme. Dupin, I expect. She was all the rage during your last visit. She's sold up, you know. Ran off to the continent with a married lover. At least, that was the gossip at the time." Jane buttered a slice of toast. "Perhaps Jenkins can alter a few of your other dresses?" she suggested before taking a bite.

Maggie was tempted. Whatever she ordered at the modiste this afternoon wouldn't be ready for a week or more. It would be lovely to have something to wear in the meantime. If only her own happiness were the sole consideration! She sighed. "It's good of you to offer, Jane, but I dare not accept. Bessie's been in high dudgeon from the moment Jenkins set foot into my dressing room. I've spent half the morning trying to soothe her injured feelings."

"How very territorial the two of them are." Jane laughed. "Like a pair of old cats. Well, never mind. I expect that Madame Clothilde will have a few dresses ready-made that you might purchase along with the rest of your order."

They planned to visit the modiste directly after breakfast. Maggie hoped she was equal to the task. Not only did she have her usual fatigue to contend with, but after a night spent with too little sleep, she had the added burden of exhaustion.

She and Jane had stayed up until nearly four in the morning discussing Maggie's visit with Lord St. Clare. Jane had wanted to know everything, from the condition of the hackney coach that had conveyed Maggie to Grosvenor Square to the far superior manner in which she'd been transported back to Green Street.

Had St. Clare really sent her home in his own carriage? With a fur-lined carriage rug and a hot brick for her feet? And was it true that he'd given Bessie a small flask of his best brandy to serve in case Maggie should feel faint again on the short journey home?

It was all true.

No sooner had she agreed to the viscount's proposed forfeits than he'd risen and rung the bell for his butler. He'd issued orders for their hired hackney to be dismissed, his own carriage to be readied, and for all to be done to assure her comfort on the journey back to Green Street.

She assumed the hot brick and carriage rug were Jessup's doing. The elegant silver flask, however, must have come from St. Clare himself, for upon examination, Maggie had discovered the letter B engraved upon it, along with some odd design which encompassed two animals that looked very much like foxes. She supposed it was the Beresford family crest.

But it hadn't been St. Clare's generosity that Maggie had lain awake thinking about until dawn, nor even his scandalous request for three forfeits. Instead, she'd been thinking of the one aspect of her visit to Grosvenor Square that she hadn't shared with Jane. The one aspect that was unknown, even to Bessie.

Lord St. Clare's unsettling resemblance to Nicholas Seaton.

"In the meanwhile," Jane continued, drawing Maggie's attention back to their conversation, "I shall lend you my new French bonnet. The white satin trimmed in blue ribbons." She paused to address a passing footman. "See that the barouche is readied, Carson. We'll be leaving in half an hour." And then to Maggie: "You must use my blue silk parasol as well. The color will suit you far better than it does me."

"That's very good of you. Though I expect your motives are somewhat less than altruistic. After all, it would do you no credit to be seen out shopping with—what did you call me upon my arrival? An unfashionable dowd?"

"No, did I?" Jane stifled another laugh. "But really, Margaret, you were used to look as neat as a pin. And now, well, it seems to me that since your dear papa died, you're past all caring. I fear that between your illness, Fred's tyranny, and the circumstances of your papa's will, your spirit has been broken altogether. I hope you'll tell me that I'm wrong."

Maggie reached for the silver pot of chocolate and silently refilled her cup. When she was finished pouring, she looked up at Jane with a taut smile. "You're quite wrong."

"My dear, I know that you've been blue deviled. Who on earth could blame you? But you mustn't allow any of these things to weigh on you. Not Fred or Beasley Park or even your poor health. You must put yourself into my hands. I have plans for everything, you see."

Maggie sipped her chocolate, regarding her friend with interest over the rim of her cup. "Oh, do you?"

"Of course! Firstly, I've been thinking that that horrid country doctor down in Somerset isn't at all the thing. He's Sir Roderick Burton-Smythe's creature, is he not? While you're here in town, you must see a proper physician. Mama consults a very competent fellow in Harley Street. Dr. Hart. He isn't particularly fashionable, for he's rather young and doesn't cater to old women's fancies, but all of his methods are the absolute newest thing, and for real illness, Mama says he's the very best."

Maggie lowered her cup. "Has Lady Trumble been ill?"

"Heavens no. It's only her megrims. And they've been much better under Dr. Hart's care. Indeed, it was Dr. Hart who recommended she remove to the country for the season. You must consult him, Margaret. At least, say you will consider it."

Maggie thought about it only a moment before saying, almost defiantly, "I don't see why I shouldn't receive a second opinion."

"Exactly so!"

"But I'd prefer it were done discreetly. And without Fred's knowledge. I wouldn't like him badgering me or...or influencing the doctor in any way."

"How could he? He's not your husband! Which brings me to another idea of mine." Jane waited until the maidservant who was clearing away the dishes had left the room. "One of my cousins is married to a solicitor, Mr. Wroxham. Do you suppose that, if you were to consult him about your father's will—"

Jane broke off abruptly as the doors to the breakfast room were unceremoniously pushed opened and her elder brother sauntered in.

George Trumble was a thin gentleman of medium height, with an amiable countenance and the same fair hair and closely set brown eyes as his sister. He'd been a sort of admirer of Maggie's during her come-out season, and though he hadn't waged a vigorous campaign for her heart—as Jane often said, George was no Wellington—he'd trailed after her quite loyally and had always been happy to be of service. When it had finally occurred to him that Maggie didn't return his, or anyone else's affections, his lukewarm ardor had cooled, quite naturally, into brotherly regard.

Now, as he greeted her, a slight reddening of his cheeks was the only indication that she'd ever been anything more to him than just another of his sister's many friends.

"What are you doing here so early, George?" Jane asked as he kissed her cheek. "I didn't expect we'd see you until much later in the evening."

George leaned around his sister to help himself to a large slice of plum cake. "I've been out riding and—"

Jane slapped his outstretched hand. "If you're going to eat that, pray sit down."

With a sheepish grin, George joined them at the breakfast table. He dropped his plum cake onto a plate and allowed his sister to pour him out a cup of coffee.

"You have the worst timing, George," Jane told him. "We're just on our way out. Indeed, I've already ordered the carriage."

"Out? Out where? And where is Aunt Harriet? Isn't she supposed to be chaperoning the pair of you?"

"Aunt Harriet's in her room with a breakfast tray. And Margaret and I are only going shopping, not to promenade along the Dark Walk at Vauxhall. We shall have our maids with us. And a footman as well. Of course," she continued, "if you're very concerned for our safety, you may accompany us yourself."

"I might at that," George replied severely. "The two of you out and about with nothing but two useless abigails and a lone footman? Recipe for disaster if I've ever heard one. I remember a time when there were so many gents crowding round Miss Honeywell, she could scarcely draw breath."

Maggie laughed. She remembered it, too. It had been an oppressively stuffy ballroom and George had taken her delicate lace fan from her hand and wafted it about her so vigorously that the sticks had broken. "Those days are long gone, I assure you. I'm six and twenty now."

"By Jove, are you? You don't look it." George took a swallow of coffee. "Not that it will make a bit of difference with the gossip going round after this morning. People bound to stare and whisper. And plenty of old tabbies won't scruple to question you outright, you mark my words."

Maggie's smile faded. "Gossip? What gossip?"

Jane's eyes narrowed at her brother. "Yes, George. Exactly what *are* you talking about?"

"That's the very thing I've come to tell you. I was out riding this morning in the park. I've bought a new gelding, Miss Honeywell. A prime goer. Not unlike that blood chestnut you had back when—" He broke off at a stern look from his sister. "Yes. Quite. As I was saying, I was out in the park this morning. All the fellows were talking about it. It's not quite the thing to speak about in front of ladies, but I daresay Jane has already told you—"

"Yes, yes. She knows about the duel." Jane waved him on with an impatient hand. "What did you hear?"

Maggie leaned forward in her chair, her attention fixed on Jane's brother. St. Clare had promised not to hurt Fred. And he'd given her no reason to doubt his word. It had all seemed to be settled.

"A lot of the gents in the park were present at the duel," George went on between bites of his plum cake. "I wish I'd been! There's not many who've seen St. Clare shoot, excepting Lord Vickers and Lord Mattingly. They traveled a bit with him on his grand tour, you know, and they said he was as deadly as all the rest of the Beresfords. Not that St. Clare's reputation meant a thing to Burton-Smythe. But then, as I told Vickers, Burton-Smythe's so full of self-importance that it would never even occur to him that any man could best him."

"Oh, go on!" Jane demanded.

"Well, the short of it is, the handkerchief was dropped and Burton-Smythe fired. His shot went a touch wide. Nearly singed the viscount's sleeve, I heard. And St. Clare didn't even flinch! Just stood there and without batting an eye, fired a bullet straight through Burton-Smythe's shoulder."

Maggie's mouth fell open. "*St. Clare shot Fred*?"

"To be sure, he did, but that's not even the best part." George's eyes were bright with excitement as he entered into the spirit of the tale. "Burton-Smythe was lying on the ground with the surgeon kneeling over him, and St. Clare walks up to him as cool as you please and says, 'Let this be a lesson to you, my good man. If you're going to act the brutish country squire, best stay in the country.' And then he leapt into his curricle and drove off." George laughed appreciatively. "If that don't beat all!"

Maggie felt a sickening flicker of dread in her stomach. One didn't have to be killed outright in order to die from a gunshot wound. Why, if Fred's shoulder festered, he could expire within the week! And then what was she to do? "Where is Fred now? Is he all right? Oh, Jane... Do you suppose I should go to him?"

"I say, Miss Honeywell, don't put yourself into a taking," George said. "Burton-Smythe is holed up at his lodgings. He's not hurt too badly—the bullet went clean through—but I hear he's in as foul a mood as anyone ever saw him. You'd be wise to leave him be for a while." George cleared his throat, giving an uncomfortable tug at his cravat. "Besides that, there's some who already think you have an agreement of some sort with Burton-Smythe—"

"Indeed, I do not!" Maggie objected.

"—and if you arrive at his lodgings to nurse him through his injury you may as well put a notice of your betrothal in the paper."

"Is that the subject of the gossip you mentioned?" Jane asked. "Well, is it?"

George groaned. "You know how things are. It'll begin with a few old tabbies stopping Miss Honeywell in Bond Street to ask after Burton-Smythe's health and end with all of the *ton* saying that the duel was fought over her honor." He shook his head in disgust. "Some of the fellows are already talking. Wouldn't you know it, that infernal gabster Beauchamp was at the duel, and by the time I arrived at the park, he was already there, telling the other gents how Burton-Smythe and St. Clare had looked as if they *hated* each other, and how he'd give a monkey to know what the duel had *really* been about. 'No doubt it's a woman,' he says. What a heap of rubbish. Everyone knows they fell out over a game of cards."

"I may as well go home," said Maggie.

"You most definitely will not," Jane replied. "Nor will we postpone any of our pleasure. If there's gossip going round connecting you to this duel…well, as far as I'm concerned, that's even more reason for us to be seen abroad. We shall go shopping just as we planned."

George heartily agreed, even going so far as to offer to escort them to the dressmaker himself, and afterward, if they weren't too worn down from their exertions, to take them both to Gunter's for an ice. "And if anyone dares inquire after Burton-Smythe's health," he said, "I'll send them off with a flea in their ear."

Maggie could do nothing but agree. In short order, she and Jane were tugging on their gloves and tying the ribbons of their bonnets, and George was handing them up into the Trumbles' barouche.

"I don't even really care about the gossip," Maggie confessed to Jane in a whisper while George stepped away to have a word with the coachman. "The truth is… Dash it, I don't like to think of myself as cold-blooded, but the only emotion I feel at the possibility of Fred succumbing to his wounds is worry over Beasley Park and my inheritance. Am I very awful?"

"No indeed." Jane unfurled a pale-yellow parasol. "Fred has been an inconsiderate clodpole. If I were you, I'd be white with rage."

"I should be, I know. And I *am* angry. But somehow... somehow I'm far more upset with Viscount St. Clare than I am with Fred. I can't think why."

Maggie recognized the untruth as soon as she said it.

She *did* know why she was more upset with St. Clare, even if she couldn't admit it to her friend. The fact of the matter was that, though she'd often felt powerless in the years since her father's death, she was wholly unaccustomed to being made to feel a fool.

Three forfeits indeed.

What a country bumpkin St. Clare must have thought her. No doubt he'd been laughing at her the entire time. And she so disposed to think well of him for no more reason than that he bore a passing resemblance to Nicholas Seaton!

5

After shooting Frederick Burton-Smythe through the shoulder, John Beresford, Viscount St. Clare returned to his grandfather's house in Grosvenor Square. He had a brief word with his groom, an even briefer word with his valet (who gaped at the singed sleeve of St. Clare's shirt with blank horror), and then, as he did after all of his duels, he withdrew to the breakfast room and ate an exceptionally large meal.

It was while he was drinking his coffee and reading the newspaper that his grandfather strode into the room.

"Out!" Lord Allendale growled at a lingering footman. The servant scurried away as the earl took a seat across from St. Clare at the table.

A taut silence permeated the room, so ominous that, at last, if for no other reason than mere curiosity, St. Clare was compelled to lower his newspaper. "Well, sir?"

The Earl of Allendale's once golden hair had gone silvery white, and except when his blood was up, the fire in his distinctive gray eyes had dimmed, but a life of activity and adventure—a life that had bronzed his skin and strengthened his body—had left him free of many of the maladies of old age. He didn't suffer from rheumatism or gout. He was never confused or forgetful. And though he was the first to admit that he walked a bit slower than he once had, he stubbornly did so without the aid of a stick.

He'd never been a typical English aristocrat. Some even called him an eccentric. Cursed with an insatiable desire to travel the world, he'd spent the better part of his life abroad, the last years of which he'd dragged his grandson along behind him. It had only been recently—as St. Clare approached his thirtieth birthday—that the earl had begun to show signs that he wasn't so very different from a typical English aristocrat after all.

"I have it from Jessup that you fought a duel this morning," Allendale said.

St. Clare saw no reason to deny it. His grandfather of all people should understand. He was no stranger to affairs of honor. Proficient with pistols and swords, it was he who had honed St. Clare into the uncannily lethal shot that he was today. "I did."

"With an inconsequential squire from the country." Allendale's tone held an unmistakable note of warning.

St. Clare gave his newspaper a regretful glance before folding it and laying it down on the table beside his plate. "An heir to a baronetcy if that makes any difference."

"A baronetcy in Somerset."

He met his grandfather's formidable gray glare. "Your point, sir?"

"Be careful."

"I am exceedingly careful."

"I believe you know what I mean."

St. Clare leaned back in his chair. "As you see, I have survived the encounter without a scratch."

"Have you?" Allendale's mouth tightened. "I was given to understand that the pistol ball singed your shirtsleeve."

St. Clare inwardly cursed Jessup. There was a reason his grandfather often referred to the elderly butler as Argus. Just like the mythical giant, Jessup seemed to have a hundred eyes. "A trifling thing," he said stiffly.

"And what of your opponent? This Somerset heir to a baronetcy. How did he fare?"

"Better than he deserved."

Allendale fixed him with a long look. "You got him through the shoulder, did you? Which shoulder? The right?"

St. Clare gave a curt nod.

"And with which hand does this fellow wield his weapons?"

A slow smile edged St. Clare's mouth. "Up until this morning, his right one."

"That pleases you, does it? Tell me, my boy, what was it that this squire, or whatever in blazes he is, did to earn your notice? Cheat at cards?"

St. Clare shrugged one shoulder. "He might have done."

"And I suppose you realized that, when you hinted at that fact in the middle of a crowded gaming hell, he might be provoked into calling you out?" Allendale didn't wait for an answer. "Well, you've paid this country nobody back quite handsomely for whatever small offense he's given. For the next month, he'll be hard pressed to raise his spoon for soup let alone his pistol or his reins and whip. Are you satisfied now? Indeed, I hope you are, sir, for you've fought your first and last duel in England."

St. Clare met his grandfather's burst of ire with silence. The same silence with which he'd endured the earl's explosions of temper many times before.

"One month! That's how long we've been back. Have you no self-control, man? No sense of purpose? What were you doing in a blasted gaming hell in the first place?" Allendale's face reddened with anger. "Do you think I've wasted all of these years with you so that you could go the way of your father? The Earls of Allendale have descended in an unbroken line for over two hundred years! Straight down from Ivo Beresford himself! Do you imagine I'll allow that line to be broken? That I'll allow the title to pass to that idiot son of my second cousin? I tell you, sir, I will see us both damned first!"

St. Clare poured out a cup of coffee, and without a word, pushed it across the table to his grandfather.

Allendale scowled but nonetheless lifted the cup and took a sip. After a moment, the redness receded from his face. "I told you when we left Florence that the time had come to do your duty. There's to be no more mucking about, my boy. You'll find yourself a wife and get yourself an heir. It's what you owe to the title. *It's what you owe to me.*"

St. Clare didn't argue. He knew very well the duty he owed to the title. For years, his life had been one long, grueling exercise in preparing for his role as the next Earl of Allendale. Anything his grandfather thought he should learn, he had learned. Any skill that had to be mastered, he had mastered. In time, St. Clare's own ambitions had receded, dimmed by the constant need to prove himself. To excel at every challenge set before him.

And he *had* excelled. No study had been too difficult for him. No sport too daring. He'd grown—by his grandfather's own admission—into a fine figure of a gentleman.

But they weren't in Florence now, nor in Paris, Cairo, or Bombay. They were in England.

"I'm not insensible of my duty," St. Clare said. "I've done everything you bid me."

"Not everything," Allendale snapped.

St. Clare continued unperturbed. "I've engaged a new tailor and bootmaker. I've set up my stable. I've joined the right clubs and attended the right balls and parties. I've even been forced to endure the company of those very men who once ostracized my father."

At that, Allendale frowned deeply. "Jackals, every one of them," he muttered. "A pack of bloody jackals. They drove him to his death."

"As I'm well aware."

St. Clare's father, the late James Beresford, Viscount St. Clare, had in his youth engaged in countless affairs of honor and had earned for himself a reputation as an excellent shot. But when, as a result of a foolish dispute over a carriage accident, he'd dueled with and killed the youngest son of the Duke of Penworthy, the *ton* had accused him of taking advantage of a weaker opponent.

The viscount's honor had been tarnished. His friends, such that they were, had deserted him.

His *father* had deserted him.

It was a fact that Allendale never mentioned—and one that St. Clare could never forget. The late viscount had needed Allendale's protection, and Allendale—a man who had valued familial pride over his actual family—had thrown his son to the wolves.

Facing arrest, St. Clare's father had fled to the continent. It was there he'd lived out the remainder of his short life, dying in his thirty-third year of an insidious wasting disease.

"Your father was a damned sight too trusting. Fell in with the wrong sort of people. But you... You know better. I believe you don't trust anyone."

St. Clare's mouth hitched in a half smile. "Nonsense. I have a great deal of trust in my valet and my groom."

"There's a lot to be said for loyal retainers," Allendale agreed, temporarily diverted. "But you won't distract me. I want your word. Your word as a gentleman. You're to leave off dueling until you've secured the title. If you've got a disagreement with someone—confound it, I don't see why the devil you should have, but if you do—sort it out some other way. From this day forward, your sole purpose is to marry some suitable female and get yourself an heir. By gad, I'll choose the gel myself if it comes to it."

"I'm obliged to you, sir," St. Clare said. "But I shall choose my own wife."

An image of Margaret Honeywell sprang into his mind.

He recalled the way her face had looked in the firelight, shadowed and beautiful. The way she'd felt when she'd fainted into his arms. A shapely scrap of femininity—altogether too weak and frail. He'd had an overpowering urge to gather her close. To hold her and never let her go.

She'd been ill, that much was plain.

It shouldn't matter. He had no patience with delicate, swooning females. But Miss Honeywell's late-night visit had upset the balance of his mind. She'd left him restless and unsettled. His thoughts were full of her.

Indeed, he was sorely tempted to call on her at the Trumbles' residence in Green Street. Later that day, after his grandfather finally left him in peace, he even made several attempts at writing a note inviting her to take a drive with him in his curricle.

Dear Miss Honeywell. Would you do me the honor of accompanying me—

My Dear Miss Honeywell. Please put me out of my misery and consent to join me—

None of his impulses seemed appropriate. He hadn't been properly introduced to her. Showing up at her door would be extremely bad *ton*. And a personal note from an unmarried gentleman to an unmarried lady was borderline scandalous.

He was going to have to find someone to present him to her. Either that or disregard the conventions altogether. Unfortunately, no matter how much he considered the matter, he couldn't determine the best course.

The result of his uncharacteristic indecisiveness was that he didn't see Miss Honeywell again until three days later, and very much by chance.

Amongst the many activities afforded in town, the theater was the only one that the Earl of Allendale genuinely enjoyed. The previous week, he and St. Clare had seen Edmund Kean in *Macbeth*. So impressed was the earl by Kean's performance that he proposed getting a small party together to see the play a second time.

That party included an elderly dowager and her two unmarried granddaughters, a middle-aged matchmaking mama and her unmarried daughter, and St. Clare's friend Lord Mattingly and Mattingly's younger, unmarried sister.

"Sorry, old chap," Mattingly muttered from his place near St. Clare in the earl's theater box. "You're the matrimonial prize of the season, you know, and my mother would insist that I throw Astrid in your path."

The young lady sitting on the other side of his friend was just out of the schoolroom, and at present, all arms, legs, and blushes. A child, merely.

She looked up from her program, caught his eye, and promptly turned crimson. "Have you seen Mr. K-Kean perform before, my lord?"

St. Clare offered her a smile. "Only last week. And you, Miss Mattingly?"

"Oh, no! This is my first t-time at the theater."

St. Clare arched a brow in Mattingly's direction.

Mattingly had the good grace to look sheepish. He mouthed another apology.

St. Clare didn't regard it. The truth of the matter was that Astrid Mattingly was the least offensive female in the box. The dowager's granddaughters were a pair of giggling henwits, and the other young lady, a Miss Louisa Steele, had all the charm of a viper that had once crawled into his tent while camping in the Egyptian desert.

According to Miss Steele's mother, who'd been extolling her daughter's many virtues since the moment they arrived at the theater, Louisa was humble, sweet, and kind. As skilled at the pianoforte and harp as she was at riding and dancing. And so far superior to other young ladies in both looks and accomplishments that she'd often been the target of spiteful, jealous gossip.

The bulk of this chatter was directed to the old dowager who sat beside her, but St. Clare was in no doubt that Mrs. Steele's words were meant for him alone.

"A diamond. That's what the duke called her at her come-out ball. He said that Louisa was the most beautiful girl anyone had seen in five seasons. Can you imagine?"

"No," said the dowager frostily.

Miss Steele herself, who was sitting at an odd angle in front of him, turned in her chair and whispered, "You must ignore Mama. I'm not interested in the duke."

St. Clare refrained from asking which duke.

"Although it's true that he said I was the most beautiful girl he'd seen in years," she continued. "I don't know why he would. I see nothing out of the ordinary in my appearance. Do you, my lord?"

What St. Clare thought was that Miss Steele was a remarkably accomplished flirt for a girl who couldn't be any older than one and twenty. She simpered, she pouted, and she batted her lashes. No doubt her tactics worked on a great many of the men she met. They didn't work on him. "You look very well, Miss Steele."

"You look divine," Mattingly said.

"Flatterer!" She laughed. "I know I do not. Not in this gown. And not with this necklace. I would have worn my pearls, for they look best with my hair, but Mama insisted I wear the diamonds. The duke said I must always wear diamonds because I am a diamond myself."

While Miss Steele directed her attentions to Mattingly, St. Clare's gaze drifted around the packed house. He didn't require a set of opera glasses to see into the tiers of boxes across the theater. It was easy enough to make out the titled and the wealthy, the famous and infamous.

Ladies draped in jewels sat at the forefront, gentlemen in gold and silver waistcoats behind. He recognized women he'd met at balls and parties, and men he'd seen at his club. There was even a famous Cyprian or two.

And then, just as the play began, he saw her.

Margaret Honeywell.

A jolt of simmering recognition shot through him.

She was seated in the front of a box opposite, one tier below his own, in the company of a slender fair-haired gentleman, an equally slender fair-haired young lady, and an elderly female who appeared to be asleep in her chair.

Observing St. Clare's arrested expression, Mattingly discreetly handed him a pair of mother-of-pearl opera glasses.

St. Clare took them without a word, training them on Miss Honeywell. The lenses were powerful. Through them he could make out every curve and contour of her flawless ivory countenance. The deep blue of her eyes—like melting sapphires. The straight, elegant line of her nose and the delicate cleft in her stubbornly set chin. It was a face one didn't easily forget. A face to haunt a man's dreams.

And not only a face. She had a figure to rival it. One he hadn't fully appreciated when she'd called on him in Grosvenor Square. Then she'd been clad in a dark, shapeless dress. But now...

Now she wore a gown of champagne silk, with tiny puffed sleeves dropping loosely off of her bare shoulders, and a neckline cut low along the swell of her bosom.

His fingers clenched reflexively on the opera glasses.

Her gown exposed a wide expanse of pale, creamy skin. And her hair, caught up in jeweled pins to reveal the slender column of her throat, was artfully disheveled, looking as if at any moment it might fall down around her in a mass of dark curls. When combined with the rosy flush in her cheeks and the equally rosy hue to the wide, full softness of her mouth, the entire effect was that of a woman rising from bed after a passionate interlude with her lover.

And who the devil was the young gentleman beside her? Some confounded coxcomb who had schemed his way into escorting her to the theater?

The young man turned and whispered something into Miss Honeywell's ear. She tilted her head to listen, giving the young man her full and undivided attention. And then she smiled.

St. Clare felt a bitter surge of jealousy.

"What are you scowling at?" Mattingly asked in a low undertone. "Haven't caught sight of another country squire worth calling out, have you?"

St. Clare thrust the opera glasses at Mattingly. "Who is that fellow opposite?"

"Which fellow?" Mattingly peered through the glasses. "Him? In the gold-embroidered waistcoat? That's Trumble's heir, George. He's a tolerable chap. Not a bit like Burton-Smythe. No need to... Ah. Wait a moment. Well, fancy that. I'd heard Miss Honeywell was back in town. Haven't seen her in—let me think—going on four years."

St. Clare turned his gaze on his friend. Mattingly was dark-haired, nearly as tall as St. Clare was himself, and generally considered to be quite handsome. "You know her? How?"

"Met her during her come out."

"Good." St. Clare retrieved the opera glasses from Mattingly and once again fixed them on Miss Honeywell. "You can introduce me to her at the interval."

6

Entering Miss Honeywell's theater box, St. Clare and Lord Mattingly found her engaged in conversation with a tall, fair-haired young lady who Mattingly identified as Miss Jane Trumble. The two ladies' elderly companion was snoring softly in her chair, and George Trumble was nowhere to be found.

"My brother has gone to fetch us some lemonade," Miss Trumble explained after Mattingly made the introductions.

St. Clare supposed he should have felt a pang of conscience at that. No doubt the flock of females in the earl's box were expecting that he and Mattingly would procure them refreshments as well. But as he looked at Margaret Honeywell, he couldn't summon the slightest twinge of remorse at abandoning his responsibilities.

Let some other enterprising gentleman tend to the needs of Miss Steele and the dowager's granddaughters.

"I say, what did you think of the first act?" Mattingly asked, deftly maneuvering himself into the seat beside Miss Trumble.

He wasn't the brightest of fellows, but St. Clare credited him with good instincts when it came to assisting his friends. As easily as he'd lent his opera glasses, he now occupied Miss Trumble, leaving the field with Miss Honeywell open for St. Clare. "Saw Kean in *Othello*," he continued. "Not sure his Macbeth is up to the same standard."

"He seems to be doing an excellent job," Miss Trumble replied. "But then, I have nothing with which to compare him. Was his portrayal of Othello really as brilliant as everyone says?"

While Mattingly and Miss Trumble discussed Shakespeare, St. Clare approached Miss Honeywell. There was a strangely unwelcoming expression in her blue eyes. "May I?" He gestured at the empty seat next to her.

"If you like," she said coolly.

He sat down beside her in the chair that had lately been occupied by George Trumble. This, too, was the view he'd enjoyed. A diaphanous gown clinging to gently rounded bare shoulders and falling in shimmering folds down to delicately slippered feet. Creamy skin illuminated by the flickering candlelight from the chandeliers. A provocative décolletage accented at its center with a small cluster of wildflowers. And that unforgettable face. Wide eyes, soft lips, and a stubbornly cleft little chin, all framed by escaping tendrils of glossy mink hair.

Up close she was even more ravishing than she'd appeared from across the room.

She was also very much on her dignity.

St. Clare felt oddly off balance. As if he were an impertinent schoolboy soliciting the hand of a beautiful young lady at his first country assembly.

A ridiculous notion.

What had he to be nervous about? He'd dined with nobility on the continent. Had waltzed with a princess and danced the quadrille with an archduchess.

But Miss Honeywell had a frank way of looking at him. As if she could see past his elegant, black evening clothes and intricately tied white cravat. As if she could see straight to the center of his being. "What do you make of me?" he wanted to ask her. But he already knew the answer. She didn't make much of him at all. And yet...

After a few moments' consideration, it occurred to him that the rigidity of her spine and the martial light in her eye likely had more to do with some incidental grievance she'd laid at his door than with a thorough indictment of his worth as a human being. Had she heard something about him, perhaps? That he was a rake? An adventurer?

He was immeasurably cheered by the thought.

"Are you enjoying the play, Miss Honeywell?" he asked.

"Yes, thank you."

"Kean is a rare talent, don't you think?"

"As you say."

"I had the privilege of seeing this very play only last week. Mrs. Bartley's performance as Lady Macbeth was particularly good. I didn't think another actress could compare, but Mrs. Hill has done a creditable job of it so far. It will be interesting to see how she handles the sleepwalking scene in Act V." St. Clare waited for a response. None was forthcoming. "I beg your pardon. Have I done something to offend you?"

She at last turned to address him, her voice dropping to a low, accusing whisper. "You know that you have."

His brows lifted. "Indeed, I do not."

"Do you think me a complete ninny, my lord? I knew about the duel, did I not? Do you suppose for a moment that I didn't promptly learn the result of it?"

"I suppose nothing of the sort."

"Well, then?" she demanded.

He regarded her thoughtfully. "I begin to think that the results of the duel didn't please you."

"No, they most certainly did not!" Miss Honeywell leaned toward him, her voice dropping even lower. St. Clare caught the subtle scent of her perfume. "You *shot* Mr. Burton-Smythe. You promised me, on your honor that—"

"That I would not kill him. And I didn't."

"You *shot* him."

"In the shoulder."

"And did it not occur to you that your shot might have inadvertently gone too high or too wide? In a high wind, I daresay you might have accidentally blown his head off!"

St. Clare failed to suppress a smile. By God, he liked her show of temper. It was a refreshing change from the frailty she'd exhibited when she'd called on him in Grosvenor Square. "My shooting doesn't allow for accidents, Miss Honeywell. My bullet went exactly where I meant it to go. The place where it would hurt him the most."

She gave him a skeptical look. "His shoulder?"

"His pride. You know as well as I do that had I allowed him to emerge unscathed it would only have emboldened him. Your Mr. Burton-Smythe needed to be taught a lesson. He needed to be humiliated. I hope he'll be a much better person now."

Miss Honeywell bristled. "He's not *my* Mr. Burton-Smythe."

"I'm very happy to hear it."

"And if you think anything could make him a better person, then you're very much mistaken."

"Yes. Perhaps I am. In truth, I suspect he'll need to be shot a great many more times in order to effect a noticeable change."

Miss Honeywell swiftly looked away from him. A smile quivered on her lips. She visibly struggled to suppress it. "I think you're a scoundrel."

St. Clare grinned. For a moment, he forgot the countless number of opera glasses that were no doubt fixed upon the two of them. "A scoundrel to whom you owe three forfeits."

"Oh, do I?"

"Come, Miss Honeywell. I refuse to believe that you're the sort of lady who would fail to keep her word."

"*My* word?" she repeated. "How can you expect me to fulfill the terms of our agreement when you have not?"

"I did precisely as you asked me. I did not kill him."

She occupied herself with straightening one of her long gloves. "You kept to the letter of the agreement, I'll grant you," she admitted grudgingly. "But you failed to honor the spirit of it."

"Tell me then. Are you and I at point nonplus? I certainly hope not. I've very much been looking forward to claiming my first forfeit."

She proceeded to smooth her other glove. "I didn't think you were serious about any of that. The forfeits, I mean. Indeed, for the last three days I…" She hesitated before continuing. "For the last three days, I've assumed you were making sport of me."

St. Clare's brows snapped together. "I wasn't. Nor would I ever."

"You say that, but—"

"Miss Honeywell, if you don't stop fidgeting with your gloves and look at me, I shall be compelled to take your hand and hold it in mine."

Her eyes shot to his. "You wouldn't dare."

St. Clare was gratified to see the return of her temper. "Try me."

She folded her hands primly in her lap. "Satisfied?"

"Not by a long chalk. Now tell me, in earnest, will you come for a drive with me in the park tomorrow afternoon? I have a new curricle and the finest team of bays you've ever seen. It would be my pleasure to put them through their paces for you."

"What makes you think any such thing would appeal to me?"

"Would it not?"

"For all you know I may be frightened of horses."

His lips twitched. "You? Afraid of horses?"

"I might be."

"All horses? Even match-bays? With faultless shoulders and first-rate legs?"

At his coaxing tone, the corner of her mouth trembled. But she didn't smile. Instead, she cast him a thoroughly reproving glance. "Are you inviting me, my lord, or are you calling in a forfeit?"

"Whatever is necessary," he answered.

She exhaled a breath. "You needn't waste a forfeit. An invitation will do." She added quickly, "But only because I'd like to see your cattle."

"Naturally." His heart thumped heavily. "I shall come for you at five if that's agreeable."

"It is. Thank you, my lord."

"What a crush it is out there!" George Trumble entered the box. "Oh, I say! Didn't know anyone else was here." He handed a glass of lemonade to Miss Honeywell and another to Miss Trumble. "Everything all right, m'dear?"

"Perfectly," Miss Trumble replied. "George, you've met Lord Mattingly, I presume? And Lord St. Clare? They've been keeping us company for the interval."

St. Clare and Mattingly both rose and made their bows to him.

"Couldn't resist coming to pay our respects to Miss Trumble and Miss Honeywell," Mattingly said.

"I'm obliged to you," Trumble replied.

"We were just about to take our leave. I'm afraid we've been neglecting the ladies in our own box, haven't we, St. Clare?"

"Whereabouts are you sitting?" Miss Trumble asked.

"Straight across the way. One tier above and a little to the right."

Miss Trumble raised her opera glasses. "Oh! Is that Miss Steele I see? She's quite the belle of the season, I understand."

"Brought my sister, Astrid, too," Mattingly said. "The young lady in the front. She's fresh from the schoolroom, you know."

"She's lovely," Miss Trumble responded graciously. She lowered her glasses. "It seems you have a bevy of young ladies waiting for you. How selfish of us to keep you as long as we have."

"We won't keep you any longer," Trumble said.

St. Clare ignored him. His attention was riveted on Miss Honeywell, and unless he was very much mistaken, her attention was equally engaged with him. He reached for her gloved hand and she gave it to him willingly. He bowed over it, retaining it in his grasp a few seconds longer than was proper. "Until tomorrow, Miss Honeywell."

She met his gaze. "I look forward to it, my lord."

He reluctantly let her go, and after taking his leave of Miss Trumble and her brother, left the theater box with Mattingly close behind him.

The passage was crowded with people bustling about during the interval. St. Clare navigated through the crush, proceeding toward the stairway that would take them back up to their own box. At the first opportunity, Mattingly drew level with him. "The Honeybee," he said.

"What?" St. Clare asked, distracted.

"That's what Margaret Honeywell was called during her come out." Mattingly chuckled. "Not at first, mind. When she first arrived, all the gents were calling her the Pocket Venus. You never saw a girl so beautiful. And with such a figure! She drew quite a court around her, too. Then the first chap got stung. And then the second." Mattingly reflected on this with evident appreciation. "Used to deliver some of the sharpest set-downs you ever heard. Rather indecorous as well. Galloping her horse in Hyde Park. Firing a pistol during a country house party. And that temper of hers! More spleen than sense, Miss Honeywell."

St. Clare listened to his friend's words with avid attention, all the while wondering how to reconcile the picture Mattingly painted of a fiery, hoydenish hellion with the wan, quiet figure who had fainted into his arms in his library. An illness, her maid had said. What sort of an illness? And did she suffer from it still?

"Miss Honeywell doesn't strike me as a temperamental sort of female," he remarked absently.

"No? She was buzzing about you a fair bit just now. What was she saying, St. Clare? Looked to me as if she was calling you to account for something."

"Did it? How odd. We were simply discussing the play. Miss Honeywell is quite passionate about Shakespeare."

"Hmm. Well, it stands to reason that she's not going to be as high-spirited as she once was. Advanced age, you know."

St. Clare flashed his friend an amused smile. "She's hardly in her dotage."

"She's five and twenty if she's a day. And still unmarried, by Jove. Hardly seems possible."

"No, it doesn't." He'd been perplexed by that fact himself. "Were there never any serious admirers?"

"Loads of 'em! I know of at least six chaps who made her an offer. Decent fellows, too, and all but one of them with a respectable fortune. Miss Honeywell refused them out of hand. As for the rest… Timid chaps all. Quickly stung and easily dispatched. Not that it mattered in the end. Come to find out, she was wearing the willow for another fellow."

St. Clare looked at him sharply. "Who?"

Mattingly shrugged. "Some soldier. I never met him. And seeing as how she's still unwed, I suppose nothing came of it. Perhaps the poor sod died in the war?" He cast a brief glance at St. Clare as they shouldered past a group of raucous young men. "Burton-Smythe's an admirer of sorts."

"I'm aware."

"The way I hear it, he's been trying to fix his interest with her for ages."

"And failed, it seems."

"She's poorly suited for him, anyone can see it. He needs a nice quiet mouse who'll never say a word against him." Mattingly chuckled again. "Now you… Well, I should have known you'd take an interest. Miss Honeywell fits the pattern card."

"What pattern card?"

"Miss Honeywell is your type is what I mean."

St. Clare gave an abrupt laugh. "I won't deny it. But I can't think how you would know one way or the other."

"Quite easily. When Vickers and I first met you in Italy, the only females that ever caught your attention were the ones with dark hair and blue eyes. The bluer the better. Vickers used to make a joke of it. Anytime a fair-skinned gel with dark hair and blue eyes passed by, you'd do the most damnable about-face. As if you'd seen a ghost. Never failed to send Vickers and me into whoops." He laughed at the memory, but at the sight of St. Clare's grim expression he quickly schooled his features into more somber lines. "Not that I'm comparing Miss Honeywell to a continental light-skirt, mind. She's a lady. No one would dare say otherwise. All I'm trying to say—and badly, apparently—is that Miss Honeywell fits the pattern card."

St. Clare was silent for a moment. When he finally responded, his words were quiet ones, inaudible to his friend and quickly lost in the noise of the crowded theater. "Miss Honeywell *is* the pattern card."

7

The following afternoon when Maggie and Jane returned to Green Street after a morning of shopping, culminating in a lengthy visit to Hookham's Library, they were met by a note from Lord St. Clare.

"Rather presumptuous of him to write you, don't you think?" Jane asked, stripping off her gloves. "But then, perhaps such things are done with ladies on the continent? What does he say, Margaret? Is it a love letter?"

"No, indeed." Maggie skimmed the note. "It's the veriest commonplace. He'd like to pick me up for our drive an hour earlier. I prefer it, actually. But it hardly gives me any time to get ready. I shall have to go up and change directly."

Jane ushered her toward the drawing room. "There's time yet for a cup of tea. Carson? Tea and biscuits, if you please."

Maggie sank down on the sofa, the note still held in one hand. She looked at it again. Properly looked at it. And then she stared.

"Is anything the matter?" Jane came to sit next to her. "Margaret?"

"What?" Maggie glanced up, startled. "Oh, no. It's nothing. I only thought…for a moment…" Her heart was hammering so swiftly, she scarcely knew what she thought.

"You've gone as white as the paper that note is written on. Here—" Jane plucked the missive from Maggie's fingers. "What has he said to upset you so? Let me see…" She quickly read the note. "He's only requesting you respond and tell him if four o'clock will suit. There's nothing shocking in that. No doubt you misread his handwriting." She squinted at the scribbled blotches of ink. "Heavens, what an atrocious scrawl. It's a bit like those Egyptian hieroglyphs one sees in the British Museum."

"Yes. It's very untidy," Maggie said distractedly. She moved as if to get up. "I shall have to write out a reply."

"Don't trouble yourself, dear. I'll play secretary." Jane rose from her seat.

Maggie was grateful for her friend's solicitude, even as she regretted the necessity of it. Her head was spinning, her mind tumbling over itself at the possibilities raised by that note. The very real—very stark—possibilities. She prayed Jane wouldn't press her on the subject. Not now. Not when Maggie could barely comprehend the matter herself.

"Hold a moment, Carson." Jane went to a small escritoire in the corner, pulled out a sheet of paper, and took up her quill pen. "A single sentence stating that four o'clock is agreeable?" she queried Maggie. "And I'll sign your initials, shall I?" She wrote out a few brief lines, folded the paper, and sealed it with a wafer. "Take this round to Lord St. Clare at once," she instructed the footman. "He's presently at the Earl of Allendale's residence in Grosvenor Square."

"Yes, ma'am," Carson said before exiting the room.

"Clearly he's trying to get you alone in the park before the fashionable hour." Jane resumed her place beside Maggie on the sofa. "It may be that he doesn't want the two of you to be observed by all of the *ton*. Or I suppose there's always the chance he has some nefarious scheme in mind. A kidnapping, perhaps. Spiriting the unmarried heiress away to Gretna Green so that he can gain control of her fortune."

Maggie managed a wry smile. "If that's his plan, he's in for a very unpleasant surprise. At any rate, I don't believe the viscount to be a fortune hunter."

"Nor do I," Jane admitted. "And yet... I don't know exactly what to make of him. Oh, he's gentlemanly and polite, to be sure. Not but that I don't think he's sneering a bit at everyone under all that civility. But there's something else. Something not quite right. I can't put my finger on it. Then again, I have little experience with rakes. And even less with truly dangerous men."

"Dangerous?"

Jane nodded. "Oh yes. To hear George tell it, St. Clare is absolutely lethal. The way he recounts that duel..."

"Gentlemen are far too easily impressed. To hear them talk, you'd think it was the most difficult thing in the world to hit a target at fifteen paces. Why, at Beasley Park, I've hit an empty bottle off of a fence at twenty, and a bottle is a far smaller target than a man."

"Yes, dear, but the bottle wasn't firing back at you."

"Perhaps not. But to think he's dangerous merely because of his ability to shoot straight is an utter absurdity."

"It wasn't merely that. It was his cold-bloodedness. He stood still as a statue as Fred's bullet whizzed past." Jane held her arms stiffly at her sides, affecting an air of boredom as she watched a make-believe bullet go by. "And then, he raised his pistol." She lifted her hand as if holding a weapon. "And fired." Her finger pulled an imaginary trigger. "'My dear fellow, if you're going to act the brutish country squire—'"

"No more!" Maggie protested with a groan. "It's bad enough that I must hear it thirty times from George, but when you begin to recite it, it's the outside of enough."

"Come now, you can't pretend to be unimpressed."

"I'm not unimpressed. Neither do I stand in awe. According to St. Clare all of the Beresfords are skilled with a pistol. It's no great accomplishment for them. By the by, speaking of the Beresfords, I must remember to return Lord St. Clare's flask to him."

"And you must take your new parasol," Jane advised. "The sun is out today, and as pale as you are, without it you're likely to burn. And you mustn't overtax yourself. No matter how ardently Lord St. Clare presses to prolong your outing—"

"Ardently," Maggie scoffed. "Really, Jane."

"Why not? I don't claim he's after your hand, but your late-night visit to see him has clearly aroused his interest. Perhaps he means to make you one of his flirts? You needn't look put out by the idea. There are worse ways to spend the season than being chased after by a golden-haired viscount, you know. And only consider, while he's pursuing you, I shall no doubt have the constant company of Lord Mattingly." Jane paused, before confessing, "I had the most awful *tendre* for him the year of my come out."

"Lord Mattingly?" Maggie gave her friend a quizzical smile. "You never mentioned that before."

"Considering that the highlight of my first season was Lady Barbara Latimer christening me 'Spindleshanks' and all the rest of the young ladies, and most of the young gentlemen, gleefully taking up the moniker, it has seemed to me that those few months of my life are best forgotten." Jane's own smile became rueful. "Besides, it's a dreadfully depressing story. Lord Mattingly was a dark and dashing Corinthian, and I was then much as I am now. Too tall, too plain, with nothing to recommend me but my brains. And you know how gentlemen feel about ladies with brains."

Before Maggie could make a reply, the door to the drawing room creaked open and a rustle of twilled silk announced the entrance of Jane's aunt Harriet.

A small woman with snowy white hair and a wrinkled face that put one in mind of a bleached walnut, she shuffled into the room with the aid of her ebony cane. "There you are, my dears," she said in a warbling voice.

"How was your nap, Aunt?" Jane asked.

"What's that?" Aunt Harriet slowly lowered herself into a wing chair. "My cap?" She touched a blue-veined hand to the delicately beribboned bit of lace tied over her thinning locks.

"Your rest!" Jane said a little more loudly.

"Yes. Quite right. It is the best of all my caps." Aunt Harriet leaned her head against the velvet-upholstered wing of her chair. "I shall close my eyes for just a moment until tea. You must rouse me when the tray comes, Elizabeth."

Maggie cast a bewildered look at Jane.

"Elizabeth is my mother," Jane whispered, stifling a grin. "Did I not tell you my aunt Harriet would be the best chaperone in the world?"

At promptly four o'clock, before the drawing room clock had even finished chiming the hour, St. Clare arrived in Green Street driving a dashing black curricle drawn by a pair of glossy, temperamental-looking match-bays. Maggie had been watching for him, and as he pulled up in front of the Trumbles' townhouse, she hurried down the front steps to meet him.

At the sight of her, St. Clare ordered his tiger to go to the horses' heads and jumped down from his curricle. "Miss Honeywell," he said solemnly, making his bow.

"Lord St. Clare."

He surveyed her fitted blue kerseymere pelisse and matching bonnet with an appreciative eye. "You look very well."

"As do you." And it was true. St. Clare's figure was marvelously displayed, from the crown of his beaver hat to the mirror shine of his Hessians, and all the powerfully muscled, expertly tailored acreage in between.

He gave a sudden, slightly sheepish, grin. "I'd intended to come to the door and call for you properly."

"Had you?" She was a little chagrined. Why had she run out to meet him so impetuously? So eagerly?

It was just the sort of thing she was used to do when Nicholas would call at the front entrance of Beasley Park, begging her company on a drive into town in the gig. "I've been charged with delivering these preserves to the vicarage," he would say. "Pray come with me, Maggie, and lend me a bit of countenance."

At the memory, Maggie felt the same sense of bewilderment and uncertainty that she'd felt when she read St. Clare's note. "Well, it doesn't matter, in any case. My chaperone, Miss Trumble's aunt Harriet, is fast asleep and you've already made the acquaintance of Miss Trumble herself. So there's really no need to go inside. Unless…you don't feel as if you must, do you?"

"No," he answered after a moment. "As you say, there's really no need."

Maggie walked ahead of him to the curricle's step and waited. When he stopped beside her and didn't immediately offer his hand, she looked up at him inquiringly. And she had to look up, up, up, for he was infuriatingly tall. How had she not noticed before how diminutive she was when compared to him? She scarcely reached his shoulder!

As if to illustrate their vast difference in size, he didn't simply hand her up into the curricle as any other gentleman might do. Instead, he clasped his large hands lightly round her waist, and without the least visible effort, lifted her up onto the seat.

Maggie's cheeks flushed at the intimate contact.

St. Clare gave no sign that anything was out of the ordinary. He leapt into the curricle beside her, and before taking the reins, paused to spread a rug over her knees. "Comfortable?"

Maggie wasn't comfortable. St. Clare's muscular thigh was brushing against her leg. And her waist was still tingling from the pressure of his hands. "Yes, thank you." She was mortified by the squeak in her voice.

St. Clare gave a curt nod. His own smile had faded. His gray eyes were a bit more watchful. Perhaps he was feeling the effects of her closeness just as she was feeling the effects of his? "Stand away from their heads, Enzo," he called to his tiger. And taking up his whip, he gave the horses the office to start.

The tiger, a thin, dark-haired boy with obsidian black eyes, ran behind them for a few strides and then hopped onto his perch.

Maggie hadn't been for a drive in an open carriage in many years. Her own phaeton had been sold long ago, and at Beasley Park, since her illness, she'd been restricted to riding in a closed coach lest she overexert her lungs. She'd missed the freedom of it most dreadfully, and as St. Clare put the bays through their paces, her embarrassment at being so close to him was rapidly replaced by exuberance.

She sat up tall in her seat, the wind whipping the curled feathers in her bonnet and playing havoc with her carefully pinned hair. "Oh, is it not glorious!" she exclaimed. "To be up so high and going so fast!"

"You're not afraid?" St. Clare asked, expertly maneuvering his team through the streets.

"Why should I be? Your curricle is well sprung and you seem skilled enough with the ribbons. And your horses..." She gazed at them in frank admiration. "What sweet goers they are. Devilish quick and not a bit choppy."

"At this speed, most ladies would be holding white-knuckled to the side."

"Would they indeed, my lord? What poor-spirited ladies you've been driving with."

St. Clare's bays chose that moment to take exception to a passing carriage pulled by four matched chestnuts. They skittered and danced, ears flattened and teeth bared. He steadied them easily, guided them past the carriage, and then, with awe-inspiring expertise, feather-edged a corner as he turned toward the entrance into the park.

"You mistake me, Miss Honeywell. I was speaking in generalities. In truth, you're the first lady I've taken driving since my arrival in London."

Maggie's smile dimmed. It wasn't true, of course. How could it be? Even last night at the theater, he'd been in the company of beautiful women. "How long have you been in London, my lord?"

"A month, approximately."

"And before that?"

He cast her a fleeting glance. "I was most recently in Italy."

They passed through the gates of Hyde Park at a brisk trot, St. Clare's bays exhibiting a forward-action that any connoisseur of fine horseflesh would envy.

Maggie unfurled her dainty silk parasol and tipped it back against her shoulder as she looked around. There were quite a few other carriages about, including a barouche occupied by three young matrons, and a high-perch phaeton driven by a gentleman who clearly had no idea what he was doing, but the traffic was nothing like it would be during the fashionable hour. "Why did you ask me to come at four o'clock instead of five?"

"Why did Miss Trumble respond to my note instead of you?" he retorted.

Maggie stilled, feeling a faint trembling in her stomach. "How do you know it was Miss Trumble who responded? It was signed with my initials, wasn't it?" She waited for him to answer her, but he did not. Goaded, she said, "There's no great mystery, I assure you. Miss Trumble often does little things to assist me if she fears I've overtaxed myself. She's the best-natured creature in the world."

St. Clare focused on calming his horses as they trotted around the young matrons' slow-moving barouche. Once past it, he began to direct his team farther away from the rest of the afternoon traffic.

"When I invited you for a drive yesterday evening," he said, "I was hoping you and I might have a bit of privacy. A few uninterrupted moments in which to talk to one another. It didn't occur to me until this morning that at five o'clock, with all of the *ton* in attendance, privacy would be impossible. That's why I requested that we drive at four. I hope the change in time hasn't inconvenienced you too greatly."

"Not at all." Maggie expected he might say something more about Jane's note, but he did not. With a sigh, she turned her head to view the passing scenery.

It was a beautiful sunny day with just enough breeze to rustle the branches of the trees. There were fewer carriages now. Fewer people. St. Clare was driving farther and farther away from the other inhabitants of the park.

"Where are you taking me?" she asked.

He eased his team down from a spirited trot to a brisk walk. "That little cluster of trees at the end of the avenue. It's a distance yet."

Maggie didn't care for the slower pace. It only served to emphasize the prolonged silences between them and the rather erratic beating of her heart. She cast about for something to say, deciding at length that she may as well be straightforward with him. "When you were in Italy—"

"During your come out—" he said at the same time. And then, "Forgive me."

"No, please. What were you saying about my come out?"

"Only that I've heard that during your come-out season you received a great many offers of marriage."

Maggie was taken aback but saw no reason to deny it. "Yes, I suppose I did."

"I also heard that you refused them all."

"You seem to have heard a great deal."

"Society will talk, Miss Honeywell. And when a subject interests me, I can be a prodigious good listener."

"Is society still talking? My come out was nearly six years ago. I would have thought it all forgotten by now."

"Nothing in London society is ever forgotten. The *ton* has the collective memory of an elephant."

"Then I suppose there's no use in denying it. Not that I would. There's nothing so out of the ordinary about a young lady refusing all of the offers she receives during her first season, surely."

"I understand there was a particular reason for your refusals. That you were, at the time, wearing the willow for another gentleman. A soldier."

Maggie's pulse accelerated. She ventured a glance at St. Clare. His eyes were focused on the road ahead, his jaw tense. "In a manner of speaking."

When it became clear that she wasn't going to expound on the subject, St. Clare asked, almost irritably, "Shall you tell me about it? Or must I call in a forfeit?"

"It means that much to you, my lord? I can't think why. It's ancient history."

"You may mark it down to my abominable curiosity."

Maggie knew enough of men to recognize the sound of jealousy when she heard it. The irony didn't escape her. "As you wish. For the price of one forfeit, then. It's true. I *was* wearing the willow for a gentleman. But I don't know if he was a soldier."

St. Clare scowled. "You don't know?"

"He and I were childhood friends. We were parted very unhappily ten years ago."

The horses suddenly broke stride, causing the curricle to lurch forward. St. Clare muttered a blistering oath as he caught up the reins more securely and steadied them.

"He was my first love," Maggie continued. "My only love, really."

St. Clare's attention appeared to be fixed entirely on quieting the horses, but Maggie would have had to be blind not to notice the tension in the set of his shoulders. "Young lovers, tragically parted," he remarked sardonically. "An all-too-common tale."

"We weren't lovers."

"Of course not."

"Not but that we wouldn't have been had he stayed."

His gloved hands tightened on the reins, causing the already nervous horses to commence an agitated dance. "You shock me, Miss Honeywell."

"Why is it shocking? I loved him. I expected to be with him always."

"Many young ladies have no doubt felt the same about their first loves. Young gentlemen, too. It passes as one grows older."

"Does it?"

His face was grim. "In most cases, I believe."

"Perhaps I've trivialized it by saying that I loved him. I didn't mean to, but how else can I explain?" She paused. "The fact is, he and I were more than friends. More even than lovers. We were soul mates. As essential to each other as light or air. From my earliest memory, I existed only for those moments when I could see him next, and he did the same. Neither of us was complete outside the presence of the other." She looked out at the slowly passing landscape of the park as she combated an unexpected wave of sorrow. "I often think that, in the years since he left me, I've been living as only half a person. Waiting…" Her mouth curved in a small, rueful smile. "You wonder that I refused every offer of marriage. How could I wed any of the gentlemen who offered for my hand when I knew that the other half of my heart may yet come back to me?"

"But he didn't come back."

"No. I've always assumed that he became a soldier." There was a slight tremor in her voice. "I believe he must have gone off to fight on the continent and…died there."

"A cheerful thought," St. Clare said.

"It's been easier for me to bear than the alternative."

"And that is?"

"That I never meant anything to him. That after we parted, he went on with his life and forgot all about me."

"Impossible."

"Is it?"

"No man who loved you in the way that you describe could ever forget you." St. Clare brought the horses to a halt. "I believe you're right, Miss Honeywell. This childhood friend of yours is dead. Allow me to offer my sincerest condolences on your loss. Enzo!" he shouted abruptly to his tiger. "Hold their heads." St. Clare turned at last to look at her. "Will you walk awhile with me on the grass?"

Maggie searched his face. His expression was cold, his features as hard and unyielding as granite. Only his eyes—those dearly familiar gray eyes—betrayed the smallest flicker of emotion. It was fleeting. Practically nonexistent. But it was there. "I'm a bit tired from shopping this morning, but if you don't mind my leaning on your arm, then yes. I'm pleased to walk with you."

St. Clare jumped from the curricle and came around to assist her down. This time, she didn't wait for him to extend his hand, but reached out immediately to grasp his broad shoulders. As she clung to him, he caught her around the waist and lifted her out of her seat, setting her down gently onto the grass.

He held her there a moment, his strong hands resting on the flare of her hips and his gaze locked interminably with hers. Any passerby seeing them would have mistaken it for an embrace. The result would be gossip. Scandal. Damage to Maggie's reputation. And worse, to poor Jane's.

Maggie knew she must put a stop to it. It would be easy enough. St. Clare wasn't forcing himself upon her after all. A word or a gesture would be sufficient to discourage him. Indeed, with one firm backward step, she might be out of his arms.

But Maggie couldn't bring herself to move away from him. She stood there, staring up at him as if in a dream.

And then she lifted her hand and lightly touched his cheek.

A tremor went through St. Clare's large frame. He closed his eyes briefly as he leaned into her touch. "Don't," he said gruffly.

Ignoring his halfhearted protest, Maggie brought her other hand to his face and gently caressed the side of his jaw. In response, she felt St. Clare's arms encircle her waist. It was the only movement he made. He held himself still as she touched him, his head half-bowed. A muscle worked in his throat.

Slowly, she reached up to smooth a lock of golden hair from his forehead, her gloved fingers tracing a delicate, soothing path over his brow.

His arms tightened reflexively around her. "Margaret——"

"Maggie," she whispered.

St. Clare's breath caught as if he had received a blow. "Maggie," he repeated. And having said her name, he bent his head and captured her mouth in a kiss so fierce and full of longing that Maggie's knees weakened beneath her.

She wound her arms around his neck, pressing her body close to his as she returned his kiss with soft, half-parted lips. He was warm and strong, and even after ten long years, so wonderfully, achingly familiar. "Nicholas," she breathed. "Oh, Nicholas, Nicholas. I knew you'd come back to me."

8

For the barest moment, St. Clare held Maggie tightly, crushingly against him, and then—before she fully understood what was happening—he removed her arms from his neck and gently but firmly set her away from him.

His face was taut and white, his expression void of all emotion. "Miss Honeywell," he said with excruciating civility. "You seem to be laboring under a misapprehension."

Maggie's lips were still swollen from his kisses, her body still warm from being held against his. She was slow to register the change in his demeanor. He'd drawn himself up to his full, intimidating height. He looked every inch the disdainful, cold-blooded aristocrat. He sounded like one, too. Indeed, his words, when he spoke them, hit her like a dash of icy water.

"Do not mistake me, ma'am. Your willingness is very tempting, and I have half a mind to encourage it, but my reputation is black enough already without perpetrating such a ruse. Besides, I flatter myself that I have no need to pretend to be another man in order to seduce a pretty girl." His lip curled into a faintly mocking smile. "This Nicholas of yours was a fortunate fellow to have inspired so much devotion, but alas, I am not him."

"Yes, you are." Her temper sparked to life. "Do you take me for a fool? Did you think I wouldn't know you? I recognized you from the moment we met. Why in heaven do you suppose I swooned?"

"Because you're unwell," he said.

Maggie flinched, and then, in typical fashion, bristled with outrage. How dared he? Using her illness as a means to win an argument! It was a tactic often employed by Fred, and one she deemed wholly unworthy of the man standing before her now. She opened her mouth to tell him so.

Just then, her attention was arrested by the sight of St. Clare's tiger. The boy was watching the two of them with undisguised interest as he walked the horses.

Maggie felt a rush of mortification. Had he heard her call his master Nicholas? Had he seen them kissing? Her cheeks flamed. She turned abruptly away from St. Clare and walked briskly across the grass.

St. Clare was at her side in an instant, silently offering his arm. She took it grudgingly. "Enzo understands only enough English to mind my cattle," he said as if reading her mind.

"Oh? Is he blind as well?"

"I'm afraid not. But you needn't worry that he'll tell tales. Even if he could come up with enough English to gossip amongst the servants, he wouldn't lower himself to do so. He's loyal to a fault."

"That's comforting."

"Miss Honeywell——"

"I recognized your handwriting, you know." She felt him tense slightly against her as they walked. "How could I not? I was the one who taught you how to read and write. Did you imagine for even one second that I'd forgotten?"

"You are mistaken," St. Clare said quietly.

"And how did you know that I wasn't the one who responded to your note? No, you needn't answer. It's plain enough. After all those hours spent writing out words and phrases for you to copy in your copybooks, my particular style of handwriting must be emblazoned on your brain."

Her chest was beginning to feel heavy, her heart pounding harder as her lungs worked to accommodate the strain of walking and talking.

"I'd begun to convince myself that you couldn't be him," she said, hearing the first traces of breathlessness in her voice. "That it was merely a strong resemblance. I told myself that the real Nicholas would have come to find me. That the moment he set foot back on English shores, he'd have made for Somerset. He wouldn't have spent a month in London gambling and engaging in duels." She shot him an accusing glance. "But it wasn't just any duel, was it? It was a duel with Frederick Burton-Smythe. Apparently, your hatred for him has outlived your love for me."

St. Clare's expression hardened. "You don't know what you're talking about."

"Then explain it to me! Tell me which parts I've got wrong!"

"Everything. That's what you've got wrong. Everything."

"I don't pretend to understand how you came to be here, or why it is you're pretending to be a viscount—"

"I *am* a viscount."

He said it with such conviction that Maggie almost believed him. Almost. "If you didn't trust me enough to tell me the truth, why did you seek me out? You must have known that I'd recognize you."

"You sought *me* out," he reminded her. "To beg for Burton-Smythe's life, if you'll recall."

"Not then. After that. At the theater and today and..." Maggie faltered. "If I'm a stranger to you, then...why did you kiss me?"

"If you must ask me that, I can only assume that you've vastly underrated your charms." St. Clare looked down at her with studied nonchalance. "Consult your glass. You're an uncommonly beautiful girl. What gentleman wouldn't kiss you if given encouragement?"

"And I encouraged you, did I?"

"Didn't you?"

Her brows knit together. "No... Perhaps... I don't know! Are you trying to provoke a quarrel? Or is it simply that you wish to hurt me?"

A shadow of some unidentifiable emotion passed over his face. "I wouldn't hurt you. Not now. Not ever. If you believe nothing else, you must believe that."

"You have hurt me every day for the last ten years. You have broken my heart."

Color rose in St. Clare's face. Once again, he turned away from her to stare out at the grassy path ahead of them. His profile might have been carved out of stone. "I beg your pardon. I've behaved badly. That kiss was entirely my fault. I apologize for any distress it may have caused you."

"And now you're mocking me."

"I am not—" He broke off, muttering something under his breath that sounded very much like a frustrated oath. "This conversation is madness. Complete and utter madness."

"Yes, I daresay it is." Maggie raised a gloved hand to press against her flushed cheek.

If Bessie were here, she'd warn Maggie that she was working herself up into a state. That all of this excitement was going to send her straight into a swoon. And it was true. But it wasn't only the excitement. She'd walked too far with Jane this morning, and now, already weakened, she was walking again with St. Clare.

Was it any wonder that she couldn't catch her breath?

"Perhaps I am mad," she said. "I suppose I must be to mistake you for Nicholas Seaton. Stark raving mad. You shall have to keep clear of me from now on. You shall have to cut my acquaintance."

"I shall do nothing of the sort." He paused before adding, "I mean to court you."

If he'd taken out a mallet and struck her on the head, she couldn't have been more astonished. "Court me? But…why?"

"Why does any gentleman court a lady?"

"You can't mean…?" *Marriage*. She couldn't bring herself to say it. It was ludicrous. Unthinkable.

And utterly impossible.

In six months' time she was to marry Fred. She *had* to marry Fred. There was Beasley Park to consider. The house, the land, and the tenants. It was her home. Her birthright.

He was too late. Nicholas Seaton had finally come back to her, and he was too late.

"I believe I've rendered you speechless," St. Clare murmured.

Maggie gazed vacantly around the park. Her head was swimming. How far had they walked? There were no carriages about them, nor any other person out for an afternoon stroll. Where was Enzo with the curricle? Gracious, she couldn't breathe. Her lungs were on fire.

"There's a fallen tree just up ahead that will serve as a seat." St. Clare's deep voice interrupted her thoughts. "Can you make it that far? Or shall I carry you?"

Maggie's eyes flew to his. "I am not ill!" The exclamation—which she'd intended to be forceful—came out weak and breathless. She cringed at the sound of it. Good lord, what must he think?

But as St. Clare stared down at her, the expression on his face left no doubt that he recognized the flush in her cheeks and the hitch in her breath for exactly what they were. "Four nights ago, when you fainted in my grandfather's library, your maid admitted to me that she'd once been your nurse. She said that, if not for her care, you might have died."

"It's true that Bessie was my nurse. But it was many years ago and…" Maggie looked ahead of them to the broken trunk lying just outside a cluster of trees.

St. Clare put his arm around her waist. "A few more steps."

And then they were there, and Maggie was sinking gratefully onto the tree trunk, gloved fingers tugging at the ribbons of her bonnet. "I can't breathe," she whispered, tears springing to her eyes.

St. Clare sat down beside her. "Let me." Ignoring Maggie's faint protests, he untied the ribbons himself and gently lifted her bonnet from her head. "Better?"

Maggie nodded weakly. She closed her eyes and took a breath. And then another and another. Bit by agonizing bit, the frenzied beating of her heart slowed and the constrictive heaviness in her chest began to ease. "I felt as if I was suffocating. Forgive me. I shall be all right directly."

She exerted all of her will toward calming herself. Toward breathing. It was soothing really. Being out of doors like this. The breeze rippled through the trees and she could smell the scent of horses and fresh, damp grass. And then there was St. Clare, the strength of his presence at her side so big and warm and comforting.

He'd fallen into a brooding silence. It was some time before he spoke again, and when he did, it was in tones of grave self-reproach. "I shouldn't have taxed you to walk with me. And I certainly shouldn't have argued with you while you did so. I find I must apologize once again."

She looked up at him in order to respond. Her heart skipped a beat. While her eyes had been closed, he'd removed his tall beaver hat. He was watching her now, tousled golden hair glistening in the afternoon sunlight and gray eyes fathomless beneath deeply knit brows. Next to him, Maggie felt small and vulnerable and disconcertingly female. Worst of all, as she met his gaze, she had a sudden, visceral memory of his warm lips closing over hers. It sent a shiver up her spine.

"Good grief," she said, flustered. "I hope I'm not yet so infirm that I can't walk across the grass leaning on a gentleman's arm. I've already given up riding, driving, and most every other activity that brings me pleasure. If I'm now too frail for walking, I can't think what's left for me."

"And yet…you claim you are not ill."

"Nor am I. Not now, at any rate."

"When?" he asked quietly.

"Three years ago." Maggie answered his next question before he could ask it. "It was influenza. And according to our village doctor, it has left me frail and enfeebled with a set of what are, apparently, the weakest pair of lungs in the West Country. It's why I haven't attended any balls since I came to town. I can't manage dancing any longer, or any manner of overexertion. I daresay you'll be lucky if I don't expire in your curricle on the journey back to Green Street."

St. Clare saw no humor in her words. Indeed, he seemed to stiffen with something very like anger. "How? Was there an epidemic in the village?"

"Nothing so dramatic as that, thank goodness. An elderly tenant on the outskirts of Beasley Park contracted a virulent strain of the fever. He lasted only four days, and after he was dead, his wife became ill. It was difficult. She had no family or friends. No one to nurse her. I couldn't let her die alone. I wouldn't have. My father forbade me going, naturally, but nothing could prevent me." She swallowed, her mouth suddenly dry. "I stayed with her until she died three days later. By that time, I had the fever myself."

"And almost succumbed to it."

"Yes, well, it was a very near thing until Bessie came."

And just like that, the aristocratic façade dropped and the icy coldness of St. Clare's countenance melted under a smoldering explosion of temper. "What in blazes were you thinking? Did your own well-being mean nothing to you? Had you no care at all whether you lived or died? My God." He raked a hand through his hair. "To risk your own life for… who? The village pariah? A person who'd be mourned by no one? Whose death would go unremarked? I cannot credit it. And now you're ill—"

"No!" she objected.

"*You're ill*," he repeated, glaring at her accusingly. "For nothing. For no bloody reason."

"Oh, stop ripping up at me! It's true, my own well-being wasn't foremost in my mind, but it wasn't for 'no bloody reason.' I had every reason to go to her when she was dying. I had an *obligation*."

"Because you must play lady of the manor," he said scathingly.

"No. No. Not that I wasn't… But ministering to the sick was never… Oh, drat you! If you must know, I went because the tenant's wife…" Her palms were damp beneath her gloves. "I'm sorry, Nicholas, but the tenant's wife was Jenny Seaton."

This time St. Clare didn't object to her use of Nicholas's name. He merely stared at her as if she'd said something to him in a language he couldn't understand. "What?"

"The year after you left, she married Ned Jensen. Perhaps you remember him. The cantankerous old recluse who used to shout at us whenever we rode past his cottage?" She swallowed. "He was looking for someone to keep house for him and Jenny told him that marrying her would be less expense than hiring a woman from the village."

"How touching."

"It was no love match, but they contrived to rub along. Indeed, I think they were both fairly content for the years they had left."

"They contrived to rub along." St. Clare's mouth curved into a slow, derisive smile. "What an epitaph."

Maggie wasn't sure what to make of his reaction. At first, he'd seemed to be almost stunned. But now…Good lord, he was *furious*.

Nicholas had never had a close relationship with Jenny Seaton. He'd never even called her mother. Not that she'd deserved the title. She was ignorant and neglectful, notoriously loose with her favors, and prone to unpredictable mood swings that shifted between maudlin bouts of self-pity and shrieking rages during which she often struck her young son with whatever implements were close at hand.

But whereas injuries inflicted by Frederick Burton-Smythe could send Nicholas into a towering fury, injuries inflicted by his mother had affected him in an entirely different way. Maggie remembered one particular afternoon when, after suffering an awful beating from Jenny, Nicholas had come to their meeting place in the woods at Beasley Park, and laying his head in her lap, had wept with painful, racking sobs while she stroked his hair.

The memory provoked a peculiar feeling inside her. She felt for a moment that she might weep herself.

Perhaps she shouldn't have told him about his mother's death. Perhaps Jenny Seaton wasn't worth even a second of his grief. But the Nicholas she'd known had desperately needed something from Jenny. Unconditional love, Maggie had always thought. That bottomless well of emotion that in the absence of feeling from his mother, Maggie had poured into Nicholas herself.

"I'm so sorry," she said once more. And, undeterred by the coldness she saw in St. Clare's face, she held out her hand to him, palm up in invitation. Again, she saw that peculiar shadow flicker across his hard features, but whatever feelings he had about her or his mother or the past didn't prevent him from taking her hand and holding it protectively in his.

"You shouldn't have done it," he said huskily. "You might have died."

Ah. So that was the source of his fury. Not the untimely death of Jenny Seaton, but that Maggie had risked her own life to care for her. "I did it for your sake."

St. Clare shook his head. "No."

"Jenny was all that I had left of you. The last link in the whole world. So, I sat with her. Holding her hand just as I'm holding yours now. I held it until she took her very last breath. I did it because of you. Because I loved you so very much."

"Confound you, Maggie."

Her heart gave a mad leap. It was far from a pronouncement of his true identity, but to her ears it might as well have been. She lifted his hand and pressed it to her cheek. "Nicholas—"

"No," St. Clare said in a low, hard voice. He cupped the side of her face. "No more of this."

"No more of what? The truth?" Her heart skittered wildly as he touched her. She could feel the heat of his hand through his glove, could sense the tightly controlled power lurking behind the tender stroke of his fingers.

Jane had said he was dangerous. Lethal.

And perhaps he was.

But Maggie wasn't afraid. "Am I to pretend that the past never happened? That you and I first met the night that Bessie and I came to Grosvenor Square?"

"As far as I'm concerned, we did meet for the first time that night," St. Clare said. "There's no need to pretend anything."

As far as he was concerned.

Her breath stopped. It was the closest thing to an admission he'd given her. An admission—and a warning. He didn't want to talk about the past. Didn't want to acknowledge who he was, or what they'd been to each other.

She supposed he had his reasons. Indeed, some of them were obvious. He was pretending to a position that he didn't have. Portraying himself as a wealthy viscount for heaven's sake. And Lord Allendale, of all people, seemed to be encouraging this deceit!

Was it some kind of swindle? A ploy to gain money or power?

"You're asking me to forget the past," she said. "But I haven't forgotten. Not once during all these years. I could never—"

"Miss Honeywell—"

"Maggie."

"Maggie." He drew his hand down the edge of her jaw, catching her cleft chin lightly in his fingers. And then he whispered her name again, his low baritone voice holding a softness that bordered on reverence. "*Maggie*."

She looked deeply, searchingly into his eyes. "I don't even know what to call you."

"Is St. Clare not to your liking?"

"It's a title."

"It's *my* title," he said. "But if you prefer it, when we're alone together, I give you leave to use my Christian name."

Maggie brightened. "Do you mean—?"

"John."

She frowned. Not Nicholas then. It was to be John Beresford, Viscount St. Clare. He would admit to being no one else. "John," she said.

John. St. Clare. My lord. What difference did it make? Whatever he wanted her to call him, he was Nicholas. *Her* Nicholas. And yet...

And yet, as she said his name, she trembled. She trembled as if he were the stranger he pretended to be. As if he were not Nicholas Seaton at all.

St. Clare's mouth tugged into a crooked smile. "You needn't look as if you'd just swallowed poison." He tipped her face up to his, his thumb caressing the voluptuous edge of her bottom lip. "Here. Say it again."

A warm blush rose in her cheeks. "John."

His hand still holding her chin, St. Clare lowered his head to kiss her.

Maggie's eyes closed. Her pulse was soaring just as it was used to do when one of her hunters was approaching a particularly treacherous fence. That unique mixture of fear and joy and primitive exhilaration. It was mother's milk to a Honeywell. Her lips parted softly in breathless anticipation.

But before St. Clare could capture her mouth, he froze. The sound of carriage wheels and faraway laughter drifted on the afternoon breeze. He gave a short, rueful laugh. "The fashionable hour has begun."

Maggie stiffened. She wasn't a young miss just out of the schoolroom whose reputation must be zealously guarded, nor was she one of those unfortunate souls whose every movement was governed by the dictates of propriety. Nevertheless, there were rules.

She was an unmarried lady sitting with an unmarried gentleman. Sitting *intimately* with an unmarried gentleman. And not just any unmarried gentleman, mind. The Viscount St. Clare. The very man who had put a bullet through Frederick Burton-Smythe's shoulder.

She gave an inward groan. George Trumble had warned her about the gossip, and what had she done but gone and thrown fuel directly onto the fire.

"We must go." She pulled away from him, rising so quickly that she nearly toppled over on the skirts of her pelisse.

St. Clare was up in a flash, steadying her. "Easy," he murmured. "They're a few minutes away yet. We have time."

"To exit the park completely unobserved?"

"That, I'm afraid, would be impossible. But there's time yet to get you and your reputation safely back in my curricle. After that, we shall be nothing more than another couple out for an afternoon drive."

"But everyone is already talking. If Fred hears—"

"What does that signify?" He swept up her bonnet and placed it back on her head, swiftly tying the ribbons before she could formulate an objection. "Burton-Smythe isn't your father."

"No, but…Beasley Park and my money and…Papa's will…" She looked up at him. "Oh, you don't understand how things are now!"

St. Clare paused a moment in the act of putting on his own hat. His mouth was set in a grim line. "No, likely not. But I very soon shall, make no mistake."

9

The Earl of Allendale had often remarked upon his grandson's extraordinary cold-bloodedness. It was a trait St. Clare had learned in hard school. Never to be a slave to his Beresford temper. Never to let emotion get the better of reason. In most cases, he'd discovered, an icy reserve could disarm an opponent more effectively than harsh words or a show of physical strength.

Still, he'd never been entirely certain whether his grandfather approved of his glacial demeanor.

Until now.

Seated in the earl's lavish drawing room in Grosvenor Square—two sets of shrewd, blatantly acquisitive eyes examining him as if he were a forged painting—St. Clare would have wagered a great deal that his grandfather not only approved of his coldness, but that he admired it, too.

Pity the old earl was incapable of exercising the same degree of restraint. It hadn't taken but one mention of his long-deceased son for him to fly straight up into the boughs.

"Why in blazes would you have heard of my son's marriage? You cut his acquaintance, along with the rest of society. Did you expect him to send you a formal announcement of his betrothal? An invitation to his wedding?"

Mrs. Lavinia Beresford, the widow of the earl's second cousin and mother of the man who, but for the existence of St. Clare, stood to inherit the earldom, was a painfully thin woman with birdlike features and a deceptively feather-brained air. Upon arriving at Grosvenor Square with her son fifteen minutes before, she'd perched herself on the edge of the drawing room sofa and set up an endless chirp of sharp-edged chatter.

"What have I said?" she asked with a titter. "Surely you didn't think I meant to imply…? I merely wondered…" She turned her sharp eyes back on St. Clare, the quick movement of her neck causing the ostrich plumes in her hat to quiver. "As one does wonder, you know. Having never met your mother myself. And not knowing any of her family."

St. Clare looked steadily back at her. He'd known this was coming. His grandfather had prepared him for it. They were to meet such accusations head on. Calmly, but decisively, and without undue protestation.

At least, that had been the plan.

"How would you know them?" Allendale bellowed. "My son was living in exile! He wasn't courting girls at Almack's!"

"Oh dear. I have put it badly, haven't I?" She looked to her son for assistance. "Lionel?"

At nearly thirty years of age, Lionel Beresford bore little resemblance to the "young pup" that St. Clare had heard his grandfather raving about for so many years. He was, in fact, a fairly large gentleman. His height was only an inch or two below St. Clare's own, and his width was presently straining at the confines of a brightly striped waistcoat and skintight pantaloons.

He had light brown curls brushed into careful disorder. A fleshy chin resting on an elaborately folded neckcloth. And he bore about himself an air of well-practiced indolence.

St. Clare had initially identified him as some manner of aspiring dandy. Within fifteen minutes of meeting him, however, it had become clear that Lionel Beresford was another sort of creature altogether.

"Madre means no offense," he said lazily. "She's simply curious. As are we all."

Allendale glared at Lionel from under ominously lowered brows. "Curious, are you? Damn your impudence. What right do you have to be curious about my heir?"

"We are family, Uncle."

"Uncle, is it!" Allendale exploded. "I'm no uncle of yours, you encroaching young jackanapes!"

"Oh," Mrs. Beresford tittered again, this time at St. Clare. "How coolly you look at us, my lord. What you must think. That I would cast aspersions on your parentage! I daresay your mother was an excellent sort of woman, if not, perhaps, as *gently* bred as one might like. And as for your father, well, he was always wild. Up to all manner of pranks, I'm told. And what he did, dueling with that poor feebleminded boy of Penworthy's was—as many still say—*dishonorable*—" She stopped and tittered once more at her own tactlessness. "But I shall say no more on the subject. The past is such a delicate subject for us Beresfords, is it not? And yet"—she paused, smiling—"one cannot help unearthing it at every turn."

"Can't they?" Allendale growled. "If you've come up to town to dig up some sort of a scandal, Lavinia—"

"Scandal? But surely you don't expect anything like a scandal? People may talk, naturally. But you must rest assured, Lionel and I shall do our parts to put down any doubts— that is to say any *rumors*—about Lord St. Clare's legitimacy. Won't we, Lionel?"

Lionel paused in the act of perusing a valuable-looking curio to pronounce himself at St. Clare's service. "I stand ready to assist you on every front. We Beresfords must stick together."

"You? A Beresford?" Allendale gave a crack of laughter. "Your distant ancestor was a Beresford, I grant you, but what you are, my boy, is the descendant of four generations of tradesmen. You're no more a Beresford than Jessup here."

The elderly butler, who had just entered the drawing room, graced his employer with a deferential bow. He then proceeded to announce the arrival of Lord Vickers and Lord Mattingly.

"Show them in, Jessup," Allendale said. "The only thing this farce lacks is an audience."

"Tradesmen?" Mrs. Beresford echoed when Jessup had withdrawn. "It is true that my late husband's great grandsire married an heiress, but—"

"A cit's daughter."

"Oh no," Mrs. Beresford protested. "Her father was a wealthy gentleman, yes, but he was no cit. He might have *dabbled* a bit in trade, but—"

"He owned a manufactory in Leeds," Allendale said.

St. Clare had heard the story frequently. There had been four Beresford brothers all those generations ago. Charles, the eldest, had inherited the earldom. Harold, the youngest, had married a cit's daughter. Harold's own sons had prospered in trade and their sons too, thus supplying the fortune on which subsequent descendants of Harold's line had lived.

But this, by itself, wasn't the source of the present earl's prejudice. As he often said, "Everyone knows that Harold Beresford bore more resemblance to one of the footmen than to his own father."

Whether Lionel Beresford was, in fact, a blood relation to him, St. Clare couldn't be certain, but at face value there didn't seem to be one drop of Beresford existing in the man. It was no wonder his grandfather exploded at the mere mention of his second cousin's son. The very things Allendale prided most in the Beresford line were conspicuously missing from Lionel. He had no looks, no bearing, and no trace of the infamous athleticism and daring that had characterized generations of Beresford men before him.

What he had instead was a certain low cunning, quite evident in the flintlike eyes that peered out from under deceitfully lazy lids. By St. Clare's measure, those eyes had already calculated the relative value of the artwork and the furnishings down to a ha'penny, and were presently making the same not-so-subtle evaluation of St. Clare himself.

"Lord Vickers and Lord Mattingly," Lionel said with seeming disinterest. He drew out an enameled snuffbox, flicked it open with one hand, and took a pinch of snuff. He promptly sneezed. "Friends of yours are they, my lord?"

"Friends? Indeed, so distinguished," Mrs. Beresford said. "Have you met them, Lionel? No? But then, we're not up to town as often as we would like. Shall I ring for tea, Allendale? I will pour, of course, being the most senior Beresford lady present. But then, there are no ladies present, are there? Dear me, so many single gentlemen! But that must be the reason you are come back to England, Lord St. Clare. To find a wife and set up your nursery. Lionel will be marrying soon, will you not, Lionel? Standing ready to do his duty by the title if things should not go quite as you have planned."

St. Clare fixed the woman with an implacable stare. He was pleased to see her artificial smile dim by several degrees.

"There will be no tea this morning, madam," Allendale informed her. "You and this young pup of yours have stayed quite long enough."

The very next moment, Mattingly and Vickers were shown in, and after introductions all around, the earl, very curtly, instructed Jessup to see Lionel Beresford and his mother out.

"Mushrooms," Mattingly pronounced as he watched them go. "Come up from the country to sniff around your claim to the title, have they?"

"That seems to be the case," St. Clare said.

Mattingly nodded. "No doubt they'll attempt to attach themselves to you for the duration of their stay."

At this, Vickers was properly horrified. "I say, St. Clare, you won't be obliged to spend much time in that fellow's company, will you?"

St. Clare grimaced. "Good lord, I hope not."

"I'll say this." Allendale addressed his grandson with a measure of pride. "If they've come up to town expecting to rattle you, they know better now. By gad, sir, but you can keep your countenance. Such phlegmatic coldness I've never had the privilege to behold. I would have done well to follow your example. I might have done, too, if that woman hadn't had the effrontery to mention my son to me. And then that whelp of hers, calling himself a Beresford! I was hard pressed not to throttle the pair of them."

"They've taken a house for the season," St. Clare said. "In Half Moon Street, I believe."

"They may engage as many houses as they please," Allendale replied acidly, "but if they think to presume upon my acquaintance—"

"Unless you intend to give them the cut direct, you must acknowledge them some time or other."

Allendale glowered at this bit of reasonableness. "Off with you. Go call on some of the young ladies you've met or take a gel for a drive. After what I've seen today, if you don't soon make some advances toward matrimony, I shall be forced to take a wife and sire the next heir myself."

Vickers stifled a choke of laughter. "He wouldn't, would he?" he asked as they made their exit.

St. Clare shook his head. He didn't elaborate. Unbeknownst to Vickers—or to society at large—a carriage accident during the early years of Lord Allendale's marriage had robbed him of his ability to sire more children. He'd fathered only the one: James Beresford.

If the line was to survive, it must continue through James's son. Through St. Clare himself. Indeed, it was the sole source of St. Clare's value to his grandfather, and one that Allendale took pains that St. Clare should never forget.

As if he ever could.

10

Dr. Felix Hart was by no means the most fashionable physician in London, but after he spent an hour examining her, Maggie was convinced he must be the most thorough one. He was a young man with a kind face and a slow, thoughtful manner. He didn't merely listen to her heart and her lungs, he asked a great deal of questions, and unlike the village doctor who had treated Maggie during her illness at Beasley Park, he seemed to be more interested in her answers than in the sound of his own voice.

Looking at him now, sitting across from her in the Trumbles' library, his hair sticking up at odd angles and his spectacles twinkling in the sunlight that shone in through the tall windows, she felt a guarded sense of hope.

"Cases like yours are all too common, Miss Honeywell," Dr. Hart said as Jane handed him a cup of tea. "Well-meaning family, and if you'll forgive me, wrongheaded country physicians, who respond to any near brush with death by wrapping the patient in cotton wool. If I've said it once I've said it one hundred times, the sooner one resumes their normal day-to-day activities after such an illness, the sooner one is restored to health."

"But how can I resume my normal life?" Maggie asked. "I'm not bedridden, it's true, but I'm far from being able to walk all over the countryside, or gallop my horse, or any of the number of things I was used to do before I fell ill. Why, I nearly fainted after a simple stroll in the park last week."

Having finished presiding over the tea tray, Jane took a seat beside Maggie on the library sofa. "Margaret is light-headed and faint whenever she overexerts herself. It's my constant fear that she'll swoon during one of our outings and crack her head open on the paving stones."

Dr. Hart nodded in sympathy. "You *are* weak, Miss Honeywell. That I will not dispute. But while there's certainly a portion of your weakness that can be attributed to the influenza, the majority, I believe, is a result of three years of enforced invalidism."

Maggie listened as the doctor went on to explain how her already weak lungs had been made weaker still by her lack of activity, and in his opinion, two successive bouts of mourning that had kept her confined to the house with little opportunity for fresh air and sunlight—two items he deemed essential for recovery from any illness.

"I don't hold with keeping my patients in darkened rooms with fires burning all year round. The outdoors is the place for healing. The countryside, ideally. Fresh air, sunlight, and short bouts of exertion several times each day. A turn about the garden, perhaps, or a walk down the drive. It needn't be strenuous."

"Then you believe Margaret can recover?" Jane asked. "That there's a chance she'll be well enough to do all that she did before?"

Dr. Hart scratched the side of his nose. "Well...No. Not precisely." He looked at Maggie. "By your own description, your life preceding the influenza was a very active one. It's unlikely you will ever be strong enough to resume that level of vigor. But you're still relatively young. There's no reason to say you won't recover enough to ride again or to go for walks. It's a matter of building your strength by slow degrees. Pushing yourself just enough without going too far, if that makes sense."

The doctor remained another quarter of an hour, outlining his course of treatment while he finished his tea. He might have stayed longer if the butler hadn't entered to inform Jane that Lord St. Clare and Lord Mattingly had come to call.

"I told them that you were not at home to callers today, Miss Trumble, but..." He gave a discreet cough. "Lord St. Clare was most insistent that I tell Miss Honeywell he was here."

A smile threatened at the edge of Maggie's mouth. In the week since St. Clare had first taken her driving, she'd seen or heard from him nearly every day.

One morning he'd contrived to accidentally run into her and Jane at Hookham's Library. Another morning he'd crossed their path as they were exiting a shop in Bond Street. He'd twice sent her a large bouquet of flowers. And on two separate occasions, he'd come to call on her in Green Street.

Their interaction in town had been limited to a cordial greeting and an equally cordial "I'm obliged to you, my lord" when he'd offered her some assistance. Whether it was reaching a book for her from a high shelf at Hookham's, or handing her up into the barouche outside the milliner's in Bond Street, St. Clare never lost an opportunity to do her some little service.

All the same, it was clear to Maggie that what St. Clare really wanted was a moment alone with her. Another chance to talk as they'd done that day in the park. She suspected it was the reason for his calls to Green Street.

Thus far, he'd been consistently thwarted in that regard. His visits to the Trumbles' townhouse had been brief and heavily chaperoned. Not only had Jane been present, but Jane's aunt Harriet as well, and on the second occasion, even George.

As a result, St. Clare's conversation had been restricted to the veriest commonplace. He'd talked civilly with Jane and exchanged a dry witticism or two with George, all while keeping his voice low so as not to disturb a sleeping Aunt Harriet. When he'd addressed Maggie at all it was to remark on such unexceptionable topics as the weather or the quality of the new hunter he'd lately purchased at Tattersall's.

He was courting her, to be sure, and his conduct in doing so was beyond reproach. But Maggie could see that he was becoming frustrated with the excessive formality.

"You'd better show the pair of them in, Olmstead," Jane said to the butler.

"But we haven't yet finished speaking with Dr. Hart," Maggie objected.

"That's quite all right, Miss Honeywell," the doctor said, rising. "I have another appointment I must get to before the hour."

"Thank you, Doctor," Jane replied with a smile. "I haven't yet seen Lord St. Clare out of temper. All the same, I'm not foolhardy enough to provoke him."

"I'd like to speak to him alone, if I might," Maggie said after the doctor had gone. "If you can contrive it."

Jane frowned. "I don't see how I can. Not without risking both of our reputations. Unless... I suppose we could walk in the garden? I could steer Lord Mattingly away, and if you and the viscount lingered a few steps behind, I wouldn't draw attention to it."

Maggie pressed a swift kiss to Jane's cheek. "Bless you."

Jane wasn't so easily placated. "Do you truly like him? He's handsome, I grant you. And rich, if reports are to be believed. But there's something else..."

"What?"

"Something beneath the surface—something cold and unforgiving. He doesn't seem to possess any warmth about him. It quite frightens me."

Maggie recalled St. Clare's embrace in Hyde Park. The way his arms had closed around her, his sinful mouth capturing her lips in a slow, and thoroughly devastating kiss. "He's warm enough."

Jane's brows shot up. "Upon my word, Margaret. You haven't been indiscreet with the man, have you?"

Before Maggie could answer, the butler ushered St. Clare and Lord Mattingly into the library. He may as well have ushered in a tiger, for that's how St. Clare appeared standing in the midst of the wood-paneled walls, thick Aubusson carpeting, and polished bookshelves filled with somber, leather-covered volumes. It was all very proper and civilized. And St. Clare wasn't civilized. Not entirely.

Jane was right. Something lurked beneath the surface of him. Something cold and predatory. It wasn't obvious at first glance. Indeed, he looked immaculate as always, clad in biscuit-colored pantaloons and a coat of impeccably cut super-fine. Next to him, Lord Mattingly paled into insignificance.

Not to Jane, however. Though she kept her composure and played the dutiful hostess, Maggie could sense her friend's attraction to the dark-haired gentleman at St. Clare's side.

"We've been shut up inside all morning," Jane said. "It seems a shame to let this fine weather go to waste. Shall we take a turn about the garden?"

St. Clare's gray gaze was settled on Maggie. It had been ever since he'd stepped into the room. He looked at her as if no one else existed.

It gave her an odd, fluttery feeling. Nerves, she suspected. Either that or some manner of giddy girlish excitement. This was, after all, a man she'd kissed. A man who had kissed *her*, more deeply and intimately than she'd ever been kissed before in her life. It was impossible to stand in front of him and not think of it.

Impossible not to want to do it again.

She'd spent years dreaming of Nicholas coming home. Years envisioning what it would be like to reunite with him. To hold him, love him, marry him.

"Do you feel equal to a stroll?" he asked.

Her mouth was dry. Great goodness. Had she been staring at him? "Of course." She moistened her lips. "The exercise will do me good."

He studied her face. It seemed as though he wanted to say something more. And no doubt he would when they were alone. Their encounter in Hyde Park hadn't been her finest moment. She'd come very close to fainting. Again.

Was it any wonder he was disposed to think her an invalid?

She tucked her hand into his arm as they followed Jane and Lord Mattingly out into the Trumbles' back garden. The sun was shining, a faint breeze ruffling through the branches of the fruit trees, just cold enough to merit the cashmere shawl Maggie wore draped round her shoulders.

St. Clare moderated his stride to match her own. He was solicitous. Gentlemanlike. As attentive to her frailty as Bessie often was.

Maggie stole a glance at his handsome profile, only to look away. Her happiness at seeing him again was shadowed by a nagging sense of self-consciousness.

If only she could be more like her old self for him. The Maggie Honeywell he must remember. A girl with a fiery temper and a wild, reckless heart.

Then, she'd been ready to dare anything. There had been no thought to her own human frailty. No consideration that she might do herself an injury.

Papa had been just the same. A true force of nature. His death, when it had come, had been sure and swift. His heart had given out midgallop during the autumn hunt at Beasley Park. He'd toppled from his horse, dead before he hit the ground. It was precisely how Papa would have wanted to meet his end. Snuffed out in full flame.

Meanwhile, Maggie had been reduced to seeing her own flame weaken and die—a mere cinder left to flicker in the ashes of what had once been her life.

If only Nicholas had come back sooner. If only he could have seen her in the months before the contagion of Jenny Seaton's illness had wrapped its suffocating fingers around Maggie's lungs. If only...

"You're very quiet," St. Clare said.

She looked up at him, managing a slight smile. "I have a great deal on my mind."

"Anything you'd like to share?"

Up ahead, Jane and Lord Mattingly disappeared down a path to the right. The Trumbles' garden wasn't large, but what it lacked in size it made up for in ornamentation. Wherever one looked there were arbors, trellises, and artfully placed topiary providing hidden spots of intimacy among the trees and flowerbeds.

Maggie came to a halt beside a stone bench. A trellis of roses shielded its back from view, and climbing ivy shrouded the sides. It was a perfect place for a private conversation. "Shall we sit down?"

A look of almost comical relief crossed over St. Clare's face. "Yes. Please. I've been trying to get you alone all week."

She laughed. "It's rather more difficult now, isn't it? We're not children anymore." Taking a seat on the bench, she arranged the skirts of her sprigged muslin gown.

It was one of her new dresses, made by Madame Clothilde. The fashionable modiste had been everything Jane had claimed—a small, sharp-eyed Frenchwoman of indeterminate age, who wielded her needle rather like a fairy godmother might wield a magic wand.

Maggie had lost the first bloom of her youth, it was true, and illness had robbed her of her once famous figure, but Madame Clothilde's designs had managed to bring her back to life with colors that flattered and cuts that clung in just the right places.

St. Clare sank down at her side. Close. *Too* close. "Miss Honeywell—"

"You can't keep denying it."

"I must," he said. "I've already told you. I'm not this child-hood friend of yours. Mister whatever his name was."

"Nicholas Seaton." She angled to face him, and her knee brushed his. It was the barest touch. Hardly an intimacy—her muslin-covered limb against his linen-covered one—but she felt it all the way to her core. Her heartbeat quickened. "Strange then, that you resemble him to such an extraordinary degree."

"A resemblance proves nothing. If there *is* a resemblance. I believe you said that it's been ten years since you saw your friend?"

"Ten, yes. Not twenty or thirty. It's hardly any time at all if one thinks of it."

"Ten years is a lifetime."

"It doesn't make one a stranger. I still recognize you. You haven't changed *that* much."

The corner of his mouth ticked up. "Your Mr. Seaton was my copy, it seems. My twin."

"No. Not twins. Not entirely. You're bigger than him. Taller, too. But your face—"

He looked down at her, amused. "What about my face?"

"Your eyes." Her gaze held his. A shivery warmth pooled low in her belly. She *knew* him. Recognized him with every fiber of her being. A stranger wouldn't have this effect on her. No man ever had before. "I think I know my friend."

His head bent to hers, close enough that he might kiss her. "As I said before," he murmured, "your friend is a fortunate fellow."

Mingled disappointment and frustration warred within her. She drew back from him. "If you will insist upon this fiction—"

"It's not a fiction, my dear. It's an incontrovertible fact."

My dear.

The rogue. He was enjoying this, whoever he was. Seeming to drink in her every expression, her slightest change of mood. To relish the very sight of her.

"Very well, then," she said, piqued. "Where were you born?"

He answered without hesitation. "In Venice."

"And your mother?"

"A lady of northern Italian extraction. My father married her abroad, and she died bringing me into this world."

Maggie's lips compressed. She didn't believe him. She couldn't. It would mean disbelieving the evidence of her own eyes—her own heart. "What was her given name?"

"Giovanna."

"Not Jenny Seaton, then."

He smiled. "Not remotely."

"And your father was Viscount St. Clare before you? The gentleman who fled London after killing a man in a duel?"

St. Clare's expression sobered. "You've heard the tales, I take it."

"Whispers," she said. "Is it true, what they say?"

"True enough." He was silent a moment. "My father shot the youngest son of the Duke of Penworthy. The boy was fee-bleminded, barely twenty at the time. He had a reputation for being hotheaded. Most everyone had learned to ignore his insults. But my father..."

"You said he was a rather famous shot."

"He was. Too famous by half. Every young pup with something to prove wanted to duel with him. It was something of a rite of passage."

"But he didn't duel with everyone who challenged him, surely?"

"I don't know." St. Clare frowned. "According to my grandfather, my father was a bit hotheaded himself. He didn't always exercise the best judgment. When Penworthy's son died from his wounds, my father was obliged to escape to the continent. He died there some years later."

"You never knew him?"

He shook his head. "My grandfather had the raising of me."

For the first time, Maggie felt a flicker of doubt. She tried to ignore it. It wasn't possible that his story was true. That he really was Lord St. Clare, heir to the Earl of Allendale.

He was Nicholas Seaton. He looked like him. He wrote like him. Smiled like him and smelled like him. Even the way he'd held her—the way he'd said her name. *Maggie*.

There were differences, it was true. Marked differences. He no longer carried himself as Nicholas had. And he no longer sounded like him, either. He spoke in the cultured tones of a gentleman, conversing with ease about art and music and history.

Nicholas had been neither well-read nor well-traveled. But he hadn't been cold. He'd been warm and affectionate. Passionate in his anger, but always ready with a teasing, lopsided grin. Indeed, despite the hardships of his young life, he'd laughed with her easily and often.

She wondered what he'd suffered to turn himself into the Viscount St. Clare. What he'd sacrificed to become the gentleman he was today.

But she feared she already knew the answer.

He'd sacrificed his past. Blotted it out entirely, and her along with it.

"We traveled a great deal," St. Clare said. "My schooling was haphazard at best. But the adventures I had. No man could wish for a better education."

"Tell me," she encouraged him.

And he did.

He told her about his youth. About the Grecian Count with whom he'd raced yachts in the Mediterranean. The dangerous little Italian who had taught him swordplay in Venice. And the perpetually foxed scholar his grandfather had employed to tutor him, a man who had doggedly followed them from Italy to Egypt and back again before, at long last, expiring of drink outside a disreputable tavern in Rome.

"I met Lord Mattingly and Lord Vickers not long after Napoleon was exiled to St. Helena," St. Clare said. "We traveled together for over a year before I was obliged to rejoin my grandfather."

"And then...?"

He shrugged. "And then I came home to England."

She felt a sudden flush of anger toward him. "But it's never been your home, has it? Indeed, it must seem very strange to you after a lifetime spent abroad."

"It isn't strange at all," he said. "Not a day of my life has passed that my grandfather hasn't spoken of England. He's described every facet of fashionable society. Every stone and timber of our estate. I always knew it was my destiny to return here."

She had to look away from him for a moment, else risk losing her temper. Good lord above. What a pantomime this was. What an absolute farce. She wanted to shake him until he admitted the truth to her.

But she couldn't force him to do anything.

She didn't dare try, not when there was the faintest shadow of uncertainty about who he was. And she *was* uncertain, more now than she'd been before he'd started his tale. How could she not be when he looked as he did and talked as he did? When he had wealth, and a title, and the support of the Earl of Allendale?

"Does it not get tedious living with your grandfather?" she asked. "A man of your age?"

"In Grosvenor Square?" He shrugged. "On occasion. But I'm not bound to stay there."

"You have another residence?"

For a moment it seemed he would not answer. And then: "I keep a set of rooms at Grillon's. A place I can go when I want a bit of privacy." His mouth hitched in an apologetic smile. "It's not something I generally make known."

A set of rooms at Grillon's.

Heat crept into Maggie's face. She was no green girl. She knew why a gentleman might keep rooms at a hotel. Privacy indeed. "Why did you come back? Do you mean to settle here?"

"I told you," he said. "I mean to court you."

She huffed an exasperated breath. "To what end?" She was resolved to be as blunt as he was mysterious. "I can't marry you."

St. Clare went still. His eyes searched hers.

"And yes," she said quickly, to stave off embarrassment, "I know you haven't proposed, or even mentioned marriage, but the natural goal of any courtship is—"

"Why not?"

"Because I can't, not even if I wanted to. Don't you understand? You're too late." She stood from her seat, her heart twisting on an unimaginable spasm of anguish. "Whoever you are, you're a year and a half too late."

11

St. Clare caught Maggie gently by the wrist and drew her back down to his side. She came reluctantly, resuming her seat on the bench, closer to him now than she'd been before.

"Talk to me," he said. "I want to understand."

She couldn't look at him. She wouldn't. The reality of her situation was too fraught with emotion. It was bad enough that she must contemplate marrying Fred, but to lose Nicholas forever? He'd only just come back into her life. How could she let him go? The unfairness of it was enough to drive anyone to tears. And she didn't wish to cry.

"What else is there to say?" she asked. "I'd have thought it was abundantly plain."

His fingers slid from her wrist to engulf her bare hand. His own hand was bare as well. He'd left his hat, cane, and gloves inside with the butler. There was nothing untoward about it. The two of them were in a private garden, not a public promenade. But it didn't feel entirely proper. Quite the opposite.

His skin pressed so intimately to hers. It felt dangerous. Illicit. Sensual beyond permission.

He didn't have the soft hands of a pampered aristocrat. His hands were large and strong, his long fingers almost elegant, with callusing from where he held his reins and whip. The hands of a sportsman. A Corinthian.

They were Nicholas's hands, she was sure of it.

"Does this have anything to do with Mr. Burton-Smythe?" he asked in a quiet voice. "You said he was something like your guardian."

She returned the warm clasp of St. Clare's fingers. She couldn't help herself. "He has control of all of my money and property."

"Until when?"

At last she turned to meet his eyes. Her heart clenched. "I must marry before six months have passed. If I don't, everything will go to Fred absolutely."

St. Clare straightened. "Well, then. There's no difficulty—"

"You don't understand. It must be with his permission. A groom of his choosing."

"In other words—"

"In other words, Fred himself. He won't approve of any other."

A muscle ticked in St. Clare's jaw. "And if you don't marry him? If you wed someone without his approval?"

"I shall lose my fortune, and Beasley Park along with it."

Were St. Clare truly Nicholas Seaton, he would have comprehended the full meaning of her words. Nicholas had known what Beasley Park meant to her. It was as much a part of her as he had been. Love of the land was etched into her very soul.

But St. Clare didn't seem to register the difficulty Fred's power over her presented. "I have no need of your fortune," he said. "I have one of my own."

Maggie stiffened. "You're suggesting that I allow him to take Beasley Park?"

"Why not? If the choice is between the estate and your happiness—"

"The estate *is* my happiness."

His hand tightened on hers almost imperceptibly. "You would marry Burton-Smythe in order to keep it?"

"I don't *want* to marry him. But Beasley must come first."

"You fear what he'll do to it if left to his own devices, is that it? You believe he'll run it straight into the ground?"

"It's not that," she admitted.

On the contrary, according to the letter she'd lately received from Mr. Entwhistle, the decisions Fred had been making in regard to Beasley Park had, thus far, been sound ones. Generous ones, too. He'd even approved a plan to replace the old roofs of the tenant cottages—a costly scheme that Maggie had advocated for herself.

"It's just that...he's put me in an impossible position."

"Nothing is impossible," St. Clare said.

"Some things are. Believe me, sir. If any of it were easy, I'd have already sorted it out for myself. As things stand, I intend to consult a solicitor. Though I don't hold out much hope. My father made his wishes abundantly clear."

"What can I do to help? My grandfather has solicitors. Private inquiry agents, too. If it's a matter of law—"

"I don't need your help, thank you. I shall deal with it. And with Fred, too. I don't require any—"

"Don't be stubborn merely for the sake of it. Pray, let me be of use to you. I shall run mad otherwise."

She gave him an ironic look. "You're very keen for someone who claims to have known me only a fortnight."

There was nothing of amusement in his face. Not any longer. "I know my own mind, Miss Honeywell."

"And I know mine. I'll sort it out myself. There's more to consider than legalities. Fred is…Fred." She withdrew her hand from St. Clare's grasp. "If you were Nicholas Seaton, you'd understand that better than anyone."

Jane chose that moment to reappear at the end of the garden path, Lord Mattingly at her heels.

Rising from the bench, Maggie pasted on a smile. "There you are. I wondered where you'd got to."

The following afternoon, St. Clare returned from Jackson's Boxing Saloon, his mind still in a state of turmoil. Exercise usually served to settle it, but not today. No amount of sparring had calmed him, not even during those minutes when he'd imagined that his opponent was Frederick Burton-Smythe.

Entering the marble-tiled hall at Grosvenor Square, he divested himself of his hat and gloves and handed them to Jessup.

"Lord Allendale requests your presence in the library, my lord," the antiquated butler said.

St. Clare ran a hand over his rumpled hair. "Now?"

"Immediately upon your return. He was quite clear on that point."

St. Clare made for the library. If his grandfather wanted to see him so urgently, it was nothing to the good. Best to get it over with.

He entered without knocking, finding his grandfather seated behind his carved mahogany desk. His head was bent over what looked to be a newspaper.

"You wished to see me?" St. Clare crossed the thickly carpeted floor to stand in front of him.

The library at Grosvenor Square was a masculine room, smelling of pipe smoke and leather. Wooden shelves lined the walls, sagging under the weight of old books and new ones. Volumes on travel, archaeology, and natural history abounded, stacked on every available surface. They were complemented by inlaid tables draped in maps of the world, and a magnificent terrestrial globe standing in a tall carved frame.

Allendale looked up from his paper. He scowled. "Back at last, are you?" He gestured to the leather-upholstered chair in front of his desk. "Sit."

St. Clare sat down. "You expected me sooner? I can't think why." His grandfather had known he was going to Tattersall's this morning, and then to Jackson's Saloon after that. "We agreed at breakfast that we'd dine together before attending Lady Colchester's ball."

"That was this morning. Before I saw this." Allendale thrust his newspaper across the desk.

St. Clare retrieved and opened it. But it wasn't a newspaper at all. It was a gossip rag. One of the most unsavory, too. A veritable scandal sheet. He skimmed the small, smudged black print before looking up at his grandfather with a scowl. "What—"

"The second page," Allendale said. "Quarter of the way down. Under that bit about the opera dancer."

St. Clare looked again. This time he saw it. Indeed, he wondered that he hadn't noticed it the first time. It was written there, plain as day, under the heading Tittle Tattle of the Fashionable World:

> *At long last, the Earl of A— has returned from exile, accompanied by his golden heir. But was the mysterious Lord S— born on the right side of the blanket?*

St. Clare lowered the paper back to the desk. A chill settled into his veins. "Is that all?"

"What? Not pointed enough, for you? Never fear, my boy. It soon will be." Allendale tapped the offending report with his finger. "This is how it always begins. Small. Just a few lines of suggestion. Of innuendo. But it won't be small for long. Not if Lavinia and her boy have anything to say about it."

"You hold them responsible?"

"Who else?"

St. Clare was silent. Who else indeed.

Allendale's eyes narrowed. "You haven't been doing anything you shouldn't have, have you?"

"I don't know what you mean."

"I warned you, no more dueling with country squires. No more personal vendettas. You and I have bigger matters to contend with."

"So you've said."

Allendale leaned across his desk. His face reddened. "By heaven, if you've faltered—"

"Calm yourself," St. Clare said. "There have been no more duels. Nothing that would cause remark."

Indeed, as far as he was aware, Burton-Smythe was still holed up in his rooms in St. James's Street, nursing his wounds. St. Clare looked forward to the moment when he emerged.

"I told you to be careful," Allendale said, frowning. "All you must do is find a bride and secure the title. I've drawn up a list. Suitable ladies of breeding years. Each of them of good stock." He withdrew a sheet of paper from a drawer of his desk and extended it to St. Clare. "You met several at the theater last week, Miss Steele among them."

St. Clare took the paper and set it down, unread. "I told you, I'll find my own bride."

"And what efforts have you made in that regard? Have you called on Miss Steele? On the dowager's granddaughters? Even that young chit, Mattingly's sister, might do if you insist upon having her. Only make up your mind—"

"I *have* made up my mind," St. Clare said with uncharacteristic heat.

Allendale came to attention. "And? What's the gel's name?"

"Miss Margaret Honeywell."

It was in this very room she'd appeared to him not two weeks before, cloaked in a shapeless gown, her face shadowed in the firelight. He'd caught her in his arms as she swooned. Had held her so very close to his breast. He'd understood then what he knew now absolutely. There could be no one else. No other lady, save her.

"Honeywell. Honeywell." Allendale murmured the name as if he was on the cusp of recalling some troublesome memory. "Who's her father?"

St. Clare hesitated. "A wealthy country squire, recently passed away."

Allendale's expression darkened. "Whereabouts was his property? Not Somerset, I trust."

St. Clare was silent.

"Foolish boy—"

"I'm not a boy. Not any longer. And she's the one I want. The *only* one I want."

"*Want*," Allendale echoed derisively. "What does that have to do with anything? You know your duty. You claimed to have accustomed yourself—"

"I thought I had until I saw her. And now I can't..." St. Clare struggled to express the emotion he felt whenever he looked at Miss Honeywell. The way his heart swelled with longing at the sight of her face. The way his blood heated when she argued with him. And when they'd kissed...

Everything had clicked into place. Settling perfectly, as if she was the missing piece that made the puzzle of his restless life complete.

"I can't imagine marrying anyone else but her," he said.

"Then you lack imagination, sir. Any of these gels would make you a conformable wife." Allendale pointed to the topmost name listed on his paper. "Miss Steele is as handsome a female as you're likely to find. Don't tell me you can't rouse yourself to sire an heir—"

"I'm not a stud horse on one of your farms, sir," St. Clare shot back. "And you haven't even met Miss Honeywell yet."

Allendale's gray eyes were hard as flint. "I don't need to meet her. Indeed, it seems to me that the wider a berth you give the gel, the safer you'll—"

"She wouldn't—"

"Oh, wouldn't she? Gossiping with her friends? Whispering in front of her servants? Before you know it, the scandal sheets will be rife with outright accusations. And when I die—"

"You're not dying anytime soon."

"*When I die*, where will you be? How will you defend your claim? No. I'll not have it. You must do your duty—for duty it is. I won't permit you to ruin my plans for some country nobody."

St. Clare clenched his jaw. There was no more point in arguing. He stood from his chair.

"Miss Steele will be at the ball this evening," Allendale said. "You'll secure the waltz with her, and the supper dance as well. Make it your particular priority. I want an heir by next year."

"You leave little time for courtship."

"Blast your courtship!" Allendale bellowed at St. Clare's departing back. "Do your duty so I can die in peace!"

The Trumbles' carriage rattled toward Green Street. Both Maggie and Jane sat silent within it. They'd uttered not a word between them since leaving Mr. Wroxham's office in Fleet Street. What was there to say? The solicitor had made Maggie's situation plain enough.

She stared out the carriage window, her thoughts drifting, as they often did, toward Beasley Park. To the household servants she'd grown up with, and the tenants she'd come to look on as her own family. She had a responsibility toward all of them. They were her people.

"You're not too dreadfully disappointed, are you?" Jane asked.

Maggie turned to look at her friend seated across from her in the carriage. "I am, rather. Not but that I didn't expect—"

"It's my fault. It was I who gave you reason to hope."

"Hush. You did only what a friend would do. A very dear friend."

Jane sighed. Clad in a slate-colored carriage dress and plumed bonnet, she appeared the very picture of an elegant and sensible lady. One who was accustomed to addressing problems with efficiency. "I do think that Mr. Wroxham might have found some way to extricate you from the restrictions of your father's will. It's an injustice if I've ever seen one. And the law is supposed to concern itself with fundamentals of fairness, is it not?"

Maggie smoothed the skirts of her pale blue pelisse. It was fitted tight through the bodice, with a decorative belt fastened high at her waist, and military-style braiding trimming the collar and sleeves. The sort of garment one wore when embarking on a campaign. She'd felt guardedly optimistic when she'd put it on this morning. As if she might conquer the problem of her father's will as readily as a general conquered a foe on the battlefield.

More fool her.

"Fundamental fairness for men, perhaps. But not for ladies."

"No, indeed," Jane said. "We must seek justice elsewhere, it seems."

"Where?"

"By petitioning other men, I suppose. Powerful men who might argue on our behalf."

"Why would any of them trouble themselves over me? I made no allies during my younger days in town. Quite the reverse. I daresay there are many gentlemen who would be glad to see Fred take me in hand."

"Oh dear. I hadn't considered that. You *were* much talked about. And when you refused every offer of marriage—"

"You know why I did—"

"Yes, yes. I know. At the time, I thought it rather romantic."

"It was headstrong and foolish is what it was. What I wouldn't give to go back and do it over again, knowing what I know now."

"You would have accepted one of them?"

A knot formed in Maggie's stomach as she recalled her previous suitors. Perhaps she should have chosen one of them. A gentleman who would have been kind. Someone she could have managed, who would have allowed her to run Beasley Park as she saw fit. It needn't have been a romance. It needn't have been *him*.

Nicholas.

Viscount St. Clare.

Shadowed images of the two men intermingled in her mind. She couldn't think of one without seeing the other. And yet, St. Clare still refused to acknowledge the truth of his identity.

Maggie was beginning to wonder if maybe she'd got it all wrong.

What if St. Clare was telling her the truth? What if her long illness and dual periods of mourning—all those months of darkness and solitude—had addled her wits? Had left her longing for Nicholas so keenly that she was seeing him in a man who was nothing but a stranger to her? An attractive, dashing stranger, but a stranger nonetheless.

"Margaret?" Jane prompted.

Maggie exhaled a deep breath. "No. I wouldn't have married any of them."

"And you won't marry Fred, will you?"

"I want to say no."

"Then say it."

"I can't. Not if it means relinquishing my estate." Maggie clasped her gloved hands tightly in her lap. "Beasley Park means everything to me, Jane. I won't allow Fred to take it from me."

"He'll take it anyway," Jane said. "He's not going to become more manageable once you're wed. He'll become worse. Men like him always do. Odious men who would use the law to oppress the ladies in their care. Oh, but I do think he's awful, Margaret. An absolute tyrant." She glanced out the window as the carriage came to a halt in front of the Trumbles' town house. Her face tightened. "Speak of the devil."

Maggie followed her gaze. It was Fred, or rather, the back of him, ascending the steps to the door and disappearing inside. She'd have recognized that coppery hair and those brawny shoulders anywhere. "What is he doing here? I'd have thought he'd still be abed."

The footman opened the carriage door and handed them both down.

"Something must have happened to drive him from his rooms," Jane said as they climbed the front steps to the house. "We shall soon find out."

Inside, the butler informed them that Fred was waiting in the drawing room.

Maggie stripped off her pelisse, bonnet, and gloves, and smoothed her hair into order. "I'll go to him, Jane. It's best he and I speak alone."

"Very well," Jane said. "But only for a quarter of an hour. You know you shouldn't be seeing him without a chaperone. And certainly not if he's in a mood."

"I'll be fine," Maggie promised. "If there's anyone I know how to handle, it's Frederick Burton-Smythe."

Bold words and ones that she reminded herself of as she entered the Trumbles' drawing room. Fred was standing near the bank of green damask-draped windows. At the sound of her footsteps, he turned. His right arm was bound up in a cloth sling, held close against his chest. She supposed it was meant to take the weight off of his injured shoulder.

"Margaret." His eyes raked over her. The cut of her new muslin day dress showed off her figure better than anything she'd worn in years.

"Fred. This is a surprise." She crossed to a petit-point chair near the marble fireplace and took a seat. She couldn't risk the gilded silk settee. It would only encourage him to sit beside her. "I wouldn't have thought it advisable for you to be out as yet. Has your physician allowed it?"

He came to join her, lowering himself into the delicate chair across from her. The carved legs gave a creak of protest at his bulk. "I'm hale as a horse. Only a trifle sore." A frown darkened his brow. "I expect you've heard what transpired."

"The day of your duel? I've heard that Lord St. Clare bested you."

Fred's already mulish expression transformed into a scowl. "It was dumb luck. The wind was high, else my bullet would have struck him first. It came very close to doing so. His sleeve was singed. But I don't expect Miss Trumble and her brother will have told you that part of the story. Gossiping busybodies always get their facts wrong."

She looked at him steadily. He was angling for a fight. No doubt his pride was hurt. "Is this what you've come to see me about? Gossip about your duel?"

"Not about my duel," he said. "The gossip has been about you."

Her brows lifted. She affected a look of unconcern, even as a flicker of uneasiness set her on her guard. "Oh?"

"I've been hearing countless tales. Indeed, people have been at great pains to bring them straight to my door. Tales of you and the man responsible for this." Fred lifted his elbow in its sling only to drop it back against his chest with a thump. "I've come to find out if the tales are true."

"How on earth should I know?" she asked. "I don't even know what it is you've heard."

"That he's been making advances toward you," Fred replied sharply. "I demand that you tell me what's been going on. I have a right to know. If he's been coming here—"

"Is that what they're saying?"

"Yes, dash it all. They say he's been calling on you here. That he's been seen with you in Bond Street, and at Hookham's Library. That he's even taken you driving in Hyde Park. And all of this—"

"Really, Fred."

"*All of this*," Fred raised his voice, "*after the blackguard shot me through the blasted shoulder!*"

Maggie's nerves jumped. From childhood, Fred had been a hothead and a tyrant. As a grown man, however, he'd rarely shouted at her, preferring to exert his dominance with high-handed edicts and masculine condescension.

But not now.

Now, he was, once again, the formidable bully of her youth.

"Be reasonable," she said. "It was you who issued the challenge. You who shot first. What else was he to do but return fire?"

"Has he called on you here? Have you received him?"

There was no point in lying. It would be easy enough for Fred to discover the truth, if he didn't know it already. "Yes. On both counts."

His face darkened like a thundercloud. "I forbid it."

"You have no right—"

"Try me," he said. "You'd be hard-pressed to stay in London with no funds of your own."

"Rubbish." Her gaze locked with his. She refused to be intimidated. "You can withhold my money, but you have no control over my person. I can go where I like and see whom I like. I can marry anyone—"

"Marry him!" Fred launched from his chair. "You wouldn't—"

"I might."

"Margaret—"

"And pray don't loom over me in that overbearing manner. You'll give me a cramp in my neck."

He reluctantly dropped back into his seat. "I won't ask if he's proposed to you, for I know full well he hasn't. He's made no secret that he's courting Miss Louisa Steele."

Maggie stared at Fred. For a moment, she wasn't sure if she'd heard him correctly. St. Clare was courting Miss Steele? That beautiful porcelain doll of a girl Maggie had seen him with at the theater? The young debutante in the first bloom of her youth?

She shook her head. "I don't believe it."

"It's true. He took her driving yesterday and escorted her to Lady Colchester's ball that same evening. To hear tell of it, the pair of them were inseparable. Waltzing together, dining together."

Maggie hadn't attended the Colchesters' ball. She was saving her strength for Lady Parkhurst's ball on Saturday. It was to be a grand affair. Maggie's first and only ball of the season, and one where she had hoped she might attempt a waltz with St. Clare. Then again...

He hadn't called yesterday. And he hadn't come today. Not yet. He hadn't even sent his usual bouquet of flowers.

"Miss Steele is this season's incomparable," Fred went on. "Her father is the younger son of the Earl of Lindsey, which makes her more than suitable as a match for a viscount. The *ton* is already talking about her marriage to St. Clare. If he's paying attention to you at all, it's not because he wants to wed you. It's because you're—"

"What am I?"

"Come, at your age, you can't expect—"

"I *beg* your pardon!"

"You're six and twenty. If a man like St. Clare is paying attention to you at all, he can have only one thing in mind, and it's not to make you his wife."

"How dare you!" Maggie's temper boiled over at last. "To make such insinuations. You don't know anything about him."

"No one does! He's never been seen before in England. There are reports he's not even legitimate. Why else would the Earl of Allendale have kept him away so long?"

She looked at Fred in disgust. "Is that the rumor your spreading now? I knew you were spiteful, but this is the absolute limit. To accuse someone of—"

"Not me. It's in the papers where anyone can read it." Fred leaned toward her. "And I won't be called spiteful, not when I'm only endeavoring to protect you."

"To protect me from St. Clare, you mean."

"And others of his ilk. So long as you're in town, you're fair game to them. A lady past her prime, who makes a show of herself at the theater and in Hyde Park—"

"Past my prime!"

"You're obviously not angling for a husband. The whole of society knows you're meant to marry me. It's what your father wanted."

"My father never understood the first thing about you." Maggie moved to rise.

Fred anticipated her, catching her by the arm in a harsh grip. He hauled her up in front of him, far too close for her comfort.

An unaccountable jolt of fear went through her. Despite his bluster, Fred had never resorted to brute force. Not where she was concerned. "Let go of me," she said.

"You *will* listen to what I have to say." His grasp tightened, as if he could force her to obey him by a show of physical strength. "Go home, Margaret. You've had a fortnight's holiday. Let it be enough. Go home," he said again. "Ready yourself for our wedding."

"I never said I'd marry you."

"We both know that you will. You'll do anything to keep Beasley Park." A peculiar light shone in his eyes. "Can you not find it in yourself to love me a little? I'm not the ogre you make me out. All I require is that you——"

"*I said let go of me.*" She wrenched free from his grasp. "Do you think anything in the world could ever induce me to love you after what you did to Nicholas Seaton?"

Fred froze where he stood. It was as if the name had turned him to stone. A name Maggie hadn't uttered in nearly ten years. "What did you say?" he asked in a dangerous whisper.

She took a step back from him. Her heart beat swift as a hare caught in the sights of a hunting hound. "I believe you heard me."

Fred advanced on her. "That boy—that *bastard*—was a thief and a liar. He stole your jewelry——"

"Spare me that old story, if you please. I'm not as gullible as my Aunt Daphne." She glared at him. "I see you for exactly what you are."

There was no remorse in Fred's face. No sign of regret over what he'd done to Nicholas so long ago. Quite the reverse. "He should have been hanged."

"If he had been," Maggie said, "you'd be no better than a murderer."

Fred gave her an accusing look. "Is this why you continue to refuse my hand? Because of *him*? Because you're still pining for him after all these years?"

"Did you think I'd forget? You stole my happiness away from me."

"A stable boy." He gave a derisive snort. "And for his memory you'd relinquish Beasley Park? I don't believe it."

Her spirits, already so low after the visit to the solicitor, sank even further. "No. I'm not stupid. I may yet marry you. You've given me little choice in the matter. But make no mistake. Whatever the future holds for us, I shall never, ever love you."

The Parkhursts' estate was located just outside of Chiswick. Maggie and Jane traveled there Saturday evening in the company of Jane's brother and Aunt Harriet. It was a long drive from Green Street, but not a lonely one. The usually dark road was alight with elegant carriages bound for the ball, the glow of their lamps leading the way to the drive of a grand house emblazoned with torches.

At a quarter past ten, guests were still arriving steadily. Traffic was backed up in the drive, coachmen only able to move their horses a few feet at a time.

George rapped at the roof of the carriage, signaling the driver to stop. "We'll get out here," he said. "If you all don't mind winding our way to the front steps? It will be quicker."

He handed each of them down onto the cobbled drive. It was a balmy evening, scarcely worthy of the light wrap Maggie had brought. She was glad to leave it behind in the carriage. Her new gown wasn't meant to be covered up. It was made to be shown off—every shimmering, clinging inch of it.

Indeed, Madame Clothilde had outdone herself for the occasion, creating a stunning confection of Clarence-blue silk, cut low at the bosom with short, fluttering sleeves and an overskirt embroidered with delicate beadwork that flashed and glittered in the candlelight.

When she'd first come to London, so many years before, Maggie had never worn anything half so daring. But as Fred had taken pains to point out, she wasn't a young girl anymore. She was a woman of six-and-twenty. A veritable artifact. Surely no one could object if her ball gown clung to her curves, antiquated as those curves must be.

As she stepped into the entry hall, she felt numerous sets of eyes upon her. Her pulse quickened. Was Lord St. Clare here? It was difficult to tell in such a crush.

Jane caught hold of Maggie's hand. "Stay close."

Maggie was grateful for the security of her friend's grasp. Jane and her aunt Harriet were each in possession of one of George's arms, but Maggie had no such support.

She passed through the receiving line and into the ballroom. A sea of faces greeted her, both familiar and unfamiliar. It had been many years since she'd last appeared at such a grand event. Beasley Park was a long way from Chiswick, and even if Maggie had been in London for more than a flying visit, her health wouldn't have permitted attendance. Crowded ballrooms were anathema to invalids, and dancing was all but out of the question.

"Heavens." The plumes on Aunt Harriet's fashionable turban quivered as she looked about the crowded room. "So many people."

"We shall find you a comfortable chair, Aunt," George said.

Jane craned her neck. Her own modest dress—a dove-gray creation, trimmed with a pattern of seed pearls—made her look every bit the mature, elegant lady. "There, George. I see Lady Featherstone and Mrs. Herron by the window. You'll wish to sit with them, won't you, Aunt?"

"Mrs. Herron?" Aunt Harriet brightened. "Oh yes. Do take me to her, my love."

After leaving his elderly aunt with her friends, George offered his free arm to Maggie. The orchestra was tuning up for the first dance. A country dance, by the sound of it. "Miss Honeywell? May I have the honor?"

Jane opened her mouth to object only to shut it again. She'd promised not to be too much of a mother hen this evening. Not that she hadn't clucked aplenty during the days since Dr. Hart's visit, warning Maggie to take things slowly.

Maggie supposed she *had* been pushing herself. But her health wasn't so easily recovered. It was going to take time. More time than she had at her disposal during this particular visit. "Best not," she said. "I must save my strength."

"How about you, m'dear?" he asked Jane.

Jane hesitated. "I don't like to leave Margaret on her own."

"Nonsense," Maggie said, urging her friend off. "I'll not permit you to play nursemaid."

Jane departed with George to line up at the center of the ballroom. Maggie remained at the edge of the floor. The music commenced with a swell of violins, and the dance began. Maggie stood to watch awhile. As she did so, her excitement over the evening was briefly dampened by a weight of self-pity.

Before the influenza, she'd loved to dance. Indeed, in her memory, her come-out season was one long string of country dances, cotillions, and scotch reels. The music had sung in her veins, and as she'd had no particular attachment to anyone, dancing had been the chief pleasure of every ball she'd attended.

She only regretted that she'd never waltzed. During her youth, it hadn't yet been deemed respectable. It was a close dance—scandalously close. Some claimed it was akin to embracing on the dance floor. Maggie had hoped she might experience it this evening. That is, if the right gentleman came along.

Had St. Clare had the courtesy to call on her in Green Street in the past three days, she'd have given him advance warning of her desire. But he'd been noticeably absent since that afternoon in the Trumbles' garden. To hear Fred tell it, St. Clare was too busy paying court to Miss Steele to trouble himself with Maggie.

And perhaps he was.

The very thought of it caused Maggie pain, but there was nothing to be gained by hiding her head in the sand. She forced herself to be realistic. Had she not surprised St. Clare that night in Grosvenor Square—had she not met him so totally by chance—would he ever have sought her out? Would he ever have returned to Beasley Park to find her?

"*Wait for me, Maggie,*" Nicholas had said all those years ago. "*No matter how long it takes, I will come back for you.*"

But Nicholas hadn't come back. Not for her.

And St. Clare showed no sign that he'd ever intended to. Rather the opposite. He was settled here in London. Settled, and looking for a bride. She'd thought that bride was to be her, but now…

Well. What did it matter anyway? She was as unable to marry him as he was unwilling to marry her. There was no point in repining.

Still, she couldn't help wondering if all of her questions about Nicholas had had some small part in driving St. Clare away. If she hadn't pressed him so relentlessly, would he have returned to her side? Or would he have grown bored with her regardless?

A depressing thought.

Unfurling the painted fan that hung at her wrist, Maggie wafted her face. More guests had arrived, and the ballroom was becoming stuffy. She made her away along the edge of the floor, toward the doors that led out to the terrace.

"Margaret," a familiar voice called out.

It wasn't the voice she'd been hoping to hear.

Steeling herself, she stopped and turned. "Fred. I didn't know you'd be here."

He stood in front of her, garbed in fashionable evening dress. *Too* fashionable. His neckcloth was folded in a fantastical design, and his ivory satin waistcoat shimmered like a jewel. It suited his brawny frame not at all.

There was no sign of the sling he'd worn on his arm during their last encounter. No concession to his recent bullet wound at all, save a certain stiffness in the way he carried himself.

"Naturally I'm here. You said you'd be attending. Though not to dance, I trust. You can't mean to exert yourself."

"I may dance," she said. "The waltz is, I understand, not terribly fatiguing."

Fred's face tightened. But he didn't argue. Instead, he gestured to a gentleman behind him. Like Fred, the man was extravagantly attired—high shirt points, an even higher neckcloth, and a black coat and knee breeches cut so snugly he minced when he walked. "Miss Honeywell, may I present Mr. Lionel Beresford. Beresford, Miss Honeywell."

"Beresford?" Maggie inquired as the man bowed over her gloved hand. "Are you any relation to Lords Allendale and St. Clare?"

"Distantly, ma'am. Distantly." Mr. Beresford released her hand, affecting an air of fashionable boredom. "I claim the honor of calling the earl my uncle, and Lord St. Clare—a relative only recently brought to my attention—my cousin."

"We met at Tattersall's," Fred said. "Beresford likes a bit of hunting. I've invited him to come and enjoy the shooting down at Beasley Park."

Maggie's eyes narrowed. "Have you."

Fred already acted as if Beasley was his own, making decisions about the estate that should rightly have been left to her, but inviting guests down to stay was a new level of presumed ownership.

"Is Letchford Hall not a more appropriate place to entertain your guests?" she asked.

Located next door to Beasley Park, Sir Roderick's estate was equally as grand and had the added benefit of being Fred's actual home.

"Not with the renovations. There's plaster and stonework everywhere. Isn't safe for company. Besides"—Fred turned back to Lionel—"you can't beat Beasley for hunting and shooting. The best in the West Country, that's what I always say. You may bring your mother, too," he added magnanimously. "Miss Honeywell could do with a bit of female company."

"Obliged to you, sir." Mr. Beresford gestured to someone in the crowd. "There's Madre now. Allow me to introduce you, ma'am."

There was no way Maggie could politely refuse. She permitted Fred to escort her back through the crowd to a row of chairs populated with elderly ladies and wallflowers. Mrs. Beresford sat among them, a thin, bird-like woman with unsettlingly sharp eyes. She regarded Maggie with a thin smile as Mr. Beresford made the introductions.

"You're not dancing, Miss Honeywell?" she asked. "A shame to have dressed in such a singular gown and not dance. To be sure, the design looks quite French." She tittered. "I can't say I've ever seen anything like it on any of the young ladies of *my* acquaintance."

"Miss Honeywell cannot dance," Fred replied. "She's an invalid."

Maggie's fingers clenched so hard on the ivory handle of her fan, she feared she might crack it in half. "How droll you are, Fred. Indeed, Mrs. Beresford, I *can* dance. I'm merely conserving my energy for the waltz." She inclined her head. "Good evening."

Turning sharply, she made her way back through the clusters of elegantly clad ladies and gentlemen that lined the ballroom. "Excuse me," she murmured. "I beg your pardon."

The music swelled as the dance came to a close, the orchestra playing so loudly that she could hardly think.

"Margaret." Fred caught hold of her arm—the same arm he'd clenched so brutally during his last visit to Green Street.

She couldn't conceal a wince.

He dropped his hand. "Where do you think you're going? You can't charge off alone." His gaze flicked down the length of her in disapproval. "Not dressed like that."

"I'm not alone. I came here with Miss Trumble, and with her brother and aunt."

"None of whom are anywhere to be found."

"Here I am!" Jane hurried, breathless, from the dance floor. "Is everything all right?"

Maggie had never been more relieved to see her friend. "Fred is objecting to my lack of a chaperone."

Jane laughed. "Nonsense. She has three chaperones altogether. My brother has just gone to fetch us some punch, and then we'll be rejoining my aunt."

"Exactly so," Maggie said. "I don't need you hovering over me all night, Fred. You'll only cause a scene."

Fred glowered. "Very well. But I'll be keeping an eye on you, Margaret, make no mistake." He strode away to rejoin his friend.

"What was that about?" Jane asked.

"Possessiveness," Maggie said. "And worse. He's befriended a distant relation of Lord. St. Clare's."

"Oh?" Jane shot Maggie a look. "What mischief can he be up to?"

"I don't know. But Fred never forgets a slight. I wouldn't put it past him to be brewing some manner of trouble for the viscount."

Jane sighed. "Men and their petty grievances. How tedious they can be." She linked her arm through Maggie's. "Come. Let's find George."

The evening continued in a flurry of music and dancing. More people arrived, and the ballroom was soon packed full to bursting. It was hot under the flickering lights of the crystal chandeliers, the air heavy with the cloying fragrance of perfume, pomade, and perspiration. One could scarcely draw breath. Indeed, midway through the evening—in a sure sign that Lady Parkhurst's ball was a success—a woman dancing the scotch reel fell into a dead faint from the lack of circulation.

Maggie felt a trifle light-headed herself. She hated to think how much worse it would be if she was dancing.

But she didn't dance.

Not even when the waltz was finally played. It was the supper dance—a dance coveted by any gentleman with aspirations toward a deeper familiarity with his lady. And not only because the waltz was an intimate undertaking, but because afterward he would have the privilege of dining with his partner. Of sitting beside her for an hour or more.

Maggie stood near to Aunt Harriet's chair, watching the dancers swirl about the room. It was then that she saw him.

John Beresford, Viscount St. Clare.

Clothed in an elegant black-and-white evening ensemble, he was waltzing with Miss Steele. All but embracing her as they swirled to the music.

Maggie's breath stopped.

When had he arrived? She hadn't seen him. Hadn't heard any talk to indicate he was present. He must have come just before the dance began. Which meant he'd likely reserved it with Miss Steele ahead of time. An agreement the pair of them had come to at a prior engagement, perhaps, or during the course of one of their drives in the park.

Maggie rested a hand at her midriff, willing herself to breathe, even as her heart clenched with hurt and jealousy. She was ashamed to admit to the latter. She had no formal claim on St. Clare. He'd said he intended to court her, it was true, but he'd made her no promises. Had sworn her no oaths. Only Nicholas had done so, and that had been too many years ago to count. He'd been little more than a lad then. What had he known of the world? What had he known of women?

Across the ballroom, St. Clare looked as experienced as any world-weary rake. He smiled down at Miss Steele as they danced. She was talking to him. Flirting with him, more like. Garbed in a shimmering silver dress, she fairly glowed in the candlelight. Twinkling like a diamond. Young and pretty and vigorous.

Maggie had been so once.

But not now.

She felt a sudden flush of embarrassment at her daring blue dress. She should have taken a page from Jane's book, dressing in a modest ball gown more appropriate to her years.

Jane herself looked elegant and graceful, waltzing with Lord Irvine, an elderly widowed gentleman. She was closer to Maggie than St. Clare was. Close enough to flash her a beaming smile.

Maggie forced a smile in return. A brighter smile than she thought herself capable of, given the circumstances. She wouldn't have her friend worry over her. Jane had already wasted the first half of the evening in looking after Maggie's comfort.

It was when she was smiling with such artificial brilliance that the twirling pattern of the dance brought St. Clare and Miss Steele closer. A dip and a swooping turn, and then his stormy gray gaze caught Maggie's across the floor.

Their eyes locked for an electricity-charged instant. For that timeless moment, he looked stunned. Stricken to his core. Maggie saw the emotion in his eyes, as plain as anything. But as quickly as it manifested, it was gone, lost beneath an air of glacial reserve.

He waltzed Miss Steele past, his attention once again fixed firmly on his partner's face. He even smiled at her, though there was nothing of warmth about his expression.

Maggie looked after him for the space of a heartbeat before forcibly turning her attention back to Jane. It wouldn't do to publicly pine after the season's most eligible bachelor. Not when the entire fashionable world knew that he'd recently fought a duel with Fred. It would only spark further gossip.

"Has Harold returned?" Aunt Harriet asked, blinking owlishly about the ballroom. "He promised to take me into supper."

Harold Trumble was Jane's father. Aunt Harriet frequently mistook the younger generation for those who had come before them.

Maggie didn't bother to correct her. "He's in the gaming room playing cards, ma'am. I'm certain he'll be here soon."

The final notes of the waltz sounded, with St. Clare and Miss Steele ending their dance at the far side of the ballroom. Maggie could no longer see them through the crush of people.

She didn't *want* to see them.

Though she'd resolved to keep her countenance, she didn't think her heart could bear to witness St. Clare escorting his comely young partner into supper.

"Aunt Harriet." George appeared out of the crowd, a little short of breath. He came to stand in front of his aunt. "Are you ready to go down to supper."

"Yes, yes. I'm famished." Aunt Harriet took George's arm.

"Miss Honeywell?" He offered his other arm to Maggie.

She shook her head. "Thank you, but I must have some fresh air. I feel a trifle light-headed."

When Jane returned with her partner, she offered to accompany Maggie outside. "It will be no trouble at all."

"Nonsense," Maggie said. "I'm fine on my own."

"But if you're going out into the garden—"

"I won't venture that far," Maggie promised. "I'll only step outside onto the terrace for a bit, and then I'll come and join you. You'll scarcely notice my absence."

As her friends and the rest of the guests made for the dining room, Maggie pressed toward the opposite end of the ballroom. Glass-paned doors led out onto a wide stone terrace. A liveried footman opened one of them for her.

She passed through and kept walking until her hands found the cool edge of the railing. Lit by torches, the terrace looked out over an expansive tiered garden. No one else seemed to be about. Except for a few lingering servants tidying up in the ballroom, she was alone.

The evening air was cool on her exposed skin. Far cooler than it had been when they'd arrived. She leaned over the rail, breathing deeply. Her eyes closed on a sigh.

It had been foolish to come here. Foolish to imagine she was well enough to dance with anyone, let alone St. Clare. Perhaps Fred was right. It was time to go home to Beasley Park. Time to resume the normal course of her life.

London had been a welcome distraction from reality. It was full of energy and industry. Alive with entertainments. But it was no place to recover one's health. It was too dusty and dirty, the air filled with smoke and damp with fog. What she needed was the fresh air of Beasley Park. She needed to walk in the countryside. Perhaps even to ride again, if she could convince Fred that it was safe for her to do so.

Fred.

The prospect of a life spent under his thumb depressed her spirits. It would be no life at all. But many women endured worse. Many carved out lives for themselves in spite of brutish, bullying husbands. She was more equipped than anyone to do so. With her temperament and backbone, she'd never permit Fred to break her spirit, or to get the better of her.

As for the rest of it—

Maggie's melancholy thoughts were arrested by the sound of the terrace door opening and closing again. Footsteps echoed on the stone as someone approached.

She went still, a shiver tracing its fingers down her spine.

It was St. Clare.

14

Maggie sensed him before she saw him, too afraid to turn and look lest he disappear in a puff of smoke. Indeed, it seemed like another dream. As if she'd conjured him out of the ether. A manifestation of her unrequited longing.

But he was no dream. He came to stand beside her at the rail, his body big and warm and breathtakingly real. His arm brushed hers. "You shouldn't be out here alone."

"Nor should you," she said with creditable calm. "Your partner will be waiting for you."

"Miss Steele? She's seated quite comfortably in the dining room. Lord Mattingly is looking after her."

"I wasn't aware Lord Mattingly was here."

"He's been in the card room. As have I, until the waltz."

"Ah yes. The waltz. You dance it very well."

He brushed the back of his knuckles over the small expanse of exposed skin that resided between the bottom of her sleeve and the top of her elbow-length glove. "I'd rather have been dancing it with you."

Butterflies fluttered wildly in Maggie's stomach. That anyone's touch should have such an effect on her! "You might have been. If you'd asked me."

"I didn't know you'd be here. You said that you no longer attended balls."

"I don't. That is, I haven't. Not since my illness. But Madame Clothilde made this dress for me, and I thought—if there was a chance that you and I—" She stopped herself.

"You look beautiful this evening. You always look beautiful."

"How kind of you to say so," she replied dryly. "And how spontaneous."

"I mean it. I've never known any lady who shines as brightly as you do. When I saw you in the ballroom—"

"You may keep your compliments. Save them for Miss Steele, or whoever else you—"

"Miss Honeywell." His voice deepened. "Maggie."

"Don't."

"I want to explain. About Miss Steele. About my absence these past days. There are things you don't understand."

"Undoubtedly," she said. His fingers fell from her arm. She felt the loss of his touch too keenly for words.

"My grandfather has very specific plans for my life. He doesn't allow for any deviation. And I *have* deviated since coming to London. First by dueling, and then by paying court to you."

At last she looked at him. "He classes courting me in the same column as dueling?"

St. Clare's brows lowered. "Unfortunately, yes." He paused. "My grandfather's concern—his sole concern—is securing the title with as little talk as possible. He wants me to marry and sire an heir. It's the only thing he can think of."

"What about you?"

His mouth quirked. "All I can think of is you."

Maggie's chest constricted on a pang of unutterable longing. She so wanted to believe him. "I'd never know it. It's been, what? Three days since I saw you last? Four?"

"And every one of them a misery."

"Please do me the courtesy of being honest. You haven't been miserable. You've been squiring Miss Steele about. All of London is talking about it. Even this evening, when you were waltzing—"

"That wasn't real," he said. "None of it's real."

"It looked very real to me."

"It's...it's a game."

Her brows lifted. "And what is Miss Steele in this game of yours? A pawn? A prize?"

"She's nothing. Just a child. A silly, spiteful chit of a girl. I have no interest in her save pacifying my grandfather."

Maggie hesitated to ask. "And what am I in your game?"

An inexplicable emotion crossed St. Clare's face. "You're everything," he said. "*Everything*."

They were pretty words. Just the sort designed to pacify a jealous female. Maggie didn't want to believe them. And yet...

Every instinct within her told her he was speaking the truth.

She could see it in his face. In his gray eyes, soft as smoke. The way he looked at her, so very different from the way he looked at anyone else. But she didn't dare trust her instincts. Not entirely. "How very flattering. Three days ago, I might have believed you. But that was before I saw you dancing with Miss Steele."

He studied Maggie's face. "You're not jealous?"

She laughed—a hollow sound in the cool, torch-lit darkness. It was an answer in and of itself.

"You have no reason to be," he said.

"No reason except that she's young and vital, with her whole life in front of her. Except that she was able to dance the waltz with you. I'd hoped that I—" Maggie broke off. She straightened one of her long gloves on her arm, smoothing it back over her elbow. "It doesn't matter. I couldn't have waltzed anyway. One must face facts."

His expression softened a fraction. There was deviltry in his eyes. And something else, too. Something from the very depths of him. It brought a huskiness to his words that hadn't been there before. "You wanted to waltz with me?"

Her stomach trembled with longing. "I said it didn't matter." She stood from the railing. "I must go down to supper. I promised Jane—"

"Miss Honeywell." St. Clare extended his hand to her.

She gave it a guarded look before slowly, cautiously sliding her hand into his. "You can't escort me down. Not when you're already bound to Miss Steele."

"I don't want to escort you to supper. I want to dance with you."

Her gaze jerked to his. "Don't be absurd. The orchestra is gone for the hour. There's no music."

"We don't need music."

Her mind immediately leapt to that long-ago dancing lesson in the clearing at Beasley Park. They hadn't had music then either. She searched St. Clare's eyes, wondering if he was thinking of that day, too. Did he remember how they'd twirled about the clearing? How they'd laughed?

She cleared her throat. "If you're trying to placate your grandfather—"

"My grandfather is at supper. And no one else is about. Not here. We have the whole terrace to ourselves."

"I suppose…"

"Waltz with me, Maggie. I'll claim it as my second forfeit if I have to."

She exhaled. "Very well. For a forfeit. Though it seems silly. You know we can't—" Her breath caught as his right arm circled her waist.

Heavens.

This couldn't be a good idea. Not when his very touch turned her limbs to melted treacle.

He held her left hand tight in his. "Put your other hand on my shoulder."

She did as he bid her. Her heartbeat quickened into a gallop. "I'm afraid you're too tall for me."

"Nonsense. We fit each other perfectly."

"I mean it. You've grown too big. And I haven't grown at all— Oh!" She gasped as he spun her into a turn.

He grinned down at her. "You do know how to waltz, don't you?"

"Do *you?*" she countered. "This isn't the way you were waltzing with Miss Steele."

"That was an English waltz. Not exciting at all." St. Clare tipped his head to hers. "The waltz is danced differently on the continent. A man and woman hold each other close." His arm tightened around her. "Like so."

Her pulse fluttered at her throat. "Goodness. How daring."

"It is, rather." He spun her round.

A thrill went through her as he waltzed her across the terrace. Her skirts swirled about his legs in a cloud of glittering blue silk. There were no missteps. No clumsy fumbles. It was easy. Effortless. Like something from one of her girlhood daydreams.

She gazed up at him in the torchlight, a smile spreading over her face. "We're waltzing together."

He looked steadily back at her. There was nothing cold in his countenance now. It was warm and open. "That we are, my darling."

The casual endearment sent a flush of warmth through her. She wanted to fling her arms around his neck. To stretch up and kiss him. To call him Nicholas.

But she didn't do any of those things.

She merely danced with him, letting him guide her through steps quick and slow, through turns that made her stomach quiver with excitement. All the while he stared down at her with single-minded attention, holding her in an unyielding grip—strong and sure and safe.

"Is a continental waltz longer than an English one?" she asked at last.

A look of immediate concern crossed his face. "Have I tired you out?"

"On the contrary." The giddiness of the dance made her bold. Foolishly so. "I wish it might last forever."

He smiled. "Until you wear through the soles of your dancing slippers?"

"Like a princess in a fairytale."

They both laughed, so consumed by their own pleasure that Maggie didn't hear the sound of one of the terrace doors opening. It was only as St. Clare steered her into another swooping turn that she saw Fred. He was standing at the door, frozen to the spot, watching them.

He looked just as he had so many years before when he'd discovered them laughing and dancing in the clearing. His brawny fists were clenched at his sides, his brow clouded with equal parts anger and resentment. And in his eyes—

But no. The look in Fred's eyes wasn't the same as it had been so long ago. This time, there wasn't murder in his gaze There was something worse.

Maggie very much feared it was recognition.

15

St. Clare followed Maggie's startled stare. The smile faded from his lips as he brought their dance to an untimely close. "Mr. Burton-Smythe. This is an unexpected pleasure."

Fred's muscular bulk filled the doorway. The light from the ballroom illuminated his reddening face. He was angry, and getting angrier by the second. A big brawny bully unchanged by time or circumstance. "Get your hands off of her."

St. Clare was slow to obey, only gradually loosening his arm from Maggie's waist. He still held her hand in his. He was loath to let it go. "How is your shoulder these days?"

"I said unhand her." Fred's voice was practically a snarl.

Maggie's hand slipped free from St. Clare's as she moved between them. "Don't be ridiculous, Fred. We were only waltzing."

St. Clare stood behind her, towering over her small frame. The tableau the three of them presented was visually ludicrous. Both he and Fred dwarfed Maggie in height and breadth. Yet she behaved as if she were physically strong enough to prevent the two of them from coming to blows. As if the mere fact of her feminine presence could restrain them.

In other circumstances, St. Clare would have been tempted to laugh. But he didn't feel much like laughing now. Indeed, he was glad Maggie couldn't see his face. All traces of warmth were gone. He felt quite cold to the heart. "A wound like that, it must be exceedingly painful to move your arm. Any luck yet driving your curricle? Holding your whip?"

"I'm recovered enough to protect what's mine," Fred replied through gritted teeth. "Come here, Margaret." He beckoned her to him with an imperious flick of his fingers. It wasn't too dissimilar from the way a farmer might summon his dog.

"Really, Fred," she objected. "I—"

"*Now.*"

Maggie reluctantly crossed the terrace, her spine stiff with dignity. "You needn't make a scene," she said under her breath. "Nothing untoward was going on."

"I'll be the judge of that." Fred caught hold of her arm and hauled her the rest of the way to his side.

She sucked in a sharp breath at his rough handling.

And St. Clare saw red.

He strode forward. "*Let go of her.*"

"Don't!" Maggie turned to block his path. "You'll only make things worse."

St. Clare came to an unwilling halt. A smoldering rage built within him, long banked but never extinguished. It wouldn't have taken much more provocation for him to pitch Fred straight over the rail of the terrace. "Let go of her," he said again. The fingers of his right hand curled into a fist. His knuckles cracked. "I dislike repeating myself."

Fred relinquished Maggie's arm. "Go back inside, Margaret."

"She's not yours to command," St. Clare said.

"And there you're wrong." Fred's eyes glinted with smug satisfaction. "I stand as her guardian. The man who holds power over her home—her very existence. She'll do as I say if she knows what's good for her."

"Oh, for heaven's sake," Maggie said.

"You have an advantage on me there," St. Clare said. "I've never had to blackmail a lady to my side. They generally come willingly."

Maggie shot St. Clare a warning look. *Don't provoke him.*

It was too late. Fred was already puffing himself up like an enraged toad. "*Blackmail?*"

"You heard me."

"You dare to insult *my* honor?"

"I'd be happy to offer you satisfaction," St. Clare said.

"You, a man who no one has ever seen before? Who may be an imposter for all we know?"

"Or to demand satisfaction of my own." St. Clare took another step forward. "If you keep talking."

"Enough." A note of exasperation sounded in Maggie's voice. "The two of you are *not* going to engage in another duel."

"I say, is everything all right out here?" Lionel Beresford appeared behind Fred in the doorway. He wore an expression of vague surprise. As if he'd stumbled upon the scene purely by chance.

St. Clare brought his anger under ruthless control. It wasn't easy. His heart was still pumping heavily, his muscles bunched with tension. The realization of what he'd almost done—what he'd very nearly put at risk—ricocheted through his consciousness like a rifle shot.

Good lord.

What had he been thinking? Another second and he'd have throttled Fred in plain view of Maggie, the Parkhurst servants, and Lionel Beresford, too.

The knowledge shook St. Clare to his core. He'd lost his temper. He *never* lost his temper.

What in blazes was wrong with him?

"A minor disagreement," he said.

Fred regarded St. Clare with all-too-familiar contempt. "There's nothing minor about a man's honor. A gentleman would know that."

"*Enough.*" Maggie placed a staying hand on Fred's sleeve. "I mean it. I'm bored to tears with all this bluster. You will oblige me by escorting me down to supper."

"Have no fear," Fred replied tersely. "I'll look after you." Tucking her hand into his arm—an unmistakably proprietary gesture—he cast a malevolent look at St. Clare. "You and I will meet again."

"Undoubtedly." St. Clare watched them depart through the terrace doors. Maggie was saying something to Fred, her voice too soft to be heard. St. Clare made no attempt to discern her words. He walked to the rail of the terrace, conscious of Lionel following behind him.

"An old enemy of yours?" Lionel asked.

St. Clare leaned back against the railing, his arms folded. "What do you think?"

"What I think, Cousin, is that you're not the man you seem."

"And you are?"

Lionel removed his enameled snuffbox from an inner pocket of his coat. He flicked open the lid. "The difference being that I can produce evidence of the legitimacy of my birth. While you"—he took a pinch of snuff—"cannot."

The torches that flanked the terrace flickered and snapped in the darkness. St. Clare's anger flickered, too. This time he managed to contain it. "Is my grandfather's word not enough for you?"

"No," Lionel answered. "I'm afraid it isn't."

And there it was. The unvarnished truth of the matter.

St. Clare had suspected as much, but he hadn't anticipated his cousin would admit it quite so plainly—or quite so offensively. "I should call you out for that."

"You should," Lionel agreed.

"I might, if I was confident you knew how to hold a pistol straight. As it stands, I may as well be calling out a child. And I don't engage with children in affairs of honor, offensive as they may be."

"Your father had no such scruples."

St. Clare drew himself up to his full height. For a moment, he didn't trust himself to speak.

"He had a temper too, they say." Lionel extracted his handkerchief to wipe the remaining snuff from his nostrils. "I've heard the stories. He was reckless and foolish. Wasting his fortune on whores and drink and gambling. Playing ridiculous pranks. According to Madre, your grandfather had had enough of him. And when your father shot Penworthy's boy—"

"Penworthy's son was no child. He was a man grown."

"In years, perhaps. But not in reason. Madre says the boy hadn't the sense of an addled pea goose. By consenting to a duel with your father, he all but signed his death warrant."

"Your mother knows nothing about my father. Nor do you."

Lionel shrugged. "Merely stating the facts."

St. Clare shot a narrow glance back toward the ballroom. A few footmen and housemaids were busy tidying up near the glass doors. Conspicuously busy. There didn't appear to be any guests lurking about, but one never knew. "By the by, where is your esteemed mother?"

"Enjoying her supper when I left her. Madre's found a kindred spirit in your Miss Steele. They've become fast friends."

St. Clare supposed Lionel's statement was meant to put him on his guard. As if Louisa Steele was in possession of any of St. Clare's secrets. During the past days, as he'd squired her about town, he'd done little but smile as she rattled on about herself in tiresome detail. All the compliments she'd received from men and all the ladies who were—inevitably—jealous of her.

It had been a small sacrifice to appease his grandfather, but a sacrifice nonetheless. Every minute spent with Miss Steele was one St. Clare might have spent with Maggie. And now, to know that Maggie had misunderstood him. That he might have hurt her in some way.

It wasn't what he'd intended. Not by any stretch of the imagination.

More and more he was beginning to feel like one of those hapless street performers he'd seen in Venice as a lad. A juggler with too many balls in the air. It took all of one's focus to keep the balls from dropping. A single fumble could mean catastrophe.

"I congratulate you, Cousin," Lionel went on. "Miss Steele is a great beauty. The prize of the season, I understand, and that set on marrying a title. It would be too bad if she were disappointed in that regard."

Too bad, indeed.

St. Clare's mouth curled into a humorless smile as he crossed to the terrace doors. His shoulder narrowly clipped Lionel's as he passed. "Do your worst."

Inside the ballroom, the servants who had been eavesdropping scattered in his wake. St. Clare paid them no mind. He'd said nothing that couldn't be repeated.

No. It was Lionel who had provided the gossip. An outright accusation that St. Clare wasn't who he said he was. It was only a matter of time before that accusation made the scandal sheets. An unambiguous charge made from one member of the Beresford family against another.

His grandfather would want to know.

St. Clare didn't look forward to the conversation. Not tonight. He had other things on his mind. Maggie and Frederick Burton-Smythe for one. He nevertheless descended the stairs leading down to the dining room. At the foot of them, he found George and Jane Trumble, their heads bent together, deep in whispered conversation.

Miss Trumble straightened at the sight of him. "Lord St. Clare. Good evening."

Her brother inclined his head in a stiff greeting. "St. Clare."

St. Clare looked between the two of them. A frisson of uneasiness went through him. "Is something amiss?"

"Not at all," George replied.

"It's Miss Honeywell," Miss Trumble said at the same time.

St. Clare's pulse leapt with something like alarm. He took a step forward. "What about Miss Honeywell?"

"Jane," George whispered a warning.

"It's all right," Miss Trumble whispered back to him. "He's Margaret's friend." She looked up at St. Clare. "Mr. Burton-Smythe insisted on taking her back to Green Street in his carriage."

St. Clare's alarm grew exponentially. "Alone?"

"No, no," Miss Trumble answered quickly. "Nothing like that. My Aunt Harriet has gone with them as chaperone."

The same elderly, enfeebled aunt who had been asleep on every occasion that St. Clare had chanced to meet her? What kind of chaperone was she? No chaperone at all, as far as he was concerned.

"We offered to take Miss Honeywell home ourselves," George said, "but she wouldn't allow us to suspend our pleasure on her account."

"I'm sure everything's fine," Miss Trumble said. "She can look after herself. It's only that…Mr. Burton-Smythe was in such a temper, and it's such a long drive back to Green Street."

It was fifteen miles, in fact. Fifteen long miles of dark, isolated road.

St. Clare's chest tightened with apprehension. Maggie was, indeed, more than capable of taking care of herself. But Fred had been pushed to his limit. He'd grabbed her roughly on the terrace and crudely ordered her about. And that had been in full public view.

What might he do to her when the two of them were, effectively, alone in a darkened carriage?

St. Clare wasn't going to wait to find out.

16

Maggie drew her wrap more firmly about her shoulders, mindful to conceal her gown's low décolletage. Beside her in the carriage, Jane's aunt Harriet snored softly. The motion of the coach, rolling steadily down the deserted road, had lulled her to sleep only moments after they'd set off from Chiswick.

"There's something familiar about the man." Seated across from Maggie, Fred's face was lit by a single carriage lamp. It cast his ruddy complexion in a pattern of shifting shadows. "Something I can't quite put my finger on."

Maggie had blown out the candle in the other carriage lamp so as not to disturb Aunt Harriet's slumber. It had seemed a courteous thing to do, initially. Now, however, alone in the semidarkness with Fred, she had cause to regret her decision. The shadowy interior of the carriage lent an intimacy to their discussion that she neither wanted nor welcomed.

"In what way familiar?" she asked.

"Something about his eyes. When I saw you dancing with him…" Fred's mouth hardened into a disapproving line. "If you can call it dancing."

She flicked a glance out the velvet-curtained carriage window. The starless midnight sky was black as pitch, and there was no full moon to light their way. Had they left the ball at the same time as the rest of the guests they might have benefited from the blaze of lamps swinging from the dozens of carriages returning to town. Now, however, there was no traffic at all. Nothing ahead or behind them save a long, lonely expanse of dark road. It was impossible to see a thing.

Perhaps it had been unwise to allow Fred to accompany her home early.

He'd insisted on doing so, and at the time, she'd thought it easier not to argue with him. He'd been in such a foul mood. On the verge of making a scene. Besides, she hadn't relished the thought of remaining at the ball. Of seeing St. Clare dining with Miss Steele. Dancing with Miss Steele. Not after Maggie had danced with him herself.

But Fred's anger hadn't been assuaged by her compliance. Indeed, since she'd climbed into the carriage with him, his sullen mood had grown worse.

"It was the waltz, that's all," she said.

He snorted. "Not any waltz I've ever seen."

"How could you have? You've never traveled outside of England. Whereas Lord St. Clare—"

"Beresford says he was born on the continent. In Italy, apparently." Fred's brow furrowed. "I wonder…"

Maggie didn't like the look on his face. Not one little bit. Fred wasn't a great thinker, and his memory was nothing to boast about, but unless she was very much mistaken, some part of him had recognized St. Clare, just as Maggie had recognized him that night in the library at Grosvenor Square.

It was the dancing. The way she and St. Clare had been looking at each other and laughing. Fred was a man who needed things spelled out for him, and tonight on the terrace, Maggie and St. Clare had unwittingly written the truth out in capital letters.

How long before Fred made the connection? He was struggling for it now. Straining his feeble wits to put the pieces together. At the moment, those pieces remained just out of his reach, but soon…

Soon he would realize that St. Clare bore a startling resemblance to Nicholas Seaton.

And then what?

Maggie regarded Fred from across the carriage. There was little she could do to protect St. Clare from Fred's vindictiveness, save try to nip his laborious process of deduction in the bud. "You're obsessed with him. That's what it is."

Fred's nostril's flared. "I am not."

"You are. It's excessively tedious. I'd sooner we changed the subject."

"If I speak of him at all it's only because you insist upon being in the man's company. As your guardian—"

"You are *not* my guardian. Not in the way you presume. And if you won't oblige me by changing the subject, then pray be quiet. You're incessant harping is giving me a megrim."

A muscle twitched in Fred's cheek. "This isn't a game. You're my responsibility, like it or not. What do you suppose a man like that wants from you? I'll tell you what—"

"Please, spare me the gruesome details of your wild imaginings."

"He wants to bed you," Fred blurted out. "To take his pleasure of you and leave you ruined."

Maggie reflexively drew back in her seat. She was no sheltered child. She nevertheless felt a quiver of uneasiness at Fred's bluntness.

Ladies hadn't much to protect them in this world. Little else but the rules of polite behavior. It was those very rules that made gentlemen treat them respectfully—almost deferentially. Maggie had never valued such deference. Not when it was offered purely on account of her sex. But now...the absence of it left her feeling peculiarly vulnerable. As if Fred had issued an unspoken threat.

"You mustn't speak of such things to me," she said. "It's not decent."

Fred continued undeterred. "You may not care one way or the other. You've made no secret how little score you set by your own reputation. But know this, I won't wed a woman who's been playing the light-skirt, nor will I support one."

Heat rose in her face at his crass words. Her temper rose as well. "Is that what it will take to rid you of this ridiculous desire to marry me? If only I'd known sooner."

"I mean it, Margaret. If you're to be my wife, you're to come to my bed untouched or not at all. And if I find out—"

"*Untouched.* There's a word. It can mean so many things." Maggie knew she was playing with fire but couldn't seem to stop herself. "Am I never to have embraced another gentleman? Never to have kissed him? Or is it only the marital act that you object to?"

Fred's face reddened in the dim light. He leaned forward in his seat. "*Have* you kissed him?"

"You're not a feudal lord, Fred. You're no lord at all. You're not even a baronet. Not yet. And if you think you can dictate to me—"

"*Have you kissed him?*"

She lifted one shoulder in a careless shrug. "I can't recall. One kisses so many gentlemen."

A predatory glint shone in Fred's eyes. "You've never kissed me."

Maggie didn't register the danger until it was too late. One second Fred was sitting across from her, and the next he'd caught her by the arms and pulled her from her seat, straight into his lap. She gave a muffled yelp of surprise.

"Perhaps that's the trouble," he said. "You don't know what you're missing."

She shoved his chest. "Let go of me, you great oaf."

"Just one kiss." His grip on her arms tightened painfully. "It's the least you owe me."

"I don't owe you anything." She fought to break free of his bruising grasp. Her hand found his injured shoulder in the struggle. She pressed hard against his bullet wound.

Fred let out a hoarse yelp. For a split second she managed to get loose, but then he seized her again, more roughly than before. The delicate sleeve of her new ball gown tore in his hand.

"Oh!" she cried. "Now look what you've done!"

He didn't seem to hear her. He was too intent on his purpose. "Hold still," he muttered as his mouth sought hers. His breath was hot on her face. "You may enjoy it."

At that very moment, the air was rent by a thunderous crack.

The horses screamed and the carriage veered sharply to the right. Maggie was flung from Fred's lap straight into the door.

Aunt Harriet woke with a start. "Good gracious! Have we lost a wheel?"

Maggie struggled to her seat. Her hair had come loose from its pins during her tussle with Fred. She pushed it back from her face. "That wasn't the wheel," she said breathlessly. "It was a pistol shot."

"Nonsense," Fred said. "Something's merely happened to the carriage." He hammered on the ceiling. "Coachman? What the devil is going on?"

The coachman made no answer.

But someone did.

A deep masculine voice broke through the darkness. "Stand and deliver!"

Aunt Harriet's rheumy eyes grew wide as saucers. "Heavens!" she cried. "It's a highwayman!"

Fred dropped back into his seat. His face was ashen. "Stay calm, ladies. Leave this to me."

Maggie's heart pounded in her ears. She told herself that she wasn't afraid. Not terribly so. Highwaymen didn't kill ladies, not as a general rule. "It's all right," she said to Aunt Harriet. "He'll only want our jewelry."

Aunt Harriet's blue-veined hand flew to the diamond necklace at her throat. "Can our outriders not protect us?"

Maggie shot a look at Fred. "We don't have outriders. Only the coachman and a footman."

"I said leave it to me," Fred snapped. He reached for the carriage door. His hand had no sooner touched the handle than the door was wrenched from his grasp.

It flew open, revealing a sinister figure enveloped in a heavy black cloak. His face was covered by a mask, his eyes shadowed by a tricorne hat pulled low over his brow. In his hand he held a horse pistol of truly startling proportions. He leveled it straight at Fred.

"Evening, guv," he said. "Mind stepping out of the carriage?"

"We don't want any trouble," Fred said. "We'll do whatever you ask of us."

"Then do it." The highwayman gestured with his pistol. "Out you come."

"Ooh," Aunt Harriet moaned.

The highwayman glanced at her. "Madam." He touched his hat in a mock salute. And then he looked at Maggie. His large frame seemed to still for an instant.

And no wonder.

She knew how she must appear. Without her wrap, there was no hiding her disheveled state. The torn sleeve of her ball gown was plainly visible in the light from the carriage lamp, as was her loosened coiffure.

"It seems I've interrupted something." Turning his attention back to Fred, the highwayman very deliberately cocked his pistol. "Step out, guv, before I haul you out myself."

Fred hastily exited the carriage. "Have a care how you point that thing," he said as the door slammed shut behind him. His voice was muffled. "If it's money you want, I can give you—"

There was a heavy thud. It was followed by a grunt and the sound of a large person hitting the ground.

Maggie clasped Aunt Harriet's hand. Her pulse was racing so she could hardly catch her breath.

"Do you suppose he's killed him?" Aunt Harriet asked.

"I don't think so. We'd have heard the pistol discharge."

The carriage door opened again, framing the highwayman's cloaked figure in the darkness.

"You can't take my diamonds, sir," Aunt Harriet said with a surprising degree of composure. "They're a family heirloom."

"Never fear, madam, I don't steal from aged ladies. Nor from young ones." His gaze caught Maggie's. "But I've been known to take payment by other means." He extended his hand to her. "Step out, love. Let me have a look at you."

She stared at his gloved hand, and then back at his face—at his eyes. Some of the tightness in her chest eased. Slowly, she slipped her hand into his.

"Miss Honeywell!" Aunt Harriet objected.

"I'll be fine," Maggie said as the highwayman assisted her out. "He won't hurt me."

"So long as you stay where you are," the highwayman warned Aunt Harriet. He shut the door of the carriage, leaving her alone inside.

Maggie blinked, trying to acclimate herself to the darkness. In the light of the lantern that swung from the coachman's box, she could just make out Fred on the ground, his slumped figure half-propped against the carriage wheel. He didn't appear to be dead. He wasn't even unconscious.

The coachman himself remained on the box, the liveried footman immobile at his side. Maggie didn't understand why they hadn't put up a fight. Not until she saw that there was another masked man standing in the shadows pointing a pistol at them. He was a great deal smaller than the first highwayman, but no less effective.

"What do you want from her?" Fred demanded. "Margaret—"

"What I want's a bit of privacy to claim my prize." The highwayman ushered Maggie behind the carriage. "This way, my beauty."

As soon as they were alone, Maggie reached to tug down the highwayman's cloth mask. He permitted her to do it, putting up no fight at all. St. Clare's handsome face was revealed by inches.

As if she'd had any doubt.

From the moment he'd reached for her, extending his hand in that age-old way, she'd known exactly who he was.

"Have you gone utterly mad?" she asked under her breath.

"Have you?" he replied in a sharp whisper. "Why did you leave the ball with him?"

"Because he was making a scene. It was easier to do as he asked than risk a scandal." She paused, admitting, "I thought I could manage him." Self-disgust coursed through her at her own naiveté. Fred wasn't a boy anymore. He was a man, and one she could obviously no longer control. "Is that why you came after me? Dressed like this?"

"There was little I could accomplish dressed as myself. I have no claim on you." St. Clare's fingers brushed over her torn sleeve. "Did he do this?"

"Yes. He was trying to kiss me, and when I fought with him—" She broke off, catching St. Clare by a fold of his cloak as he made to stride off. "Don't you dare do anything rash!"

"I'm going to *murder* him."

Her fingers tightened on his cloak. "Don't be stupid. You've already done enough."

"I've barely gotten started yet," he said.

There was something in his voice that made the fine hairs lift on the back of her neck. Good lord. Was he so consumed with hatred? With vengeance?

"Fred will get his comeuppance," she said. "I promise you. But not here. Not now. You must go. It's too dangerous for you to linger in this manner."

St. Clare glowered in Fred's direction. "He's the one in danger. If he so much as—"

"He won't touch me again. Not after this."

"No, he won't," St. Clare agreed. "Not once I break both his arms."

"Oh, for pity's sake. If you think this is what I want—two men pummeling each other over me—then you're very much mistaken. I'm not some damsel in distress for you to rescue."

He arched a brow at her torn dress.

She grimaced. "Yes, well… I confess, it *is* fortunate that you came along when you did. I'm not as formidable as I thought I was, not when Fred's blood is up. But I know better now. You can be sure I'll keep Jane's aunt awake during the remainder of the journey home."

"Is that meant to set my mind at ease?" he asked.

"It's the best I can offer at the moment."

It plainly wasn't good enough. St. Clare's lethal gaze once again drifted in Fred's direction. Maggie had no doubt he'd have broken every bone in Fred's body if given the chance.

"Look at me." She touched his jaw, drawing his eyes back to hers. "You're putting everything at risk. Don't you understand? It's not worth it. *He's* not worth it."

St. Clare stared down at her. "It's not about him. It's about you. It's *always* been about you."

Her heart gave a heavy thump.

And she wished—quite desperately—that she could see his face clearly in the darkness. That she could look into the eyes of the man behind the mask. Nicholas Seaton, not Viscount St. Clare or some nameless highwayman, but her friend. Her love.

"In that case," she said quietly, "you *must* go. I'll not have this reckless stunt on my conscience. If it should get out—"

"It won't."

"You're very confident. You must trust your partner excessively. It's not Lord Mattingly, I can tell that much."

"It's Enzo."

His tiger? She felt the unholy urge to laugh. "That's not very reassuring."

"He can handle a pistol as well as I can."

"Not tonight he won't." She tugged St. Clare's mask back into place. "You're both going to leave before anyone gets hurt."

"Margaret!" Fred shouted.

"I'm here!" Emerging from behind the carriage, she found Fred on his feet, cradling the back of his neck. She supposed she should feel sorry for him, but given how he'd manhandled her, she couldn't muster a single drop of sympathy.

"Into the carriage, my dove." St. Clare opened the door and handed Maggie inside. He shut it firmly behind her, and then whistled to Enzo.

Abandoning his post, the tiger trotted round the carriage to join his master. They retreated to where their horses waited in the brush alongside of the road. Hooves sounded on hard earth, stirrup leathers creaking as the pair of them mounted up.

"Is there a third one?" the coachman asked the footman.

"Can't rightly tell," the footman replied. "Too dark."

"Fair warning, John Coachman," St. Clare said as he spun his great black horse around. "My compatriots might be anywhere along the road ahead. Gentlemen, all. They don't take kindly to men who abuse their women. Best keep your guvnor on the box."

With that, he kicked his horse into a canter, and along with Enzo, disappeared into the night.

"Give me that if you won't use it!" Fred shouted at the coachman. The carriage shook. "What do I pay you for?"

Maggie leaned out the lowered window to see what was going on just in time to witness Fred take aim with the coachman's double-barreled carriage pistol. He fired into the darkness.

There was a sound—an unmistakable sound. The thud of a bullet striking flesh. It was followed by a shout, and the skitter of hooves as St. Clare and Enzo galloped off at breakneck speed.

She covered her mouth to stifle a scream.

"Did you get him, sir?" the footman asked excitedly.

"I hit something," Fred said. "The big one, I think. He's who I was aiming for."

"A bullet straight through the vitals," the coachman said. "Not a pleasant way to die." He gathered up the ribbons. "There may be more of them."

"Onto the back," Fred ordered the footman. "I'll ride up front." He stalked to the door of the carriage.

Maggie looked at him, her eyes wide. "The bullet hit him?"

"Of course it did. With any luck, he'll be dead by morning." He scanned her face and figure through the lowered window. "He didn't hurt you?"

She shook her head numbly. "Fred, are you certain—"

"There's no time for talk. We must hurry. There could be others lying in wait for us along the road." He departed without another word. Within seconds the carriage sprang into motion.

Maggie sank back in her seat. Her vision blurred with tears. Fred had shot St. Clare.

It didn't seem possible. And yet, she'd recognized that sound. Had known as soon as she heard it that the bullet had struck flesh.

She'd wanted to leap out and run after him, foolish as that would be. Even now, she suppressed an overpowering urge to scream for the coachman to go back. She couldn't just leave St. Clare there. She had to see for herself that he was all right.

But what could she do?

Even if she managed to convince Fred to let her out, there would be no way of aiding St. Clare without revealing his identity. She was powerless to help him. Powerless to do anything.

"There, there, dear," Aunt Harriet said, patting her hand. "His valet will look after him."

Maggie blinked at her through her tears. "What?"

"These sporting gentlemen and their servants know how to take care of their war wounds. And I daresay Lord St. Clare knows better than most after so many years of villainy."

An icy awareness seeped into Maggie's veins. Her vision slowly cleared. "I...I don't know what you mean."

"Young Viscount St. Clare," Aunt Harriet said. "I saw you conversing with him through the back window."

"You...what?" Maggie's nerves jangled a sharp warning. She flashed an anxious look at the long carriage window behind them. It was framed by velvet curtains and lit by the single flickering lamp inside.

Standing behind the carriage with St. Clare, she'd taken no notice of it at all. It had never once occurred to her that Aunt Harriet might be peeping out at them. That she might have witnessed Maggie lowering St. Clare's mask.

"I saw him," Aunt Harriet said.

Maggie wiped her eyes. "My dear ma'am...I know how it must look. But it isn't what you think. Lord St. Clare—"

"He turned to highway robbery, didn't he?" Aunt Harriet asked mildly. "After killing the duke's son?"

"I *beg* your pardon?"

"It's what people said at the time. I always thought it was a vicious rumor myself. He was such a nice boy."

Maggie stared at her in dawning realization. "Do you mean...*James* Beresford?"

"Aye. That's right." Aunt Harriet looked at her as though it was Maggie who had lost her wits. "The Earl of Allendale's son. Jim, they called him. A handsome golden lad. Such a shame he was a wrong 'un."

18

ocated on Albemarle Street in Mayfair, Grillon's was an eminently respectable London hotel. Luxurious too, by any standard. But St. Clare hadn't taken rooms there to enjoy such luxury. If that were the sole consideration, he'd have sooner remained at his grandfather's house in Grosvenor Square. No. It was privacy he wanted. And privacy for which he paid a tidy sum.

The hotel's manager, Mr. Fordyce, was the soul of discretion. He didn't utter so much as a peep when St. Clare appeared in the dead of night, shrouded in a cloak and leaning on Enzo for support.

No doubt the man assumed he was foxed. An assumption aided by the fact that, upon reaching his rooms, St. Clare immediately sent down for two bottles of brandy.

Enzo busied himself filling a basin in the dressing room while St. Clare stripped off his linen shirt. He sucked in a sharp breath as his sleeve—stuck fast with dried blood—peeled away from his arm. Fred's bullet had merely winged him, but that didn't mean the wound didn't hurt like the very devil. And it hadn't stopped said wound from bleeding profusely.

It was no less than he deserved for behaving in such a reckless manner.

The moment he'd heard that Fred had taken Maggie away in his carriage, St. Clare had lost the remaining hold he'd had on his temper. For the second time that night, he'd seen red.

His grandfather often warned him of the dangers of his Beresford temper, both in words and with visual displays of his own poorly controlled ire. St. Clare had prided himself on his ability to manage that temper. To hold his emotions close, like a card player who never revealed his hand.

Even when he'd dueled with Fred so many weeks before, St. Clare had kept a tight leash on his emotions. He'd been cold and calculating. Never once permitting the anger—the hatred—that roiled within him to melt through the glacial exterior he'd forged for himself.

Until tonight.

"*Acqua, signore.*" Enzo brought a porcelain basin from the dressing room, placing it on a low table near the bed. Water sloshed over the rim. "*E un panno.*"

St. Clare wet the proffered cloth and used it to clean his wound, rinsing the blood away over the basin until the water was tinted red with it. "*Portami una bottiglia di brandy.*"

Enzo obediently fetched a bottle of brandy from the sitting room and brought it back to him.

Uncorking it with his teeth, St. Clare poured a liberal amount over his wound. He may as well have doused it with liquid fire. It burned like the dickens. He clenched his jaw against the pain. "Blast Burton-Smythe to hell and back," he muttered wrathfully.

"*Stupido inglese*," Enzo echoed in sympathy. He craned his head. "*Ago e filo?*"

St. Clare angled his arm to examine his wound. The bullet had taken a chunk out of him. It wouldn't be easy to stitch it back together, but he supposed it was worth a try. "*Sì*," he said. "And Enzo? Try and find a sharper needle than the one you used in Rome."

Enzo flashed a grin before disappearing once again into the dressing room.

This wouldn't be the first time he'd sewn his master back together. After an Italian street brawl several years ago, he'd rather ruthlessly stitched a gash on St. Clare's shoulder using what could only be described as the dullest needle in Christendom. At the time, St. Clare had considered it a just punishment for his own bad judgment.

Tonight, however, he was in no mood for additional pain.

He took a long drink from the bottle of brandy.

And then another.

By the time Enzo began to sew him up, St. Clare had half a bottle in him. And by the time Enzo finished, St. Clare had half a bottle more.

He sat down in a chair for Enzo to pull off his boots. "I'll have to send word to my grandfather. *Puoi consegnarlo a Grosvenor Square.*"

Allendale had known St. Clare was leaving the Parkhursts' ball early, but he hadn't known why. There'd been no chance for a private word. No opportunity for anything save a glaring look of disapproval from his grandfather, silently indicting him for abandoning Miss Steele in the middle of supper.

St. Clare would have to think of something to tell him. An excuse his grandfather would deem acceptable. But to what end?

He didn't know anymore.

Everything had changed since returning to England. Since that fateful moment Margaret Honeywell had walked into that darkened library and fainted into his arms.

Recalling the way she'd looked tonight in the glow of the carriage lamps, his temper once again threatened to get the better of him.

Fred had torn her dress. Good lord, he'd been in the process of forcing himself on her when St. Clare had ambushed them on the road. If he hadn't arrived when he had...

It didn't bear thinking of.

He ran a hand over his face. "Fetch me ink and paper."

Enzo brought him his writing implements and St. Clare dashed off a short message to his grandfather:

> *Spending the night at Grillon's. Can't be helped.*
> *Will explain tomorrow.*

After dispatching Enzo with the note, St. Clare lay down upon his bed, one arm draped over his brow. His eyes fell shut. He might even have drifted off awhile, for when next he opened them, it was to the sound of someone rapping softly, but rather insistently, at the door.

He roused himself with a groan. His arm was stiff. A bone-deep ache that threatened swelling and fever. He'd have to clean it again, and soon. Either that or summon a doctor to do the job.

St. Clare prayed it wouldn't come to that.

He wasn't anxious for anyone else to discover he'd been shot. The last thing he needed was Fred realizing that it wasn't some random highwayman he'd encountered on the road.

Rising from his bed, shirtless, St. Clare tugged on a silk banyan over his breeches and went to the door. "It's half two in the morning," he muttered as he opened it. "This had better be…" The words dissolved on his lips.

It was Maggie Honeywell.

She stood on the threshold, garbed in a blue velvet cloak, the sable-trimmed hood drawn up to conceal her features. She looked up at him, naked relief on her face. "Oh," she said on a breath. "Thank heavens you're all right."

St. Clare stared down at her, stunned. For a moment he wasn't certain she was real. And then it hit him. Not only was she real, she was standing in the corridor outside his rooms. In a dratted hotel of all places.

Ducking his head out the door, he glanced quickly to the left and right, assuring himself that the hall was empty, before pulling her inside his room and shutting the door behind her. "What in blazes are you doing here?"

She pushed her hood back from her face. "Looking for you, of course."

His pulse stuttered. She was too beautiful for words. Too unutterably dear. It almost hurt to look at her. Especially now, tonight, when his self-control was already on a razor's edge. "How did you know—"

"You told me you kept a set of rooms at Grillon's. When you weren't at your grandfather's house, I assumed you'd be here."

A jolt of alarm shot through him. "You visited Grosvenor Square?"

"No, I sent Bessie. She went to the kitchen door this time. One of the scullery maids told her you hadn't come home yet. And I thought—"

"This is a hotel, Maggie," he said roughly. "Good God. If someone saw you enter—"

"You're concerned about my reputation?" She was incredulous. "How can you be? After what happened tonight—"

"Of course I'm concerned! Respectable ladies don't visit hotels. If they did, they wouldn't be considered respectable for long."

She stretched out a hand to touch him, but he backed out of her reach.

He shook his head. "You can't be here." He was half-dressed. Half drunk. And his emotions—usually under such rigid control—were as raw and vulnerable as they'd often been when he was a lad. "This isn't... This isn't a good idea."

She advanced on him. "Don't be stupid. You haven't anyone else to look after you. Naturally I came. Wild horses couldn't keep me away."

"I mean it. I've drunk nearly two bottles of brandy. I'm not..." He ran a hand over his disheveled hair. "For pity's sake, I'm not even dressed."

Her gaze flicked from his banyan to his breeches and back up again. A blush rose in her cheeks, but she didn't fluster. If anything, her tone became even more businesslike. "I'm not a green girl, you know. And besides, you're not just anyone." She came closer. "Where did the bullet hit you?"

"My upper arm. But that doesn't signify. You—"

"Here?" She touched him lightly.

He flinched and sucked in a breath.

"Poor darling," she murmured. "Does it hurt terribly?" She stripped off her gloves and removed her cloak, revealing the same ill-fitting blue dress she'd worn to visit him that night in Grosvenor Square. "You'd better let me have a look at it."

St. Clare marshaled his addled wits. She'd all but backed him into a corner. "Does Miss Trumble know you're here? Does Burton-Smythe?"

"No one does. No one except Bessie. She accompanied me here in a hackney cab."

He exhaled a breath. Her maid was with her. That was something, at least. "Where is she now?"

"Gone back to Green Street, I expect. I told her to wait in the lobby for ten minutes, and if I didn't come back from your room——"

"You *what*?"

"I'll make my own way home in the morning. You can put me in a cab yourself if you like."

"Have you lost your mind? If someone were to discover you——"

"I begin to think that's it's *you* who doesn't want me here."

Multiple wood-paneled doors led off of the sitting room. The one to his bedroom stood open, providing a glimpse of the rumpled coverlet on his four-poster bed and the clothing littering the carpeted floor—his shirt, stockings, and boots tossed at random.

Her eyes narrowed. "You don't have someone in your bedchamber with you, do you?"

"What?" The suggestion was so ludicrous—so far removed from the truth—that it took him a moment to comprehend her meaning. He huffed an astonished laugh. "A woman, do you mean?"

"Do you?"

"Of course not. I'm alone. That's what I've been trying to tell you. Even Enzo has gone. That's precisely why you can't——"

"Oh, can't I?" she shot back. "I've spent the last hours frightened to the heart that you were injured somewhere on the road from Chiswick. Do you have any idea what that feels like? To know I couldn't go back for you? That I couldn't help you? I couldn't even ascertain if you were alive or dead. And now you expect me to leave. To just…what? Hail a hackney to take me back to Green Street?" Her face crumpled slightly. "Confound you. I thought I'd lost you all over again."

His breath burned in his chest. He hadn't thought—hadn't considered. It had been too long since anyone cared about him. Not the title or the succession, but him. "I'm sorry I caused you distress."

"Don't be sorry. Just…let me look after you. I won't be satisfied until I see for myself that you're going to be all right."

He could do little else but stare at her, his jaw clenched hard against the emotion dammed up within him. She couldn't possibly comprehend the danger she was in. Not only the fact that she was here, at a hotel in the dead of night, but that she was *here*. Alone with him when he was in such an unpredictable mood.

He wanted her, damn him. He needed the solace of her arms. To lose himself in the sweet-scented feminine softness of her body.

It was already impossible to be near her without longing for her like a lovestruck pup. Thus far, only the respectability of daylight—of mannerly visits in the Trumbles' parlor and polite encounters on Bond Street—had kept that longing in check. And even then, he'd faltered. The day they'd kissed in Hyde Park, and then again when he'd waltzed with her on the Parkhursts' terrace. With each touch of her lips and clasp of her hand, he'd lost a little more of his implacable resolve. The very resolve that was meant to see him through this.

If only she'd waited until the morning to call on him, he might have regained some semblance of control over himself. But now...

"Let me see." She stretched out her hand to loosen the tie of his banyan.

This time he made no attempt to stop her. He didn't back away, merely stood there, holding his breath as the silken garment slipped over his shoulder and down his bare arm, exposing the bullet wound to her view.

But it wasn't the bullet wound that caught Maggie's eye. It wasn't his arm at all. It was his naked chest.

She froze in front of him, her gaze riveted to an old scar that slanted from the bottom of his neck down over his pectoral muscle. Long faded, but still quite visible, it was the sole reminder of who he was and where'd he come from. The lone memento of a past he'd tried very hard to forget.

Bloody blasted hell.

He hadn't meant to reveal it to her. Not here, not now. Had he been thinking clearly—

But it was too late.

A strange expression came over her face. She went pale and flushed by turns. And then she touched him. The slightest brush of her fingertips against his exposed flesh. It sent an earthquake through his vitals. A shudder he could neither hide nor suppress.

She inhaled a ragged breath, as though she felt it too. That deep bond of connection, forged so long ago, unbroken by time and distance. "Great God, I knew it." Her eyes found his, a glimmer of triumph shining in their liquid sapphire depths. "It really is you."

19

Maggie had scarcely touched him before St. Clare was, once again, moving away from her.

He pulled his banyan back over his shoulder, and tying it with a jerk, strode into his bedroom. A table beside the bed held a bottle of brandy and a single glass. He poured out a generous measure and drank it down in one swallow.

She followed after him. Surely he wasn't going to continue to deny it? Not now. The scar across his chest was definitive proof. She'd recognized it instantly, remembering the bloodied gash left by Fred's whip as if it were yesterday.

"*Look at what he did to me,*" Nicholas had said on that fateful night so many years ago. "*I ask you, is this the work of a gentleman?*"

St. Clare slammed his glass down on the table. "I told you that you shouldn't have come here."

Maggie knew she shouldn't have come. It was reckless and wild. A very real risk to her reputation. Worse than that, it was unfair to Bessie (who Maggie had told), and doubly unfair to Jane (who Maggie hadn't).

But Maggie hadn't cared about burdening her servant, or keeping secrets from her friend, not when St. Clare's well-being hung in the balance.

Nicholas's well-being.

They regarded each other across the short distance of his bedchamber like two adversaries on the verge of battle. A pulsing heat throbbed between them. A palpable tension that was as much a product of hurt and anger as desire.

"You lied to me," she said.

His gaze was locked with hers, his heavy-lidded eyes almost sullen. "I know."

"You made me doubt myself. When all the while—"

"I *know*." Bitterness and frustration sounded in his voice, along with a raw edge of genuine regret. He raked a hand through his golden hair. His tousled locks, usually combed into meticulous order, stood half on end.

She'd never seen him less poised. Less in control of himself. "Why did you do it?" she asked.

He turned away from her for a moment, his countenance half-hidden in the shadows cast from a branch of guttering candles on his bedside table.

And she felt it, the tremor that went through his body. The anger and frustration and soul-deep remorse. The roiling conflict that warred within him between the past and the present.

"Is it so terrible to recall it? To remember who you were?" She took a step toward him. "Who we were to each other?"

He shook his head, his face taut with some inexplicable emotion.

"I knew it was you. All I wanted was the truth. For you to acknowledge—"

"Acknowledge what?" The question was practically a snarl. "I never expected to see you again. How was I to know you'd be here? That you'd come to me as you did that night?"

"You must have been surprised."

He made a choked noise. It might have been a laugh. "You've developed a talent for understatement."

"And you've developed a skill for hiding your true feelings."

"Whatever skill I had has left me. I am as you see me now, without a shred of my armor." He poured himself another drink. "You've taken it all from me."

Her heart skipped a beat. "You can hardly blame me for your present condition. It wasn't I who—"

"No. It's my own fault. I have no control at all where you're concerned. I never have." He drained his glass. "You should go," he said. "I'm not myself."

She gave him a wry look.

"I mean—"

"I know what you mean. You're upset with yourself for acting so impulsively on my behalf. And you're in pain, I suspect, which accounts for your drinking."

He scrubbed his face with his hands. "You have to go," he said again. "I mean it, Maggie."

"Undoubtedly. But first things first." She came closer, backing him against his bed. "Let me have another look at your wound. A proper one this time."

"Haven't you seen enough?" he growled at her.

"Sit down." Her pulse was fluttering madly, but her voice was under admirable control. "No more nonsense."

Muttering something that sounded like an oath, he grudgingly sank back onto the edge of his mattress. His hands were braced at his sides, his feet planted firmly on the floor.

Maggie stepped forward between his legs. When he was seated, the two of them were of a similar height. It gave her a sense of command over the situation she didn't entirely feel. "You're like a great lion with a wounded paw. A wounded paw and a sore head." She untied his banyan and pushed it off of his shoulders. "You don't often drink too much, do you?"

"Rarely."

"I'm pleased to hear it." She moistened her lips. Her mouth had gone dry. And no wonder. He was bared to the waist in front of her. An arresting sight. It made her cheeks heat and her stomach quiver. She forced herself to focus on his arm. To behave in a clinical fashion, not in the manner of a lady on the verge of having the vapors.

It wasn't easy.

His chest might have been chiseled from a slab of marble. Every hollow and groove of his naked flesh was perfectly defined. As elegant with power as a statue of some Grecian God or hero. All lean muscles and tightly coiled strength.

The Nicholas of her youth had been spare and lanky. Far less intimidating to her senses. She wondered what he'd done to earn all these muscles. Jane had said he was a sportsman, but the smattering of faded scars on his chest and shoulders spoke less of pleasure than survival.

And he *had* survived.

More than that. Somehow, someway, he'd forged a life for himself—an entirely new identity. He'd become, in these ten years, a completely different man.

Maggie frowned as she examined the wound on his arm. The torn flesh was stitched together rather neatly with black thread. "Enzo's work, I presume. I trust you cleaned it thoroughly beforehand?"

St. Clare made a hoarse sound of assent.

She touched the edge of his wound. He flinched under the brush of her fingertips, and again when she drew her knuckles down the hard length of his bare arm. She doubted whether his reaction was entirely provoked by pain. Indeed, the more she touched him, the more she suspected that, underneath his taut exterior, he was as dry-mouthed and quivery with longing as she was.

Her gaze met his. "Does it hurt very much?"

He looked steadily back at her. "It's an agony."

Her heart thumped hard. "For me, as well." She slipped her hand into his, gratified to feel his fingers engulf hers. His clasp was hard and firm. Possessive. His head lowered as she leaned into him. "Nicholas—"

His mouth found hers, silencing her with a kiss. There was nothing gentle about it. His lips shaped to hers, rough with heat and want and raw masculine demand. A desperate kiss, far more than a sweet one.

And she melted.

There was no other way to describe it.

Her knees weakened and she melted against him. Into his arms, and into his kiss. Clinging to him as his mouth captured hers.

"Maggie," he murmured low in his throat. "I can't—"

"It's all right." Her arms circled his neck. And when he might have drawn away—mustering some scrap of gentlemanly restraint—she pulled his face back to hers and kissed him again.

He didn't require a great deal of encouragement. Indeed, the more she responded to him, the more he demanded. She gave it willingly, her half-parted lips molding to his. He tasted of brandy and male heat. A thrilling combination. It swiftly robbed her of her senses.

St. Clare appeared to be experiencing a similar effect. He was breathing heavily, his big hands moving at her waist and back, curving around her neck to hold her steady as his mouth fused with hers.

One kiss led to another and another, the next one beginning before the first had come to its natural end. All the while, an ache built within her—a longing for something she couldn't express. It made her as wild and desperate as he was, kissing him until she couldn't catch her breath. Until she couldn't seem to support the weight of her own body.

His arms wrapped around her in a powerful embrace. He lifted her onto the bed, settling her back against the rumpled pillows and coverlet. She had but a moment to gather her wits before he came down over her, caging her in his arms and kissing her again, hot and deep and breathless.

Goodness.

Goodness.

She gasped against his mouth. "Wait."

"I've waited too long already."

Her fingers twined in his hair, tugging at him weakly. "You'll smother me."

"I want to devour you." He pressed hot kisses to her cheek and jaw and throat. "If you knew what I've suffered—"

"And what about me? What about what I've suffered?" She gave another tug to his hair, forcing him to meet her eyes. Her body was trembling with yearning for more of his kisses. More of his touch. But she yearned for something else even more. She wanted—needed—the truth. "Why didn't you come back to me?"

He stared down at her for a long moment. The heat of passion slowly faded from his face. It was replaced by an emotion she couldn't identify. His throat spasmed on a swallow. And then he lay down at her side, his head coming to rest on the pillow next to her. "I wanted to."

"But you didn't. You didn't send me so much as a single letter." She looked at him in the waning candlelight, their faces only inches apart. "Why?"

"Because…" There was a peculiar sheen to his gray eyes. "In order to move forward…I had to let you go."

20

St. Clare had never contemplated saying the words aloud, let alone uttering them to Maggie Honeywell herself. Confessing to her that once he'd left Beasley Park—once he'd begun his transformation into John Beresford, Viscount St. Clare—he'd been obliged to think of her as an inextricable part of his unfortunate past. A past that had been better left forgotten.

I had to let you go.

It had been the only way to survive.

"I understand," she said. That didn't prevent the hurt from welling in her eyes.

The sight of it made his chest constrict. He touched her cheek. Her skin was soft as warm silk beneath his fingers. "Maggie—"

"I do. I even understand why you sought out Fred."

The mere mention of his rival's name was enough to make St. Clare's muscles tense with anger. "I didn't seek him out." He hadn't. Not initially. "I saw him quite by chance one afternoon in Bond street, not long after I arrived in London."

Fred had been strolling down the opposite side of the street in company with a fashionable companion. It was impossible to mistake that bulldog gait and copper-colored shock of hair. Impossible to forget that look of smug entitlement.

In that moment, emerging from Weston's after having just been measured for a half dozen new coats, the long-suppressed reality of St. Clare's past had rushed upon him with a frightening power. All the slings and arrows of his youth. All that roiling anger. The deep sense of unfairness about it all, and the bone-deep desire to, one day, balance the scales.

He'd thought he had put those feelings behind him. Locked them away and thrown the key into the depths of the Tiber. He'd left them there, buried in Italy—a necessary sacrifice in order to affect the transformation into the gentleman he was today. But in Bond Street, those feelings had been brutally resurrected.

"And later?" Maggie asked. "At the gaming hell?"

"That, I'm afraid, wasn't as much of a coincidence as it seemed."

She didn't appear surprised. "You contrived the whole of it, I gather."

"I did."

It had taken little effort to discover where Fred spent his evenings, and even less for St. Clare to arrange to be there himself. The gaming hell had been smoke-filled and dark, and Fred's powers of recognition none the better for drink. He hadn't known St. Clare at all.

But St. Clare had known him.

Indeed, there had been little in his life more satisfying than putting a bullet through Fred's shoulder.

"You could have contrived to meet me," Maggie said.

"I couldn't." St. Clare paused, adding darkly, "And not because of what you said in Hyde Park, about my hate for him outlasting my love for you."

"Then why?" A glimmer of vulnerability shone in her eyes.

He held her gaze. Lying beside each other on the curtained bed, the two of them face-to-face in the shadows, it felt as if they were children again, sharing secrets.

But not quite children.

He was a man grown—shirtless, injured, and half drunk. And she was a beautiful, alluring woman. *His* woman.

It was impossible to be anything but honest with her.

"Because...I knew if I saw you again, I'd go all to pieces. Everything I've worked for—my title, Allendale's support, the very life I live now. If I saw you again, I knew I'd risk it all to get you back, even if it meant destroying myself in the process."

She gave him a reproving look. "What a bleak way you have of viewing the matter. You saw me again that night in Grosvenor Square and your world hasn't ended."

His mouth twisted. She didn't know. Couldn't comprehend the power she had over him. The way the sight of her had affected him that night. One moment he'd been John Beresford, standing in front of the library fireplace after a night at his club. And the next he'd been Nicholas Seaton again. As if a crack had opened up in the universe and wrenched him back to Somerset. Not to the loose box in Squire Honeywell's stable, but to the forget-me-not covered grass where he'd lain with his blue-eyed love, his heart full with the promise of tomorrow.

No, his world hadn't ended, but the landscape of it had changed dramatically. Maggie's late-night visit had conjured the past for him more vividly than could a dozen encounters with the likes of Frederick Burton-Smythe. Not the anger and the rage of it, but those singular moments of sweetness. Of warmth, and unwavering devotion.

It had been all he could do to keep his countenance. To maintain the coldness of his reserve, and to preserve in his voice the hard-earned accents of a gentleman. The only saving grace had been that she hadn't seemed to recognize him.

Or so he'd thought, until their drive in Hyde Park.

"Weren't you at all curious about where I was or what I'd done with my life?" she asked. "Even if you didn't wish to see me, you might have at least made inquiries."

"To what end? I assumed you'd be long married. Settled down with a husband and children of your own." He grimaced. "I'd rather not have known the precise details."

A faint smile touched her lips. "You did think of me, then?"

"In the beginning, I did nothing *but* think of you. It was years before I was able to put my dreaming behind me." He'd been older. Wiser. More capable of self-discipline. "Even then…"

"What?" she asked.

He was silent for a long moment, his fingers stroking the curve of her cheek. When next he spoke, his voice was husky with memory. "Sometimes, when I was standing on the deck of a ship at midnight or driving alone along some deserted moonlit road, I'd feel the oddest sensation. A sharp tug pulling at my heart. As if a thread was anchored there, linking me to some other person, somewhere out there in the wide world. I always imagined it was you. Imagined it, and wondered if you felt it, too."

A rogue tear slipped down Maggie's cheek. "I did feel it. I still do."

He brushed the tear away, cursing himself for provoking it. "I'm sorry, Maggie. So sorry that I've hurt you. That I didn't keep my promise."

"I waited for you. For so long."

A burning prickle stung at the back of his eyes. "I'm sorry," he said again. "I wanted to come home, but...there was no way back to you. Not as the boy I was. Not as Nicholas Seaton."

"You make him sound like he was quite another person."

"I've come to think of him as such. A young, unfortunate fellow who I laid to rest somewhere in Italy."

Fresh tears threatened. "And Lord St. Clare?"

"Born in the same place. From Seaton's ashes, you might say. The man I was meant to be. Who I would have been, had things been different." He realized how nonsensical he must sound. "It's all become so bloody complicated."

"It has, rather." She set a slim hand on his bare chest, her palm sliding upward, brushing over the decade-old scar from Fred's whip. Her fingers curled around his neck. "But you're here now. That's all that matters to me at the moment."

He bent his head and kissed her very softly on the mouth. Their breath mingled, their lips parting and clinging. His pulse throbbed. It took all of his strength of will to draw back from her. "Can you ever forgive me? I know I don't deserve it—"

"Of course, I forgive you. I only wish you'd had the good sense to confide in me earlier. To trust me enough to explain who you really are."

"Who I really am," he repeated with a wry huff. "It's more complicated than you might think."

"I'm beginning to see that." She frowned. "Lord Allendale's son, James Beresford—the man you claim is your father... He truly was your father, wasn't he? He was Gentleman Jim."

St. Clare's fingers stilled on the curve of her cheek. He felt a disconcerting mixture of relief and alarm. "How did you know?"

"Something Jane's aunt said. She's forever mistaking people for their forebears. She caught a glimpse of you tonight through the carriage window and thought you were your father—Jim, she called him." Maggie searched his face. "It *is* true, isn't it?"

"It's true," he admitted. "James Beresford was Gentleman Jim."

He hadn't realized how much of a burden the truth was until he confessed it to her. No one else knew of it, save his grandfather. And the Earl of Allendale wasn't much for talking about the past. Not St. Clare's past, anyway. His boyhood in Somerset was a subject the earl had discouraged almost from the first moment they'd met.

"How ever did you find out?" Maggie asked. "The night you left Beasley Park, all you had was the merest suspicion. And that was only that a highwayman was your father, not a nobleman." Her eyes widened on a sudden thought. "Did you ask after him at the hedge tavern in Market Barrow? The one where Jenny used to work?"

St. Clare's thumb moved over her jaw in a slow caress. And then he dropped his hand. He exhaled heavily. "I didn't go to Market Barrow. I couldn't risk it. It would have meant riding inland, instead of to the coast."

"But how—"

"I went to Bristol, just as I'd planned. I asked after Gentleman Jim at every tavern I passed. All the while, I was dreading the moment the authorities would catch up with me and haul me back to Somerset to face the noose. And it wasn't only them I feared. On one occasion, two sailors from His Majesty's Royal Navy nearly impressed me into service. I managed to get away from them, but it was a very near thing."

"I thought you must have joined up. I thought you'd become a soldier or a sailor and gone away to fight Napoleon."

"Nothing so noble as that. I carried on with my search for Gentleman Jim. Kept looking—kept asking. Nearly got myself killed once or twice venturing into the wrong places." He still had the scars to prove it. Grim mementos of his early days searching for his father. "He wasn't as romantic a figure as you and I made him out to be, Maggie. He was an out-and-out rogue who kept dangerous company. Rumor was he'd escaped to the continent. To Italy some people said, by way of Geneva."

"So you traveled there yourself?"

He nodded. "I bought passage on a merchant vessel bound for Amsterdam." He could still recall, with gut-clenching clarity, how sick he'd become on the voyage. And then, that first taste of rye bread and herring when the ship had finally docked. The flavors so different from anything he'd ever eaten in England. "Thank God for that money you gave me. It saved my life more times than I can count. Kept a roof over my head and food in my belly while I trekked across the Alps to Milan."

"Such a long way," she said. "Were you ever afraid?"

"Frequently. It was a perilous journey, and for the better part of it, I was reliant on guides and the traveling companions I met along the way. I was in constant fear that one of them might slit my throat as I slept. It was a devilish incentive to learn as many languages as I could. A little German. A little Italian. Even a little French. Enough to keep me from being helpless—and from sounding too English. At the time, an English tongue was a liability."

"I wish I could have been there with you."

"You were with me," he said. "Every day. Every night." That, too, he recalled with painful clarity. The longing for her. The soul-deep yearning, worn to rawness from years spent trying—and failing—to forget. "There was so much I wanted to tell you. To share with you. Everything I saw and heard. All the funny little stories that I knew would make you laugh."

Tears glistened in her eyes. She blinked them away. "I envy you your adventures."

"Don't be too envious. My grandfather was a brutal taskmaster. I sometimes wondered if I'd have been better off taking the King's shilling."

"When did you first hear news of him?"

"Not until I reached Milan. There was an English-speaking fellow at a *pensione* there. He directed me to Venice—to the villa where the Earl of Allendale was staying."

Her brows knit. "But how did this man know where to send you? You're not saying he knew the truth of Gentleman Jim's identity?"

"He didn't know anything about Gentleman Jim at all. It was *me* he recognized. Some years earlier, Allendale had come to Italy looking for his son. He'd shown people a miniature." St. Clare's mouth hitched in a brief and bitter smile. "It turns out, Mrs. Applewhite was right all those years ago. I do bear an uncanny resemblance to my father. Some might even mistake us for the same man. Allendale knew as soon as he saw me that I was his grandson."

"His illegitimate grandson."

"His *only* grandson. He'd very nearly resigned himself to the title being passed to Lionel. It's a very sore point with my grandfather. All he's ever wanted is to secure the Beresford line. When I appeared, he realized there might be a chance to do it. He's unable to sire more children himself. And with my father dead—"

"*Is* he dead?"

"He is," St. Clare said. "I never got the chance to meet him. He died several years before I arrived in Italy, the victim of a wasting disease brought on by drink and whoring. Had my grandfather softened toward him sooner, he might have come home. But the Beresfords are stubborn—vindictive. Grandfather thought that a time in exile would be good for my father. That it would build his character. He was a disappointment to him, you see."

"A wrong 'un. That's what Jane's aunt called him."

"I daresay he was. Drinking. Fighting. Engaging in ill-conceived pranks. He was always getting himself into scrapes. When my grandfather cut him off for a time, my father resorted to robbery. I suspect it was all a lark to him."

"And Jenny?"

"One of his many conquests. No different from the other tavern wenches he struck up with during his time on the run."

Maggie didn't appear convinced. "I think there must have been more to it than that. Papa always said your mother was a rare beauty in her youth. And when she was at the hedge tavern in Market Barrow—"

"Plying her trade."

"My point is, I don't ever recall hearing Gentleman Jim's name linked with another woman. It was only ever Jenny. Which would lead one to believe—"

"That it was some grand love affair?" St. Clare scoffed. "If that was the case, then why—" He stopped himself from giving voice to the questions that had plagued his unhappy childhood.

Why hadn't Jenny loved him?

Why had she hit him and shouted at him and told him he'd ruined her life?

Maggie seemed to know what he was feeling, just as she always had. Her hand stroked the back of his neck in a soothing caress. "I think that, perhaps, she was disappointed by your father. Disappointed in life. It's unfair that she took it out on you, but…I do believe she loved you in her way."

"Oh, do you?" He gave a humorless laugh. "I'd wager she never lost any sleep over my disappearance."

"You're wrong," Maggie said. "She spoke about you in the end."

He flinched from her words as if they caused him physical pain. Jenny had often been cruel to him. And worse. She'd left him feeling as though he wasn't worthy of a mother's love. Even so, the thought of her dying—of speaking of him in her final moments—was almost too much to bear.

Maggie pressed on. "It was when I sat with her during the fever. Most of what she said in her final moments didn't make any sense. But she mentioned your name, and she asked for a priest. Not Mr. Applewhite, but someone else. A man she called Father Tuck. I'd no idea she was religious."

St. Clare hadn't either. Jenny had never attended church services and had never encouraged him to do so. As far as he could remember, she'd been at odds with God. Bitter about her lot in life and the scorn she faced as an unwed mother. "I suppose death makes believers of us all."

"Yes, well, regardless of religion, it was you she was thinking of at the last. That must mean something."

"What it means, my dear, is precisely nothing. Less than nothing. It's so much ancient history to me. Not worth discussing at all."

"And that's that, is it? You have no intention of talking about the past?"

"No," he said frankly. "I don't."

"*I'm* a part of your past."

"No, you're not." He looked at her in the darkness. "You're a part of me."

Her mouth wobbled.

"The very best part," he said. "The only part that matters. I may have given up the hope of seeing you again, but not a day has passed that I haven't thought of you. That I haven't wished…"

"What?" she asked softly.

"That I could be with you again. Like this. As the man I am now." He slid his arm around her waist and drew her close. "That I could finally make you mine."

She touched his face, tracing the curve of his brow with her fingertips and stroking the hard line of his jaw. "My first love," she murmured to him. "My only love. I am yours. I've *always* been yours."

Something inside him—a tightly held coil of worry and tension—slowly eased. He leaned into her words. Drinking them up like a man too long deprived of water.

She'd always known what he needed, what it took to make him whole. And she gave it to him now unreservedly. Her love. Her friendship. The exquisite reassurance of her touch.

He turned his face into her hand and pressed a kiss to her palm. "What about Beasley Park?"

"I could ask you the same about your grandfather and your title. Unless… You don't have a plan, do you?"

His expression turned rueful. "None of this has been planned. Not since the moment you walked into the library at Grosvenor Square. As for what comes next…I only know one thing." He loomed over her on the bed, his words as solemn and weighty as a sacred vow. "Whatever happens with my grandfather, with Beasley Park and all the rest of it…I'm never letting you go again."

21

St. Clare had to let her go, of course. Not an hour later, in the foggy, bronze-streaked minutes before dawn, he bundled her into a hackney and accompanied her back to Green Street.

It was for the best. The two of them had enough to worry about without tempting scandal in the bargain. If he and Maggie were to have any kind of future together, their courtship must proceed as properly—and as publicly—as possible.

He returned to Grillon's alone, where he cleaned his wound and went back to bed. The sheets smelled of her. Of soap and lavender water, and the sweet-scented pomade used to style her thick tresses for the ball.

It made for a restless sleep.

Rising some while later, he bathed and changed before making his way to Grosvenor Square, resolved to face the full force of his grandfather's ire. Instead, he found an empty house.

"His lordship has gone out," Jessup said.

"To where? His club?" St. Clare handed off his hat, coat and gloves to the butler.

"I couldn't say, my lord. He left in something of a hurry."

St. Clare scowled. He was in no mood for vagaries. His head was throbbing from too much brandy the night before, and the bullet wound in his arm ached liked the devil. "This isn't the time to make a mystery of things, Jessup. If something's happened to upset my grandfather, you may as well spit it out."

Jessup gave a discreet cough. "If I was to hazard a guess, sir, I would say it had something to do with the copy of *Bell's Weekly Messenger* he was reading at breakfast."

St. Clare closed his eyes for a moment. *Bell's Weekly Messenger* was a scandal sheet—one of the many his grandfather had fallen into the habit of reading since their arrival in London. It came every Sunday morning like clockwork and was presented to the earl along with his coffee.

"Fetch it for me," St. Clare said as he strode into the library. "At once."

Jessup brought it directly. It was folded over on a report about Lady Parkhurst's ball.

St. Clare leaned back against the edge of his grandfather's desk, the newspaper in his hand. He skimmed the small black print. It began with the usual drivel—who had attended and what they had been wearing. From there, it advanced to rumor and innuendo.

His fingers clenched on the paper as he read the offending passage.

> *Questions about Lord A——'s mysterious heir abound. While we have been reluctant to intimate anything nefarious, we can now confidently convey that the prevailing rumors place his origins not in Italy, but squarely in the West Country. Can that be the cause of his animus toward a certain Somerset squire?*

MIMI MATTHEWS

*And, too, for the attention paid to a certain Som-
erset beauty?*

St. Clare tossed the newspaper onto the desk with disgust.
The report was no stab in the dark. It had to have been suggested by someone. Someone with firsthand knowledge of
his dealings with Fred and Maggie.

Had it been Lionel? At the ball, he'd asked outright if Fred
was an old enemy of St. Clare's. Or had it been Fred himself?
Had he at last managed to put two and two together?

St. Clare thought the latter unlikely.

Fred was—and always had been—thick as a fence post. A
mindless bully, reacting more on instinct than sense. Never
mind that on each occasion he'd crossed paths with St. Clare
the visibility had been poor. It had either been dark or shadowed by smoke and flickering candlelight. Even on the
morning of their duel conditions had been murky, a heavy
fog billowing over the heath.

No. Fred hadn't recognized him. Not yet. But a man like
him could be easily led by the right person. Someone who
was sly and calculating, who knew how to play on Fred's
vanity and insecurities.

Someone like Lionel Beresford.

Exiting the library, St. Clare promptly called for his curricle.

Driving was a bit difficult with a wounded arm. The
stitches pulled whenever he tightened his hands on the reins.
But it wasn't too long of a journey to manage. Only a little
over a mile.

Lionel and his mother had taken a modest house in Half
Moon Street. It was a respectable address, if not an ostenta-
tious one. As St. Clare arrived, he fully expected to see some

sign of his grandfather. But the earl's elegant black lacquered carriage was nowhere in sight.

"Walk the horses, Enzo," St. Clare said as he jumped down from the leather-upholstered seat of his curricle.

The tiger trotted forward to take the reins.

St. Clare rapped on the front door. It was opened immediately by a young footman garbed in garish pink livery.

His Adam's apple bobbed. "Yes, sir?"

"Lord St. Clare to see Mr. Beresford." St. Clare didn't wait for an invitation. He walked straight into the small hall, removing his driving gloves and slapping them impatiently against the palm of his hand. "At once, man."

The footman scurried up the staircase to the second floor. Seconds later, Lionel appeared on the landing. He was wearing a tightly fitted coat with equally tight pantaloons. His starched shirt-points were as high as his ears, and the great bulk of his neckcloth had been tied in some overblown approximation of the Waterfall style. "Cousin," he said. "I wasn't expecting you."

St. Clare ascended the stairs. "Then you're not half as intelligent as I gave you credit for."

Lionel's eyes gleamed beneath his heavy lids. "Ah. You've read the report in *Bell's Weekly Messenger*, I gather."

"A report that you're responsible for."

"As you say, Cousin, you give me too much credit." He gestured for St. Clare to join him in the townhouse's well-appointed drawing room. "Madre will be pleased to see you. She's been grieved that neither you or Lord Allendale have yet seen fit to call on her. An oversight, I'm sure."

Lavinia Beresford was perched on a plump-cushioned settee, a beribboned lace cap upon her head and a scrap of embroidery in her hands. "Lord St. Clare!" Setting aside her needlework, she rose and executed a curtsy. "Do come in, my lord. And pray sit down." She flashed her son an arch look. "How naughty you are, Lionel. You might have told me your cousin was expected."

"He wasn't expected," Lionel replied.

"I should have been," St. Clare said, "after that scurrilous report in the paper."

"You've read it, have you?" Mrs. Beresford made a clucking noise as she resumed her seat. "Such a shock! To insinuate that you were born in Somerset of all places. An imposter they seem to believe. Not half-Italian at all. I wonder where they can have got such an idea?"

Lionel sat down, uttering a languid sigh. "Lord St. Clare believes it was we who gave it to them."

"*We?*" Her eyes went wide. "But we know nothing at all about you, my lord. Nothing about your life in Italy, nor in Somerset." She tittered. "Though I see no great difficulty in clearing up the matter. All you need do is present your parents' marriage lines. They have such, don't they? Even on the continent, I believe."

St. Clare made no move to sit. This wasn't a social call. "By what right do you demand proof from me?"

"Oh no. We would never *demand*. Not from Allendale's heir. What must you think of us?" Another titter. "To be sure, it's only a bit of advice. If an heir—a *presumptive* heir—is accused of being illegitimate, why, it stands to reason that the simplest course is for him to show his papers. Why wouldn't he produce them if he has nothing to hide?"

"My grandfather won't take kindly to your demands," St. Clare said. "Simple or otherwise."

"They're quite unobjectionable," Mrs. Beresford said. "And made in the familial spirit."

"They are, madam, equivalent to calling my grandfather a liar. To calling *me* a liar." St. Clare stepped forward. "And we neither of us take kindly to being called liars. Indeed, I find I can't abide the charge with any degree of equanimity."

She blinked rapidly. "We would never——"

"Which is why I must ask you, madam," he said in the same cold voice, "which one of you spoke to the papers?"

Lionel cleared his throat. "If you mean to call me out, St. Clare, know this: I'm unskilled with pistols, and equally so with swordplay. You'll get no satisfaction——"

"Your cousin wouldn't call you out, my love," Mrs. Beresford said. "What a notion!"

"Which one of you?" St. Clare asked again.

For the first time, Lionel seemed to falter. He looked a trifle white about the mouth.

Mrs. Beresford had gone a bit pale herself, but she was quick to rally. "I may have mentioned an incident or two I observed at the ball. There's no harm in talk. Not when facts, properly presented, can so easily disprove the rumors."

Some of the tension in Lionel's expression eased. "Just as Madre says," he agreed. "People will talk, you know. And if it should become cumbersome—these rumors about your legitimacy—you've only to produce your papers. That's not so much to ask, is it? The way you're behaving now, you'd think I'd done you an irreparable harm."

St. Clare turned on him. "*Was* it you, then?"

"He misspoke," Mrs. Beresford said hastily. "I already admitted it was I who talked to the paper. My son is blameless."

St. Clare didn't believe her for a minute. "What manner of man are you," he asked his cousin, "to hide behind the skirts of your mother?"

Lionel's cheeks flushed. "This from a man who has no mother at all. No mother anyone's ever heard of." He jutted his chin. "I'll not be lectured to by you, sir. If you mean to call me out—"

"No one is calling anyone out today." The Earl of Allendale's voice rang out.

St. Clare's head jerked to the drawing room doorway just in time to see his grandfather walk into the room. He came to a halt at St. Clare's side, giving him a sharp look of warning.

"Lord Allendale!" Mrs. Beresford leapt to her feet again, executing another curtsy. Her son rose to stand beside her. "What a surprise this is. That is to say, an honor. You never came to call before, not even when invited. And now, here you are—you and Lord St. Clare both—within minutes of each other. One can hardly countenance—"

"Enough of your forked-tongue pleasantries, Lavinia," Allendale said. "There's nothing I despise more than a serpent who walks upright."

Mrs. Beresford's mouth opened and closed and opened again. "Well! I never—"

"You've done enough damage with your infernal gossip. And you too, sir." Allendale glared at Lionel. "Your scheming stops today. Do you hear me? I'll have no more of it."

Mrs. Beresford drew herself up. "Really, Allendale, if you continue in this manner, I will have to ask you to leave."

"And if *you* continue," Allendale said, "you will see how I deal with snakes. Even those who bear the name of Beresford."

"And what of my cousin?" Lionel asked. "If we must be classed as serpents, how would you class him? He's no Beresford."

"He's a wolf in lamb's clothing is what he is," Mrs. Beresford said.

"A fox, more like. Isn't that the animal that graces the Allendale coat of arms? The trickster?" Lionel's mouth curled. "I don't have a mind to be tricked, Uncle. Not out of my title."

"*Your* title!" Allendale stalked to Lionel, only stopping when they were nose to nose. "I'm not dead yet, my boy. And when I go, make no mistake, it's my grandson who will inherent my title, no matter how much hissing you and your mother do."

St. Clare stood silent, his blood pumping hard in his veins. He didn't dare say a word. His grandfather wouldn't thank him for interfering. Not at this stage.

"I've been to see my solicitor this morning," Allendale said. "He leaves for Italy tomorrow to collect proof of my son's marriage, and of my grandson's birth—proof that he'll return with directly. In the meanwhile, if I hear so much as a single whispered word shared with a scandal sheet, I'll ruin the pair of you. And don't doubt that I have the power to do it. My name still counts for something in this country."

Mrs. Beresford's lips thinned. She'd long given up any pretense of civility. "You expect us to keep mute until you produce evidence of Lord St. Clare's legitimacy? To say nothing of the scheme you're perpetrating against my son, your true heir?"

Allendale regarded her with unvarnished contempt.

"For how long must we wait?" Lionel asked.

"My solicitor will return within a month's time," Allendale said.

"A month?" Mrs. Beresford's gaze shot to her son. "Lionel—"

"It's all right, my dear. We'll be well occupied elsewhere." Lionel looked to St. Clare. "Madre and I are going away for a time. A visit to the country. Someplace you might be familiar with."

A flicker of foreboding put St. Clare on his guard.

"Mr. Burton-Smythe has invited us to Beasley Park as his very special guests," Lionel said. "We leave for Somerset tomorrow."

It was all St. Clare could do to keep his countenance. The fact that Lionel and his mother were traveling to Somerset—the very place St. Clare had been born and raised—was bad enough. But there was something even worse. Something that chilled St. Clare to his heart.

Fred would never go to Beasley Park without Maggie. Which meant...

She was leaving, too. Not in a week or a month. But tomorrow.

Tomorrow.

"Your travel plans are of no interest to us, boy." Allendale's hand closed around St. Clare's uninjured arm in an iron grip, steering him to the door. "Mind well what I've said."

They didn't take their leave of Lionel or his mother, not by so much as a bow of acknowledgment. Allendale was in no mood for pleasantries.

"Take it back to Grosvenor Square," he snapped at Enzo as they walked past St. Clare's curricle in the drive.

The earl's carriage was waiting in the street. St. Clare climbed in after his grandfather. A footman shut the door behind them.

"What did you hope to achieve by that display?" Allendale asked as the carriage set off.

St. Clare sat back in his seat. His arm twinged as his shirt brushed over his wound. He could barely suppress a grimace. "The same thing you did, I imagine."

"To warn them off? It sounded to me as though you had something else in mind. Another duel, in fact."

"It was Lionel who broached the topic of a duel, not I."

Allendale frowned. "What's he playing at, I wonder?"

"I'd have thought it was obvious. He's attempting to dig up the truth. And he's doing a damned good job of it."

"On the scent like a bloodhound," Allendale muttered from his place across from St. Clare. "All because of that duel of yours with Burton-Smythe. And because of your dealings with that Honeywell female." He scowled at him. "You've been careless."

"Perhaps I have."

"You've forgotten your duty."

A swell of bitterness took St. Clare unaware. "I beg your pardon, but I have not. How could I forget? It's been hammered into my head every minute of every day for ten years."

"Self-pitying claptrap. You may have been obliged to work hard and train hard, but look at what you've gained in the bargain. You came to me a raw country lad, nothing but unchecked emotion, and I've made you into a gentleman of restraint and refinement. My heir. My *true* heir. And you would throw it all away? Cast it to the wind the very moment we stand on the brink?"

"We *are* standing on the brink," St. Clare said. "But not of success, I fear."

"Nonsense. My solicitor will manufacture the proof required. After which—"

"After which, I shall be beholden to the man for the remainder of my life." The prospect left a sour taste in St. Clare's mouth. "I'm amazed you're willing to trust him with our secret."

"What's the alternative? You've yet to make a match with a suitable gel. Had you proposed to Miss Steele—or one of the dowager's granddaughters—"

"Not this again."

"Yes, this," Allendale snapped. "If you'd managed to contrive a betrothal with Miss Steele, it wouldn't only be my influence you'd have on your side. It would be the influence of the gel's father."

"I'm not going to marry Miss Steele. It was a mistake to act the part of her escort these past days. I thought I could stomach it—"

"Stomach it!" Allendale repeated, outraged. "You talk as if the gel's an antidote."

St. Clare folded his arms. His stitches strained across his wound. The bite of pain only sharpened his resolve. "She may as well be as far as I'm concerned."

"Bah! She's an acknowledged beauty."

"She's not for me. Only one lady is. And I've a mind to have her, by whatever means. Even if I must—"

"Don't dare say another word," Allendale warned. His face was red, his jaw clenching and unclenching with barely controlled fury. "By heaven, I never thought I'd see the day you'd go the way of your father. Throwing everything away for the sake of your basest impulses."

"For love."

"*Love!*"

"Love," St. Clare affirmed.

"*We were soul mates,*" Maggie had said. "*As essential to each other as light or air. From my earliest memory, I existed only for those moments when I could see him next, and he did the same. Neither of us was complete outside the presence of the other.*"

St. Clare's chest constricted to recall it. It was the truth. He'd only ever been loved but once in his life, and had only ever loved once in return. "I tried to forget her," he said. "To leave her behind with all the rest of my past. I thought I *had* done. But I hadn't. I can't. I'd sooner cut out my own beating heart."

Allendale studied his face. "Because you love her."

St. Clare nodded grimly.

"You'd give up the title? You may as well do. You'll be leading the papers straight to Somerset. Any enterprising reporter could find out the rest. Question the servants at that estate where you lived. What was it called?"

"Beasley Park."

"Just so. You won't have been forgotten completely. Some groom or groundskeeper will sell their secrets for a shilling. 'Aye, that's him,' they'll say. 'That's the scullery maid's bastard.' And when that much is known, you may bid goodbye to the title."

"It's not mine," St. Clare said. It was the bitter truth. He *was* a bastard. A drunken mistake. He had no right to any of this. "Not by law."

"You had no scruples about that when we began this venture. No more than I did."

"That was before."

"Before you saw this Honeywell gel."

St. Clare fell silent.

"Think well on it, my lad," Allendale said. "If you abandon the claim, you'll receive nothing from the estate. Nothing from me. Not a single penny. I won't support my son's bastard."

St. Clare's felt a twinge in his midsection—the veriest ache somewhere in the region of his heart. Stupid, really. He supposed he'd begun to believe that his grandfather cared for him. Not for what he could do to secure the title, but for *him*. The man. "I'd expect nothing from you, of course."

Allendale inclined his head. It was impossible to tell what he was thinking. His expression was inscrutable, his gray eyes cold as hoarfrost. "So long as we understand each other."

22

Maggie paced from the marble fireplace to the tall damask-curtained library windows and back again, her arms folded at her waist. It had been hours since Fred had called on her in Green Street. Long, anxiety-filled hours during which Jane had persuaded her to exercise patience.

Patience!

Every instinct within Maggie had told her to leave at once for Grosvenor Square. To find St. Clare and to tell him everything. But Jane had warned against it.

"Your recklessness will only expose the both of you to further censure," she'd said.

It was sound advice. Reasonable and wise. It was also deeply infuriating. Maggie wasn't accustomed to inaction. And in the present circumstances—

"I'm certain he'll come to you, Margaret," Jane said from her place on the library sofa. A leather-bound book lay open at her side. "If you will but wait a while longer."

"And if he doesn't?" Maggie had no sooner posed the question than the Trumbles' butler materialized at the door carrying a silver salver. A calling card lay upon it.

"Who is it, Olmstead?" Jane asked.

"Lords St. Clare and Mattingly, ma'am," he said. "Shall I show them in?"

Maggie stopped where she stood on the thick Aubusson carpet. She shot an anxious glance at Jane.

"Yes, do." Jane rose from the sofa to smooth her pale green day dress. "And have Carson bring in the tea tray, if you please."

"He's brought Lord Mattingly with him," Maggie said. "I wonder why?"

"For me, obviously." Jane smiled slightly. "He's meant to distract me from my duties as chaperone. Not that my role has made one jot of a difference in this affair."

Maggie sighed. Jane wasn't deaf to the gossip that had begun swirling about town. Much more of it and it would begin to reflect on her. Maggie was her houseguest after all.

A rather poor one, at that.

She felt a flare of guilt for putting her friend in such a precarious position. "Oh, Jane. What a trial this all must be."

"It's rather an adventure, truth be told." Jane moved to stand next to Maggie. "But you must take care, my dear. At present there are only whispers about the pair of you, but it wouldn't take much to instigate a full-blown scandal. Not now that the papers are on the scent."

"I know that," Maggie said.

Lord St. Clare appeared a moment later, with Lord Mattingly close behind. The pair of them were as impeccably dressed as always, looking as though they might have come straight from a strut on Bond Street or a promenade in the park during the fashionable hour.

It gave Maggie to wonder whether St. Clare had heard about her departure at all. Perhaps his visit was nothing more than the natural consequence of their romantic interlude at Grillon's? A brief interview to ascertain that she was well, and that her feelings were unchanged?

"Miss Trumble," he said, bowing. "Miss Honeywell." It was impossible to tell that he'd been injured. There was no stiffness about his arm, no awkwardness in the way he held himself.

Maggie suspected that he was used to ignoring his pain. "Lord St. Clare. Lord Mattingly." She curtsied along with Jane.

Lord Mattingly smiled, revealing a flash of perfectly straight white teeth. "I trust we're not interrupting anything?"

"Not at all," Jane said. "Do come in."

Upon entering, Lord Mattingly wasted no time in singling out Jane for his attention. On her invitation, they sat down together on the sofa and commenced an animated discussion about the theater.

Maggie didn't join them. Instead, she walked to the cushioned window seat at the far end of the library. Framed by heavy claret-colored curtains, the diamond-paned glass faced out toward the garden—a view that had grown dusky in the approaching twilight.

St. Clare followed her in silence, and when she sat down, he took an immediate seat at her side. "I came as soon as I could," he said. "As soon as Mattingly was free to accompany me."

"Do you think it makes any difference?" she asked. "This fig leaf of propriety?"

He frowned. "I don't know. But I'd as soon not add fuel to the fire. Not until we know where we're at."

Maggie had a good idea where they were at. And it wasn't anywhere she wished to be. Quite the reverse. She cast a distracted glance at his arm. "How is your wound?"

"Tolerable," he said. "At present, it's the least of my worries."

She winced. "You saw the report in *Bell's Weekly Messenger*?"

"I did. As did my grandfather. He's none too pleased."

"It must have been Fred. Who else—"

"It wasn't Fred," St. Clare said. "It was Lionel Beresford. He and his mother are intent on sowing doubt about my legitimacy. It's the whole reason they've come to town. They'll do anything to protect Lionel's position as heir."

"But Somerset? How would they know about it if not for Fred? If not for me?" Her heart ached as she looked at him. It had been less than a day since he'd admitted the truth of his identity. Not more than fourteen hours at the most. She keenly remembered how he'd held her in his arms and kissed her.

"*My first love*," she'd called him. "*My only love*."

And love wasn't meant to be selfish.

She exhaled a tremulous breath. "I fear our connection has put your claim to the Allendale title very much at risk."

His frown deepened. "Maggie—"

"Ever since I read that passage in the paper this morning, I knew..." She hesitated. For hours she'd been fretting over how she would explain things, and yet now, sitting face-to-face with him, she felt as ill-prepared as ever. "I won't be the cause of you losing everything that you've worked for."

"What are you saying?"

"I'm saying that...if my mere presence jeopardizes your claim, perhaps it's best if I return home."

His gaze darkened. "So, you *are* going, then."

"You knew?"

"I paid a call on Beresford and his mother this morning. They said they were traveling down to Beasley Park tomorrow as Fred's special guests."

"Did they indeed." She felt a sharp stab of irritation. The same irritation she'd felt when Fred had dropped in unannounced to tell her of his plans. "Fred's never before made free with invitations to Beasley. The insufferable swine. I expect he's trying to get a rise out of me."

"Not out of you. Out of me." A wry smile curved St. Clare's lips. "He believes that by aligning himself with my enemies he can do me some harm."

Maggie didn't see how St. Clare could be so calm about it all. "Can't he? If he takes the two of them down to Beasley and they begin to ask questions—"

"Questions about what?" He lowered his voice. "I haven't been back to Somerset since the night I left. No one knows me as I am now."

"They know you as you were then," she whispered back, conscious of Jane's and Lord Mattingly's presence across the room. "And Lord St. Clare isn't so different from Nicholas Seaton as you imagine. Fred might be blinded by your fine clothes and gentlemanlike manner—he could never see past the surface of things—but I knew you from the first moment I set eyes on you. And so might others at Beasley. There are still servants remaining from your time there. Mr. Entwhistle, for one."

"That old relic," St. Clare said. "He must be pushing ninety."

"Eighty, more like. But there's nothing wrong with his faculties. He's still the steward, and sharp as a tack besides. He knows everything about everything at Beasley. If your cousin and his mother take to asking questions—"

"You believe you can prevent them? They'll be Fred's guests, not yours."

Her spine stiffened. "I'm still mistress of Beasley Park. And I can handle Fred—so long as I'm not obliged to be alone with him in a darkened carriage again."

St. Clare's smile vanished. It was replaced by a forbidding look, almost frightening in its intensity. "What had he to say for himself on that count?"

"He claimed he'd had too much to drink at the ball. An excess of champagne, he said, combined with the feelings— the *overpowering* feelings—he's cherished for me since childhood." She made a sound of disgust. "It was a rubbish excuse as excuses go. And so I told him."

She *had* done, and Fred had promised that he'd never take such liberties again. He'd even had the good sense to look ashamed of himself.

But Maggie was no fool.

The line Fred had crossed couldn't be uncrossed. Emboldened by his power over her, it was only a matter of time before he crossed another and another. His bullying nature practically guaranteed it.

"That's all very well," St. Clare said tightly, "but what if he should—"

"He won't have the chance. Jane's already agreed to convey me back to Beasley in her carriage. Her aunt is coming, too, and they've both promised to stay a week, at least. It's all been arranged."

"Rather hastily arranged, it seems."

"Fred didn't give me much choice in the timing."

"You aren't obliged to dance to his tune. He's the guardian of your fortune, not your person. He can't prevent you from staying in London if you wish to." St. Clare took her hand, cradling it gently in his. "Isn't it better to remain here? Close at hand, where I can see you? Touch you?"

Her pulse briefly lost its rhythm. "I want to be with you," she said softly. "More than anything."

"Then stay. Please." His voice was a husky caress. "Don't make me call in my last forfeit."

It would have been easy to say yes. To give in to the longing she felt for him. But she refused to lose sight of reality. "I can't," she said. "Not even for a forfeit. I won't risk your cousin and his mother poking about the estate. It wouldn't take much digging for them to learn about you and Jenny."

His head bent closer to hers. "And what if I told you that the title didn't matter? That none of this mattered except you?"

Her breath stopped for a moment. She stared up at him. "You don't mean that."

"Have you already forgotten what I told you at Grillon's?"

"I haven't forgotten." He'd said he was never letting her go again. And she'd believed him. She *still* believed him. "But this separation isn't permanent. It will only be for a little while. Just so that we can get a handle on the gossip. With Fred and I out of London—"

"Maggie—"

"I need to go back," she said. "I need fresh air and wide-open spaces. It's the only way I'll ever get well."

He stilled. "Did the doctor tell you this?"

"Yes. He didn't promise I would recover completely, but he gave me reason to hope. Once I'm home—"

"Home," St. Clare repeated. "To Beasley Park."

"It *is* my home. And at the moment, it's where I can do the most good for you. You can't go there yourself. It would be too dangerous. But I can go in your place. I can protect you from whatever it is Fred and your relations are up to."

Something fractured in his expression. An emotion lurking just behind his eyes, briefly breaking to the surface. It was pain. Regret. Raw feelings from youth that had long been under ruthless control. "You haven't changed," he said gruffly. "Even as a girl, you were as brave as you were small. Always trying to save me."

"A false bravery. I had my father at my back. He was the one with the power, not I." She smiled slightly. "I suppose I must thank him. He raised me to be as bold as any son. And a little boldness never goes amiss."

"'Though she be but little, she is fierce.'"

Her brows lifted. "Is that Shakespeare?" she asked, momentarily diverted.

"My grandfather made me read an appalling amount of the stuff. He considers himself something of a scholar." Drawing her hand to his lips, he brushed a light kiss to her knuckles. It was an old-fashioned gesture—and one that made her heart turn over. "How long do you plan on staying in Somerset?"

"I don't know. A fortnight, possibly. Perhaps longer. It depends on what happens there."

St. Clare didn't look at all pleased by her answer. "And I must wait here, must I? Wait and hope that you'll come back to me."

"Wait and hope. Just as I did for so many years after you left Beasley."

He gave her a piercing look. "The difference being, my dear, I'm not half so patient as you are."

23

Beasley Park
Somerset, England
Summer 1817

Maggie tugged on her gloves as she descended the grand, curving staircase at Beasley Park.

Bessie followed after her at a trot, down the stairs, through the expansive marble-tiled hall, and out the tall, carved oak front doors into the warm, early afternoon sunlight. "Slow down, Miss Margaret!"

Maggie stopped on the stone front steps, inhaling a breath of fresh country air. Her lungs expanded to their utmost. It still wasn't very much. She'd only been back at Beasley for a week. Hardly enough time to effect a full recovery. She nevertheless felt better in the country. Despite the havoc created by her guests—by Fred and the Beresfords, and even by Jane and her aunt Harriet on occasion—Maggie was glad to be home.

"You'll make yourself ill with all of this striding about." Bessie adjusted Maggie's chip bonnet, settling it more firmly on her head, and retying the cornflower-blue ribbons in a jaunty bow at her chin. "And don't pretend you've recovered. You forget I was your nurse. I can see when you're overexerting yourself."

"Don't fuss, Bessie." Maggie swatted her maid's hands away. "I haven't time for it today. I told Mr. Entwhistle I'd call on him at one o'clock precisely."

Maggie had sent the note round yesterday. Mr. Entwhistle had replied at once, seeming to understand her need for discretion. If Fred knew she desired to visit the old steward, he'd insist on accompanying her. Which is exactly why Jane had contrived to enlist him as an escort into town this morning.

She'd departed earlier, along with her aunt, and the Beresfords. Fred had ridden alongside their carriage on horseback. Maggie had watched them go from her bedroom window.

Looking up at her from the drive, Fred had touched his riding whip to the brim of his hat in a brief salute. He believed she was overtired. Too ill, in fact, to endure the exertion of an outing.

It was the first time Maggie had ever used her ill health to her own benefit. She wondered that she'd never thought of doing it before. "If they should chance to return before I do, tell them—"

"I'll say you're sleeping and can't be disturbed," Bessie replied. "They shan't get past me, Miss Margaret. And as for Mr. Beresford's valet…" Her expression turned fierce. "He won't be poking about today. Not if me and Mrs. Wilkins have anything to say about it. Nor will that hoity-toity maid of his mother's."

Maggie couldn't conceal her relief.

It was bad enough that Lionel Beresford and his mother must be kept occupied every minute of the day to prevent them from snooping, but their busy servants must be kept occupied as well. The two of them seemed to work as malicious extensions of their employers. Like scent hounds or terriers, set loose at Beasley Park to sniff out and dig up whatever secrets they could find and carry them back to their masters.

Indeed, Mrs. Beresford's lady's maid always seemed to be lurking about the halls, and Lionel Beresford's sly, sallow-faced valet was forever popping up in the oddest places. More than once Maggie had had the unsettling suspicion that he was watching her. Following her, even.

Thank goodness for Bessie and the housekeeper, Mrs. Wilkins. With their help—and with the help of Jane and Aunt Harriet—Maggie had, thus far, managed to keep things under control.

She flashed a parting smile at Bessie over her shoulder as she made her way down the front steps to the drive. Mr. Entwhistle had a small cottage on the estate. It wasn't too far of a walk. Not if one knew the landscape of the park.

And no one knew it better than Maggie did.

She cut across the wide expanse of manicured lawn and down through a thicket of trees. Wildflowers were blooming, and bees buzzing about in the sun to drink their nectar.

Her half-boots crunched on the grass as she followed the winding path that ran along the edge of the stream that flowed through the grounds. Ahead, the gently sloping banks were covered in a familiar wash of blue.

Years ago, she'd lain there with Nicholas Seaton, upon a bed of forget-me-nots. She'd held his hand, her young heart so in love with him it was fit to burst.

She'd heard nothing from him since leaving London. She hadn't entirely expected to.

But no matter. She didn't have time to pine. Her guests had kept her busy.

Too busy, frankly.

With any luck, the Beresfords would soon grow tired of their stay in the country and head back to town, taking their equally nosy servants along with them. None of them appeared to be enjoying themselves, Mr. Beresford least of all. He wasn't much for shooting or other country pursuits, not as far as Maggie could tell. She'd rarely seen a man so out of his element.

"Miss Honeywell!" Mr. Entwhistle hailed her from the garden gate of his stone cottage. A thin, balding gentleman with a stooped figure, he'd been the steward of Beasley Park for as long as Maggie could remember.

She smiled at him in greeting. "Good afternoon, Mr. Entwhistle."

"A pleasure to see you, ma'am. But what's this? I expected you'd come in the carriage."

Her smile dimmed. Goodness, the way he looked at her, one would think she was on her last prayers. "I'm quite well enough to walk. The fresh air has done me a world of good."

His bushy white brows lowered. "Best come in and sit down. I'll have Mrs. Square fetch you a cup of tea. Nothing better to revive a body."

Maggie followed him inside. The cottage was clean and cool, scented with the fragrance of lemon oil furniture polish and freshly baked bread.

Mr. Entwhistle's elderly housekeeper, Mrs. Square, awaited them in the modest entry hall. Gray-haired and plump, with a pair of half-moon spectacles perched upon her nose, she was another familiar face from childhood.

Maggie recalled accompanying her father to see Mr. Entwhistle when she was just a little girl, barely out of leading strings. While Papa had talked with his steward, Mrs. Square had plied Maggie with candied fruit and sugared biscuits.

"Poor little lamb," she'd used to say. "And you with no mother to look after you."

Maggie hadn't liked to be babied, not even then. She'd preferred to remain with her father. To listen to the adults talking—or arguing, which was more often the case where Papa was concerned.

"Miss Honeywell!" Mrs. Square cried. "Bless me. What a sight for sore eyes you are. Oh, but this does bring me back—"

"Enough of that, Mrs. Square," Mr. Entwhistle said as he ushered Maggie into the cottage's small parlor. A pair of overstuffed chintz armchairs were arranged in front of a curtained bow window. A low table stood between them. "Fetch some tea for us, and then leave us be. Miss Honeywell and I have estate matters to discuss."

Once the tea tray had been brought in, and Maggie had poured them each a cup, Mr. Entwhistle settled down to business. He held nothing back from her. He told her about the recent expenditures for improvements to the tenant cottages, and repairs to the water wheel at the mill. About the increase in earnings for this years' crops. And about the benefits of joining with the Burton-Smythe estate.

"It's what your father always hoped for," he said from his seat in the armchair across from Maggie. "Both estates working together as one. It's why we've managed to get better prices this year. It's all owing to the Burton-Smythes. Sir Roderick in particular. He always did have a level head. Never allowed any emotion to get in the way of business."

Unlike her father, he might have said.

Maggie returned her teacup to the tea tray. "People loved my father."

"Aye, he was a rare character. A good friend, and the best sportsman for miles. No one had a better eye for horseflesh than Squire Honeywell."

"Yes, but I'm talking about the estate. About the management of Beasley Park."

Mr. Entwhistle took a sip of his tea before slowly clinking his cup back into its saucer. "I often find, Miss Honeywell, that some things are better left unsaid."

She suppressed a flare of irritation. "Come, sir. You needn't spare my feelings. I value a bit of plain speaking. It's why I came here today."

He was quiet for a moment. "Very well. To put it plainly, then. Your father was not an easy man to do business with. The Honeywell temper, you know. It's legendary around these parts."

"Not in a bad way, surely." Maggie waited for him to reply, but Mr. Entwhistle remained silent. A knot of anxiety formed in her stomach. "I know he could be difficult, but people made allowances. It was something of a joke, wasn't it? The way he lost his temper? I always found it amusing."

"Oh yes, we all had a laugh about it now and then, but when dealing with estate matters—matters of business—a temper like that is no laughing matter." He took another sip of tea. "Sir Roderick, on the other hand, has a nice steady temperament."

For an instant, Maggie forgot herself. "Sir Roderick is thoroughly disagreeable."

Mr. Entwhistle took her outburst in stride. "He's not a pleasant man, I grant you. Not one you'd like to share a pint with down at the tavern. But he's a reliable sort, the same man on one day as he is on the next. In business, men come to count on reliability. They trust it."

"And what about his son? What about *his* temperament?"

"Master Fred? He does have his moods, right enough. But still…" Mr. Entwhistle seemed to consider. "He keeps it out of estate business. And the Burton-Smythe name *is* respected around these parts. People like continuity. Makes 'em feel safe."

"It's *my* name that provides the continuity, not his. As a Honeywell—" She stopped short. "But I suppose the Honeywell name doesn't carry as much weight here as I thought it did. Never mind that my father single-handedly built Beasley Park into the estate that it is today."

Mr. Entwhistle gave her a look of sympathy. "The Honeywell name still carries weight. People were fond of your father. They're fond of you, as well. But unlike Master Fred, you—"

"What?" she demanded.

He shrugged. "You're a lady."

Maggie was temporarily rendered speechless. The fact that she was a female had never made a difference before. At least, not when it came to Beasley Park. As a girl, she'd accompanied Papa all over the estate. Had learned at his knee how to run it—how to care for it—as he did. No one had ever treated her differently because of her sex. She'd been Papa's right arm. His chosen successor. Or so she'd believed until the day his will had been read.

"An unmarried lady at that," Mr. Entwhistle added. "Most folks would prefer to deal with a man."

"Well that's just... That's just ignorance, is what it is. Any one of them should know by now that I'm as capable as a man. More capable than Frederick Burton-Smythe. More to the point, Beasley Park is in my blood. It's...it's my birthright."

Mr. Entwhistle sighed. His heavily lined face was the picture of an old retainer on the verge of delivering some very bad news. "You must understand, Miss Honeywell, after your illness, you quite disappeared from public life. During those years, what with your mourning and—"

"I hadn't much choice on that score. First Papa died, and then my aunt. Would the villagers have rather I flouted the rules than adhered to them?"

"No, but—"

"It begins to seem to me, sir, that as a female, there's nothing I can do that won't bring public censure down on my head." The unfairness of it all chafed at Maggie's soul.

Mr. Entwhistle set his teacup and saucer on the tray. He threaded his fingers, resting them on his slim midsection. "I would advise you to try and see it the way the outside world has come to see it. You, inside that great house for years on end. Yes, yes. I know it was illness, and then mourning your father and aunt. But to everyone else it seems that you've long been an invalid. Someone too frail and weak to be taxed with the management of such a great estate."

She stared at him. "Is that what you believe?"

"What I believe, ma'am, is that your father—God rest his soul—should have never let that Seaton woman come to Beasley Park. If not for nursing her, you would still have your health, and perhaps be in a position to maintain a more tangible hold on the estate. I did warn Squire Honeywell. For such a creature to come here, in her wretched condition, and spouting such fanciful tales—"

Maggie's body jerked to attention. "Tales? What tales?"

"Eh?" Mr. Entwhistle blinked at her. He seemed to have lost his train of thought.

"Jenny Seaton," she reminded him. "You said she came to Beasley Park spouting tales."

"Ah, that old yarn." He rubbed the side of his face. "I only heard it secondhand, mind you. And a woman like that will make up all manner of things to excuse her conduct, especially when that conduct results in—"

"Yes, yes, I shall take it with a grain of salt. Only tell me what it is you heard."

Mr. Entwhistle's expression turned weary. "It's a tale as old as the hills, Miss Honeywell. She claimed to have thought herself married to the fellow who left her in that condition. That it was only later—far too late to rid herself of her sinful burden—that she discovered it had all been a wicked trick on the fellow's part." He shook his head. "An improbable story. One that conveniently absolved her of any guilt in the matter."

Maggie looked at him in disbelief. She'd never before heard any such thing. Not from her father or anyone. Could it be true? Had Gentleman Jim truly convinced Jenny Seaton that the two of them were married?

But how?

And to what end?

St. Clare had said that his late father had been fond of ill-conceived pranks, but to trick a young woman into a sham marriage? And why would he need to? It couldn't have been in order to have his way with her. Jenny was already plying her trade in Market Barrow. Her favors would have come cheaply enough. Marriage wasn't at all required. Unless...

Had Gentleman Jim known Jenny was with child?

The possibility struck Maggie like a lightning bolt.

It would certainly explain why Jenny had felt such animosity toward her child. If she believed Nicholas to have been responsible for inspiring such a trick—if she blamed him for driving away her lover—it would be natural for her to resent him.

But even if Gentleman Jim had known, why bother with a fake marriage? Why not simply abandon Jenny full stop? He was already escaping to the continent to avoid the noose. Escaping the burden of a pregnant mistress was minor in comparison.

Surely, he wouldn't have toyed with her merely for his own amusement? A prank was one thing, but to convince the woman who was carrying your child that the two of you had married—that the child's name was secure...

That was no masculine prank. It was an outright cruelty.

And it made no sense at all.

"You claim you heard this tale secondhand," Maggie said. "Who told it to you?"

"Why, it was Squire Honeywell. He mentioned it not long after Miss Seaton arrived at the Park. I warned him that girls in that sort of trouble often conjured outrageous fictions out of whole cloth. He knew it to be true. But he was a big-hearted man, your father." Mr. Entwhistle's mouth dropped into a frown. "He came to regret that kindness after you took ill."

"That wasn't Jenny's fault. It was mine. I'm the one who insisted on nursing her during her final days." She'd spent endless hours seated beside Jenny's cot. She'd held her hand

and sponged her brow. Had listened to her ravings about Nicholas and Father Tuck.

A priest, Maggie had thought. Someone to whom Jenny wished to confess. But what if…

What if…

Maggie's lungs seized on a breath. All at once, the small parlor felt even smaller. She forced herself to breathe.

Mr. Entwhistle rose. "Are you all right, Miss Honeywell?"

She waved him back. "Fine. Perfectly fine. I need a little air, that's all."

He put a hand under her elbow, assisting her to her feet. "I'll have the gig readied. Thomas can drive you back to the Park." He turned to go but Maggie forestalled him.

"Mr. Entwhistle, I wonder…"

"Yes?"

"Have you ever heard of a clergyman hereabouts by the name of Father Tuck?" It was a stab in the dark, but she'd never forgive herself if she left without asking. "It may have been a long while past. Possibly before I was born."

Mr. Entwhistle beetled his brows. "Can't say I have. Is it something to do with the estate?"

"Nothing like that. Merely my own curiosity." A curiosity that hadn't been satisfied yet. That wouldn't be satisfied until she'd found out the whole of the matter.

Which was precisely what she intended to do.

24

London, England
Summer 1817

St. Clare set down his fork. He was seated, along with his grandfather, at one end of the long, polished mahogany dining table at Grosvenor Square. A row of liveried servants lined the silk-papered wall behind them, standing at the ready. Supper had been served early this evening to accommodate their engagement at the theater.

Allendale shot a narrow glance at St. Clare's unfinished meal. It sat before him, the sturgeon à la broche and French beans and white sauce on his plate all but untouched. "Something wrong with your fish?"

"Nothing's wrong," St. Clare said. "Other than the fact that I have no appetite for it."

The dining room was awash in light. Two branches of dripping beeswax candles graced the table, and on the walls evenly spaced sconces glowed with dancing flames. Shadows played across the enormous oil paintings that hung over them—

gilt-framed Beresford ancestors looking down at them with all-too-familiar expressions of hauteur.

"Off your feed, are you?" Allendale asked.

"Something like that." St. Clare leaned back in his chair. He was in no mood to eat. No mood to do much of anything save bark and growl at everyone around him. A lion with a wounded paw and a sore head, wasn't that what Maggie had called him?

He could only imagine what she'd think of him now.

One week without her and he was already too cross for company. No longer icy and implacable, but sullen and short-tempered and restless as all hell.

Allendale gave the signal for the servants to leave. The line of footmen swiftly filed out, shutting the door behind them.

St. Clare looked at his grandfather, brows raised in question.

Allendale fixed him with a disapproving glare. "If this is how you mean to conduct yourself, you may as well go after the gel."

As permission went, it was lukewarm at best. It nevertheless sent a jolt through St. Clare's vitals. Go after her? *Yes*, he wanted to say. *At once*.

But his grandfather didn't mean it. It was just another means of finding fault with him.

"You object to my conduct?" St. Clare didn't know how he could. During the past week, he'd done all that his grandfather asked of him. He'd attended two balls, four performances of Shakespeare in company with a large party of ladies and gentlemen, and even accompanied Mattingly and Vickers for a ride in the park along with Miss Steele and two of her eligible friends.

He had, in fact, done everything within his power to snuff out the gossip about Fred and Maggie and Somerset. Surely his grandfather could have nothing to reproach him with.

"You don't talk anymore," Allendale said. "You brood. Loudly." He scowled. "And what in blazes is wrong with your arm? You've been favoring it all week. I trust you haven't been dueling again?"

"Don't be absurd," St. Clare said. "Nothing's wrong with me. Not my arm or any other part of my anatomy."

It wasn't entirely a lie.

His wound *was* healing. That didn't stop it from causing him pain. It still ached on occasion, and the stitches made movement uncomfortable. He wasn't surprised that his grandfather had noticed.

"Absurd, am I? I've been watching you since that Honeywell female departed London. You've been sulking like a lad after his first woman."

"If you're attempting to bait me—"

"I'm attempting to bring you up sharp, my boy. Have you forgotten everything I've taught you about self-discipline?"

St. Clare inwardly sighed. "What would you like me to say? I've tried to master my feelings for her. To rid myself of this restlessness." He gave his grandfather a wry look. "Have you not wondered why I've passed so many hours sparring at Jackson's?"

Allendale frowned. "That bad, is it?"

It was worse. Far worse than St. Clare had expected it to be when he'd promised Maggie he would stay in town.

Wait and hope, he'd said.

But he'd also warned her that he was impatient.

"It's been a week," he told his grandfather. "I don't know when she's coming back."

If she was coming back.

Beasley Park was the great passion of her life. She belonged there, far more than she belonged in London. Not only because of her health, but because it was her home. The place she loved best in all the world.

What if she never came back? What if she decided to remain there? To marry Fred in order to keep her claim on the estate?

Good lord.

She wouldn't, would she?

The very notion made his heart seize as if it were being tightened in a vise.

"I should have gone with her," he said. "An oversight on my part. But it's not too late. If I leave in the morning—"

Allendale's brow clouded with outrage. "Don't be daft. You'd risk being recognized. I've warned you—"

"It doesn't matter," St. Clare said in a burst of impatience. "Can't you see that? Not if she needs me. I'm doing nothing for her here. And she's there, at the mercy of Burton-Smythe, and Beresford and his mother."

"She has a chaperone, hasn't she? Trumble's daughter, I thought."

"You don't understand." St. Clare fell silent for a long moment, reluctant to give voice to what it was that troubled him so. "She hasn't written," he said finally. "She wouldn't. Not when we're trying to quell the gossip. But I can't help worrying about her. She...She hasn't been entirely well."

"Not well? What the devil's the matter with her?"

"She took ill some years ago. A bout of influenza weakened her lungs. Sometimes, when she's exerted herself, she finds it hard to catch her breath."

Allendale returned to his supper. "You know how I feel about frail, sickly females."

"She's not frail. She's the strongest person I know. The strongest, the bravest." A lump formed in St. Clare's throat. "She saved my life in Somerset. If not for her…"

"A gel with spirit. That's something, at least. Only natural you should feel gratitude toward her."

"It's more than gratitude. I told you. My feelings for her—"

"Feelings, bah! You appeared willing enough to forget those feelings before we came here." Allendale speared a piece of sturgeon with his fork. "You weren't moping about Rome or Venice, as I recall."

St. Clare's expression hardened. There had been precious little time for moping when his grandfather had first taken him in hand. Indeed, in the beginning, every waking moment had been absorbed by lessons. Lessons upon lessons from an endless string of pitiless foreign tutors.

He'd had to learn everything over again. More than just the reading and writing that Maggie had taught him as a boy. He'd had to re-learn how to walk and talk. How to think. Most importantly of all, he'd had to prove that he had the aptitude to change. The raw material, as his grandfather had called it.

"No use wasting my time if you haven't the capacity for it," he'd often said. "You can go straight back to where you came from. I've no patience with a lad who won't put in the effort."

St. Clare had put in the effort and more.

He'd studied ceaselessly, his hours in the schoolroom broken only by hours spent with his fencing instructor or practicing his shooting. In time, he'd mastered pistols and sword-play. Even more difficult, he'd learned how to master his own unruly temper.

None of it had been easy. Every day had ended in physical and mental exhaustion. And then he'd gone to sleep, only to start over again the next day and the next. Training and studying and learning, until he didn't only look and act different, he *was* different. Until Nicholas Seaton was dead and a new man had risen in his place. A gentleman. A *nobleman*.

It had taken ten years to effect the transformation. A complete one by outward appearances. But one small part of Nicholas Seaton had resisted the change. A piece of his heart had remained, beating as strongly as ever, pure and true and steadfast for Maggie Honeywell.

No matter how long it takes, I will come back for you.

"I never forgot her," he said. "She's the only person on this earth I've ever loved."

"*Love.* You bandy that word about a good deal in relation to your Miss Honeywell." Lord Allendale reached for his glass of wine. "Perhaps it's time she and I made each other's acquaintance."

25

Beasley Park
Somerset, England
Summer 1817

"You've been vicar here for some time, it seems." Lionel Beresford's tone was deceptively lazy, but there was no mistaking the glint of alertness in his gaze. Seated beside his mother on the scrolled-arm silk sofa in the Beasley Park drawing room, he'd long given up any pretense of casual conversation.

"Going on four decades," Mr. Applewhite replied from his place near the dwindling fire. "Isn't that right, Miss Honeywell?"

Maggie glanced up from her embroidery. She'd been attempting to sew ever since they'd removed from the dining room. A fruitless occupation. She had no skill with a needle. "It is. Mr. Applewhite was vicar here before I was born."

Aunt Harriet snored softly from her chair across from the vicar. She'd drifted to sleep almost as soon as she'd sat down.

GENTLEMAN JIM

Across the room, Jane tinkled quietly on the keys of the pianoforte, mindful not to wake her.

Fred stood nearby, flipping through a stack of sheet music.
He was incredibly proud of his singing voice and had threatened to entertain them after dinner.

"Four decades?" Mrs. Beresford tittered. "Such a long while!
I daresay you know the people here better than anyone."

"I expect I do," Mr. Applewhite conceded. "Though not
as well as my wife did, God rest her soul. She could recite
chapter and verse on everyone in the county."

Maggie never thought she'd live to see the day when she
regretted the passing of Mrs. Applewhite. The vicar's wife
had been a font of local knowledge. She'd also been the bane
of Nicholas Seaton's existence, and a great critic of Maggie's
behavior, too.

In his wife's absence, the vicar had seemed like the next
best person to question about the mysterious Father Tuck.

Maggie had wanted to call on him at the vicarage, but
after returning from Mr. Entwhistle's, and finding that Fred
and the others had come back early from their visit to town,
there had been no possibility of getting away. Not alone. She'd
had to settle for inviting Mr. Applewhite to dinner the following evening.

Unfortunately, between Fred and the Beresfords, she'd
scarcely managed to get a word in edgewise, let alone a
moment for private conversation.

"I wonder if she ever knew my cousin?" Lionel asked.
"John Beresford, Viscount St. Clare. A strapping blond fellow.
Quite tall."

Maggie's muscles tensed. The past week had been one long
fishing expedition on the Beresfords' part. Abetted by their

sneaking servants, the two of them wheedled and probed, casting about for any scraps of information that might reveal some connection between St. Clare and Somerset.

"Was he a resident here?" Mr. Applewhite asked, frowning. "I don't seem to recall the name."

"Indeed not," Maggie replied. "Lord St. Clare has never been to Beasley Park, or to anywhere hereabouts that I'm aware."

Fred scowled. "Must we speak of him? This is meant to be a merry party."

Mrs. Beresford affected not to hear him. "I believe the viscount must have visited the region sometime or other," she said. "Perhaps he used an assumed name? Young gentlemen will have their pranks. To be sure, his father indulged in many such amusements when he was a young man. And blood will tell, they always say. Like father, like son."

"An assumed name?" Mr. Applewhite appeared utterly perplexed by this line of inquiry. He turned to Maggie. "Who did you say this fellow was again?"

"It's not important. Quite the opposite." She set aside her needlework. "It's late, Vicar. Shall I call for your carriage?"

Mr. Applewhite gave her a look of relief. "Yes, thank you, Miss Honeywell. You are very good."

Maggie rang for a footman. And when, a short time later, the same footman returned to announce that Mr. Applewhite's carriage was ready, she insisted on accompanying the aged vicar out herself.

"I'm obliged to you, Miss Honeywell," he said as they descended the curving staircase and passed through the entry hall. "Such hospitality. You're to be commended for the fine meal. And the wine—from your father's cellar, I collect. A splendid vintage. I haven't tasted—"

"Mr. Applewhite," Maggie interrupted. "There's something particular I've been meaning to ask you."

"Eh?"

A footman opened the front doors for them, and Maggie and the old vicar passed out onto the wide stone steps. The night was cool, the evening sky dusted with stars. An old carriage pulled by two equally old chestnuts awaited the vicar in the drive.

There was little privacy to be had. Only the space of seconds between the top of the front steps and the bottom. Maggie took full advantage of them. "Have you ever encountered a clergyman in the district by the name of Father Tuck?"

"Who's that?"

"Father Tuck. It would have been some thirty years ago, I suspect."

"Don't know of a Father Tuck." Mr. Applewhite's brow creased. "I've heard of a Friar Tuck, of course."

She frowned. "Quite. But this man wasn't a character in Robin Hood."

"Certainly not. Though I daresay that's why he was called such. Expelled from his order, I believe it was. Never met him myself but heard the tales, a long time past. Something to do with that hedge tavern in Market Barrow."

"Market Barrow!" Maggie's pulse skipped.

"Love of drink is at the heart of many of the world's sorrows, Miss Honeywell," Mr. Applewhite said. "I won't say a man can't enjoy it, but one mustn't ever become a slave to the grape."

At that, they reached the bottom of the steps. Maggie stood, unmoving, as a waiting footman helped the vicar into his carriage and shut the door after him. She raised her hand in a gesture of farewell. But her mind wasn't on Mr. Apple-white's departure. It was on Market Barrow. On Friar Tuck and Jenny Seaton.

It was on Gentleman Jim.

She was so distracted by her thoughts that she didn't notice Fred coming down the steps to join her. She started in sur-prise when he appeared at her side. "Good lord, you gave me a fright."

He was dressed in an evening ensemble, his coat tight across his shoulders and his silk neckcloth as lavishly arranged as ever. He'd long ceased wearing his sling. "I came to escort you back to the house."

"That was unnecessary."

"On the contrary." He took her elbow. "You've been over-exerting yourself."

She shrugged out of his grasp. "By walking the vicar to his carriage? Hardly."

Fred kept pace alongside her, up the stone steps and back through the marble entry hall. "I'm not talking about the vicar. I'm talking about your visit to Entwhistle yesterday. A visit you made when you were supposed to be confined to your room with a megrim."

Her gaze jerked to his. "Who told you I'd been to see him?"

"His housekeeper, Mrs. Square, came to tea with our Mrs. Wilkins this afternoon. Their conversation was overheard."

Our Mrs. Wilkins. As if the housekeeper at Beasley Park already belonged to him. Or, even worse, to the both of them. As if they were already a married couple.

"Overheard by whom?" she asked.

"Beresford's valet. A canny fellow. He keeps his ears open."

"I'll bet he does," Maggie said acidly.

"And a good thing, too," Fred went on in the same officious tone. "I don't like you walking off alone in your condition. If you wanted to go over estate matters, you should have told me. I'd have accompanied you in the carriage."

Maggie stopped at the foot of the main staircase. Her voice sank to a whisper. "I'm never getting in a carriage with you alone again. Next time I might not be lucky enough to have a highwayman happen along to save me."

Fred's face reddened in the light of the crystal chandelier that hung overhead. "Must you make everything an argument? You force me to take you in hand."

"Is that what you call it?"

He again grasped her arm. "If you'd exert yourself to be sweet to me on occasion—"

"I shall exert myself to slap your face if you don't let go of me."

His body went stiff as a poker at her words. Taut seconds passed before he grudgingly released her. "Your temper is unbecoming."

"Then you must take care not to rile it." And clutching the heavy skirts of her silk dinner dress in her hand, she turned to climb the stairs.

Early the next morning, before the guests—or their servants—had risen from their beds, Maggie crept down to the Beasley Park stables. Made of stone, with strong wooden doors and red-clay roof tiles, they housed the Honeywell coach horses, riding horses, and what remained of her father's bloodstock. As a girl, the stables had been her second home. Now however, there was a distinctly unwelcoming air about the place.

"What do you mean my carriage isn't available today?" she asked, outraged.

The stablemaster, Mr. Tilley, shuffled his feet. He held his cloth cap in his hands in front of him. "Mr. Burton-Smythe says as how I'm not to allow any use of the vehicles unless it's on his authority."

Tilley had been employed at Beasley Park for only two years, the majority of which Maggie had been either ill or in mourning. No doubt he'd come to look on Fred as his master.

"That's all very well," she said, "but Beasley Park belongs to the Honeywell family. To me, in fact. And I need my carriage this afternoon."

Fred and his guests would be lunching with Sir Roderick at Letchford Hall, and then driving down to view a neighbor's collection of etchings. Their absence would provide the perfect opportunity for Maggie to embark on an errand of her own. An errand that required her maid and her carriage.

And perhaps one of Papa's pistols.

He had a smallish one in his collection. An old Queen Anne that would fit nicely inside Maggie's reticule.

Tilley fidgeted with his cap. "I'd like to oblige you, Miss Honeywell, but I did promise Mr. Burton-Smythe I'd do as he told me."

Maggie's blood commenced a slow boil. She endeavored to keep her temper. She wouldn't have anyone accusing her of being as unreasonable as her father. Not after what Mr. Entwhistle had said to her. "Well then, I'll simply have to take up the matter with Mr. Burton-Smythe, won't I?"

With that, she strode from the stable, but she didn't go back to the house. She was too angry. Besides, it wasn't long past dawn. No one was up yet, save the kitchen staff. And frustrated as she was, she couldn't condone waking Jane merely to complain to her about the injustice of it all.

Instead, she walked.

She crossed the drive and made her way out over the sloping lawn and down to the path that would take her to her sanctuary. The old meeting place she'd shared with Nicholas so many years before.

Branches caught at the skirts of her pelisse as she went deeper and deeper into the trees. The stream lay ahead, framed by the blue splendor of its forget-me-not covered banks. It was as she stopped amidst the sweet-scented wildflowers, one hand clutched at her side, panting for breath that she saw him. A fine, tall gentleman standing along the edge of the water.

He was clad in breeches and top boots, the broad lines of his shoulders outlined by a dusky blue coat that had obviously been cut by a master tailor. He held his tall beaver hat loose in one hand along with his whip, looking for all the world as though he was waiting for someone.

For her.

At the sound of her tread on the grass, he turned to look at her. But she already knew who he was. There was no mistaking that golden hair glinting in the morning sun. No mistaking those stormy gray eyes and that lean, panther-like grace.

His name formed on her lips as she ran to him. His *real* name.

He reached her in two strides and caught her up in his arms, lifting her straight up off of her feet.

She clung to him, uncertain whether to laugh or to sob. "You're here," she whispered, breathless, against his cheek. "You've finally come home."

26

St. Clare wrapped his arms around Maggie, holding her so close against him that the toes of her leather half-boots no longer touched the ground. He buried his face in her hair. She wasn't wearing a bonnet. He had the vague idea that she'd dropped it when she ran to him.

Good lord, she'd *run* to him. And she shouldn't be running at all. Not in her present state of health. Even now, he felt her struggling for breath.

"What are you doing here?" she asked. "Why did you come back? You know you can't—"

"Hush, love." He slowly lowered her back to the ground. His concerned gaze moved over her face. Every curve and contour was as precious to him as his own life. More precious than any title ever could be. "Come and sit down."

"Where?"

"Here. On the bank." He stripped off his coat and laid it down upon the damp grass.

"You gallant idiot. You'll ruin it."

"Sit," he commanded. As if he cared one jot about his coat. He had dozens more where that one came from, each of them as elegant as the last.

"Very well. But only because you insist." Maggie reluctantly sank down onto his coat. She was wearing a fitted dark blue pelisse over a plain muslin gown, her thick hair tied back in a simple knot at her nape. Her cheeks were flushed, her blue eyes extraordinarily bright. "What do you mean by coming here?"

"And what do you mean by striding about in this manner?"

"I'm walking off a temper fit."

His lips quivered. "Already? At this hour of the morning?"

"Don't change the subject." She gave him a worried look. "I thought we agreed it was too dangerous for you to come home?"

"We did. There was only one problem." He dropped down at her side. "I couldn't stand another second apart from you."

Her expression softened. "Was it very awful?"

He grimaced. "I was working myself into a state apparently." Pining like a lad after his first woman, his grandfather had said. Ridiculous.

She touched his cheek, her fingers as light as butterfly wings brushing over the hard edge of his jaw. "I missed you, too." Her hand curved around his neck, tugging him closer. "Dreadfully."

He bent his head and kissed her. Or possibly, she kissed him. He wasn't entirely certain. All he knew was that his blood suffused with warmth at the touch of her lips, and every restless part of him sighed with relief.

She was here. Back in his arms.

"Maggie..."

"I nearly didn't come here this morning," she said. "If I wasn't so angry—"

"You and your temper."

Her fingers slid into his hair. "I've lately heard it's unbecoming."

"Not to me." He nuzzled her cheek. "My fierce, beautiful girl." He felt her mouth curve in a smile. "You burn so very brightly. Is it any wonder my life has been so cold without you?"

"I don't wish you to be cold. But I still don't think this is a good idea. Your coming here." That didn't prevent her from kissing him again.

He was vaguely conscious of the breeze rippling through the trees along the stream, and of his hired horse milling about nearby, cropping grass along the bank. A reminder that he was not, in fact, in a private room somewhere with his beloved, but under a clear blue sky, in the great wide open of Beasley Park.

It was the only thing that kept him from prolonging their embrace.

Drawing back, he rested his forehead gently against hers. "It's all right. No one saw me riding up. The house looked all but deserted."

Her eyes widened. "You rode up to the house?"

"I did," he said grimly.

He hadn't expected it to affect him. Seeing the sprawling Palladian manor house of honey-colored limestone. Walking over the sloping grounds blanketed in forget-me-nots. But it *had* affected him. Quite deeply, really. Indeed, every stone and timber provoked another storm of memories.

Coming home, Maggie called it.

But this had never been a home to him. It had been a place where he'd worked. Where he'd suffered. Where he'd felt the anguish of not belonging. The pain of rejection, even from his mother—of stifled hopes, and of dreams that would never ever come to pass.

If he'd had a home at all, it hadn't been here at Beasley Park. It had been *her*. Maggie Honeywell had been his home. His only harbor in the storm.

All those years abroad, wandering the world, St. Clare wondered how he'd ever managed to go so long without her. Ten long years, with nothing but his memories to sustain him. It didn't bear thinking of, not now that he'd seen her again. Not now that he knew she was free. That she'd been waiting for him all this time. His love. His Maggie.

"Is it the same as you remembered?" she asked.

He pulled a face. "Smaller."

"It stands to reason. You've grown bigger, after all." She lay back on his coat, her head resting just over the edge of the collar on a tuft of forget-me-not covered grass. "Do you remember us lying here together that day? Before it all went wrong?"

"How could I forget?" He was tempted to lie down next to her. In for a penny, in for a pound, wasn't that how the saying went? But there had to be limits. Even for him. He cleared his throat. "Have you come here often down the years?"

"Too often for my own good." She turned her head to look at him. The collar of his coat brushed her cheek. "I believe most of these wildflowers have been watered by my tears at one time or another."

He took her hand. The thought of her weeping over him made his chest constrict. "That's all over now."

"Yes." Her fingers curled around his.

"I thought of this place a good deal," he said. "Especially in the beginning. I wanted to come back here again. To see if I'd feel the same."

"Do you?"

He huffed a breath. "No."

She lifted her brows.

"It was never this place that made me happy." He brought her hand to his lips. "It was you."

Her eyes glistened. Good lord, the way she looked at him. As if he were, indeed, as essential to her as light or air. Her soul mate. The other half of her heart.

It both electrified and humbled him. More than that, it filled up the emptiness inside him. Made the broken pieces of him whole.

She'd been right that day in Hyde Park. Neither of them could exist outside the presence of the other. He knew he couldn't. Not anymore.

"I love you, Maggie Honeywell," he said huskily. "You do know that, don't you?"

"Yes."

"And you love me? Not just the memory of me…of him… but me, as I am now?"

"Yes. For all eternity." Her voice was a velvet promise. A vow that had never been broken. That couldn't be broken. Not by time or distance. Not even by death, he suspected.

"Say it," he commanded. "I need to hear it."

"I love you, Nicholas Seaton." Her eyes held his transfixed. "I love you, John Beresford. Whatever you call yourself, however much you've changed, you're mine."

He bowed his head, setting his face against her hand. Her words were a salve upon his soul. "I *am* yours."

"Well," she said, "now that we have that settled."

"Yes, now that we have that settled…" He hesitated as he looked at her, choosing his next words with care. He'd already mulled them over on the journey down. Now it was only a matter of getting them out, and in the right order. "I know how you feel about this place. How much it means to you—the land and all of your tenants, but…" He faltered.

How could one man weigh himself against an entire estate? An estate that was synonymous with the Honeywell name?

But he didn't have to formulate the right words.

Maggie saved him the trouble.

"My father always told me that the land would go on. That people didn't matter. *We* didn't matter. Nothing mattered but Beasley Park." A frown puckered her brow. "I daresay he hoped it would persuade me to accept Fred. To think only of the estate and what our marriage might mean for it."

Her marriage.

St. Clare's mood soured at the edges. "You don't still intend—"

"No. But Papa was right. The land *does* go on. And it has, all through my illness, and while I was in mourning. It's gone on without me." She gave him a bleak smile. "I've had an epiphany, you see. I'm not as indispensable to Beasley Park as I've always believed."

He pressed a consoling kiss to her wrist, that delicate place where her pulse beat so valiantly. His heart ached for her, but he couldn't be sorry. Beasley Park was as much a rival to him as Frederick Burton-Smythe had always been. "I've had a similar epiphany."

"Oh?"

"That night, when I left here, when I struck out on my own, had I found Gentleman Jim, I'd have gladly joined him in whatever criminal enterprise he was engaged in. I had no particular principles. And later, when Allendale proposed to take me under his wing—to pass me off as his heir—it never occurred to me to refuse. And it wasn't because I aspired to riches or the trappings of notoriety or nobility. It was because... all I ever wanted was to belong somewhere. It didn't much matter where."

"You belong with me," she said.

Her words, spoken so simply, were his undoing.

What self-control he had left fractured on a surge of emotion. It crumbled to dust, taking the remnants of his gentlemanly resolve right along with it.

Any thoughts of propriety promptly fled. There was only her. The two of them. And ten long years of restless, painful, unrequited longing.

He levered himself over her, ignoring the twinge from his bullet wound as he caged her with his arms. Her eyes went wide as he kissed her, hard and fierce. "Yes," he said. "And you belong with me. Not here, stuck on this bloody estate for the remainder of your life. Not married to Frederick Burton-Smythe."

"I told you, I'm not going to marry him. I thought I could before you came back but—"

"Marry me," St. Clare said. It was half plea, half hoarse command. Not at all the romantic proposal he'd contemplated when traveling down from London.

Her bosom rose and fell against his chest. He felt her heart beating wildly, surely as wildly as his own. "And how shall we live?" she asked.

"Does it matter? Without you, life wouldn't be worth living at all."

She briefly looked away from him. Her throat spasmed on a swallow.

"You told me that, without me, you've been only half a person, living half a life. But I'm here now. Not the same—not Nicholas Seaton—but my heart is still yours. It's always been yours. If you'll marry me—"

"Of course I'll marry you."

His eyes blazed. "Maggie—"

"But you know Fred will never approve the match. It will mean giving up Beasley Park. Giving up my fortune."

"Damn this place, and your money along with it. I'd take you in your underclothes."

She choked on a laugh.

"I may still do," he said in a low growl. "Come here."

Her arms circled his neck, and when his mouth found hers once more, she kissed him back as eagerly and as passionately as he kissed her.

Sometime later, he lay down at her side, holding her hand, just as he'd done so many years before. A foolish smile played over his lips. He was lovestruck. Thoroughly besotted. And, at present, not much inclined to address realities.

Maggie had no such aversion. "Your grandfather's not likely to approve either."

"You think not? You may invite him to tea and ask him yourself."

"*What?*" She abruptly sat up. One might think the earl himself had appeared in front of her. "Don't say he's come with you?"

So much for their respite from reality.

St. Clare propped himself up on one arm. "He has. He's at the Hart and Hound. Still abed, I expect." They'd arrived at the coaching inn late last night, sometime after eleven. His grandfather had forgone dinner and gone straight to his room. Even now, St. Clare still wasn't sure of his mood. "We intend to pay a formal call on you this afternoon."

Maggie was aghast. "You wouldn't dare."

"Why not? I have it on good authority that a little boldness never goes amiss."

"There's boldness and there's boldness. This is…" She shook her head. "Your grandfather must realize what will happen if someone recognizes you."

"He's aware."

"And yet still he's come?"

St. Clare shrugged. "I told him how I felt about you. He knew I had to see you. That I was tired of waiting. And he knew I'd come with or without him—hang the consequences."

A blush seeped into her cheeks. "Good gracious. He must think me the veriest siren."

"If he's thinking badly of anyone at the moment, it's me. His thoughts are for his title. If I'm exposed as being illegitimate, his dreams of me inheriting it are over."

She frowned. "I wonder."

He gave her an alert look. "About what?"

"About whether you *are* illegitimate."

27

S t. Clare listened in stunned silence as Maggie told him all she'd learned about Jenny, Father Tuck, and Gentleman Jim. When she got to the part about what she'd planned to do next, a chill settled in his veins. "You were going to visit the hedge tavern in Market Barrow?"

"Well…yes. If Fred hadn't forbidden me the use of my carriage."

"Thank heaven he did." St. Clare got to his feet, too troubled to remain sitting. He paced to the edge of the water and back again. "Damnation, Maggie. That tavern is notorious!"

"Nonsense. You make it sound as though I'll be going there in the dead of night. I intended to go this afternoon, in broad daylight. Nothing can harm me then, surely."

"And what will you find out in broad daylight? What villains will you question with the tavern standing empty?"

Maggie's face fell. "Oh. I hadn't thought of that." She quickly rallied. "Very well then, I shall simply have to plan a foray after dark. And you needn't look so appalled. I'd be safe enough. I'd take Bessie with me." She paused, adding quietly, "And a pistol."

"Good God," he muttered. "I'd credited you with more sense."

She glared up at him. "What a thing to say. You know I can shoot as well as any man."

It was true. As a girl, she'd never lacked for skill—or courage. She'd been as formidable with a pistol as she was on horseback.

"That's beside the point," he said.

Maggie stood from the grass. "It's exactly the point." She dusted off the skirts of her pelisse. "If you're going to say that the place is dangerous and imply that I'm foolish to go there—"

"You're reckless. Just like you were sitting with Jenny while she was dying. Nearly killing yourself in the bargain. And when you came to Grosvenor Square that night to stop me from dueling Fred. Or when you came to Grillon's—to my hotel room of all places. You never stop to think of the consequences."

"Must you recite a list? This is different. It's—"

"*Reckless*," he said again. "And for what? To prove some damn fool theory you have about Jenny and Gentleman Jim having been married?"

"It's not a 'damn-fool' theory. It makes perfect sense."

"That the son of an earl would marry a hedge-tavern doxy?"

She threw up her hands. "Yes! The same son of an earl who turned highwayman. If he can contemplate one, why couldn't he contemplate the other?"

St. Clare shook his head. It was too far-fetched. Too apiece with the private dreams he'd had as a boy. That one day he'd discover he wasn't a bastard after all. That he'd had parents—a mother and a father who had been wed to each other.

He couldn't believe it. *Wouldn't* believe it.

Maggie came to stand in front of him. Some of her hair had fallen loose from the knot at her nape. Mink strands curled about the edges of her face, ruffled by the morning breeze. "You're blinded by your feelings for Jenny. So angry at her for being a bad mother that you can't imagine she might have had any redeeming qualities."

"She didn't."

"She was beautiful once. That's enough for most men. And she might have had other attributes to inspire Gentleman Jim's affections."

He snorted.

She rested a hand on his chest. A soothing gesture. He felt the weight of it there, through the layers of his cloth waistcoat and linen shirt, all the way down to his skin. His blood surged in response. Only moments ago, he'd been lying with her, kissing her and holding her. Asking her to marry him.

And she'd said yes.

She'd said yes.

And now, here they were, all but arguing over...what? The decades-old relationship between Jolly Jenny and Gentleman Jim?

St. Clare might have laughed if he wasn't so irritated.

Good lord, was there nothing about Maggie Honeywell that didn't tie him in knots? That didn't leave him breathless and befuddled and struggling to keep his bearings?

"Not every relationship is a grand love affair, you know," she said. "For most people, a comely countenance and a pleasant disposition is enough."

He covered her hand with his. "It doesn't follow that they got married. Not even if Gentleman Jim admired her attributes. Not even if he knew she was with child. He wasn't an honorable man, Maggie."

"So I gather. But who's to say he married her because he cared for her? Perhaps he had some other motive."

"Such as?"

"Perhaps he married her to spite his father?"

St. Clare went still. "And then left her here, with child?" The chill in his veins turned positively glacial at the dastardly possibility of it.

"You said it yourself. He wasn't a good man. Indeed, when it comes to James Beresford, that seems to be the prevailing point of view."

"If it's true…" St. Clare didn't dare consider it. He was too wary of disappointment to hope. In his experience, when one went chasing after the past, one never found quite what they were expecting. "But how can it be? If I was legitimate, Jenny would have announced it to the world. There would have been no reason to keep it secret."

"According to Mr. Entwhistle, she told my father that she'd been tricked into believing she was married. That, in fact, she wasn't married at all. I suspect this Father Tuck or Friar Tuck or whatever it is he was called at the time may have been part of it." Maggie frowned. "Either that or Jenny simply asked for him on her deathbed because he was an old friend—someone who had once been kind to her."

"There," he said. "Do you see? You may be making a mountain out of a molehill."

"Perhaps," Maggie replied. "There's only one way to find out."

His brows lowered. "Market Barrow."

"It's unfortunate that I can't use my own carriage. But Jane has her carriage here, and her servants answer to her, not Fred. I'm certain she won't mind if—"

"I hope Miss Trumble has more sense than to aid you in such a dangerous enterprise." He tightened his grip on Maggie's hand. "Can you not imagine what might happen? A beautiful creature like you—a young, well-to-do lady—arriving at a hedge tavern in an expensive coach with a matched team of fine horses and no one but her maid to protect her? What do you suppose the villains thereabouts will think when such a plump-pocketed victim walks willingly into their lair?"

Maggie said nothing more. She merely looked at him, a challenge in her blue eyes that fired his blood as much as it frightened him for what she might do next.

He stifled an oath. "Very well. I'll go myself if it will put the matter to rest."

She brightened. "And take me with you?"

He gave her a forbidding look. "On no account. I told you, it's too dangerous. I'll go at night, and I'll go alone."

"You can't go alone," she said. "You have your injured arm to think of."

"Maggie—"

"And besides," she continued determinedly, "*I'm* the one who discovered the existence of Father Tuck. It's not fair that I should wait at home while you get to enjoy the adventure."

He recognized that subtle lift of her cleft chin. Her mind was made up. She wouldn't be swayed, neither by threats nor reason. He nevertheless made one final effort. "It's not about fairness. It's about your safety."

She smiled up at him. "You'll keep me safe. I have every confidence in you."

That afternoon, just as he'd threatened to do, St. Clare paid a formal visit to Beasley Park in company with his grandfather. It was the polite thing to do when one was newly arrived in the district, paying calls on acquaintances from town. Everything aboveboard and proper.

Indeed, there was nothing out of the ordinary about it at all. Nevertheless, when climbing the wide stone front steps of Beasley Park, St. Clare felt distinctly out of his element.

As a boy, he'd never been admitted to the house through the front doors. He'd been obliged to use the side entrance by the kitchens. Maggie may have relented on this point, but the rest of the household had not. Nicholas Seaton was never permitted to forget his place. He'd belonged below stairs, with the servants.

"You belong with me," Maggie had said.

The memory of her words—of her kisses—heartened him as he applied the brass knocker to the door.

"A pleasing prospect," Allendale remarked, glancing about the grounds. "Surprising."

St. Clare's mouth curved. "You expected a tumbledown country pig farm?"

Before Allendale could reply, the door was opened by a footman in dark green livery. He was a young man, and one who St. Clare didn't recognize.

"Viscount St. Clare and the Earl of Allendale to see Miss Honeywell," St. Clare said. "We're expected."

The footman looked at each of them, glanced past them to the earl's stately carriage, with its crest emblazoned on the door, and then—with a deferential bow—bid them enter. After taking their hats and gloves, he ushered them up the stairs and into the drawing room.

Maggie stood from the sofa as they entered. She was wearing a simple muslin dress with a ribbon sash at her waist. Her hair was caught up in a high knot, a few strands left to curl about her face. She looked extraordinarily young and extraordinarily beautiful.

St. Clare's heart thudded hard. He felt the same warm, vaguely breathless feeling he did whenever he looked at her. As if his surroundings had narrowed to a point, his entire world reduced to a single person. To her.

He endeavored not to show it and flattered himself that he succeeded. It was bad enough to be accused of behaving like a lad with his first woman. He wouldn't allow himself to act the part.

"Miss Honeywell," he said, bowing. He swiftly dispensed with the introductions.

Not that either of them appeared to be listening.

His grandfather approached Maggie without preamble, responding to her neat curtsy with a stiff inclination of his head. "Miss Honeywell, at long last. I understand you've thoroughly ensnared my grandson."

"No more than he's ensnared me, my lord," Maggie replied without missing a beat. She gestured for them to sit down.

Allendale sank into a chair, his attention fixed on Maggie as she resumed her seat on the silk-cushioned sofa.

"Lord St. Clare tells me that you've taken rooms at the Hart and Hound," she said. "I trust you're comfortable there?"

"Comfortable enough," Allendale said. "Where's that supposed nephew of mine and his mother? They're staying here, aren't they? Presuming on some threadbare acquaintance?"

"Indeed. My neighbor, Mr. Burton-Smythe, invited them down for the shooting. They're out at present, visiting his father, Sir Roderick, at Letchford Hall."

St. Clare wandered to the fireplace. His gaze drifted around the drawing room. It was a large space, richly carpeted, with silk-papered walls covered in oil paintings of horses and hounds, and furnished with elegantly upholstered sofas, settees, and chairs. Everything was just as he remembered.

But something seemed off.

It was the light. There wasn't quite enough of it. The heavy plum-colored damask curtains were closed against the midday sun, leaving the room dim and cool.

He looked at Maggie, frowning.

"Burton-Smythe is your guardian?" Allendale asked her.

"Something like that." She flashed a glance at St. Clare. "Will you not sit down, my lord?"

He walked to one of the rosewood chairs and took a seat.

When contemplating his visit to Beasley Park, he hadn't considered how strange it would be. How unsettling the intersection of his past and his present. More than that, he hadn't taken into account how Maggie might feel about his return. She wanted him, he had no doubt. Accepted him exactly as he was. And yet…

And yet the drawing room was as dark as it could possibly be in the middle of a blazing summer afternoon.

Was she so worried about what Fred might do if he recognized who St. Clare really was? If he saw him in the unflinching light of day?

The thought irritated St. Clare to an extraordinary degree.

He was more than capable of handling Frederick Burton-Smythe. Didn't Maggie know that? Or did she think him still a boy—a servant lad who was in danger of falling victim to a thrashing? Someone she must protect at all costs?

"When will your guests return?" Allendale asked.

"Not for several hours, I expect," she said.

St. Clare folded his arms. The stitches in his bullet wound tightened painfully. "Perhaps we'll wait for them."

Maggie's smile dimmed. "If you like. Or you could postpone the pleasure until tomorrow evening."

His brows lifted. "Burton-Smythe will be here?"

"He will," Maggie said. "And Sir Roderick, as well. They're coming for dinner. I hope you and Lord Allendale will be at liberty to join us."

A dinner party, attended by Fred and his father. It would mean arriving after dark to dine in a room illuminated only by flickering candles. A setting almost guaranteed to disguise any hints of his true identity.

"An excellent notion," Allendale said.

"And Fred has approved of this?" St. Clare asked. "He knows I've arrived in Somerset?"

"He does not," Maggie admitted. "If he had, he wouldn't have been so willing to leave me unattended this afternoon."

"Thereby letting a fox loose into the henhouse."

Maggie's lips compressed. "A metaphor that flatters neither of us."

Yet an apt one, St. Clare felt. "When do you plan to tell him?"

"I won't have to tell him. He'll learn of your visit all on his own. There's always someone about watching and reporting back to him."

"This Burton-Smythe fellow," Allendale said. "Treats your home like his own, does he?"

She didn't deny it. "He's had the running of the estate since my father died. It's not ideal, but—"

"It's far from ideal," St. Clare said. "And it's not just her home he has the running of. It's the rest of her life as well."

"Really," she objected. "I'm certain Lord Allendale doesn't want to hear—"

"I'm certain he does." St. Clare turned back to his grandfather. "Burton-Smythe must approve her marriage, else she forfeits her claim on her father's estate. A legal device employed by Squire Honeywell to force her to marry the man of his choosing."

"And why shouldn't she?" Allendale asked. "If that's what her father wished?"

"Because she's marrying me," St. Clare said. "I proposed to her this morning."

His words were greeted with a sudden and very obvious silence. Indeed, had a pin fallen at that moment, he was confident he would have heard it drop.

Both Maggie and Allendale stared at him, but before either of them could muster a word in response, the silence was broken by the arrival of the tea tray. It was carried in by a footman—different from the one who had opened the front door, and equally unrecognizable. He put the tray down on a low table near the scrolled-arm sofa where Maggie sat.

"That will be all, Salter," she said. And then, her blue eyes still throwing sparks over St. Clare's abrupt announcement, she asked, quite civilly, "Tea, anyone?"

They waited to speak as she poured them each a cup. As if the polite ritual held them in thrall. It was only after she'd returned the porcelain teapot to the silver tea tray, that Allendale finally responded.

"So," he said, "my grandson has proposed marriage to you, has he?"

"He has."

"And you've accepted, I gather?"

Maggie raised her teacup to her lips. "I have, my lord." There was a hint of a challenge in her voice.

It brought a faint smile to St. Clare's lips. Perhaps he should have warned his grandfather that Maggie had been raised by the biggest bully in the West Country? Squire Honeywell's temper had all but inoculated his daughter. When it came to overbearing men, she was accustomed to giving as good as she got.

"And what if he should forfeit the title? What then?" Allendale addressed St. Clare. "You haven't the coin to keep a wife. Not one who's accustomed to living in a fine house with a full staff of servants, and...what else?" He gave Maggie a hard look. "A string of hunters, and a coach and four? Trips to London for the season?"

"You mistake me," Maggie said. "I require none of those things."

"And what of my grandson? What about what he requires? A lad meets a gel in his youth, puts her on a pedestal. Doesn't mean she's suitable for the gentleman he becomes."

Maggie lowered her teacup back into its saucer with a sharp clink. "There's no one more suitable for Lord St. Clare than I am. And surely it's his choice?"

"It *is* my choice," St. Clare said. "And it's been made. Miss Honeywell and I are to be married, as soon as we can contrive it."

"No matter the consequences?" Allendale asked.

"I hope," Maggie said, "that the compensations of the match will outweigh any consequences."

St. Clare's gaze met hers. And he felt it there, the love for her anchored deep inside him, as elemental as his own heart's blood. It didn't seem possible that it could grow stronger. And yet it did; the more he was with her, the closer he came to making her his.

He prayed she was right. That marrying him, giving up her claim to Beasley Park, wasn't something she'd regret for the remainder of her days.

A better man—a nobler man—might have prevented her from making such a sacrifice. He might have withdrawn his suit and saved her from giving up her home and her fortune.

But St. Clare was neither good, nor noble.

This time, when he left Somerset, he was taking Maggie Honeywell with him.

28

"St. Clare was here?" Fred's enraged voice exploded from the door of the Beasley Park library. He stormed across the room to where Maggie was sitting by a tall window, curled up in an oversized armchair. "And you received him?"

She glanced up from the book she'd been reading. "You're back early." She looked past him. "Where's Miss Trumble?"

"To blazes with Miss Trumble," he said harshly. "Is it true? You entertained him here? Alone?"

"I was in no danger. He was accompanied by the Earl of Allendale. Unless you mean to suggest that Lord St. Clare would ravish me in front of his own grandfather?"

A wash of color darkened Fred's face. "Did you know he was coming? Is that why you claimed to be too tired to join us on our outing? Did you have an assignation with the man?"

Maggie turned the page of her book. "This may come as a surprise to you, Fred, but I have no desire to be traipsing about the countryside on a hot day. I'd far rather stay at home. And yes, when acquaintances from town come calling, I invite them in and offer them tea. Would you prefer I have the servants cover the windows and remove the door knocker?"

Fred gave an enraged snort, like a bull preparing to charge an unseen enemy. "He's followed you down here, the blackguard."

"My cousin has arrived?" Lionel Beresford came into the library. He looked from Maggie to Fred and back again. His normally languid gaze was alive with calculated interest. "And my uncle with him? Now that *is* unexpected."

"They had tea here." Fred's tone was thick with insinuation, making the act sound like some kind of debauch.

Jane followed not far behind Mr. Beresford. Her bonnet was still in her hand. "There you are." She went straight to Maggie, plumping down in the chair beside her. "What's this I hear about Lord Allendale and Lord St. Clare coming to call?"

"They're staying at the Hart and Hound. I wonder…" Maggie mused. "Do you think they'd be more comfortable here? We could make a house party of it."

"We'll do no such thing," Fred said. "I forbid it, absolutely. The sooner St. Clare returns to wherever it is he came from, the better. I'll not have him in this house making advances toward you."

Advances.

Maggie's blood warmed to recall her early morning meeting with St. Clare on the banks of the stream. "Don't be ridiculous, Fred. His lordship behaved in a perfectly proper fashion, and I intend to reciprocate. I've invited him to dinner tomorrow."

Fred's fists clenched at his sides. "You wouldn't—"

"He'll be here at seven, along with Lord Allendale." She gave him a stern look. "And I'll hear no more on the subject.

You've fought with him, and he's won. It's time to accept your loss with good grace."

Jane made a strangled noise.

Perhaps that *had* been pushing Fred a bit too far.

His red face grew redder still, his breath puffing out of him. "My loss? *My* loss? What do you know of what transpired? These are gentlemen's affairs."

"Come, sir," Lionel said, coaxing Fred away with a hand on his arm. "Let us leave the ladies to their novels. I've a matter or two to discuss with you. Perhaps over a glass of port?"

Fred grudgingly obliged his guest, exiting the library—but not before casting one last glower in Maggie's direction.

"I've never seen him so angry," Jane said. "Is it wise to bait him so?"

Possibly not. Fred's temper had been getting worse since Maggie arrived in town. The more she resisted him, the angrier and more frustrated he seemed to become. It had culminated in his attempt to kiss her in the carriage, and now, with St. Clare's arrival, Fred was all but ready to snap.

Maggie supposed she should be afraid, but she wasn't. She was in love. Engaged to be married. And after tonight, she may even have solved the riddle of Nicholas Seaton's birth. For once, the future looked bright—and the present along with it.

"Fred can't harm me," she said, closing her book with a snap. "Today I feel as though nothing can."

That night, as the longcase clock in the hall chimed the eleventh hour, Maggie slipped out the back door of Beasley Park and made her way to the end of the darkened drive. A rickety two-horse carriage awaited her, driven by a very small man in an oversized greatcoat and hat.

She had but a moment to examine him in the silver glow of the full moon before the door of the carriage open and St. Clare jumped out.

"Is that Enzo?" she asked.

"Never mind him." St. Clare tossed her into the cab and then climbed in after her, shutting the door behind him. "Did anyone see you leave?"

"No. I don't believe so." She'd been quiet as a mouse, only lighting a candle long enough to get dressed in one of her old gowns and her cloak. Only Bessie was aware of what Maggie was doing. The rest of the house had been silent as the grave. Not a trace of Lionel Beresford slinking about, or his equally odious valet.

Or so Maggie hoped.

"Good." St. Clare sat down in the seat across from her. He was wearing a caped greatcoat, his hat and cane on the dingy cushion beside him.

"It was wise of you to think of hiring a gig for the night," she said. "No one will remark this vehicle, surely."

He didn't reply.

She looked at him in the weak light of the carriage lamps, attempting to make out his face in the shadows. "If you're going to sulk—"

"I'm not sulking."

She lifted her brows but said nothing more. What more *could* she say? He hadn't wanted her to come with him, which was understandable. She privately acknowledged that visiting a hedge tavern after dark *was* a trifle dangerous. Dangerous for him as much as her. He wasn't invincible, after all.

And so she'd told him.

But if his arm was paining him now, he certainly didn't show it. He seemed to be made of stone, sitting there, across from her, still and quiet, as if he had more important things on his mind than a midnight foray into the past.

Meanwhile, Maggie's own nerves were fairly crackling with anticipation.

How many times in their youth had she and Nicholas speculated about the famous hedge tavern in Market Barrow? Too many times to count.

And now, they were almost there.

The carriage rattled and jolted along the road, seeming to connect with every stone and pothole. It was a poorly sprung vehicle—a poorly sealed one as well. The cold of the evening seeped through the edges of the doors and windows.

Shivering, Maggie wrapped her cloak more firmly about her.

St. Clare sighed. In the next instant, he was up from his seat and sinking down next to her. His arm came around her shoulders, gathering her close inside the warmth of his great-coat. "Better?"

She snuggled against him, shaping herself to the side of his body. It was akin to cuddling with a furnace. "Much better, thank you."

They seemed to be the only coach on the road, but occa-sionally, Maggie thought she heard the clip clop of hooves echoing behind them. As if a horse and rider were traveling by the same route. She fervently hoped it wasn't a highwayman.

"How long is it to Market Barrow?" she asked.

"Some seven or eight miles." St. Clare's lips brushed over her hair. "When we arrive, you're to stay close to me. Do you understand?"

"You mustn't worry about me." Before leaving the house, she'd tucked the Queen Anne flintlock into her reticule. It had been a long while since she'd fired a pistol, but one didn't forget, surely.

"Of course I'm worried," he said. "If anything should happen to you—"

"It won't, I promise. I'll stay right with you the entire time." She set a hand on his midsection. The buttons of his cloth waistcoat brushed over her palm. Her stomach fluttered. There was something extraordinarily intimate about being with him this way, inside a darkened carriage, enfolded in his greatcoat and sheltered by his arm "Did Lord Allendale have anything to say about your going out?"

"He retired early."

"He doesn't know?"

"About this Father Tuck fellow?" St. Clare frowned. "No. I didn't tell him. There seemed little point."

"I hope that after tonight there will be something worth the telling."

Some forty minutes later, their rickety carriage finally rolled into the yard of the legendary hedge tavern in Market Barrow.

Maggie drew back the edge of a moth-eaten curtain to peer out the dirty carriage window. She admitted to a certain disappointment. The tavern was nothing like she'd envisioned it would be. This was no shadowy den of thieves from a gothic novel, but a small, obscure stone building located alongside the highway amidst a tangle of trees and brush.

"The Crossed Daggers," she read aloud from the swinging wooden sign as the carriage came to a halt. "How ominous."

"It's certainly not the Hart and Hound," St. Clare said grimly. He moved to open the door, but she forestalled him.

"A kiss for luck?" she suggested.

He stilled. "You're enjoying this, aren't you?"

"I am," she admitted.

"It's dangerous, Maggie."

"Yes, dangerous. Like a cross-country gallop on a hot horse—a jump over a tall gate or a leap across a too-wide ravine." She hadn't ridden in ages, but she well remembered that feeling of speed and daring, of utter abandon. It called to her primitive Honeywell soul. "I've been wrapped in cotton wool for too many years. Locked away inside Beasley Park. The night you returned to me is the night I came alive again. There's no going back now."

He bent his head. "No. There isn't." He kissed her, hard and fierce.

She clutched weakly at his greatcoat, her heart thumping heavily as his sinful mouth claimed hers.

It was he who ended the kiss, a blaze of fire in his gray eyes. He drew her hood up to veil her face before opening the carriage door. "With me," he said.

She nodded, and when he leapt down, she allowed him to grasp her waist and lift her out of the cab as easily as if she were a bit of thistledown.

He set her gently on the ground, tucking her hand in his arm. "Keep an eye out," he commanded Enzo.

The tiger dipped his head.

"Will he be safe out here?" she asked.

"Safe enough." St. Clare led her across the yard to the tavern's darkened entrance. There was no one about save for a portly man in an oilskin coat. His hat was pulled low over his face, obscuring his features as he mounted a rather depressed-looking chestnut horse.

Maggie suppressed another shiver. She clutched her reticule close to her, feeling the reassuring weight of the flintlock within it.

It was nearly as dark inside the tavern as it was without—and darker still as the heavy wooden door slammed shut behind them on hinges that were desperately in need of oiling.

At the sound, every man in the room seemed to look up. And there were a great many men present. Three grizzled, white-haired fellows were hunched over a table in the corner, nursing tankards of ale. Two slightly younger men were near the fire, smoking pipes. And yet another group—younger still—huddled at the high wooden counter of the bar.

Their faces were uniformly sinister in the shadows cast from an overhead oil lantern that swayed on a chain. And most sinister of all, the barman—a hulking figure with a balding pate and a crooked nose that looked as if it had been broken at least half a dozen times.

She shot a worried glance at St. Clare, but he didn't appear to be at all concerned. To be sure, his face was as cold and implacable as it had often seemed in London.

Maggie tightened her hand on his arm as the two of them approached the counter.

The barman looked between them, his flinty gaze at last settling on St. Clare's face. "Can I help you, milord?" A heavy strain of sarcasm colored his words.

"My companion has one or two questions for you," St. Clare said. "Try to keep a civil tongue in your head."

Maggie's heart clutched on an unexpected surge of gratitude. She'd thought that St. Clare would handle the questioning. That he'd prefer her to remain mute—a silent observer to their adventure rather than a participant in it.

But that wasn't how he felt about her at all.

She was his companion, he'd said. Just as she'd always been. His equal, and second self. Not someone to be silenced. But someone he would help to be heard.

If she could have flung her arms around his neck and kissed him in that moment without causing a furor, she would have done so, and gladly.

The barman looked at her. "Questions about what?"

She moistened her lips, focusing her mind on the task at hand. "Are you the proprietor?"

"Who wants to know?"

"Well...*I* do, of course." What a thing to ask! "I'm looking for someone."

Some of the younger men at the bar hooted. "Will I do, missus?" one of them called out.

St. Clare gave them a cool glance. The men quieted.

Maggie ignored them. "I'm looking for a man who frequented the tavern many years ago."

"How many years?" the barman asked.

"Thirty, approximately. A trifle less, perhaps. It was long before my time."

"And mine," he said. "Wasn't but a babe thirty years ago, was I?"

Her spirits dimmed.

"Who can we speak to?" St. Clare asked. "There must be someone about." He cast a pointed glance at the three old men in the corner. They were watching him—had been ever since Maggie and St. Clare had entered the tavern. "What about them?"

"Nah. It's me father you want." The barman spat on the ground. "But can't think why it'd be worth it to trouble the old man at this time of night."

"You'll be compensated, of course," Maggie said.

The barman's gaze narrowed. "Secrets don't come cheap around here, milady. And you won't find none of us willing to sell out one of our own."

"There's no question of that." St. Clare's voice deepened—projecting through the tavern, though he didn't raise it one jot. "This is a family matter."

A swell of whispers rose in response to his words.

Maggie gave St. Clare a frowning glance. But there was no time to inquire what he was playing at.

He slid a gold sovereign across the bar. "There's another for you once we've spoken to him."

The barman picked up the sovereign and bit it. Seemingly satisfied, he dropped it into the pocket of his stained waistcoat. He walked out from behind the counter, jerking his head toward a dark, narrow staircase. "He's upstairs in his room."

St. Clare didn't budge. "Summon him. We'll speak to him here."

"Can't do," the barman said. "He don't come downstairs no more."

Maggie felt St. Clare's arm tense under her hand. She understood why. It could very well be a trap. A means of isolating them so that they could rob them of *all* of their money, not merely the promised gold sovereigns.

"And why not?" she asked.

"Because," the barman said, "the old codger is blind."

29

St. Clare cursed himself for agreeing to bring Maggie to this godforsaken place, and doubly so for permitting her to accompany the barman up the narrow wooden staircase. The whole of it went against his every instinct. Against every bit of his better judgment.

And yet, here they were.

He followed close behind her, the stairs creaking with every booted footstep. They were ascending into darkness, met by an odor fouler than the stink of sour ale and perspiration that permeated the taproom. It smelled of stale urine, rotten meat, and unwashed male bodies.

The barman stopped in front of a door at the end of the corridor. "He's in here."

St. Clare drew Maggie back to his side. He was ready for anything, but when the door opened, there was no one lying in wait. No one in the room at all, save a small man in a chair who turned his clouded eyes blindly toward the door. His wrinkled face was lit by the light of the full moon shining through a grease-streaked window.

"Who's there?" he croaked.

"It's me, Pa," the barman said. "These folks want to ask you about someone from the old days."

"What folks?"

"A fine lady and her gentleman. Paid a sovereign, they did. And they'll cough up another when they've finished talking to you."

The old man perked up. "Two sovereigns!"

"This is me father, Ed Mullens," the barman said by way of introduction. "He's owned the Crossed Daggers since...1780, wasn't it, Pa?"

"Aye. Somewhere thereabouts. Come in, come in." Mullens beckoned to them. "Don't get many visitors."

St. Clare and Maggie entered the room. The barman withdrew, shutting the door after him.

"Have you a candle?" Maggie asked.

"On yon table," Mullens said. "Not much need for it in my condition."

St. Clare found it, along with a tinderbox, and managed to strike a spark to light the wick. The candle flame flickered.

Maggie pushed back the hood of her cloak. There was a spindly chair near the unmade bed. She sat down upon it carefully, getting straight to the point. "Mr. Mullens, do you recall a man by the name of Father Tuck, or possibly, Friar Tuck? He may have come here sometime thirty years ago."

"'Course I recall him." Mullens gave a jagged, phlegmy cough. "What's he to you, missus?"

"*We're* asking the questions," St. Clare said.

Another hacking cough. "Don't like to see old Tuck in trouble."

"We don't want to cause trouble," Maggie assured him. "We merely want to learn a little more about the man."

"He was a churchman." Mullens laughed hoarsely, which only provoked another cough.

St. Clare went to the window. It looked down over the yard of the tavern. Enzo was still there, alone at his post. He was young and small, but he was capable enough. Like St. Clare, he was well armed. Not only did Enzo carry two horse pistols on his person, there was a rifle in boot underneath his seat.

"You there," Mullens gasped, still coughing. "Pour me some wine."

There was a dusty bottle on a table by the bed. St. Clare uncorked it and poured the contents into the dirty glass at its side. He put the glass into the old man's hand.

Mullens drank deeply.

St. Clare moved to stand behind Maggie's chair.

"A former churchman, yes," she said. "He was expelled from his order, I believe."

"No former about it. Went back, he did. Gave up the drink." Mullens drained his glass. "Pious fool."

St. Clare looked at him. "Went back where?"

"To his church, I reckon. Somewhere in Devonshire. Damned if I know."

"Devonshire?" Maggie's expression turned hopeful. "Do you know the name of the church?"

"Why would I?" Mullens was quiet a moment, his wiry brows beetling. "He did come back once, now I recall it. Thumping his Bible at us. Said as how we was to repent. Tossed him out on his arse, the boys did. Never saw him again after. Might be dead for all I know."

Maggie was undeterred. "He was friends with one of your barmaids, wasn't he?"

Mullens snorted. "Who says so?"

"Wasn't he?" she pressed. "I thought he might have been acquainted with Jenny Seaton."

Mullens cackled. "Jolly Jenny? There's a name I've not heard in years."

"You remember her working here?"

"Nothing wrong with my memory, missus. Hired the wench meself, didn't I? She were only sixteen—straight off the farm—but comely as a dove. Didn't know nothing about ale, nor men, that one." His mouth spread in a toothless smile. "She soon learned."

St. Clare's hand tightened on the back of Maggie's chair. He had to force his fingers to unclench.

Maggie cast him a concerned look. *Are you all right?*

He gave her a brief, tight smile. *Never better.*

A decade had passed since he'd last seen Jenny Seaton. He'd never meant anything to her, and she'd never meant anything to him. Now wasn't the time to start feeling protective of her.

"A game girl, she was," Mullens went on. "But she were never friendly with Tuck. Never met him, don't think, excepting once—a fair dustup they had."

Maggie's brows lifted. "They quarreled?"

"Something like. Saw him drinking when she came in. He was fair done for, couldn't see straight, nor walk upright. Had to be doused with the pump afore he could get himself home. 'What's that vicar doing here?' she asks. 'Him, a vicar?' we says. 'This here sot who's pissed himself?' Crying with laughter, we were. Then she commenced crying herself, flew at the man with her fists. Had to pull her off him, we did, the mad cow."

St. Clare gave him an alert look. "When was this?"

"Don't rightly know." He shrugged. "A long time hence."

"Was Gentleman Jim still her beau at the time?" Maggie asked.

"Her beau!" Mullens laughed. "Is *that* what you heard?"

St. Clare went still. For an instant his breath seemed to stop in his chest. "Wasn't he?"

"Pour me another." Mullens blindly thrust out his dirty glass.

This time Maggie took it. Rising from her chair, she crossed the small room to the table with the bottle on it, returning with a fresh drink a moment later. She helped Mullens to find the glass with his hand. "We understood that Jenny Seaton and Gentleman Jim were... That is... That she was his sweetheart."

"Oh, he fancied her, he did. But he were a strange one, Jim was. A right mysterious devil." Mullens downed a swallow of his wine with another congested cackle. "He never had no *sweetheart*."

St. Clare held the chair as Maggie sat back down.

"May I ask..." She hesitated. "When Jenny quarreled with Father Tuck... was she with child?"

"Not so's anyone would know. I did hear tell she might have been, but never did find out for certain. She disappeared not long after. Went home, some of the fellers said, to that farm she come from."

"Where was Jim?" St. Clare asked.

"Gone, some weeks before. We gave him a right send-off." Mullens breath rattled on a sigh. "The best days of me life, those were. Downstairs, with Jim and the lads. Every night were a feast when he dropped in. Oh, but the lasses were in a fair swoon over him, with his golden hair and fine gentlemanlike ways. Women came for miles to sit on his knee."

St. Clare wasn't surprised. An earl's son at a hedge tavern? With his commanding figure and his aristocratic ways? He'd been handsome, of course. St. Clare knew that much. Handsome and reckless and dangerous.

Maggie leaned forward in her chair. "Did Gentleman Jim know Father Tuck?"

Mullens shrugged. "Might have done. Old Jim knew all sorts. Had friends high and low. Recall one time, he came into the tavern, and..."

The old man ran on with his stories. Tales of the distant past—a happier time for him, clearly.

Maggie let him talk, occasionally prodding him with a question about Jim, Jenny, or Father Tuck, but no relevant information materialized from Mullen's lips. Merely more reminiscences.

St. Clare went back to the window and peered down into the yard. A man was loitering near the door, staggering about as if he were drunk.

"And you're certain Father Tuck's church was in Devonshire?" Maggie asked.

"I told you," Mullens replied, "nothing wrong with my memory."

St. Clare looked at Maggie. It was past time that they left. They'd already stayed far longer than he'd planned. The more they delayed their departure, the greater chance that something would go wrong. He opened his mouth to tell her so when a sudden movement in the yard caught his attention.

It was a carriage arriving. A fine carriage, with a team of four prime horses in the traces. Two men sat upon the box, the coachman and a second fellow wrapped in an oilskin coat. He pointed at Enzo and the hired carriage.

Bloody hell.

"Time to go," St. Clare said. He strode to Maggie and hoisted her from her chair.

She scrambled to her feet. "But I still have questions for Mr. Mullens!"

"There's no time." St. Clare urged her to the door, his hand on her arm. "We need to get out of here." He asked Mullens, "Is there another exit?"

"Through the kitchens," Mullens said.

St. Clare muttered an oath. They'd still have to descend the staircase. He opened the door and looked out into the hall. No one was about. Not yet. "Out," he said to Maggie. "Quick as you can."

Blessedly, she seemed to understand the urgency. "Goodbye, sir," she said to Mr. Mullens as she exited the room. "I'm obliged to you for the information."

"Wait!" Mullens called after them. "I didn't catch your name!"

St. Clare shut the door behind him, silencing the old man's cries. The hall dissolved into darkness again. There was only a faint glow at the end of it—the light from the taproom drifting up the stairs.

"What is it?" Maggie asked as she hurried along at his side. "Some sort of villainy?"

"The worst kind," St. Clare said. "Someone's followed us here."

"What!" She would have stopped in her tracks if he hadn't jockeyed her along to the landing.

"Put up your hood. We'll duck out through the kitch-ens. There's a chance we might be able to get to the carriage without anyone seeing you." He sensed the futility of the plan as soon as he'd given voice to it. Enzo and their hired carriage had already been spotted. Recognized, even.

Maggie drew her hood over her head, and then took his hand, clutching it tightly as she followed him down the stairs. "Who is it?" she asked. "Not your cousin?"

He didn't have to supply an answer. They'd no sooner descended halfway down the steps than an all-too-familiar voice echoed up the staircase.

"I know she's here somewhere," Fred bellowed. "Don't make me fetch the magistrate."

St. Clare's shoulders bunched with tension. The dratted fool. Threatening the inhabitants of a hedge tavern with the magistrate? As if every villain below wasn't armed to the teeth and ready to fight.

"Oh no," Maggie groaned. "What is *he* doing here?"

The answer to that question came in much the same fashion.

"We don't want any trouble." Lionel Beresford's languid words drifted up to them in the darkness. "Only tell us where we can find the lady and the rogue who's abducted her."

"Abducted!" Maggie bristled. She sounded more outraged than worried about being discovered.

St. Clare supposed it hadn't yet occurred to her how all this might look. The two of them, alone in a tavern in the middle of the night, emerging from a long while spent in an upstairs bedroom.

He led her down another few steps—carefully, quietly—until they were but two steps away from the floor of the taproom.

"Don't much like the gentry coming into my tavern making threats," the barman said. "Nor waving pistols about."

Pistols?

"The bloody idiot," St. Clare muttered. "He's going to get himself killed."

"Where are they?" Fred demanded again.

"Don't be too hasty with that weapon, my friend," Lionel said. "I think I can guess where my cousin has taken his captive." And to the barman: "You have rooms above, do you not, my good fellow? A place a man can be private with a lady?"

The barman guffawed. "Did you hear that, Bill? A *lady*? In the Crossed Daggers?"

An elderly warble answered him, Bill presumably. "Don't see no ladies here."

St. Clare squeezed Maggie's hand. There was no way to duck out to the kitchen without being observed. Their only hope was that Fred and Lionel would lose interest and back away to the other side of the tavern.

It was a scant hope, and one that was quickly dispelled.

"I'll send my valet up to have a look around," Lionel said.

St. Clare tensed. It was either wait to be discovered or reveal themselves voluntarily. Exchanging a swift glance with Maggie, he knew at once which one she'd prefer.

"No need," he said, descending the final steps with her at his side.

Fred stood by the tall counter, a pistol hanging loose in his hand. Lionel was nearby, wrapped up in a fashionable overcoat, his hat still on his head. His valet, a shifty-faced man of indeterminate age, stood next to him.

At the sight of St. Clare and Maggie, Fred's ruddy face mottled with fury. He advanced on them, his pistol half raised against any perceived interference on the part of the tavern's customers. "I didn't want to believe it," he said, giving Maggie a look of disgust. "You, sneaking out of the house like the veriest light-skirt. For an assignation at a hedge tavern of all places." He pointed his pistol at St. Clare. "You'll answer for this."

"I intend to," St. Clare replied "Though I do wonder how it is you came to find us here?"

"Ah," Lionel said. "That would be my doing."

Maggie dropped St. Clare's hand. "You set your valet after me, didn't you? Of all the cheap, underhanded tricks. And you a guest in my home!"

"He did follow you, I confess, and then returned to fetch me. I thought it only prudent to summon Mr. Burton-Smythe." Lionel gave St. Clare a lazy smile. "Apologies, Cousin, if I've interrupted your pleasure."

"My pleasure has just begun," St. Clare said. And reaching into the inner pocket of his greatcoat, he smoothly withdrew his own pistol—a nasty-looking double-barreled flintlock.

Lionel took an involuntary step back.

The table of old men in the corner laughed heartily. "Where's your magistrate now, guv?" one of them cackled.

Fred's hand trembled, but he didn't waver. "Come, Margaret. At once. I'm taking you home."

"Oh, do put that thing down, Fred," Maggie said in exasperation. "You'll never best him with pistols, and well you know it."

There was more laughter from the old men in the pub. "You tell him, missus!" one of them said. "He won't get the better of our lad."

"That's right," another cried. "You show our lad some respect."

Our lad.

St. Clare vaguely registered the words. Just as he'd registered the old men's stares and whispers when first he'd entered the Crossed Daggers. He knew what it all meant, but there was no time to dwell on it. He had his old rival to contend with.

The two of them faced each other at the edge of the shadowed taproom.

"Come here," Fred commanded Maggie. "Now."

"She's not going anywhere with you," St. Clare said. "Not tonight—not ever. She belongs to me."

"You!" Fred glared at him with something very like hatred. The same unbridled hatred with which he'd once regarded St. Clare so long ago. "Just who the hell do you think you are?"

One of the grizzled old men stood up from his seat at the corner table. "Don't you know who you're talking to, boy? Why, that's Gentleman Jim."

Another of the men laughed. "He's not Jim, you silly sod. He's too young."

"He looks like him right enough," the first man replied. "A damned mirror image. Must be his son."

Fred stared at St. Clare in dawning realization. His mouth opened and closed. His chest heaved. He shook his head, as if in denial of what was right in front of his eyes.

"I *am* his son," St. Clare said. His mouth curved in an arctic smile. But his blood wasn't cold. It was swiftly simmering to a raging boil.

This was the man who'd driven him from Beasley Park. Who'd beaten him and scarred him and separated him from the love of his life. This was the man who would have let him hang for a crime he hadn't committed.

And here St. Clare was at last, facing him, not as a cold-blooded viscount but as himself—as the hot-tempered lad who had fled Somerset ten years ago.

"Don't you know me, Fred?" he asked.

"Nicholas Seaton," Fred uttered in tones of disbelief. "It's not possible."

"Oh, it's quite possible, I assure you," St. Clare said. And he cocked his pistol.

30

Maggie's heart jumped in her throat. Until a few minutes ago, St. Clare had been in complete control of the situation. She'd been content to follow his lead. But somewhere between the last two steps on the staircase and the taut moment in which they were now embroiled, he'd let his emotions get the better of him.

She felt as though she was standing atop a tinderbox. Not only were Fred and St. Clare pointing their pistols at each other, the rest of the men in the tavern had risen to their feet. Some of them appeared to be in possession of weapons of their own. Even the barman was armed. He'd withdrawn a heavy wooden club from behind the counter, as if in eminent expectation of an all-out brawl.

"Jim's son!" one of the old men said. "Knew it as soon as I saw him, I did. Didn't I tell you, Bill?"

"A family matter, he said," another replied. "Did you ken?"

Ignoring the upraised voices, Maggie set a hand very gently on St. Clare's arm, careful not to startle him. He was entirely focused on Fred. "This isn't going to solve anything."

"Probably not," St. Clare said without looking at her. "But it will make me feel better."

Fred had cocked his pistol as well. It shook a little in his hand. Not the most heartening sight. Indeed, Maggie had more fear that Fred would fire upon St. Clare accidentally than that St. Clare would shoot Fred on purpose.

"Put it down, Fred," she said, "before you hurt someone!"

"I mean to hurt someone," Fred replied. "Him."

Mr. Beresford backed against the counter, half shielding himself behind his valet. "Pray tell, Cousin, just who is Nicholas Seaton?"

"*I'm* Nicholas Seaton," St. Clare said, without batting an eye.

Maggie winced. Good lord. This was all her fault. She'd known full well that St. Clare had wanted to leave his old identity behind. Dead and buried, he'd said. And now, because of her, he was forced to confront it again, and in the most public way possible.

"The bastard son of a whore and a highwayman," Fred said. "Born at Beasley Park, wasn't he, Margaret? He used to muck out Squire Honeywell's stables."

Maggie's fists clenched. "Shut up, Fred."

"He was a thief, too," Fred went on. "A dirty, no-good grubby little thief. He was going to be hanged for his crimes. And would have been if someone hadn't set him free." He flashed a scathing look at Maggie. "Were you letting him bed you even then?"

After that, things happened rather quickly.

Thrusting his flintlock at Maggie, St. Clare closed the distance between him and Fred in a few swift strides. He knocked the pistol from Fred's hand. And drawing back, punched him full in the face.

There was a deafening roar of approval from the men in the tavern, and a great rush forward as they all closed in to watch what looked to be the beginning of a mill.

Fred flew backward from the strength of the blow, landing against a table. He rallied immediately. One minute he was shaking his head, as though stunned, and the next he was charging St. Clare like a bull. He caught him in the midsection, nearly bowling him off of his feet.

But St. Clare was no lad anymore. Not a lanky servant boy who Fred could beat without fear of reprisal. He returned Fred's blows with powerful blows of his own, another to the face, and several to Fred's sides, making his opponent grunt and grimace.

St. Clare's flintlock still in her hand, Maggie shoved through the crowd to grab Fred's fallen pistol from the floor. She reached out for it, but Mr. Beresford's odious valet beat her to it. He swept it up in his hand, and with a triumphant sneer, withdrew back to his master, who was by this point hunkering behind the bar.

Meanwhile, St. Clare and Fred fought on, across the taproom and toward the door. Glasses shattered as they threw each other against tables, and wood splintered as chairs broke and upended onto the floor.

St. Clare's golden hair was wildly disheveled, his greatcoat torn off, and his neckcloth ripped loose. Blood stained his brow and dripped from his mouth.

Fred was in even worse condition. His hat and coat were gone, his waistcoat had lost all but two of its buttons, and his copper hair stood straight up on his head. One of his eyes was half shut, and he was bleeding copiously from his nose.

Neither of which deterred him.

He grabbed St. Clare by his shirt, and spinning him around, smashed his fist into St. Clare's jaw.

Maggie covered her mouth to stifle a cry. But St. Clare didn't appear to be hurt—not grievously.

Retaliating instantly, he struck Fred once, twice, and then—by the simple expedience of one well-delivered boot to the chest—quite literally kicked Fred out the door of the tavern.

The crowd went mad. "Hell's teeth!" one of the men exclaimed. "Did you see that?"

"He's Jim's lad, all right!" another cried.

But the fight wasn't over.

St. Clare followed Fred into the yard, and the two of them picked up straight where they'd left off.

Maggie ran after them, along with the rest of the rabble. "Stop!" she cried. "That's enough!"

St. Clare and Fred circled each other, both of them panting, deaf to her pleas. And then, Fred lunged at St. Clare again—a staggering, unsteady assault. The two of them grappled with each other, exchanging imprecise blows.

"Oh, for pity's sake!" Maggie wished she had a bucket of water to throw over them. She looked desperately around the yard. Her eyes lit on their hired carriage. It stood in the same place they'd left it. Except now...

It was completely unattended.

Worse than that. It no longer appeared to be attached to the horses.

A jolt of alarm went through her. Abandoning her place at the front of the crowd, she ran to the carriage only to discover that the traces had been cut. Panic rose in her breast. "Enzo?" she called. "Enzo, where are you?"

"Here!" a faint voice answered.

She almost didn't hear it over the roar of the crowd. It was a tiny sliver of sound, emanating from the only other carriage in the yard.

Fred's carriage.

Mr. Beresford, his valet, and the coachman stood alongside it, well out of the way of the fight and ready to make their escape. The valet was holding Fred's pistol.

Maggie fixed the trio with a glare. "I beg your pardon, is that my servant I hear inside your cab?"

Mr. Beresford smiled. "Just obeying orders, Miss Honeywell."

"Whose orders?"

"Mr. Burton-Smythe's, naturally."

"He has no authority over my tiger," she said. "Let the boy out at once."

"Can't do," Mr. Beresford said.

"Oh you can't, can you?" Her temper flared.

"Not unless it's on Mr. Burton-Smythe's say-so. And, as you can see, he's a trifle busy with my cousin at the moment."

She moved to the door to try the handle, but the valet blocked her path. "Get out of my way!"

"This lad's for the magistrate, ma'am," Mr. Beresford said.

"Rubbish. He's committed no crime. It's you who I'll have up before the magistrate if you don't release him."

He chuckled. "On what charge?"

"Kidnapping. *And* I'll report you for damaging my hired carriage. Just what do you mean by cutting the traces? And if you say you were merely obeying Mr. Burton-Smythe's orders, I shall not be responsible for my actions. Now, out of my way," she said again. Only this time, she raised St. Clare's flintlock.

It didn't provoke quite the response she'd anticipated.

The two servants laughed uproariously. Even Lionel Beresford tittered with amusement. As if she were a simpleton who didn't know one end of a weapon from the other.

"You be careful with that, little lady," the valet said. "You might harm yourself."

Maggie leveled the flintlock. "Let him out, or I shall shoot that dratted pistol straight out of your hand."

"Have a care, ma'am." Mr. Beresford moved as if to take the weapon from her. "If you do yourself an injury, how will we—"

Maggie pulled the trigger.

A pistol shot broke through the noise of the crowd—exploding in the night like a firework.

The sound wrenched St. Clare back to his senses. Tearing his attention from Fred, he looked for Maggie at the edge of the crowd. She'd been there but a minute ago, begging him to stop fighting. But now she was gone.

She was gone.

Shoving Fred away from him, St. Clare shouldered his way through the onlookers. Someone was screaming. A sound to make his blood curdle. But it wasn't a woman, thank God. It was a man. Lionel's valet, in fact.

He was doubled over next to the door of Fred's elegant carriage, clutching himself. A pistol lay on the ground at his feet. Fred's coachman lunged for it, but Maggie kicked it away before he could reach it.

She was facing them alone, still holding St. Clare's flintlock.

"Me hand!" the valet wailed. "She's blown off me hand!"

"Nonsense," Maggie said. "My aim was perfect."

St. Clare was at her side in an instant, still breathing heavily from his fight with Fred. "Are you all right?"

She looked up at him. Her brows knit as she scanned his face, a frown forming on her lips. "Are *you*?"

He ran a hand over his hair. He knew he must look a fright. There was blood all over him, drying on his face and fists, and staining the linen of his torn shirt. Only a fraction of that blood was his own. "I'm fine," he said. "In spite of appearances."

"Good." She pushed past the still-screaming valet and opened the carriage door. Enzo was inside, his hands bound together. He gave them a look of profound relief.

"What in blazes?" St. Clare stepped forward to untie him.

"They snatched him," Maggie said. "And they've cut the traces of our carriage."

St. Clare helped Enzo out of the cab. "How did they get the better of you?" he asked in a low voice. "You were armed to the teeth."

Enzo answered him in Italian, his words accompanied by an apologetic shrug.

St. Clare turned on his cousin. "What did you hope to achieve by this pitiful jest?"

"It's no jest." Fred limped toward them. He was holding a handkerchief against his mouth. Fury still burned in his face, but it was no longer made manifest. He was too bruised and battered to continue fighting. "I'm going to have both you and your tiger brought up before the magistrate for abducting Miss Honeywell. And your good name won't make one wit of difference."

Lionel's eyes glittered in the moonlight. "But you don't have a good name, do you? You're less of a Beresford than Madre and I suspected. Indeed, you aren't a Beresford at all."

"Of course he's a Beresford," Maggie said sharply. She looked to Fred. "And it's not abduction if I went willingly. You already admitted as much in front of the entire tavern, accusing me of being a—"

"Stay out of this, Margaret," Fred told her.

The valet's screams had been reduced to whimpers. "Me hand!"

"Enough, man," Lionel hissed. "The bullet only scorched you."

Fred came forward, reaching for Maggie's arm. "I'm taking you back to Beasley Park."

St. Clare barred his way. "Like hell you are."

"She has no choice." Fred gave him a look of malicious triumph. "Your carriage isn't functional. The only way she's returning home tonight is with me."

Maggie drew closer to St. Clare. "If that's the case, I'd rather walk, thank you."

St. Clare cast a swift glance at his hired cattle. The two bays were nothing very elegant, but they were big and strong. "That won't be necessary." And then to Enzo: "Ready the horses."

Enzo sprang into action. He quickly rid the bays of their harnesses, leaving only their bridles attached. It took but a moment longer to thread the long carriage reins back through the rings of the horses' bits, fashioning two pairs of make-shift riding reins.

Fred and Lionel might have attempted to stop the indus-trious tiger if the crowd of customers from the tavern hadn't gathered around. Old men and young stood watching and cheering, uttering unhelpful commentary and encouragement.

The barman was at the front of the fray, his club in his hand. "You lot better clear out before the constable arrives and reads the Riot Act."

"No fear of that." St. Clare met Maggie's eyes, an unspoken question in his own.

Her mouth tilted up very slightly. "I suppose I must ride pillion."

"Don't be absurd, my love." He tossed her up onto the back of the larger bay, and then, taking the reins from Enzo, vaulted up behind her. His arm came around her waist, holding her fast. "This way is far more efficient."

She settled back against his chest, his flintlock still clutched in her hand.

"Don't you dare go with him," Fred bellowed. "Do you hear me, Margaret? You'll be ruined!"

Enzo retrieved the shotgun from inside the box of the abandoned carriage before mounting the second horse. He pointed the weapon at Fred and Lionel.

"Where's my pistol?" Fred asked Lionel.

"Miss Honeywell shot it out of my valet's hand," Lionel said. "A fascinating display."

"She kicked it under the carriage, sir," the coachman added helpfully. "Shall I fetch it?"

"Of course you should bloody well fetch it," Fred snarled. And then: "Margaret! There'll be consequences for this! If you leave with him tonight, you'll lose everything you love!"

"Not everything," Maggie said.

St. Clare felt the sudden urge to grin. He spun his horse around, and catching the barman's eye, flipped the man his promised second sovereign.

The barman caught it easily. "Godspeed, milord."

"Farewell, young Mullens. You may tell your esteemed father that the son of Gentleman Jim sends his regards." With that, St. Clare gave his mount a hard kick, and with Maggie clasped tight in front of him, galloped away into the night.

31

They'd gone little more than two miles before Maggie made St. Clare stop. "I can't continue sidesaddle," she said. "Not bareback."

St. Clare reined his horse off of the darkened road and into a thicket of trees nearby. Insects chirped, and somewhere in the distance an owl hooted. There was no sign yet of Fred's carriage coming after them. No sign of anyone. Nothing but a wide expanse of endless night, the moon hanging above them, lighting their way in a luminous shimmer of silver.

Enzo stood guard, his back to them as Maggie hoisted her skirts to her thighs and swung her right leg over the horse's neck.

"I'm not certain you'll be any more comfortable astride," St. Clare said, his gaze riveted to her stocking-clad legs. They were slim and shapely, culminating in a well-turned pair of ankles.

"As comfortable as you are without a saddle." She straightened her skirts and her cloak, concealing as much of her legs as she was able. "That's better. Now you won't have to hold me so tightly."

His arm came back around her waist. "I like holding you tightly."

"For six more miles?"

"Forever." He rubbed his cheek against the silken softness of her hair. "That was the plan, anyway."

She covered his arm with her own. Her head was tucked just beneath his chin, the feminine curve of her back nestled snugly against his front, fitting so perfectly to his body it was an agony.

"You frightened me tonight," she said.

"Did I?"

"A little."

He nuzzled her cheek. "It seemed to me that you got right into the spirit of things."

"I was frightened when you wouldn't stop pummeling Fred. You looked quite wild. As if you'd kill him with your bare hands." She frowned up at him. "And you had no care at all for your injury. I thought the pain of it might stop you eventually, but you didn't seem to regard it."

"No more than Fred regarded his wound. It's often the way when a man's blood is up." St. Clare had felt it, of course. The stitches had pulled, and there was a burning pain, as if some of them had burst. It had been the least of his worries.

As for Fred, he *had* seemed to wince and grunt with extra vigor whenever St. Clare connected with his shoulder, but Fred's arm had worked well enough. He'd had no difficulty throwing punches—and landing them, too. St. Clare would be lucky if he could move tomorrow. He was already aching in one hundred different places.

"Do you still hate him so very much?" Maggie asked.

"No," he said. And then, grudgingly, "Yes. In that moment at the tavern, I did hate him. It all came back to me. The injustice of it. What he did to me—and what he's done to you. I'm afraid I lost my head."

An understatement.

When Fred had insulted Maggie in the taproom, something had snapped inside of St. Clare. He'd been overcome with the urge to spill Fred's blood. To make him suffer the way St. Clare had suffered. The way Maggie had suffered.

"Yes. You did." She turned her face to his. "It was rather thrilling."

He smiled. "I thought you said you were afraid?"

"I was. Thrilled. Frightened. I do believe this has been the most exciting night of my life."

A laugh rumbled in his chest. "You mad creature. What am I to do with you?"

But he knew precisely what to do.

He found her lips in the moonlight and kissed her softly, deeply. Her mouth yielded to his, lush and sweet. His heart thudded hard.

"I'm a Honeywell," she said. The words were a mingled whisper of breath as she kissed him back with warm, half-parted lips, making his blood sing. "We can't help enjoying a bit of danger."

"That was more than a bit, my love." He kissed her swiftly once more before guiding his horse back onto the road. Enzo fell in step beside them. "At any moment, one of those men in the tavern could have turned on us. Or worse. Not to mention the fact that you might have killed Lionel's valet."

"Neither possibility is very likely," she said. "Firstly, I'm an excellent shot."

"True," he acknowledged.

"And secondly, those men recognized you as soon as we walked in the door. I didn't think of it then, but your resemblance to your father must be quite striking indeed."

"Uncanny, apparently."

"Quite. And Gentleman Jim is all but a folk hero to those villains. Naturally they'd take your side in a quarrel. Especially if your adversary was someone like Fred or your cousin, coming into the place and threatening to summon the magistrate of all people."

"Fred is a fool. He's always been a fool. That doesn't make him any less of a threat." St. Clare's mood darkened. "He's going to make things very difficult for you, Maggie."

"He'll try."

"We must marry at once. As soon as I can procure a license." He wanted her away from this place. Away from Fred and the malice of the Beresfords. Somewhere St. Clare could keep an eye on her. In his bed to start with.

"Of course we must. But in the meanwhile, I won't let him drive me from my home, not one single minute sooner than Papa's will requires. Beasley Park is still mine for the time being. And the first thing I'm going to do when I return is to eject your cousin and his mother from the premises. I want them out of my house by dawn."

"By all means. But we're not going to Beasley Park."

She wiggled around in front of him, attempting to meet his gaze, even as he urged his horse into a canter. "We're not?"

He shook his head. "We're going to the Hart and Hound."

Maggie stood in front of the fireplace, warming her hands over the freshly kindled blaze. The Hart and Hound was nothing at all like the Crossed Daggers. It was a respectable inn run by respectable people—people who were slavishly deferential to the earl and his grandson.

Indeed, when Maggie and St. Clare had arrived, the husband and wife proprietors hadn't been at all cross about being rudely awakened from their beds in the early hours before dawn. Instead, they'd averted their eyes from St. Clare's battered face, from his torn shirt and blood-stained waistcoat, and all but bowed him and Maggie into a private parlor.

After seeing her settled there, St. Clare had withdrawn almost immediately to speak to his grandfather. Ten minutes passed before he returned to her, washed, groomed, and wearing a fresh suit of clothes.

Her pulse gave a little leap, just as it always did whenever she first laid eyes on him.

But he wasn't alone.

Lord Allendale entered the private parlor after him. "Miss Honeywell."

"My lord." She curtsied. The room was lit by the fire, and by a branch of candles. The flames flickered and snapped, casting patterns over the earl's face, making his already unwelcoming expression look almost sinister.

"This is a fine mess the pair of you have got us into," he said. A wooden table graced the center of the parlor, four straight-backed wooden chairs arrayed around it. Allendale drew one out and sat down. "A public declaration of my grandson's former identity? In a hedge tavern, no less?"

St. Clare pulled out a chair for Maggie. As she passed him to sit down, their bare hands brushed, fingers tangling for the briefest instant. It sent a rush of warmth through her belly, making her knees go weak.

She didn't dare meet his eyes for fear of blushing. "No one of importance was there," she said to the earl. "No one save Mr. Burton-Smythe and Mr. Beresford."

"Burton-Smythe might be persuaded to keep silent. He has your reputation to think of. But Beresford? That duplicitous jackanapes and his mother will have the tale in all the papers by morning."

St. Clare sat down in the chair next to her. "It is morning."

Allendale's frown deepened. "You must have taken leave of your senses. To be out all hours brawling, and with a lady in tow. Is this the outlandish behavior you inspire in my grandson, ma'am? And you. Look at yourself, sir. Cut and bruised. Your lip split and your eye blackened like a criminal of the lower orders. Haven't I told you that nothing can be learned from digging up the past?"

"But we did learn something." Maggie looked at St. Clare in confusion. "Didn't you tell him?"

Allendale's gaze narrowed. "Tell me what?"

St. Clare ran a hand over his face. "It's nothing. Old rumors about my father and mother."

"What rumors?" Allendale asked.

St. Clare was silent.

Maggie understood why he might be reluctant to share the results of their investigation. She, however, felt no such inhibitions. "I believe there's a chance that Lord St. Clare's parents may have been married."

"*What?*" Blood surged in Allendale's face. He turned on St. Clare.

The innkeeper chose that inauspicious moment to enter with a tray. "Beg pardon, my lords. I've brought tea and some seed cake for you." He set the tray on the table. "The wife can make you breakfast if you'd rather. Some eggs and sausage, or porridge if—"

"That will be all," St. Clare said.

"Yes, your lordship." The innkeeper bowed. "Apologies for interrupting." He bowed again, backing himself out of the room. The door clicked shut behind him.

There was a second of silence as the man's footsteps receded down the hall. And then, once again assured of their privacy, Allendale asked, "What do you mean my son may have been married?"

"It's nothing," St. Clare said. "Just something Miss Honeywell has surmised from a remark made by my late mother."

"A deathbed remark," Maggie said, on her dignity. "And that isn't all. There's more."

With that, she proceeded to tell the earl everything Jenny had said when she was in the final hours of her illness, and everything they'd since discovered about Father Tuck, including the latest bits of information gleaned from Mr. Mullens.

After she'd finished, Allendale was quiet for a long moment. When at last he spoke, it was to utter a single word: "Devonshire."

Maggie nodded. "That's what Mr. Mullens said. He could be no more specific."

"It doesn't mean anything," St. Clare said. "Nothing but the ramblings of a dying woman and an aged former tavern keeper. It's a false hope, at best."

"You disagree, Miss Honeywell?" Allendale looked at her steadily, as if her opinion mattered as much to him as that of his grandson. "You think there might be something in this business about this Devonshire clergyman?"

Maggie cast a troubled glance at St. Clare. He'd lived an entirely different life since they'd parted. Had become a man of elegance and sophistication—a well-read and well-traveled gentleman, far outside the realm of her own experience.

But this reluctance of his to entertain the idea that his parents might have been married was no mystery. It was pure Nicholas. The anxiety of a boy who had been disappointed too many times in regards to his family. A boy who wouldn't permit himself to hope.

"Yes," she said carefully. "I think there might be something to it."

Allendale's brows lowered.

Maggie took a breath. "What if Father Tuck married Jenny and Gentleman Jim—that is, Jenny and your son. And what if, after they were wed—after your son left England, Jenny went into the Crossed Daggers and saw Father Tuck there, falling down drunk? The men in the tavern laughed at her for thinking he was a clergyman, which might have led her to believe it had all been a prank. That she wasn't married to your son at all. He was known for playing pranks on people, wasn't he?"

Allendale said nothing. Neither did St. Clare. Both men were somber and still, not moving a muscle. The tea tray sat between them, untouched. A ribbon of steam drifted from the spout of the teapot, swirling up toward the beamed ceiling.

Maggie went on. "Mr. Mullens said that Jenny left after that, and that they all assumed she'd returned to her parents' farm. But by the time she arrived at Beasley Park, she was in a dreadful condition. Not only with child, but half starving, my father said. As if she'd been wandering a good long while. By that time, she believed her baby was illegitimate."

"And you suggest that my son would have married a gel like that? A tavern wench?" Allendale scowled. "Impossible. He must have known he would come home one day. That I would forgive him. To have attached himself to such an unsuitable female…" He shook his head. "No. Not James."

"Might he have done it out of spite?" St. Clare asked. "To punish you for casting him off?"

The question hung in the air for a moment. It had a strange effect, changing the very atmosphere around them. As if the suggestion opened a Pandora's box of painful possibilities.

"Spite?" Allendale echoed at last. Something in his face seemed to crumple. A light in his gray eyes dimming slightly, as if he had absorbed a blow. He grew smaller before Maggie's eyes, and for the briefest moment, looked every bit of his age. "He might have done."

Maggie averted her gaze. She felt as though she were witnessing a private moment. One she wasn't meant to observe. The moment when the Earl of Allendale fully accepted that his late son had been a rogue and a villain, not merely a lad who had gone a bit wild.

"I was too hard on him," Allendale said. "After he killed Penworthy's boy. It was the final straw, I told him. I was washing my hands of him. But the breach wasn't meant to be permanent. He was still my heir. Still my son."

"You didn't drive him away," St. Clare said quietly. "And even if you did, he was a man grown. A man with a child of his own on the way. He could have come back. He should have done, if not for you, then for me."

Allendale cleared his throat. "No point being maudlin. We are where we are. And you, Miss Honeywell—" He fixed her with a look, no longer soft with memory but hard with disapproval. "You have no business being abroad at this hour. I've ordered my carriage to see you home."

"Thank you, my lord." She affected a meek expression. "I'm sorry for the inconvenience."

"My grandson and I will call upon you tomorrow. I trust you mean to proceed with this dinner party of yours?"

Maggie blinked. "You still intend to come?" She flashed St. Clare an alarmed glance. He looked as bewildered as she was. "Mr. Burton-Smythe will be there, and so will his father."

"And that idiot son of my second cousin's," Allendale added. "And his mother."

"You're wrong on that score." St. Clare's mouth hitched in a fleeting smile. "Miss Honeywell means to cast them out."

Maggie flushed. "Well, I did think I might."

"Nonsense," Allendale said. "Let them remain for the moment. I would see them all when I arrive tomorrow evening. Every last scheming one of them."

Maggie didn't relish the prospect. "If that's what you wish but…it's bound to be uncomfortable for all concerned."

"Exceedingly so," Allendale replied, "more for some than for others, I'd wager."

32

The next day, at seven o'clock precisely, St. Clare arrived at the front door of Beasley Park, dressed in an impeccably cut black evening suit with a light-colored waistcoat and elegantly arranged cravat.

Maggie met him at the threshold. She looked behind him, down the stone steps and over the torchlit drive. There was no sign of the earl's carriage. Nor of the earl.

A flicker of apprehension quickened her pulse. "Where is Lord Allendale?"

St. Clare's expression was grim, made worse by the heavy bruising that had emerged on his face. He had a spectacular black eye, and a cut on his brow and on his lip. "Gone."

"Gone? Gone where?" A footman approached, but Maggie waved him away. She let St. Clare into the hall herself, shutting the door behind him.

"I have my suspicions." He scanned her face. "How are you?"

"Perfectly well."

"Your guests haven't been bullying you?"

"No. That is, Fred *has* been a trifle difficult. He called earlier, and then again this afternoon, trying to speak to me alone, but Jane refused to budge from my side. Fred was very nearly ready to throttle her."

St. Clare's mouth curved. "God bless Jane Trumble. And what of my meddling relations? Have they been difficult?"

"Not exactly. Not to me, at any rate. They've kept to their rooms for much of the day. I fear they've been writing letters, spreading the news of your identity to all and sundry. They came into the drawing room this evening looking as satisfied as two cats who had just stolen the cream."

St. Clare didn't appear at all worried. Indeed, he seemed far more concerned about Maggie's well-being than his own. "I would have come sooner, but I thought it better to let tempers cool. Otherwise we might have had a reenactment of that unfortunate scene at the tavern."

"Lord, I hope not. Things are quite tense enough without adding another brawl to the mix."

Tense didn't begin to explain it.

On returning home in the earl's carriage, Maggie had gone straight to Jane and told her all. Jane had been an absolute brick, sitting up with Maggie until dawn. She'd also been a little hurt that Maggie had been keeping such an enormous secret. That she hadn't trusted Jane enough to confide in her.

"It wasn't my secret to tell," Maggie had explained.

Jane had professed to understand. But Maggie couldn't help feeling as though her friend was disappointed in her.

Fred was disappointed in her, too. Terminally disappointed. This evening, when he'd arrived for dinner, he'd fixed Maggie with a contemptuous glare, condemning her without saying a word.

She didn't have to guess what he was thinking. He'd said it plain enough at the tavern. She was a light-skirt. A ruined woman. Someone who had thrown her innocence away on a scoundrel, and whose reputation was now past the point of recovery.

"It doesn't matter about any of them," Maggie said. "My only concern is for you." She searched St. Clare's eyes. There was an expression in them that was hard to read. "Will your grandfather be joining us later?"

"I don't know. He left no word for me. He was already gone when I awoke this morning. According to the innkeeper, he departed in the early hours, shortly after I retired to bed. Just climbed into his carriage with his luggage and…" St. Clare shrugged.

Maggie's heart clenched. The earl had abandoned him. Now that St. Clare's true identity had been exposed, Allendale had no more use for his grandson. No more affection for him either, it seemed. As if St. Clare were as disposable as a piece of counterfeit paper. Something that, once revealed to be a fake, had no value at all.

Anger rose in her breast. With it, came a sharp pang of guilt.

None of this would have happened if she hadn't insisted on accompanying St. Clare to Market Barrow. It was all her fault.

Grasping his hand, she tugged him down the hall and into the library. The wall sconces were lit, along with an overhead chandelier. She didn't bother shutting the door. This wouldn't take long.

Which was just as well.

The two of them had only a few moments. Everyone else was already assembled in the drawing room—Jane and her aunt Harriet, Lionel Beresford and his mother, Fred, and even Sir Roderick. They were enjoying a preprandial drink, waiting for her to return, and if she didn't do so promptly, one of them was bound to follow after her.

"Your grandfather's not coming back, is he?" she asked.

St. Clare gazed down at her, his hand still holding hers. "Does it matter?"

"Not to me," she said. And she meant it. "To put it in terms you might understand...I'd take you in your underclothes."

He huffed a laugh. "Is that what I told you?"

"You did."

"Well. Your underclothes are a vast deal more pleasing than mine."

There was a heaviness in her chest that prevented her from laughing with him. She had too much of a sense of what he'd lost on her account.

She drew his hand to her lips and pressed a kiss to his bruised knuckles. "I have a little money of my own. A small income meant to sustain me in the event that Beasley Park passes out of my control. It isn't much, but—"

His brow furrowed. "Maggie—"

"—two can live as cheaply as one, I've heard."

"I'm not a pauper, my love."

"I–I know that," she said, stammering a little. She didn't know it, actually. It was merely an assumption.

Nicholas Seaton had appreciated the value of money—the vast difference it could make in a person's life. She couldn't imagine St. Clare respecting it any less.

He'd have put something by, surely. Something to live on if ever his grandfather withdrew his patronage. She'd have bet her last shilling on it.

But whatever it was, it would never be enough to equal what he'd given up. Had she not forced him to go to Market Barrow, he'd never have been obliged to reveal himself as Nicholas Seaton. The Allendale title would have one day been his. He'd have been rich and powerful—entirely free from the unpleasant associations of his past.

"I'm sorry," she said. "I've ruined the whole scheme, haven't I? All because I insisted on going with you to the Crossed Daggers. And now—"

"Hush." He cupped her cheek, and leaning down to her, brushed a kiss to her forehead. "The game's not over yet."

St. Clare ascended the stairs to the drawing room with Maggie on his arm. She was clad in a fashionable dinner dress of dark blue-gray silk. It was cut low across her bosom, with elbow-length sleeves that gently hugged her slim arms. Glass beads adorned the fabric, making her skirts sparkle as she walked.

She was a creature of magic. A beautiful blue-eyed sylph or fairy. And she was his, at last. All his.

A smile built within him as he recalled how she'd looked last night, standing outside the tavern, a smoking flintlock in her hand.

People underestimated Maggie Honeywell at their peril. She might be weaker than she'd once been. Her health more fragile. But what she lacked in physical stamina, she more than made up for in spirit. In heart.

He glanced down at her. The grave expression on her face provoked a twinge of conscience.

She believed that what had happened in Market Barrow had driven Allendale away. That she was to blame for his leaving.

It was the furthest thing from the truth.

St. Clare knew his grandfather. If he'd really intended to abandon him, Allendale wouldn't have slunk away while St. Clare slept. The earl would have confronted him. Would have told him that he had no more use for St. Clare now that he'd been exposed as a bastard.

It was nothing less than Allendale had said countless times before.

Indeed, on many occasions during the past several years, the earl had seemed at great pains to remind both St. Clare and himself that he had no use for his grandson aside from securing the title.

St. Clare had often wondered. And when Allendale had suggested accompanying him to Somerset to meet Maggie, St. Clare had wondered even more.

No. His grandfather wasn't gone for good.

That wasn't to say that St. Clare hadn't experienced a minor shock when he'd woken and found Allendale gone. And it wasn't only that he'd left without a word, but that they were expected at Beasley Park for dinner that evening. In his absence, St. Clare had but two choices: either send his regrets or attend alone.

Sending his regrets wasn't an option. Not with Maggie depending on him.

Besides, he'd realized something last night. He wasn't afraid of facing his past. There had been something profoundly liberating about declaring his identity to the mob of villains inside the tavern. Not only his real name, but the fact of his parentage.

Maggie's hand tightened on his arm as they crossed the landing. The drawing room lay ahead. No sounds emerged from within. No voices, and no soft music from the pianoforte.

It was soon apparent why.

All of the guests were sitting in rigid silence. Jane Trumble was on the sofa beside her aunt, sipping a glass of sherry. Lionel and his mother were perched in twin armchairs. Fred was standing by the mantelpiece, scowling. And Sir Roderick was on a settee alone, hands folded across his thick midsection, frowning at the assembled company like a disapproving father.

He was the very image of Fred, only older, heavier, and grayer about the temples. St. Clare remembered him as a hard, unforgiving sort of man. A man who was as pitiless to poachers as he was toward his own son on occasion.

The first to see them enter, he rose to his feet, his knees creaking. The rest of the company followed suit, standing briefly to acknowledge St. Clare's arrival. All but Mrs. Beresford, who remained stubbornly in her chair.

Lionel sketched a bow, a smug smile spreading over his face. "Do you see, Madre? I was right. He has come after all."

Mrs. Beresford pivoted her head from Lionel to St. Clare. The long, double strand of pearls she wore at her neck made an unsettling clacking sound. "I didn't believe it. That you would show your face here this evening. Such gall. Such effrontery. But my son said otherwise. Were it up to me—"

"It isn't up to you, ma'am," Maggie said. "Lord St. Clare is my honored guest."

"*Honored*." Fred practically spat the word. His face was black and blue, one of his eyes swollen shut, and his nose—which St. Clare suspected had been broken during their brawl—looked as though it had recently been reset by the surgeon. "And what do you mean by addressing him so? He's no viscount."

"What's that?" Miss Trumble's aunt asked as she resumed her seat. "He's no what?" She was wearing a plumed turban over her white hair. The lone ostrich feather trembled as she tilted her ear to Miss Trumble's lips.

"A viscount," Miss Trumble said loudly. She gave St. Clare a rueful smile. "It's a pleasure to see you again, my lord."

"And you, Miss Trumble," St. Clare said. "Lord Mattingly requested that I convey his respects."

Miss Trumble's cheeks turned pink. "Did he? How very kind."

Sir Roderick surveyed St. Clare with a steely-eyed glare. "Miss Honeywell, you may entertain who you like while you are mistress here, but pray do not expect us to participate in this charade. This man is a former servant of your father's, is he not? The scullery maid's son?"

"A bastard," Fred said.

"A what?" Aunt Harriet turned to Miss Trumble again, who whispered something back to her in her ear. "Ah. But surely…?"

"He's Lord Allendale's grandson," Maggie said. "It's an indisputable fact."

Lionel laughed. "That's doing it a bit too brown, Miss Honeywell. The game, as they say, is up. You may as well admit he's this Seaton fellow. He admitted it himself when we met at the tavern."

"The two aren't mutually exclusive, sir." Maggie motioned for St. Clare to sit down. "Would you care for a glass of sherry, my lord?"

"No thank you." St. Clare waited for Maggie to sit before taking a seat himself in a chair next to Miss Trumble and her aunt.

"Your face," the old lady said, looking at his bruises in dismay. "You weren't engaging in fisticuffs again?"

Again?

St. Clare recalled Maggie saying that Jane's aunt was often confused. "I'm afraid I was, ma'am."

"In my day, a man in such execrable condition wouldn't have forced his company on a party of ladies." Sir Roderick shot a withering glance at Fred. "He'd have spared them the pain of looking at him."

Fred's shoulders stiffened under the weight of his father's censure.

"And you, Miss Honeywell," Sir Roderick said. "Your part in this affair hasn't escaped me. Had I not believed the Earl of Allendale would be in attendance this evening, I'd have foregone dinner in favor of a private interview with you. A discussion about your behavior is long overdue."

St. Clare glanced at Maggie. He wouldn't blame her if she was irritated. She'd only agreed to go through with this dinner after Allendale had asked her to. But she didn't appear upset. She looked defiant. Her back was straight, and her chin lifted. There was a martial glint in her sapphire eyes.

"You may speak to me if you wish, certainly," she said. "But I'll not be lectured to. Not by you, sir, or your son. Or by anyone so unconnected with my future happiness."

"Here, here," Miss Trumble said.

Sir Roderick turned on her. "Hold your tongue, young lady. I take leave to tell you that you've done a lamentable job as Miss Honeywell's chaperone. Her ruin is on your head."

"Don't you dare speak to her in that tone," Maggie said sharply.

"Where *is* Lord Allendale?" Mrs. Beresford asked St. Clare. "Why did he not come with you?"

"My grandfather has been detained elsewhere," St. Clare replied.

Lionel idly dusted a piece of lint from his waistcoat. "Undoubtedly. Now that his scheme has been laid bare, he'll have returned to London. Or is he already en route back to the continent? He never was much for England. Not after his son disgraced the family name."

"The apple didn't fall far from the tree," Mrs. Beresford remarked.

St. Clare ignored the barb. "He'll join us as soon as he's able."

Maggie looked at him, brows lifted. There was a question in her eyes. *Is he truly coming?* But she didn't ask that. To do so would have revealed her uncertainty. "Should I hold back dinner?" she asked instead.

"That won't be necessary. My grandfather wouldn't want us to postpone our meal."

"And why not?" Lionel smiled, enjoying himself. "We can wait another ten minutes, can't we? Another fifteen, for such esteemed company as my uncle?"

Fred leaned back against the mantelpiece. "Seaton can entertain us while we wait. He can tell us where he went after escaping the hangman's noose."

"A hanging. Dear me." Mrs. Beresford tittered. "Quite shocking. But necessary, I daresay, for certain crimes—and for certain men. Men of low character and low breeding."

"He stole Miss Honeywell's jewelry," Fred said. "Three priceless pieces passed down to her from her mother. I found them hidden in his room above the stables."

"Above the stables?" Lionel chuckled. "How indescribably quaint."

"Strange that you should be the one to find my mother's jewels, Fred," Maggie said. "You discovered them before I'd even realized they were missing. And on a day when my father was conveniently away from home, unable to intervene."

"Nothing strange about it," Sir Roderick replied crossly. "My son had the ear of the servants. Someone reported the crime to you, didn't they? A maidservant, I believe you said."

Fred was quiet. And then: "I don't recall."

A flicker of rage threatened St. Clare's composure. One last glowing ember that the brawl at the tavern had failed to extinguish. "Because it never happened. You knew the jewelry was there because you put it there yourself."

St. Roderick exploded. "You dare to accuse my son?"

"It's nothing I didn't say myself at the time," Maggie answered him. "And it's the truth. Fred was always trying to separate me from Nicholas, by fair means or foul."

"Then you admit this man is the servant boy born on your estate?" Sir Roderick demanded. "The one sired by that highwayman?"

"Jim," Miss Trumble's aunt said helpfully. "That's what he was called."

"Gentleman Jim," Fred said. "A rogue and a villain."

"And my son," Lord Allendale added from the doorway.

St. Clare stood immediately, along with the rest of the guests, as his grandfather entered the drawing room. The earl was still in his traveling clothes, as if he'd come directly to

Beasley Park upon returning from his journey. A frantic footman trailed behind him, too late to properly announce his arrival.

"Your *what?*" Sir Roderick asked.

"This highwayman you speak of. He was my son, James Beresford. And you're quite right. The gentleman you see before you is James's boy." Allendale's stormy gray eyes met St. Clare's. "My grandson and heir. My *legitimate* heir." He withdrew a document from his coat. "And I have the papers to prove it."

33

Maggie looked from St. Clare to Lord Allendale and back again. Something seemed to pass between them. An unspoken understanding. It suddenly occurred to her that St. Clare had known his grandfather would return. Not only that, but that Allendale would arrive in just such a dramatic fashion.

He was a wily old man, the earl. She reminded herself of that fact as she resumed her seat. Hadn't he already been attempting to pass St. Clare off as his legitimate heir? Putting it about that St. Clare was born on the continent, the son of James Beresford and an Italian lady who had long since passed away? And yet...

And yet Maggie was filled with a sense of hope at the earl's arrival. On the edge of her seat with anticipation at what he might reveal.

Jane and her aunt Harriet were equally riveted, both of them hanging on the earl's every word.

"Impossible," Fred said, plumping down on the settee beside his father. "No such proof exists."

Sir Roderick silenced his son with a wave of his hand. "Be quiet. Let his lordship speak."

Allendale settled himself in a chair next to Maggie. She had a good view of the folded document in his hand. But he didn't open it. He held it as he spoke, rather like a prop. "I traveled to Exeter this morning to consult with the bishop. To see if he could assist me in finding the Devonshire church of this Father Tuck fellow."

Maggie cast an excited glance at St. Clare, but he wasn't looking at her. He was looking steadily at his grandfather.

"Father Tuck?" Mrs. Beresford gave a trilling laugh. "And who might he be?"

Allendale fixed Mrs. Beresford with an implacable glare. "A rogue clergyman who once knew my son."

Mrs. Beresford seemed to shrink a little under the earl's regard.

"Another Banbury tale," Mr. Beresford said dismissively.

"It certainly is not," Maggie told him. "Father Tuck frequented the Crossed Daggers some thirty years ago. He was known in these parts, and if you doubt it, you may ask our vicar, Mr. Applewhite, yourself." At that, she inclined her head to the earl, bidding him to continue.

Allendale acknowledged Maggie with a nod. "The Bishop of Exeter isn't a stranger to me. He was gracious enough to see me without an appointment. After consulting the records, he directed me to a church some thirteen miles away, in the village of Thorne St. Mary. It lies not far from the main road, which was convenient to my return journey, and so I made haste to go there."

Fred was shaking his head, frowning, but he remained mute for the moment.

"You met Father Tuck?" Maggie asked.

"He goes by Mr. Tuck," Allendale said. "But yes. I was fortunate to meet the man. He's a humble fellow, near to my age, and deeply repentant of the sinfulness of his former life. The past is painful to him, but his memory is untarnished. He readily recalled my son—and the tavern wench, Jenny Seaton."

"Like hell he did!" Fred burst out.

Sir Roderick reprimanded him through gritted teeth. "Be quiet, I said!"

"Can't you see it's just another lie? Another made-up story like the last one?" Fred gestured angrily at St. Clare. "He's no heir to an earldom!"

St. Clare didn't react at all to Fred's outburst. He was still watching his grandfather.

"Ah, but he is." Allendale's mouth curved in a cold smile of triumph. "Mr. Tuck's former church in Somerset was destroyed in a fire, and most of the records along with it. But Mr. Tuck was, for most of his life, a man of order and good sense, and in his sober hours saw fit to keep copies. He stored these copies in a strongbox and has most of them still. He went through them while I waited, and at last produced the evidence which I now have in my possession." The earl raised the document in his hand. "Jenny Seaton's marriage lines."

There was a sudden silence, as if the entire drawing room had collectively caught its breath.

"Do you mean…they were married after all?" Maggie asked.

"You may see for yourself." Allendale handed her the document.

She took it, unfolding the paper in front of her. Her eyes widened and her heart skipped, tripping over itself.

Good heavens.

It was true. It was *all* true.

"Out loud, if you please, Miss Honeywell," Allendale said.

Her fingers fairly trembled on the paper as she read: "'Jenny Seaton of Colebrook Parish, Somersetshire and James Edward Beresford of Worth House, Hertfordshire were married at Southleigh Chapel, Somersetshire this seventh day of June in the year 1789 by William Oswald Tuck.'" She looked up. "It's signed and witnessed."

Mrs. Beresford leapt from her chair. "Let me see it." She snatched the marriage lines from Maggie's hands before Maggie could stop her. "Poppycock! This is a forgery." She thrust the paper at her son, who had come to stand beside her. "The witnesses haven't even signed it."

"It's a copy written out by Mr. Tuck," Allendale said. "No different than the marriage lines kept by countless women as proof of their nuptials."

Mr. Beresford was no longer affecting an air of lazy amusement. His eyes were alert beneath his drooping lids. "And who are these witnesses? Did you meet them?"

"*We* shall meet them," Mrs. Beresford said. "You may depend upon it, my lord. We shall question them without delay."

"I wish you luck, madam." Allendale plucked the marriage lines from Mr. Beresford's fingers, and folding the paper in half, passed it to St. Clare. "The witnesses are buried in the graveyard of Mr. Tuck's former church. They were acquaintances of his past—fellow rogues. When he returned to the clergy, they accompanied him as his servants but have long since passed away."

Mrs. Beresford's face fell. She looked to her son. "Lionel?"

"And I suppose," Mr. Beresford said, "that this clergyman—this Mr. Tuck—would swear to all of this in a court of law?"

"If it comes to that," Allendale said. "But I warn you, I won't take kindly to the Beresford name being dragged through the courts. I may find myself constrained to retaliate in kind—with a defamation suit."

"A defamation suit!" Mrs. Beresford slumped back into her seat with a nervous laugh. "You never would, would you? Why, the very thought of it."

"It will be more than a thought, madam, if you dare to challenge me." Allendale's brows lowered in a threatening glare. "And if I find out that the pair of you have been spreading gossip about my heir—sending letters to those scandal sheets in London—a defamation suit will be the least of your troubles."

Mr. Beresford blanched.

Fred, meanwhile, was growing redder by the second beneath his bruises. "It's all very convenient. Too convenient." And then: "Have you nothing to say, Seaton?"

St. Clare had yet to examine the document in his hands. He glanced at Fred, but his response—when he gave it—was directed at Allendale. "I find myself at a loss for words."

"Understandable," Allendale said.

Maggie nodded. "It's a great deal to take in. Indeed, you must be quite overcome."

St. Clare looked at her. There was a roguish gleam in his eyes. "Too right, Miss Honeywell."

"If all of this is true," Sir Roderick said, "why did this scullery maid let everyone believe she was unmarried? That her child was a product of sin? Was she not right in the head, this woman?"

"She was young and ignorant," Maggie replied, a trifle defensive. Jenny hadn't been perfect. Far from it. But she was still St. Clare's mother. "After her wedding, when she encountered Mr. Tuck in the tavern, drunk beyond all decency, she must have thought she'd been hoaxed."

"For that, we can only surmise. But…" The earl's forehead creased. "I suspect it's as you say. Miss Seaton had reason to think that Tuck was no clergyman, but only a nefarious associate of my son's. She left Market Barrow, pregnant with my son's child, believing herself to be unmarried."

"Young Jim did enjoy his little jokes," Aunt Harriet said.

"What's that, Aunt?" Jane asked.

"Wagers in the betting books. That kind of thing." Aunt Harriet smiled. "You know what fashionable young gentlemen are like."

"This was no joke, madam," Sir Roderick said. "This was a sacred event. A marriage. And this man's life blighted by the confusion of it." He looked at St. Clare. "You are to be pitied, sir."

Fred gaped. "You don't believe any of this? Surely, Father, you can't—"

"Pitied, I said." Sir Roderick mouth compressed in an unforgiving line. "But that doesn't excuse his other crimes." He looked at St. Clare. "To steal from the daughter of your benefactor—"

"Really, Sir Roderick," Maggie objected. "I've told you countless times—"

"I've no desire to rewrite history, Miss Honeywell," Sir Roderick said. "We've had quite enough in the way of revisions for one evening. I confess, I'm not fond of surprises."

"Regrettable," Allendale said. "For I have more news to come." Reaching back into the inner recesses of his coat, he withdrew another paper. "While I was in Exeter, the bishop was good enough to provide me with a license."

"A license for what?" Maggie asked.

Allendale handed the paper to her. The gleam in his eyes was very much like the one in St. Clare's. "A license for you and my grandson to be married."

Thus far, St. Clare had been singularly unmoved by his grand-father's revelations. He knew when the old earl was putting on a show. Everything, from the manner of his arrival to the dramatic fashion in which he'd produced his proof, had reeked of the theater. But this...

This was real.

Maggie lifted her gaze from the special license, meeting his eyes. And this time he wasn't cold and impassive, reveal-ing nothing of his feelings. Quite the reverse. He gave her a lopsided smile.

An answering smile shone in her face.

"Have you agreed to this, Miss Honeywell?" Sir Roder-ick asked. "To marry this man?"

"I have, sir. With my whole heart." Maggie went to St. Clare.

He rose to meet her, taking her hands in his. "I promise you, you won't have cause to regret it."

"Foolish man," she said, making the words a caress. "Of course I won't regret it. You're the love of my life."

Fred was up from his seat in a flash. He paced to the mantel. "An affecting scene." He turned to confront Maggie. "I'll never approve of you marrying him, you do realize that? And without my approval, you may bid goodbye to Beasley Park."

"I'm aware," Maggie said.

Allendale stood. "And why won't you approve a marriage between my grandson and Miss Honeywell?" he demanded in a growl. "You can't hope for a better match for the gel."

Fred drew himself up. "Miss Honeywell is going to marry me."

"I'm afraid she isn't," St. Clare said. "You had best accustom yourself to the fact."

"No, I'm not," Maggie agreed. "I never promised to marry you, Fred. You only assumed I would because of Papa's will."

"Two suitors to choose from," Miss Trumble's aunt said. "Who, pray, is the second lad? The ginger-haired fellow?"

"Mr. Burton-Smythe," Miss Trumble replied. "He lives on the neighboring estate."

"Who, dear?"

"Mr. Burton-Smythe!"

"As romantic as this all is," Mr. Beresford said, rising from his chair. "Madre and I must excuse ourselves." He made for the door.

Mrs. Beresford sprang up to follow her son. "Quite right. We have matters to attend to. Our departure to arrange and so forth. We won't remain where we're unwelcome." She bobbed her head to Allendale as she passed. "My lord."

The pair hastily took their leave, frantically whispering to each other as they exited the room.

"Probably trying to catch the post before all those letters of theirs go out," St. Clare murmured to Maggie.

Her mouth curved. "They shall have to be quick about it."

A footman appeared at the door, narrowly avoiding a collision with the exiting Beresfords. He cleared his throat.

"Yes, Salter?" Maggie asked. "What is it?"

"Dinner is served, Miss Honeywell."

"Splendid." Allendale offered his arm to Miss Trumble's aunt. "Shall we go in, ma'am? Give the betrothed couple a few moments of privacy?"

"An excellent idea, my lord." She took his arm, permitting him to escort her from the room. Miss Trumble accompanied them, stopping only briefly to offer a word of congratulation to Maggie.

"This is a rum business." Sir Roderick's voice faded as he departed the drawing room with the others. "Can't say I approve of the way it's transpired."

Maggie gazed up at St. Clare. She looked as though she might say something, but he forestalled her with a subtle shake of his head.

They weren't yet alone.

Fred hadn't gone in to dinner with the rest of the party. He remained by the mantel, his face contorted in a frightening mask of hatred. "I expect you believe you've won."

St. Clare drew Maggie closer to his side. He knew Fred, even after all these years. Knew that he was at his most dangerous when he believed himself to have been humiliated.

"I'm not a prize to be fought over, Fred," Maggie said. "I'm a grown woman with thoughts and feelings and opinions of my own."

Fred didn't seem to hear her. He was too incensed. "I would have done anything to have you. I'd have treated you like a queen. But all you cared about was Seaton." He bit out his words as though he might choke on them. "The two of you, with your secret meeting places and your private jokes. Always laughing at me behind my back."

Maggie shook her head.

"You were a bully then," St. Clare said. "Just as you are now."

"I was your better," Fred retorted.

"Is that what you call it? To beat a servant boy—a boy who couldn't fight back?"

Fred was unrepentant. "Someone had to put you in your place."

"I'm in my place now, aren't I?" It wasn't a good idea to provoke him, but St. Clare couldn't seem to help himself. "Despite all your scheming, all your machinations, Maggie and I are together."

"Are you? *Are you?* I still hold power here, Margaret. Over this house and over your fortune. If you marry him—"

"Enough, Fred," Maggie said. "*Enough.* I'm not going to marry you, not even for Beasley Park. I don't think of you that way. I never have, not in my entire life."

"Because of him. If he wasn't here—"

"You've already tried to get rid of me once," St. Clare said. "That didn't work out so well for you, did it?"

Fred's brawny frame quivered. "I could have killed you that night."

"Why didn't you?"

"Because I wanted you to suffer. I wanted you to hang. And worse."

St. Clare's brows lifted. *Worse?*

"I wanted you to see what it was like to be entirely alone," Fred told him. "Abandoned, with no one to shield you."

St. Clare chest tightened. Even after all of these years, the memory of that night, locked in the loose box, was as vivid to him as if it had happened yesterday. The fear of it, and the desperation. The way he'd pounded his fists on the walls until they'd bled.

And then the blessed sound of the bolts sliding back from the door, and of his name whispered in the dark.

"I wasn't alone," he said. "Maggie came for me."

Fred looked away from them. "She wasn't supposed to know you were there."

"I mightn't have," Maggie said, "if I hadn't overheard my Aunt Daphne gossiping with the vicar's wife."

"That was my mistake," Fred said, as much to himself as to them. "I should have hidden the jewelry the day before. If I'd arranged to find it earlier—"

"*Hidden the jewelry?*"

St. Clare turned his head to the open doors of the drawing room.

Sir Roderick stood there, framed in the doorway, having apparently doubled back to fetch his son rather than continue to dinner without him. "*Arranged to find it?*" he echoed. His stern countenance was swiftly mottling with barely controlled fury. "Do you mean to say that all this time, Miss Honeywell has been telling the truth? That you—*my son*—conspired to have a servant arrested for a crime he didn't commit?"

Every last vestige of color drained from Fred's face. "Father, I—"

"Be silent!" Sir Roderick's voice resounded through the drawing room like a pistol shot. "You would have seen this man hanged? The grandson of an earl?" He turned to St. Clare. There was no friendliness in his expression, only the formality dictated by his son's actions. "On behalf of my family, I beg your pardon, my lord. You may be sure that my son will make amends for his actions, beginning with his approval of your marriage. It is the very least he can do to atone for his sins."

Fred's jaw dropped. "Father, I didn't—"

"Not another word." Sir Roderick shoved Fred between the shoulder blades, marching him out the door of the drawing room. "We're returning to Letchford Hall, where we will discuss your conduct in private."

St. Clare stood next to Maggie, still and silent, as he watched them go. He had the strangest sense that a part of his life had finally come to a close. A painful, unresolved piece of his history, still raw after so many years. The duel with Fred had been a temporary salve on it, as had the brawl at the tavern. But there had been no real justice.

Not until tonight.

Sir Roderick's acknowledgment of what Fred had done didn't have the force of law, but by God, it was enough.

"My goodness." Maggie looked up at him, stunned. "Does this mean what I think it means?"

St. Clare smoothed a strand of hair back from her temple. "That depends. Will Sir Roderick keep his word? Will he make Fred consent to our marriage?"

"He's the only one who ever could. The only authority Fred's ever recognized."

"Which means…"

Tears sprang into her eyes. "Beasley Park will remain mine."

He gathered her close. "I thought it didn't matter?"

"It doesn't. Not if I must choose between you. But if I don't have to choose…" She encircled his neck in a fierce embrace. "Oh, I should so very much like to have everything."

He smiled against her cheek. "Of course you would."

"And not just for myself." She drew back to meet his gaze. "Aren't you even going to look at your mother's marriage lines?"

"I don't need to look."

Her brows knit. "You don't believe they're real, do you? You think it's just another yarn your grandfather has spun to serve his own ends?"

"It very likely is."

"And what if it isn't?" She slid her hands down the front of his waistcoat, searching for the folded paper he'd tucked into his pocket. When she found it, she pulled it free. "Here. Look at it, and tell me it isn't real."

He grudgingly unfolded the paper and read the swirling, uneven script. The writing was long faded, darker in some places than others. As if it truly had been written decades ago. His pulse accelerated against his will, against all rational thought.

Was it possible?

Could it really be true?

He swallowed hard. "It can't be."

"Why can't it?" she asked. "Don't you want everything, too? The title. The Beresford name. Me." She stretched up to press a soft kiss to his lips. "Be greedy," she said. "I intend to be."

He stared down at her, his heart thumping heavily. A rare trace of vulnerability deepened his voice. "You're already so much more than I deserve."

Eyes shining, she reached up to frame his face, cradling his jaw in the silken curve of her small hands. "What has *deserve* got to do with anything? Do you think I deserve you? That I deserve any of this? But it's mine. *You're* mine. And tomorrow, my love, we're going to take that special license Lord Allendale procured and you and I are going to get married."

A slow smile tugged at his mouth. "Is that so?"

"It is. Unless you have something else planned?"

His smile broadened. "Not a thing." He bent his head to hers, his beautiful blue-eyed hellion. And love surged within him. The same love that had led him back here like a beacon, guiding his way home. Not to a place, but to her. Back to her side where he belonged. Where he'd always belonged. "Tomorrow is yours," he vowed. "All of my tomorrows."

"Tomorrow, then," she said. And standing up on the toes of her slippers, she kissed him again, softly, deeply, promising him all of her tomorrows, too. Promising him forever. Her heart and soul. The very world.

Epilogue

Beasley Park
Somerset, England
Spring 1823

Maggie brought her bay mare to a standstill at the top of the rise. A fragrant breeze ruffled the skirts of her riding habit as she gazed out over the blooming countryside. In the springtime, the forget-me-not-covered landscape of Beasley Park was still the most beautiful place on earth. "Look at that view, my darling. Is there anything more glorious?"

The Honorable James Aldrick Nicholas Beresford slowed his plump pony to a halt beside her. His dark-blond hair was disheveled, his small hands steady on the reins. At five years of age, he was a natural equestrian, as confident in the saddle as Maggie was herself. "You're not supposed to gallop, Mama," he reminded her. "Papa says—"

"Even your Papa wouldn't forbid a gallop on such a day as this."

"Oh, wouldn't he?" St. Clare rode up the crest of the hill to join them. His jet-black horse was bigger than both hers and

James's combined. An intimidating creature, and one Maggie had been yearning to ride ever since her husband had purchased him last month.

"Perhaps after the new baby comes, and you've recovered your health," St. Clare had suggested.

He was right, of course. But the new baby's arrival was more than six months away. And in the meanwhile, Maggie was yearning for excitement.

"You promised to take care." St. Clare drew his horse up alongside hers. His expression was stern. But there was no masking the tender concern in his stormy gray eyes, the love that shone there as brilliantly as ever, even when he was at his most exasperated. "Have you already forgotten?"

"An uphill gallop isn't dangerous." She stretched out a gloved hand to him. "I told you to race me."

He took her hand in his, holding it safe. "You were gone before I could formulate a reply—and our son along with you."

James's eyes brightened. They were the same color gray as his father's. "Did you see how fast I galloped, Papa?"

"Frighteningly fast. You very nearly managed to outpace your mother."

"I *could* beat Mama if I had a horse instead of a pony." James patted his tiny steed's neck, as if in consolation for the insult. "I'm big enough now."

Maggie gave her son a speaking glance. The subject of a horse was one that had already been addressed, and often. Despite James's insistence to the contrary, he wasn't yet ready for a full-sized mount. Besides, both she and St. Clare had promised Lord Allendale that his young heir would be restricted to a pony until he was ten years of age. A minor concession to put the earl's mind at ease.

"Well, I am," James said under his breath.

He was growing up faster than Maggie would like. Indeed, the happier she was, the more quickly time seemed to pass. It felt like a lifetime ago that she'd sat inside the house in her mourning blacks, frail and restless and longing to be out from under the oppressive control of the Burton-Smythes.

Sir Roderick had passed away after an episode of apoplexy during the winter of 1820. And Fred—now *Sir* Fred—had married a sturdy village girl of eighteen, someone who properly adored him, and who had promptly given him a son.

Fred avoided Maggie's family for the most part, as much as was possible with them being neighbors. And on those rare occasions they happened to meet, in the village or on the border of their respective estates, he and St. Clare managed to refrain from coming to blows.

As for Maggie, years of fresh air and moderate exercise had strengthened her lungs and improved her health. St. Clare had been at her side the entire time, helping and encouraging her. She'd not been married to him three months before she was back on a horse, the two of them riding over the grounds of Beasley Park, just as they'd done when they were young.

He was still the love of her life. Her best friend and soul mate. The children they'd had together had only strengthened the already unbreakable bond they shared.

"A fine day, isn't it?" His thumb moved over the back of Maggie's hand in an absent caress.

"It's a perfect day," she said. "We should have had Nurse bring Ivo and Jack out for a picnic."

"We still can. The day isn't over yet."

James's lower lip crept out in the barest threat of a pout. "Not the babies."

"Come," St. Clare said. "None of that. Your little brothers look to you as an example."

"But Papa—"

"Ride back and tell Nurse that we're picnicking on the banks of the stream, and that she's to bring Ivo and Jack along directly."

"You may stop by the kitchens afterward for a cream cake," Maggie added encouragingly. If that wasn't an incentive, she didn't know what was. "And don't forget to mention that we'll need a hamper. Cook can have Salter bring it down."

James heaved a world-weary sigh. "Yes, Mama." And turning his pony, he trotted away down the hill where a groom waited to accompany him.

St. Clare's mouth hitched in a smile. "Sometimes, I think he's more Honeywell than Beresford."

"You wouldn't know it by looking at him."

James had his father's looks, as did their three-year-old son, Ivo, and their one-year-old baby, Jack. Each of them blond and gray eyed and handsome.

"No, indeed. He's my mirror image. But it's your stubbornness he's got running through his veins." St. Clare dismounted, and after looping his reins around a nearby branch, came to assist her down from her mare. His hands were gentle but firm at her waist, lifting her easily and setting her carefully on the ground.

She clutched at his shoulders. "I'm not going to break, you know."

"No." He gazed down at her. "But every time you're in this condition…" His brow furrowed. "Is it too much to ask that we remain in one place for the duration?"

They *had* been traveling a good deal. Autumn had been spent in London, with Lord and Lady Mattingly. Jane and Mattingly had married less than a year after St. Clare and Maggie, and their children were of a similar age. Their two families always enjoyed their time together.

Visiting London was, nevertheless, somewhat of an ordeal. The gossip over St. Clare's legitimacy had never been fully extinguished. It had merely been subsumed by the gossip over the scandal of his birth—the fact that his mother had been a tavern wench and that he'd been born into a life of servitude.

Even after six years, there were still stares and whispers to contend with. Maggie and St. Clare only endured it on account of their children. Making their presence known in fashionable society, however uncomfortably, in the hopes that one day James, Ivo, and Jack—and the babe yet to come— would have an easier time of it.

After London, they'd traveled north, where they'd spent the winter and most of the spring at Worth House, Lord Allendale's palatial estate in Hertfordshire. The earl doted on his great-grandchildren, delighted to have both an heir and two spares to spoil.

And then, as May drifted lazily into June, they'd finally come home. It had been at Maggie's insistence. She looked forward to the warm spring and summer months at Beasley more than anything.

"Everything is going to be fine," she promised, curving a hand around St. Clare's neck.

He bent his head. "You always say that." His lips brushed over hers. Softly, slowly. A prelude to a kiss.

She stretched up to meet it, heart beating swiftly. Her eyes closed as his mouth captured hers. She clung to him. Even after all these years, his kisses still had the power to make her knees go weak. "*Nicholas*," she breathed. It was a name she only ever used in their most intimate moments.

He made a low sound, somewhere between a laugh and a groan. "I believe this is how we got into this predicament."

"A predicament. Is that what you call it?"

"A lovely, wonderful predicament." He rested a hand on the slight swell of her belly. "I wonder if this one will be a girl?"

"I sincerely hope so. The ladies in our household are woefully outnumbered."

"I hope so, too. A brave, beautiful girl, with dark hair and blue eyes, like her mother."

Maggie smiled up at him. "Perhaps she will be."

And she was.

AUTHOR'S NOTE

I began writing *Gentleman Jim* many years ago, around the same time I wrote my other Regency romance, *The Work of Art*. The manuscript was originally titled *Gentleman Jack*, but by the time I got around to revising it, the HBO miniseries of the same name had been released, so I renamed my story *Gentleman Jim*. Not my favorite name, I confess, but still in the same spirit as the original.

The story was inspired by my love for two classic novels: Alexandre Dumas's *The Count of Monte Cristo*, published in 1844, and Henry Fielding's *The History of Tom Jones, a Foundling*, published in 1749. There are various references to these two books throughout my story, in the names of characters, such as Jenny and Mrs. Square, and in lines of dialogue, such as when St. Clare says that he must "wait and hope" for Maggie to come back to London. I've included a part of that original quote as an epigraph. The full quote from Edmond Dantès's closing letter to Maximilian Morrel reads as follows:

There is neither happiness nor misery in the world; there is only the comparison of one state with another, nothing more. He who has felt the deepest grief is best able to experience supreme happiness. We must have felt what it is to die, Morrel, that we may appreciate the enjoyments of living.

Live, then, and be happy, beloved children of my heart, and never forget that until the day when God shall deign to reveal the future to man, all human wisdom is summed up in these two words,—'Wait and hope.'—Your friend,
Edmond Dantès, Count of Monte Cristo.

As always, if you'd like more information on nineteenth century fashion, etiquette, or any of the other subjects featured in my novels, please visit the blog portion of my author website at MimiMatthews.com.

ACKNOWLEDGMENTS

This novel was painful to finish. And I mean that literally. My neck was in spasm and the whole world was in chaos. The last thing I wanted to do was meet a deadline. I'm so very grateful for the patience of everyone involved.

To my brilliant editor, Deb Nemeth. Thank you for all of your guidance. Your suggestions never fail to make my books better.

To my wonderful beta readers, Flora and Dana. Thank you for all of your feedback, and for cheerleading me on when the writing got difficult. I couldn't have asked for a better team to see this story through.

Thanks are also due to my cover designer, James Egan; to Colleen Sheehan for formatting; and—as always—to my wonderful parents, who help me so much when things get difficult.

Lastly, I'd like to thank you, my readers. When I began serializing the first chapters of *Gentleman Jim* through my newsletter, many of you messaged me and asked why I didn't just release it as a book. Your kind words and encouragement truly helped to make it happen. This story is for you.

ABOUT THE AUTHOR

USA Today bestselling author Mimi Matthews writes both historical nonfiction and award-winning proper Victorian romances. Her novels have received starred reviews in *Library Journal*, *Publishers Weekly*, and *Kirkus*, and her articles have been featured on the *Victorian Web*, the *Journal of Victorian Culture*, and in syndication at *BUST Magazine*. In her other life, Mimi is an attorney. She resides in California with her family, which includes a retired Andalusian dressage horse, a Sheltie, and two Siamese cats.

To learn more, please visit
WWW.MIMIMATTHEWS.COM

OTHER TITLES BY
MIMI MATTHEWS

A Modest Independence
Parish Orphans of Devon, Book 2

A Convenient Fiction
Parish Orphans of Devon, Book 3

The Winter Companion
Parish Orphans of Devon, Book 4

Fair as a Star
Victorian Romantics, Book 1

CPSIA information can be obtained
at www.ICGtesting.com
Printed in the USA
BVHW032120101120
593033BV00006B/32